REDEMPTION

Don't miss the first novel in this new series
by Kate Douglas

INTIMATE

Available from St. Martin's Paperbacks

REDEMPTION

KATE DOUGLAS

St. Martin's Paperbacks

This is a work of fiction. All of the characters, organizations, and events portrayed in this novel are either products of the author's imagination or are used fictitiously.

REDEMPTION

Copyright © 2016 by Kate Douglas.

All rights reserved.

For information address St. Martin's Press, 175 Fifth Avenue, New York, NY 10010.

ISBN: 978-1-250-064776

Printed in the United States of America

St. Martin's Paperbacks edition / January 2016

St. Martin's Paperbacks are published by St. Martin's Press, 175 Fifth Avenue, New York, NY 10010.

10 9 8 7 6 5 4 3 2 1

This book is dedicated with my appreciation and thanks to my agent Jessica Faust of BookEnds LLC, and my editor Eileen Rothschild of St. Martin's Press. It's really cool when the people in charge of my career actually seem to have me figured out better than I do, and for this I thank you both.

With much love to my husband who does his best to keep me on track the rest of the time. I freely admit it's not an easy job, and he's been doing it for well over forty years. There's a lot of history between the two of us, yet the man still takes my breath, and he makes me laugh. Trust me on this, ladies . . . it's a potent combination!

ACKNOWLEDGMENTS

Writing is essentially a solitary business, but turning a writer's manuscript into an author's book takes a veritable army. My thanks to those soldiers on the front lines—my intrepid beta readers, Ann Jacobs, Rose Toubbeh, Jan Takane, Lynne Thomas, Karen Woods, and Kerry Parker, who always manage to find time to tell me where I screwed up. And yes, this is a good thing.

I owe a great deal of gratitude to author Jessica Scott, whose first-hand knowledge of the military helped me develop Ben Lowell's character. And Jessica, my apologies if anything is incorrect, because I will freely admit it's me, not you making the mistakes. Thank you, too, for your wonderful books. I never would have attempted a character with a military background if I hadn't fallen in love with the brave men and women in your military romances.

CHAPTER 1

San Francisco, CA—April 30

Wind whipped the branches overhead, rain pounded the roof of the car, and dark leaves slapped against the windshield. RJ, the little shit, sat in the passenger seat, turned with his back to the door, seatbelt cinched tight, eyes wide. Staring at him. Ben took another swallow of his beer. He already had a buzz so he didn't really need it, but it was worth the sour taste in his mouth just to watch his kid brother squirm.

His kid brother . . . the family golden boy, at least as far as their parents were concerned. He used to hold that title. He'd been the one Mom was grooming to be the star, and then along came perfect little Richie, subsequently christened RJ because it sounded better. More in tune with the superstar image dear old Mom wanted the kid to have. Why not? He had everything else. Everything RJ touched turned to gold—including the three Olympic medals he'd won.

A small branch hit the hood of the car and skittered up against the windshield. RJ flinched. "Scared ya, huh, kid?" Laughing, Ben punched it, and the black Dodge Viper leapt forward, fishtailing on the wet asphalt. At least when he boosted a car, he got good wheels.

This baby was fast.

He wrapped his fingers around the gearshift. Really a sweet ride.

"Ben! Look out!" RJ braced his hands on the dash.

Ben snapped his attention back to the road, just in time to see the stricken face of a young woman and the wide, terrified eyes of a little boy. And then the child disappeared beneath the front end of the Viper and the woman rolled across the hood, slammed into the windshield, and flew off to the right, her body twisted, arms and legs flailing like a broken doll.

RJ screamed, and he kept screaming, and that was the last thing Ben heard as he lurched forward in the bed, jerked awake, his heart thundering in his ears.

He sat there in the dark, shivering from the blast of air-conditioning hitting his sweat-soaked body, thoughts scattered, wondering if he'd made any noise, if any of the guys had heard him. He raised his head, realized he was alone in a quiet hotel room.

He wasn't in Kabul, not down at Spin B.

"Thank God." He bowed his head, and ran his fingers through hair that had grown well beyond his regulation military cut. He wasn't in the Middle East; he was in a hotel just north of the airport in San Francisco where he'd grabbed a room after his delayed flight finally got in around three this morning. All of his belongings would soon be headed for storage at Camp Parks—all but what he'd thrown into his duffle for the trip home.

Except, where the hell was home? The US Army had been his home for almost twenty years. He hadn't communicated with his parents in all that time, hadn't heard from his brother.

Not that RJ hadn't made his presence known. Those damned dreams had kept the kid sufficiently involved in Ben's life ever since the last time they were together.

The night Ben Lowell totally fucked up his life, his brother's life, and the lives of two innocent victims.

Because of him, a talented young Olympian's career was destroyed.

Because of him, a young mother and her child had died.

Their blood would forever be on Ben's hands. Somehow, before the nightmares won, before he took another cowardly way out—a more permanent one—he had to try and make this right. He wasn't really sure where to start, but sometimes the most obvious steps were the best.

Telling the truth after all these years was going to kill him. But he had to do it, had to admit what a fuckup he'd been. He'd been dying inside for the last twenty years. Looking around the hotel room, listening to his own breath rushing from his lungs, the racing cadence of his heart, he knew he had to find the courage to take that first step, one apology at a time.

Lola Monroe checked the temperature on the oven, turned it down a notch, and then poured herself a glass of wine. Mandy was due home in a few minutes, so she poured an extra glass of Chardonnay for her baby sister and carried it into the living room, careful not to trip over Rico. Their aging basset hound liked to sleep in major pathways throughout their house. It made it easier for him to keep track of them.

She'd just settled into the rocker by the window when she heard Mandy's key in the lock. Lola held out the chilled glass as her sister walked through the front door.

"Oh, thank you. You must have heard me wishing for this." Mandy took the glass, dropped her tote bag on the floor by the sofa, and sat. "I'm beat, but it sure smells good in here."

"Lasagna. I'd planned to have it ready when Kaz and Jake got home."

Mandy took a sip. "I thought they'd be here by now."

"Nope. They're spending the night at Cassie and Nate Dunagan's in Sonoma County. I really thought they'd be coming back tonight, but Kaz called and said they wanted to stay over another night. There's no reason we can't eat it."

Slipping her sandals off, Mandy took another sip of her wine and leaned back against the soft cushions. "I was hoping they'd come back. I need to see Kaz to be sure she's okay. It's just awful what happened to them. I mean, she said the bullet just grazed him, thank goodness, but . . . crap, Lola. They both could have died!" She stared into her glass for a moment and then gazed over the rim at Lola.

"I know. I couldn't sleep last night. I kept thinking about what happened. What could have happened."

"Yeah." Mandy stared into her glass. "I imagine they need some time together without anything else to worry about. Jake's got to be feeling pretty guilty over the whole thing."

"He's not the only one." Lola stared into the golden liquid in her glass. "It's my fault."

Mandy was across the room and grabbing Lola's hand before she finished her sentence. "No it's not. You had no way of knowing Jake didn't take those horrible nude pictures of Kaz. They were awful. I was as mad at him as you were."

"Hon, I should have looked closer at those pictures before giving them to Kaz. I had no idea Jake hadn't taken them, but I should have. They were terrible, and he's a talented photographer, but all I could think when I saw them was that I didn't want her to go to that premiere and see them on the walls. If I'd only looked at all of them, I would have known they weren't his pictures."

If she hadn't freaked out and given them to Kaz, none of this would have happened. Not Kaz getting kidnapped or Jake getting shot. None of it. But she'd given Kaz those damned photos, exactly as that psychopath out of Jacob's past had planned.

Furious, Kaz had gone to the reception where she and Jake were featured—the beautiful model and her sexy photographer and an expensive new line of body jewelry—except Kaz had thrown the envelope filled with disgusting shots in Jake's face and stalked out of the reception, directly into the waiting arms of a madman.

"But Jake saved her, Lola. Don't forget that. She's okay and so is he, and I would guess that if they've decided to stay up there for another night in spite of their injuries, it's because they want to be together. It's been pretty intense between them, and it could be they just need to explore what they're feeling. That's a good thing. Kaz deserves some happiness, don't you agree?"

Lola raised her head and managed to smile. "Yeah, she does. But ya know what? So do we. There have got to be a couple of decent men left out there."

Mandy giggled. "Well, if you find one, let me know."

"There's always Marcus Reed." Lola raised an eyebrow. Mandy had been lusting after him since long before they knew Jake, who was Marc's best friend. She still had a picture of him on the bulletin board in her bedroom, one she'd cut out of *People* magazine. He'd been named one of the year's sexiest young millionaires.

Mandy merely shook her head. "Yeah. Right. The drop-dead gorgeous multi-gazillionaire is going to fall for the dorky little barista at the neighborhood coffee shop."

"Have you ever seen him in person? Kaz says he's a real sweetheart."

"I thought I saw him go by the coffee shop on a bicycle one time, but I doubt it was him. This guy was all by himself on an old Schwinn. Not the sort of wheels you'd expect a rich dude to have."

"Probably not." Lola stood. "C'mon. Dinner should be

ready. We need to keep up our strength in case some good-looking, smart, nice, single guy shows up at the door."

"Yeah. Like that's gonna happen." Laughing, Mandy grabbed her hand and dragged Lola into the kitchen.

"Well, if he does," Lola said, "As the older and wiser sister, I get first dibs!"

Ben walked away from his parents' Marin home, got into the rental car, and drove a couple of blocks to a small cemetery. He'd been here once before, the night before he left for boot camp. It had been right after he was cleared of any charges in that terrible wreck, before RJ had told anyone what really happened.

Another car pulled in behind him and parked near the entrance to the parking area—a dark sedan with two men sitting in the front seat—but other than that, he was alone. He went to the spot he remembered, toward the back of the cemetery where the plots were small and marked with flat headstones, and parked in a shady space beside a redwood tree. He didn't get out. Instead, he stared blindly at the dashboard.

He couldn't believe it. RJ had never told the judge the truth. When Ben knocked on the door at his parents' home, wondering if they still lived there, if they'd even speak to him, his mother had opened the door and greeted him like the prodigal son. He was welcomed home with hugs and questions about where he'd been, why he'd stayed away so long. Then she'd called his father, and the man who never put his sons ahead of his job had rushed home from work to see for himself that his long-lost son had come home.

His parents weren't the most forgiving sort—the last thing he'd expected was to be welcomed home. But their response when he'd asked about RJ had left him angry and speechless.

They didn't want to hear his name. His parents had disowned their youngest son; they hadn't heard from him since the trial ended and he'd been sent away. Not since he'd been found guilty of involuntary manslaughter for killing two people while driving a stolen car . . . a car Ben had actually stolen; the one he—not RJ—had been driving that night.

His mother had sounded disappointed that the stolen car charges had been dropped. Ben hadn't known what to say, so once again he'd taken the coward's way out and kept his mouth shut. In his defense, he had a lot to process. He'd been so certain that RJ, when faced with any kind of jail time, would have told the truth, but he hadn't. Not one word to anyone, as far as Ben could tell.

No matter how he worked it out in his head, it came out all wrong. Made him an even bigger dick. The kid brother he'd dragged with him, the sixteen-year-old Olympian he'd resented so much, had never fessed up. He'd stuck to that story Ben asked him to tell, that RJ was driving the stolen car because Ben was too drunk to drive. That RJ had been the one to kill that poor woman and her son.

He never said a word. Not to his parents, not to the arresting officer, not to the judge. He'd been sentenced to the California Youth Authority, sent away to what was essentially a prison, even though he was innocent.

RJ had done it to protect Ben. No wonder no one had ever come after him, no one had pulled him out of formation and arrested him for manslaughter.

Because RJ had taken the fall, and he'd never admitted the truth—that Ben was guilty, not him. But why?

That night of the wreck, Ben had been so drunk he'd been heaving his guts out while RJ tried to help the little kid. He remembered that much, but for almost twenty years, he'd tried to forget asking RJ to take the blame and tell the cops he'd been driving. Ben had been so god-damned jealous of RJ, of his fame, of the fact he was their parents' favorite, that he didn't care what happened. He'd rationalized it all; told RJ that since he was just sixteen and Ben was an adult and too drunk to get behind the wheel, he could go to prison for a damned long time. As much as he hated himself for doing it, he remembered asking his brother to lie, but he didn't remember much else after the mother and her child died that night.

He remembered getting arrested. Impossible to forget that. They'd both gotten out when their father had come and posted bail and taken them home, but only RJ had been charged. Ben had enlisted while RJ's case was still in court. He'd never contacted his parents to find out how it all ended. Over the years, he'd just figured RJ had gotten off. He was a kid. He hadn't been drinking. Hell, he was a damned Olympian, a media star. Girls asked for his autograph. He had an agent, for fuck's sake.

All those years, he'd imagined his brother living the highlife, while he slogged away in war zones around the world. They'd never send RJ to prison.

Except they did.

His mother said she was sure he'd gotten out a long time ago, but no, they hadn't kept in touch. Didn't know where he was, what he was doing. Didn't care.

In their eyes he had thrown away a career they'd given him. It was a slap in the face to two parents who'd sacrificed everything for an ungrateful child who hadn't cared how much his actions humiliated and embarrassed them. They didn't care that two people were dead. No, they'd been upset because he'd made them look like terrible parents, to have raised such a flawed and thankless son.

No mention of the grueling hours of training RJ had gone through, the lost childhood while he'd spent every free moment with a harsh coach, swimming, perfecting his style, building strength and endurance.

His parents said RJ had failed them.

Even Ben knew it was his parents who had failed their sons. They never should have been parents, but he didn't tell them that. He didn't say anything. He'd merely turned away and walked out the front door.

Now, sitting here in the rental car, parked at the cemetery where a mother and her son would rest forever, he realized there was only one thing he could do. He had to find RJ. Find out what happened to him. Find out if he was okay.

He would find a way to make things right.

He gazed across the shadowy expanse of green, at the wilted flowers on a few graves, and knew exactly where the young woman and her child were buried. But just like that other night when he'd come here, he didn't have the courage to walk across the grass. He was a fucking coward, afraid to stand over her grave and apologize for the terrible thing he'd done.

He'd start with RJ. Once he cleared things with his brother, maybe then he'd be able to somehow beg forgiveness of that poor woman.

Ben scanned his laptop, but he hadn't expected this to be so hard. It was after seven, the day just about shot, when he picked up a newspaper and stopped at a cafe in the Tenderloin district for something to eat. No sign of RJ. He'd tried searching under Richard Lowell and RJ Cameron, but found only a small amount of info about his Olympic wins and brief career, a short article about his time at the California Youth Authority for involuntary manslaughter, but no recent word of his brother, not when he got out or anything about him after the trial ended.

As a juvenile, the records had been sealed.

He tried to remember if RJ had any friends, but the only one he recalled was some nerdy twerp named Marc. Marc something. Started with an *R* . . .

The waitress brought him a cup of coffee and took his order. He finished the first section of the paper and opened the next, the one with more local news. A photo of a sharp-looking, dark-haired man at some sort of premiere caught his attention. He looked vaguely familiar. Ben glanced at the caption: *Marcus Reed.* Could this be a grown-up version of Marc? He was introducing some kind of fancy new jewelry business. It had to be the same guy.

Maybe he'd know how to find RJ. Now, if Ben could just find Marcus Reed. He pulled out a twenty and caught the waitress's attention. "I have to leave. This should cover the burger. Give it to someone who can use a free meal." Handing her the money, he went in search of Marc.

It was after nine when Ben pulled up in front of what looked like a converted row house on 23rd Avenue, a few blocks south of Golden Gate Park. Actually, the whole street was lined with similar houses—in all shapes, sizes, and colors—creating a colorful row of seemingly attached yet distinctly separate homes with the garages beneath, living quarters above.

The streetlight was out, which made it feel even darker in the neighborhood than it already was. It was late—too late to be knocking on a stranger's door, and he knew he should wait until tomorrow, but now that he was so damned close to finding RJ, he couldn't stop. Not after finally talking Marc into giving him the address, even though this wasn't RJ's place.

Marc Reed had been a shock. Ben remembered him as a shy, skinny kid, and he'd never really figured out the friendship between him and RJ, but according to Marc they were still close. Composed, quietly self-confident, and obviously successful, Marc had been surprised to see Ben, but hadn't said much, and wouldn't say anything at all about RJ. He was still quiet, but he'd remembered Ben.

Had RJ kept the secret from Marc as well? It was hard to tell, but he obviously wasn't comfortable giving out RJ's information. Not until Ben said he'd come looking for his brother to right some very old wrongs. Marc had studied him for a moment without any comment, nodded, and then he'd written down this address.

And here he was, at a home that was not RJ's house with a phone number that was also not RJ's. No, Marc had sent Ben to the girlfriend's house. His girlfriend's place where her two roommates also lived. He'd said the girlfriend had some sort of trouble up in wine country, and RJ might still be there with her. Marc wasn't sure what was going on, but the roommates would know.

Though Ben had asked, Marc wouldn't give up RJ's phone number. He said the last thing his friend needed at this point in his life was a cold call from the brother who'd walked out when RJ needed him the most. He had enough on his plate.

But he wouldn't tell Ben what that might be. And he hadn't tried to disguise his obvious disapproval of Ben. Which, to be honest, was only fair.

Ben glanced toward the door at the top of the stairs, got out of the car, and locked it with his duffel and laptop inside. It was late for a strange man to be knocking on their door, especially since the porch light wasn't on, but bright lights glowed through the curtains.

With luck, they'd let him in, or at least answer his questions while he stood on the front steps.

Regardless, he had to find RJ. Had to—somehow—fix what he'd screwed up so long ago.

CHAPTER 2

Rico snorted and rolled over on his back, presenting his belly for a rub. Lola scratched just the way he liked it, and he groaned, but when she stopped petting to turn the page of the latest *People* magazine, he opened one droopy eye and stared at her until she started rubbing again. She had a feeling Rico knew she wasn't thinking about him, and he demanded her attention

Actually, she was thinking about how out of it she was. And how old. Thirty-one seemed ancient, especially when she spent her days around eternally young, gorgeous models.

The stupid magazine merely reinforced it. It was almost comical how she used to know who all the celebrities were, and now they were nothing more than pretty faces. But, she had to keep up with the pretty faces because the modeling agency she managed was filled with them.

Too bad those faces belonged mostly to beautiful women or equally beautiful gay men.

Mandy wandered out into the front room, fresh from the shower with her wet hair hanging darkly blonde just past her chin, her fuzzy chenille robe looking cute instead of frumpy like it would on most women. Lola couldn't understand why Mandy so rarely dated—she was absolutely adorable with a sweet, nurturing personality.

Not that Lola was a dating machine, but there was a perfectly good reason for that. She wasn't perky and sweet like Mandy. No, she tended to be more prickly, which was a nice way of saying her snarky attitude got in her way. Her mother said she was just like her father, a man Lola had never met, but the way she said it wasn't at all complimentary. On the other hand, she'd said Mandy's father was sweet and loving. Like Lola's father, he was also long gone. Of course, so was their mother, most of the time.

Mandy paused and shot a quick glance toward the front door just as Rico raised his head and growled softly. "Someone's coming up the stairs," she said. Still talking to Lola, she started for the door. "I wonder if Kaz and Jake decided to come home early?" The doorbell rang. "Nope. It's not them."

She squinted through the little round spyglass in the door. "Who's there?"

"My name's Ben Lowell. I'm sorry to bother you so late, but I'm trying to find my brother. Marcus Reed said you might be able to put me in touch with him. His name's Richard Lowell. Goes by RJ."

"I don't know anyone by that name."

There was a long pause. Then, "His girlfriend's name is Kaz. Kaz Kazanov. Is she your roommate?"

Mandy glanced at Lola. "He looks like Jake."

"Maybe RJ's his nickname."

Mandy leaned close to the door. She still wasn't quite ready to open it to a stranger. "We know Jake Lowell. Could that be the same guy?"

"Yes! That's him. His name's Richard Jacob Lowell. We used to call him RJ."

Mandy unbolted the door and swung it open. "Okay.

You passed. You can come in." She held the door open and stepped back so he could enter. "I'm Mandy Monroe. This is my sister, Lola."

"Ben Lowell," he said, pausing in the doorway, making eye contact with Lola before glancing back at Mandy. "Thanks for letting me in. I wasn't sure what kind of reception I'd get."

"Why?" Mandy stopped and stared at him. "Why didn't you just call Jake. Don't you have his phone number?"

"No, I . . ."

"Stay, Rico." Lola kept her hand on the dog's head to hold him in place on the sofa, and stood as Ben took a step forward into their small living room. He stopped just inside the door. His face was marked with healing cuts and some older looking scars, but he was still drop-dead gorgeous. An older, wearier version of Jake, not quite as tall or as overwhelming, but from what she could tell, a pretty close but older copy of Kaz's guy, a man they'd barely met.

Ben glanced again at Mandy and then smiled at Lola. Damn. His entire look changed with that smile. Younger. Sexier. Even more interesting.

"I haven't seen my brother in almost twenty years," he said. "We have a pretty convoluted history. Marc wouldn't give me his number but said he's dating your roommate, so I guess that's why he sent me here. Any idea when he'll be back?"

"They're spending the night in the wine country." Lola waved him in to the front room while Mandy closed the door behind him. "Have a seat. Rico's safe. He might drool on you."

Ben shot a quick grin at the dog. "I can handle drool. Anyway, Marc told me RJ's girlfriend had some trouble, but he wouldn't say what." Ben took a seat on the sofa next to Rico. The basset sniffed his hand, appeared to think he was okay, and closed his eyes once again. Ben rubbed the old dog's belly, probably earning him instant membership into the household.

He wasn't the most discriminating of watch dogs.

Mandy perched on the arm at the other end of the sofa. She still looked a bit wary of him, but that was easy to understand. There was something different about Ben, something you didn't see in his brother. A ruthlessness that was lacking in Jake. An edginess, something that drove Mandy to the far end of the sofa, but for whatever reason, drew Lola closer.

Interesting. She rarely liked guys who put off that aggressive, edgy vibe. Especially not after her psycho ex.

She hesitated to say what had happened to Kaz. If Jake hadn't seen his brother in twenty years, there might be a damned good reason and they probably shouldn't have let him in. "Some personal stuff," she said.

Ben seemed to accept that. "Okay. If they're not coming back tonight, I won't take up any more of your time. I need to find a hotel room for the night, but if I leave my. . . ."

"If you don't mind the girly stuff, you could probably use Kaz's room," Mandy said. "She won't be here."

Lola shot her a frown, and she knew she sounded less than welcoming. Too bad. There was something about this guy that put her nerves on edge. "Don't you think you should call and get her permission, first, Hon? Make sure they haven't changed plans, and that it's okay with Kaz?"

"I don't want to put you out." Ben started to rise, but Mandy held up her hand to make him stay.

"I'll call Jake." She flashed a big smile at Lola. "He can vouch for you first, and we know Kaz will be with him." She quickly punched in Jake's number, but no one answered.

She left a message for him to call her back.

"What happened to Kaz?" Ben sat forward, elbows on his knees.

Lola glared at Mandy.

Mandy smiled at Lola. "It's not like it's a big secret, Lola. You know it's gonna be in the paper tomorrow. It was all over the news tonight."

Before Lola had a chance to respond, Mandy's phone rang. She put it on speaker. "Hi, Jake. You're on speaker."

"What's up, Mandy?"

"There's a man here, Jake. He looks like you and he says he's your brother, Ben. I wanted to make sure that's who he is, since he needs a place to stay the night. We were going to give him Kaz's room, if that's okay. He said he's been trying to find you, that Marc Reed put him in touch with us."

The silence was deafening. "Jake? You still there?"

Kaz came on. "I think he's just surprised. He hasn't seen Ben in years. And yes, please tell him to go ahead and use my room. Clean sheets are in the closet. We'll be home tomorrow, but not until after the rush-hour traffic winds down. With luck, before noon."

Mandy shot a know-it-all smile at Lola, took the phone off speaker, and walked out of the room to talk to Kaz. Lola stared at Ben, well aware that it wasn't her most hospitable look, which was weird, really, because what she was beginning to realize was that she didn't particularly want him to leave. That was strange, too. Not like her at all. "It appears you have a place to stay."

Ben shook his head. "That's not necessary. I don't want to make you uncomfortable. I shouldn't have a problem finding a room. Besides, I'm tall. I might not fit in her bed."

He stared at her a moment. She had no idea what he was thinking. Even worse—why did she care so much? Normally, she'd have shown him the door and wished him well, but for whatever reason, the guy fascinated her. She wanted to know more about Ben Lowell. Twenty years estranged from his brother? There had to be a story there.

She shrugged. Tried to look disinterested. "That's silly. What are you? Six one? Two, maybe? Kaz is as tall as you, and she's got a very large bed. Help me change the sheets and it's all yours."

"Thank you," he finally said. "An invitation to stay isn't what I expected."

Lola headed for the hallway to the bedrooms. With a quick glance at him, she said exactly what she'd been thinking. "I'm curious as to what you did expect. Twenty years is a long time to stay away from family."

He stared at his boots. "I know. Too long." Then he raised his head and smiled. "You really don't want me here, do you?"

He had no idea what made him say that, especially when she'd obviously given in on the silent argument she'd appeared to be having with her sister. Maybe with herself, as well. He was having a hell of a time trying to read her.

"No," she said. "Not really, but you have Kaz and Mandy's approval and I'll defer to the majority." Turning her back on him, she made an immediate right into the first bedroom.

He had to bite back a laugh. This Lola obviously wasn't a doormat, but there was something rather surreal about the current situation, following the prickly but absolutely beautiful roommate down the hall to his brother's girlfriend's bedroom. The brother he'd not seen since they were kids, a girlfriend he'd never met, and now this darkhaired beauty who'd managed to snag his attention from the very first glance.

"Here's Kaz's room." She stopped in the open doorway.

"I'm almost disappointed." Kaz's room was a surprise. Mandy had mentioned girly stuff, but the room was so plain and utilitarian that, if not for the king-sized bed with its plain white duvet that just about filled the small room, it could have belonged to a soldier. Even the picture of a beautiful young woman and a little girl on the bedside table would have been apropos in any soldier's quarters. "I expected at least a frilly pink pillow or two."

Ben picked up the picture, but Lola was already tugging the down comforter off the bed, so he set it down to help her.

"Not Kaz. Kaz is definitely not the frilly type." She dumped a pillow out of its case and tossed the pillow into the chair behind her before reaching for the sheets. She moved like a woman with a purpose, which was probably getting his bed ready and him out of her hair as soon as she could.

Though he noticed she kept glancing his way when she thought he wasn't looking.

Whereas her sister was sweet and relaxed, she pulsed with energy and a level of intensity that he somehow found absolutely fascinating. She didn't want to trust him—that was obvious—but she was too interested to ask him to leave. A challenge; he liked that. Kept his mind off his real reason for being here.

They got the comforter rolled to the end of the bed, and he glanced again at the photo. The woman was beautiful. Not as interesting as Lola, but if this was Kaz, RJ had excellent taste.

"Is that Kaz?" He nodded toward the picture.

Lola raised her head, stared at the framed print and her entire demeanor softened. He hadn't expected that. "Yeah. That was taken a couple of years ago. That's Kaz with her little sister, Jilly. We never met Jilly. She was killed in a car accident about a year ago."

"Oh." Ben reached for the fitted sheet on his side and tugged it free. The image of another child, another time and place, filled his head. He shoved it aside and concentrated on the sheets, on helping Lola.

On not thinking about that little boy or his mother, of what happened that night in the rain. Not until he had to face RJ.

They finished up the bed in silence and Ben followed Lola back to the front room. "I'm going to get my duffle out of the car," he said. Really, he had to get out of the house. Away from memories that wouldn't leave him alone, from a woman with the ability to cloud his thoughts, to make him wish that he was a normal guy, that this was a typical situation.

He was so fucking far from normal it wasn't even funny. He closed the door softly behind him and paused on the front porch to get a better look at the house. He'd always gotten such a kick out of these neighborhoods in San Francisco, with so many houses lined up so close together.

This appeared to be a larger-than-average, older style house that had been divided into two apartments. There were two garage doors below the main level, and steps leading up to living areas on opposite ends of the structure.

The place next to Mandy and Lola's was dark. In fact, the entire neighborhood was quiet and fairly dark with that burned out street lamp, and the fact that he hadn't turned on the porch light. Ben stood there in the shadows for a moment, enjoying the cool, damp air he would always associate with San Francisco. He'd had his fill of sand and sun, of scorching heat and freezing nights. Hell, he'd had it with Bosnia, Iraq, and Afghanistan. He'd spent too much of his life on the other side of the world, too many years trying to run from the truth.

In fact, it had not been all that hard to stay away when the truth was so damned ugly. He was a coward—he'd run when his brother needed him. A failure. Nothing to be proud of. He'd been a damned good soldier, mainly because he just didn't give a shit if he made it out or not. Not caring if you lived or died could make any jerk look brave. Sometimes he thought things would have been so much better if he'd just bought it on one of his missions. So many good men lost over there.

Why the fuck was he still alive?

Fog was slowly creeping in, drifting in eddies and wisps as it flowed inland on a gentle onshore breeze. The Pacific was only a couple of miles away and there was a definite chill in the air. It fit the mood that had settled over Ben like a shroud. He was worn out, exhausted, but he knew what waited for him when he finally fell asleep.

Would he ever be free of the nightmares?

The night was still, his footsteps the only sound as he walked down the stairs to the car, unlocked the trunk, and grabbed his duffle bag. He'd already locked the car and was headed toward the house when he remembered the case with his laptop on the floor in the backseat.

"Fuck." Muttering, he went back to the car and grabbed the briefcase.

As he was locking the door, a car pulled out of a driveway across the street. He watched as it slowly went by before disappearing around the corner—a dark sedan with government plates and what looked like two men in the front.

He hadn't heard them come out of the house where the car had been parked. Were they sitting there, watching him? He could have sworn it was the same car he'd seen earlier today when he'd parked at the cemetery after he left his parents' house. He stared in the direction they'd gone.

"Damn," he muttered. "Paranoia, anyone?"

He was tired and it had been a long and emotional day. Looping the strap of the duffle over his shoulder, Ben grabbed the briefcase with his laptop and went back to the house.

Lola opened the door for him as he reached the top step.

"Thanks." He stepped into the front room. "I'll go put this stuff in the bedroom."

"Have you eaten?"

"No, but I imagine there's a homeless guy over in the Tenderloin who's probably sleeping off a good hamburger." He left her standing there with her puzzled expression, and dumped his things in Kaz's room.

Mandy passed him as he stepped out of the room. "G'night, Ben. I had a really long day at work, so I'm headed to bed. I left clean towels and a fresh razor for you on top of the cabinet in the bathroom in case you need one in the morning." She pointed to a door at the end of the hallway.

"Thank you. I appreciate it. And thank you for calling Kaz about the room. My plane didn't get in until three in the morning, so I have a feeling I'll be needing that bed really soon."

She laughed. Mandy really was adorable, though she hadn't grabbed his attention the way her sister had. "Not until after you eat. Lola's heating up some lasagna for you. Take it from me —you do not want to miss her cooking."

"Thanks. I don't intend to. Good night, Mandy."

"C'mon, Rico." She snapped her fingers and the old dog waddled down to the end of the hallway and followed Mandy into her bedroom.

Ben headed in search of Lola. If he hadn't already figured out where the kitchen was, his nose would have led him. The savory scent of lasagna had his mouth watering. His last meal had been hours ago. He couldn't recall his last home-cooked meal.

He stood in the doorway and watched Lola as she got out silverware and set a place at the round oak table in the middle of the kitchen. She stretched to reach a wine glass on an upper shelf. He would have offered to help, but she was at least five eight or nine, and grabbed it easily. That went on the table with a basket of bread beside it. She used thick potholders to lift a tray of lasagna out of the oven, placed it on top of the stove, walked across the room to the refrigerator and grabbed a plate with a perfectly arranged green salad. That went on the table above the place setting, next to the bread.

Every move was made with purpose, not a single wasted step. Finally, when she appeared to have everything ready, she spun around and gasped, slapped her hand over her heart.

"Crap! How long have you been standing there?"

"Less than a minute. I'm sorry." He walked into the kitchen. "I didn't mean to startle you. I was just watching you throw it all together." He laughed. "You look like you've done this before."

"Cook?" She smiled, and it was the first time she'd looked totally relaxed since he'd arrived. "Cooking's my personal form of therapy. I love to cook." She pulled the chair back. "Sit and I'll bring you a plate."

"I show up and you need therapy?" She laughed and shook her head when he added, "Mandy said it's pretty good stuff."

"Of course it is, though I've always accused Mandy of buttering me up when I cook so she doesn't have to do it. Red or white?" She turned and smiled at him and it took a moment for him to figure out what she wanted.

"Oh. Wine?" He laughed. "Need to get my head in the game. Actually, just water, please. I got in around three this morning and haven't had much sleep. If I have any wine, my face might land in my plate."

She filled a glass with ice cubes and added water for him, and red wine for herself. He hadn't been to California for years, but he vaguely remembered the label she was pouring. "Tangled Vines? Isn't that a vineyard in Sonoma County?"

"It is. Dry Creek Valley. It's the vineyard where Jake photographed Kaz for the Intimate Jewelry collection. In fact, it's where they're staying tonight."

"RJ . . . Jake. Wow. I need to get used to his name change. He's a photographer? Professional?" When Lola nodded, he said, "I had no idea."

"He's good. That's how he and Kaz met. I'm the office manager at Top End, a modeling agency where Kaz used to work, and Jake came in looking for a model for a line of body jewelry that Marcus Reed was doing a big publicity promotion on. Kaz has piercings and she was perfect for the ad campaign."

She used a spatula to scoop out a big square of lasagna, put it on a plate, and placed it in front of him. "Now eat."

He picked up his fork. "I will, but I want you to tell me what happened that's kept Kaz and my brother at the vineyard. I want to know more about R . . . I mean Jake." He cut a forkful of lasagna and said, "I screwed him over in a big way almost two decades ago. I'm here, hopefully, to make things right, if I can. I need to know what he's doing now. Starting now and working back probably makes more sense."

He hadn't really expected her to tell him all the details, but he was shocked to learn that while Lola and Mandy barely knew his brother, they knew how much their roommate loved him. Lola told him how a psychopath had kidnapped Kaz after a number of attempts on her life, but it wasn't random.

Not at all. He'd targeted Lola's roommate because he hated Jake.

While Lola talked, Ben finished his dinner. He was vaguely aware that it was delicious, but he barely tasted the meal, he was so caught up in the story Lola was telling. She described the attempts on Kaz's life, the convoluted plot that had driven her away from his brother and directly into the arms of a madman.

The images in his mind were stark and real —Lola describing how the man had taken Kaz to the vineyard, had beaten her and tied her up in an old barn, how Jake had found her by tracking the signal between her digital tablet and her cell phone. It wasn't long before Jake had realized they were at the same vineyard where they'd done the photos for Marcus Reed's ad campaign.

"As soon as he pulled into the vineyard, Jake ran into Nate Dunagan, the vineyard manager at Tangled Vines. Nate had come out because his wife said she'd heard a woman scream. Jake told him Kaz had been kidnapped, that it had to be her. They got into the barn —it's been renovated and it's a tasting room now —and the guy had Kaz tied up. He'd beaten her, but she was still conscious. Jake rushed the guy, who got off one shot and grazed his arm, but they were all lucky it wasn't worse."

"But why?" Ben set his fork on the plate and focused on Lola. "Why would this guy hate Jake so much?"

"That's what's really sad. It turned out that years ago, this same guy had beat up his wife and she was leaving him, when she and their little boy were hit by a car and killed. Jake was the driver, and the kidnapper has been plotting to kill Jake for almost two decades. The guy hadn't been able to find him—at first because Jake was in jail, but then when he got out, Jake used a different name. Kaz told them the man hadn't made the connection between RJ Cameron and Jacob Lowell until he spotted Jake over on Battery near Marcus Reed's office. Jake drives a big Escalade with *RJ Lowell, Photography* decals on the doors. The guy saw him, recognized him as RJ Cameron and got Jake's name and number off the decal. He followed him and ended up in the coffee shop where Mandy works, where Jake had his first meeting with Kaz. For whatever reason, he decided to target Kaz."

Her words echoed, as if they came from a long distance. Ben's chest tightened until it was hard to breathe; his hands clenched tightly into fists as Lola talked. He had an almost manic compulsion to stand up and scream no, it wasn't Jake's fault. Jake wasn't driving. He hadn't hurt anyone.

But Jake had never told a soul. And because of that, he'd made both himself and a girl he loved targets of a psychopath.

Ben found himself gazing at Lola Monroe, hoping she held the key that could put an end to his pain, but of course that made no sense. There was no way she could help him. Especially now. He'd carried this burden for so damned long, but he'd had no idea the depth of pain he'd caused others. No idea how to open up, how to tell the story that would make him look like anything other than the bastard he was.

He raised his head, glanced beyond Lola and her questioning look, and saw the darkness through the kitchen window. A backyard. Quiet, he needed a few minutes of quiet. A little slice of time to find his sanity before he spun out of control.

Without a word, he pushed his chair back from the table and quietly carried his plates to the sink. Lola stared after him, frowning, but he had no idea where to start, what to say, so he didn't say anything. He felt as if he stood at the top of a high cliff with his life spread out below, but he couldn't make that leap. The compulsion had been growing, the desire to end whatever hold he had on living out a future. The war hadn't managed to kill him. He'd come close to doing it himself, except he couldn't do it to RJ. Apologizing to his brother, asking his forgiveness, was more important than dying. He had to do that first, but right now he needed to get away before he lost it altogether and scared this poor woman to death.

He walked toward the back door, opened it quietly, and stepped outside.

It was dark in the small backyard, and huge trees blocked most of the light from the streetlights on the street behind the house, but he walked down the stairs and out into a small garden area and just kept going. The back fence wasn't all that far away, and his heart seized up at the thought that he was trapped back here, that he couldn't get away.

But even if he could run, there was nowhere to go. No place to escape the weight of all that he'd done, and even more important, what he hadn't done. He stumbled over a rock border he'd missed in the dark, and then spotted a darker shadow among the bushes. A bench in a small alcove of growing things, a place to sit, maybe to find his center, a chance to regroup before he went back inside.

He'd had a plan; he'd decided to come back, hadn't he? He had to make it up to RJ. It was so simple, and he had to start now.

But when he thought of how many people he'd hurt, of how much damage he'd done, he couldn't catch his breath. Pain sliced across his chest; his lungs burned. He tried to draw in some air, but the sound he made startled him. It happened again, and it wasn't until he heard the grating noise a third time that he knew what it was. Knew why his eyes burned and his throat hurt.

He was crying.

He couldn't remember crying, not even as a kid, not when his parents turned away from him, not when he'd stood there in the rain looking at the broken bodies of his victims lying in the street. Not in all the years of war and death and loss, of fear and anger and hopeless resignation. Not once had he cried.

But tonight he discovered that once he started, there was no way in hell to make it stop.

CHAPTER 3

Lola had no idea what was going on in Ben's head. He'd gotten an absolutely stricken look on his face, quietly stood, carried his dishes to the sink, and then just kept going. While she sat there, absolutely flummoxed, he up and walked out the back door. It was dark out there, and there was no gate out of the yard.

If he was planning to leave, it wasn't going to happen through the backyard.

She cleaned up the dishes and waited, thinking he'd come back inside, but when the kitchen was done and the minutes still ticked by and he didn't return, she got worried. Grabbing an old sweatshirt, Lola pulled it on and went out.

Standing at the top of the stairs, she tried to see him, but their yard, while small, was pretty overgrown with old trees and shrubs and dark little paths. She should have grabbed a flashlight, but there was a bit of ambient light filtering through the trees, coming from the streetlight directly behind them, and she knew the paths and trails well enough.

Then she heard him—at least she thought it was Ben, but if it was, then something was terribly wrong. He'd gone to her favorite spot, an old iron bench with a wood-slat seat beneath a huge dogwood tree. The white blooms looked ghostly in the pale glow from the streetlight, and the low branches had created a shelter of twisted limbs and velvety leaves.

Lola didn't say a word. She sat beside Ben. He was turned away from her, practically doubled over, his forearms resting on his thighs, hands clutching his head, bent so low his face was between his knees. He cried hard, gasping breaths that seemed to tear from the very center of him. She had no idea what had upset him, knew nothing of his past or his obviously troubled relationship with his brother, but something in the story she'd told him tonight had brought him to this.

She didn't really think about why she did what she did, but it felt like the most natural thing in the world to curl around him, wrap her arms around his waist, and lay her cheek against his back. She held him close against her chest as he wept.

As she held him, silently comforting him, she realized she was acting totally out of character. She wasn't the nurturing type—that was Mandy's role. Lola was the bossy one, the decision maker, the one Kaz called a force of nature. Only now? Now, this felt right.

She knew it was right when Ben slowly turned and hugged her, when his harsh sobs eased into slow, stuttering breaths, and then settled into even breathing as he brought himself under control. He held her close, resting his chin on her head, not saying anything. After a minute he sniffed, pulled away to grab a handkerchief out of his pocket, wiped his eyes, blew his nose, let out one deep breath, sucked in another.

She didn't say a word. There was nothing she could say when she had no idea what hurt him so badly. She had a vague sense of guilt that she'd caused this, but he didn't seem to blame her. At least he didn't appear to mind her staying with him. They sat there in the darkness, in the misty quiet of the evening, but it was a comfortable, almost companionable silence.

Until he began to talk. Then, all Lola could do was hang on and listen.

"I'm sorry, Lola. I've never done that. Never lost it that way." He let out a long, slow breath. "All those terrible things that happened to Kaz? To my brother? It's a long story, but it was my fault. All of it."

She started to say that it couldn't be, he wasn't even around, but he softly pressed a finger to her lips. "First, I need to apologize. I shouldn't burden you with this, but I have to tell someone. I'm sorry, but you're . . . Hell, Lola, there's no way I'll ever fix everything I've screwed up." He let out another shuddering breath. "I need to explain so you'll understand. It started years ago in a classically dysfunctional household. I'm three years older than RJ. He was my baby brother and I loved him so much, but part of that was probably because he idolized me. I could do no wrong in his eyes, even though, at first, I was our parents' favorite of the two of us. He didn't care because he looked up to me. The thing is, our mother was determined that one of her sons would be famous. She started with me. She'd been a competitive swimmer in college and got it into her head that swimming was a classy sport, and I was going to be an Olympian."

Lola didn't move, but when he paused, she quietly asked, "Were you? An Olympian?"

He shook his head. "No. Not even close. I competed as a kid, but my heart wasn't in it. I wanted to play Little League. I had a mean pitch, but that wasn't the kind of sport the kids in our fancy neighborhood wasted their time on. When I refused to train to be a swimmer, she gave me the option of trying fencing or said they'd buy me a horse if I wanted to get into show jumping. Those were the sports that were acceptable to her. But I still wanted to play Little League, so I forged my father's signature—his was the easiest—and joined a team. I was a good pitcher, but my parents never saw a single game. They'd given up on me and turned their attention to RJ. I know you said he goes by Jake now, but then he was RJ, and he was one hell of a swimmer. He was also such a major a suck-up I couldn't stand him. By the time he was fifteen he was breaking records all over the place. He qualified for and competed in the Olympics in 1996, and when he won three golds, our parents were thrilled."

"What about you?"

"Me? I'd dropped out of college after my first year at Berkeley when Dad quit paying tuition. Swim coaches were expensive, but the crazy thing was, as jealous as I was of the attention RJ was getting, I missed the little shit. He was a good kid. It wasn't his fault that he was good at what he did. Hell, he was good at everything, but Mom was turning him into a freak. He was going by a stage name for the games. RJ Cameron, with bleached-blonde hair and California surfer good looks. Hollywood was interested and the world really was all his for the asking."

Ben sat there, his arms still wrapped around Lola, remembering what it was like so long ago, before everything went wrong. It was surprisingly easy to talk to her, out here in the dark with nothing but the damp mist and the distant sound of city traffic. She was warm and soft in all the right places, and she fit into his arms as if she'd been made for him.

She moved, leaned back far enough to look at him. Her eyes sparkled; the pale light reflected from the streetlight as bright as twin stars in her face.

"What happened, Ben? Something terrible, obviously."

He nodded. "Oh, yeah. It was definitely terrible. I stole

a car. No idea why. It was a brand new Dodge Viper and the guy had left the keys in the ignition and the engine running while he ran into a little market for a pack of cigarettes. I just got in and drove away, and it was like striking gold. He'd left a six-pack of beer in the passenger seat, so I opened a bottle and drove my new wheels and felt like the coolest guy around. I was nineteen, no job, no education—nothing to lose, right? I ended up near my parents' house in Marin. Hadn't been there in months, but their car was gone and I figured I might be able to find some loose cash, but when I went inside, RJ was there. He was alone, sitting on the couch, watching TV."

"Was he glad to see you?"

"Oh, yeah. He was a real little shit, but he loved me. Hell, I loved him too. I still do. He thought I was invincible, but I was just a young, stupid guy with something to prove. I talked him into going out with me. Didn't tell him the car was stolen, just that it was new and I was trying it out. I had another couple of beers but he didn't want one. He was serious about the swimming and drinking wasn't good for an athlete. I was pretty buzzed, it had started raining, and he was getting nervous. I punched the gas and spun out. I was trying to freak him out, but it didn't work the way I expected."

He raised his head, tried to pull away, but Lola held on. "What happened, Ben?"

God, he really didn't want to go there. He couldn't meet her steady gaze.

"Tell me."

He nodded. Closed his eyes, but that made the visual even sharper. "It was really stormy and I was going too fast. RJ yelled, told me to look out, but I didn't see them."

Silence settled around them. Then Lola whispered, "See who, Ben?"

"A little boy. His mother." He heard Lola's gasp, but he

kept talking, and words spilled out, words he'd never spoken aloud, not in all the years since that horrible night. "They were in the crosswalk. I plowed right into them. I think the woman died on impact. The little boy died before the ambulance arrived. I was too busy puking my guts out in the bushes to do anything. RJ tried to help them, but there wasn't anything he could do. But that's not the worst of it."

Lola kept her arms around him, anchoring him. He felt the slow, steady beat of her heart, her warm breath against his throat. It was enough to help him get through the rest of it, though he imagined her asking him to get the hell gone when he was through. Anything to be rid of him.

"I looked up and RJ was crying, kneeling next to the little boy, holding his hand. I guess he'd just died, and it was raining. RJ had taken his jacket off to cover the mother and had put his shirt over the little boy, so he was kneeling in the rain without a shirt, shivering, with their blood on his chest, and all I could think of was how beautiful he looked, like a fallen angel or some shit like that. He was all muscle and strength, and I was nothing but a skinny drunk.

"God, I was such a bastard. I begged him to tell the cops that he'd been driving. He was young and famous. I figured they'd probably let him off, but I was over eighteen and drunk, so I'd be tried as an adult and probably go to jail for the rest of my life.

"He didn't even hesitate. The cops came, asked us what happened, and he told them straight up that he'd been driving, that I was too drunk and he wouldn't let me behind the wheel in that condition, that he hadn't seen the woman and the boy until it was too late. And I just stood there, swaying, agreeing with everything he said. I remember when they asked him where he'd stolen the car and he turned and looked at me, and there was so much disappointment in his eyes, because at that point he didn't know it was stolen. Right then, I didn't care. Slick as can be, he said, 'What's the name of that place where I borrowed the car?' He kind of smirked when he said it, like a smart ass. And I told him the name of the market, and said it was really easy because the owner had left the keys in it and the engine running. And RJ just said, 'Yeah. It was like an open invitation.'"

"You never stepped forward? Never told anyone he'd lied to cover for you?"

She didn't let go of him, but she didn't give him a break either. She loosened her grasp and sat back far enough to look him in the eye. It hurt, that pure, honest stare. There was no condemnation, merely a silent demand for the truth.

He couldn't even say the words. He just shook his head. "I wasn't charged with anything. They decided I was too drunk to have made a conscious decision, or to provide any evidence, so as soon as I was free to go, I enlisted and left before the case actually went to trial. I was a fucking coward, Lola. I'm still a coward. That man went after your roommate because of the lies I made RJ tell almost twenty years ago. Everything bad that happened to her, that's happened to RJ . . . it's all my fault. I know I can't make it right, but I have to apologize, have to tell him how sorry I am."

She gazed at him, a long, steady stare that told him absolutely nothing.

"Are you? Are you really sorry, or are you tired of feeling guilty? There's a difference, you know."

For some reason, her hard-ass comment made him smile. "Believe me, that's a question I've asked myself. Honestly? I've felt guilty for years, but it wasn't until I got home and found out just how much I'd screwed up my brother's life that I realized how very sorry I really was. My parents told me he was found guilty of involuntary manslaughter and sentenced to the California Youth

Authority. They didn't say for how long and didn't even know if he served his full term or got out early, but he didn't get off the way I'd always figured he would. Our parents turned their backs on him the moment he was found guilty, but I turned my back on him, too. I had no idea they'd disowned him. I went to see them today and they haven't had any contact with him since the bailiff hauled him out of the courtroom in handcuffs. He was only sixteen years old! What kind of parents turn their backs on their son? Yet they welcomed me home like a fucking hero."

"Did you tell them the truth?"

He shook his head. "No. I want to do that when RJ's with me. I want to hear them apologize to him, and I want him to know I mean it when I say I'm going to make it up to him. I messed with his life. He could have gone on to another Olympics, and in four more years, he would have been even stronger. Or hell, he had all kinds of interest from Hollywood. He could have done so much with his life."

"I don't know anything about his legal problems, but he's done an awful lot. He's a successful photographer with a growing business and an excellent reputation. Kaz loves him, and she doesn't love easily, so that says a lot about his character."

She studied him again, that steady, unnerving stare, and it was unsettling, not knowing what she thought of the situation, what she thought of him. Of his character—or lack of it.

It was somehow very important, what Lola thought of him.

"What about you, Ben? What have you done with your life?"

What the hell had he done? One deployment after another, most recently showing an egotistical jerk for a private security firm around a couple of towns in Kandahar

Province in Afghanistan. He'd felt like a damned mule carrying briefcases of money for the guy, but everything was done in cash with the Afghanis. He'd often wondered, though, how much of that money went to securing safe passage for their soldiers, and how much went into the drug trade. It wasn't his job to question. No, it was his job to do what his commander told him to do, and keep his mouth shut.

But all he said to Lola was, "I've been in the Army since before the trial. Served in Bosnia, Iraq, and Afghanistan. I'm a master sergeant. I put in for stateside duty to have time to see RJ. This is my first assignment in the US since I enlisted. I'll be training security troops at Camp Parks, over in Dublin."

"You'll be close, then."

He nodded. "I will. Lola . . ." He sighed. "I apologize for what happened tonight, but I think it's been a long time coming. I'm just sorry you had to see me like that."

"I'm not." She rested her forearms on his shoulders. "What you told me . . . Ben, if you could live with something like that and not be affected, I'd say there was something terribly wrong with you. I don't know how Jake's going to react to your being here, but I'm glad you're here. I imagine he's missed you, no matter how awful you were to him. On the other hand, I think you owe Kaz as much an apology as you do your brother. That maniac almost killed her. He beat her up pretty badly. He shot your brother." She smiled at him. "Thank God he's a lousy shot."

"You're not kidding." He stared into the darkness, wondering about tomorrow. Realizing that if the guy hadn't missed when he shot RJ, it would already be too late.

"Are you okay?" Lola sat beside him, but she still had an arm around his waist.

Ben wrapped his arms around her and pulled her into his

lap. "I am now." He nuzzled her hair. It was coal black, but she was really fair. He was sure she'd dyed it this color. It looked really dramatic, but she wasn't that way, really. From what he could tell, Lola was pretty down home. She was bossy and self-assured, but he liked her confidence, liked the way she didn't take any crap off him.

What was RJ like now? She'd said he was successful, that his girlfriend was a beautiful model. After twenty years of trying his damnedest not to think about his brother, Ben wanted to know everything. "What's he like? My brother? Does he look like me? Sound like me? We used to be a lot alike, but I doubt we are anymore. Our lives have been so different."

"He looks like you, but he's a lot taller. Maybe six six, or even a little over. Kaz is six two, and she looks petite next to him. His hair's longer than yours, but it's the same color." She turned and looked into his eyes. "I think his eyes are dark brown. Yours look gray." She grinned. "You have beautiful eyes, by the way."

He actually blushed. Thank goodness it was too dark for her to see. "Thank you. I'm surprised they're not bloodshot. I had a long flight, an unexpected layover due to bad weather, and a rough visit with my parents. And a meltdown in your backyard."

"Not your best day, is that what you're saying?"

He liked the way she leaned against him. And she hadn't complained a bit about his pulling her into his lap. "Pretty much. It's late. I should probably get some sleep, but I need a shower. It won't keep you awake, will it?"

She shook her head. "No, but let me get in there first so I can brush my teeth and grab my nightgown. I hate to tell you, but you're the first guy to stay over in our girls-only domain."

He helped her off his lap, then stood and took her hand. "You'll have to lead the way. I just about killed myself coming out here. You've got rock borders that jump out and attack."

"I wondered why you came out here in the dark. I thought at first you were trying to leave, but there's no gate."

He stopped and wrapped his arms around her. "Actually, I could feel the meltdown coming, but I wasn't really sure what it was. I just had a feeling it was going to get ugly. I didn't want you to see me fall apart."

She turned and cupped his face in her hands. "I saw, and it's okay, Ben. I don't think any less of you. We're all allowed to have emotions, regrets, issues."

"Thank you. Damn, Lola. It's hard. I've tried to bury the entire incident, but I couldn't. I knew it was wrong to ask RJ to lie, but I didn't know how to fix it. I still don't."

Still holding his face, she forced eye contact with nothing more than her gentle touch. "You've made a good start tonight. Admitting what you did, what really happened. That's not easy, but you had to do it. And you'll have to do it again, when you apologize to Jake, when you tell your parents. Think of it as removing a terrible infection, one that can't start to heal until the wound is clean. But each time, it's going to be easier."

He sighed. Hated to admit more weakness. "I went to the cemetery today. Where they're buried. It's the second time I've gone, the second time I didn't have the balls to walk the few steps to their graves."

"You will, Ben. When you're ready, you'll be able to apologize to them, too."

"God, I hope so." He pulled her close and rested his chin on top of her head. Her arms went around his waist and she rubbed his back. So soothing, to hold a beautiful woman in his arms. To feel the comfort of her touch.

She leaned away and her steady gaze drilled him. Eviscerated him. "You don't have to do this alone, Ben. Not anymore."

There was no fighting this, not with his emotions so raw. It seemed perfectly natural to lean close and take her mouth with his. Her eyes flashed wide, and then her lips softened, her eyes closed. Her body melted into his like warm wax, the hills and valleys of their forms finding their corresponding opposite, one to the other.

He cupped her bottom in the palm of his hand, lifted her close, pressed his surging arousal against the soft curve of her belly. She whimpered, a soft sound of need that had him fighting for control. She was wearing an old sweat-shirt and soft cotton knit pants. He slipped his hand beneath her sweatshirt, beneath the cotton tank top she wore underneath, but he didn't go for her breasts. Instead he opened his palm against the warmth of her spine, his other hand still cupped her buttocks through soft, cotton knit.

Her tongue tangled with his, her lips moved across his mouth and he wanted her with a need that had him sweating in spite of the chilly fog. Lola leaned into the support of his arms, lifted her legs, and looped her heels behind his waist, and still she met him, kiss for kiss.

His erection rose high and hard between them, trapped in the warm valley of her thighs. He wanted her. Wanted her as he'd never wanted another woman, but this wasn't right, not the time, or the place, or the right circumstances. Regretfully, he eased back on his kisses until he finally pressed his forehead to hers and caught his breath. "I'm sorry. I didn't mean to . . ."

"Well, Ben . . ." She dragged the words out, and he felt the laughter behind her drawl. "I'm not sorry, and I'm re-ally glad you did, but thank you for stopping. Not that I don't want to take this further, but I don't think it would be a very good idea. Not tonight."

He held her close while she eased her feet to the ground. "Sort of what I was thinking," he said. "Too soon, too intense. When I take you to bed, I want it to be for the right reasons."

She cocked her head and gazed at him, her fair skin almost ghostly in the darkness. "When, not if, huh? So tell me, what would those reasons be?"

"Because we've both thought about it. Because we can't not do it, although I'm really close to that point right now, but I think you're special, Lola." He leaned over and kissed her—a quick little kiss. A safe kiss. "You've pretty much dissected me. I want to know more about you, but not tonight when I'm so bone tired I won't be able to follow through in the manner you deserve."

"Oooh. I like the sound of that." She took his hand and tugged him toward the house.

"You should. I can definitely make it worth your while." He was trying hard not to laugh.

"You're a tease, aren't you?"

Lola was laughing, and he loved the sound. "I'll have you know that I'm officially off men. My last boyfriend was a monumental jerk, so it's going to take not only major powers of persuasion, but the technique of a master to keep me interested."

"Sounds like a dare. I'll bone up on my love master technique. Be afraid, Ms. Monroe. Be very afraid."

"Yeah. Right."

She led him up the back stairs and through the kitchen. "I'll be out of the bathroom in a couple of minutes, and then it's all yours." They stopped in front of Kaz's bedroom door. Ben cupped her shoulders in his big hands.

"Thank you, Lola. For everything. I never expected any of this." He kissed her fast and hard. "Not the welcome, not the lasagna, not the therapy session." He laughed.

"Especially the therapy session. It's amazing how much better I feel."

"Wait until you see my bill." She kissed him just as fast, not nearly as hard. "Then we'll see how thankful you are. G'night, Ben. Sleep well."

Then she turned away and walked the few steps to the bathroom. He watched the gentle sway of her hips until she closed the door behind her.

CHAPTER 4

Ben awoke disoriented but surprisingly well-rested. Disoriented because he'd slept so soundly. No nightmares—not even dreams. He'd crawled into the big, comfortable bed totally drained after his meltdown last night and a short, hot shower. Now, sunlight streaming through the slanted blinds had him squinting, wondering why it was so damned bright this early in the morning.

He lay there a moment, thinking of all he'd shared with Lola. He couldn't recall any time in his life when he'd dumped personal shit like that on anyone, much less someone he barely knew. Nor could he remember how long it had been since he'd slept until after sunrise . . . he glanced at the clock on the nightstand beside the bed and did a double-take. "Holy shit."

It was almost ten.

He'd slept over ten hours. Unbelievable.

Still, he lay there a moment longer, listening. Sleeping so long was as unbelievable as waking up to laughter, but that's what he heard. Mandy and Lola laughing and talking, the sounds so damned joyful they made him smile. After a couple of minutes, he got up, dug a pair of clean sweatpants out of his duffle bag, and slipped them on along with a T-shirt. After a quick trip to the bathroom to wash up and brush his teeth, a quicker glance in the mirror at the healing damage to his face from an up-close-and-personal with shrapnel from an IED—and didn't that feel like a whole other life—he headed out to the kitchen where the smell of bacon reminded him that Lola's wonderful lasagna had been quite a few hours ago.

He glanced at his watch. Ten o'clock, straight up.

Mandy spotted him first. "Good morning, Ben. I was about ready to go in to see if you were still breathing." Smiling as if it was perfectly normal for a strange guy to come wandering out of the bedroom, she grabbed a cup, filled it with fresh coffee, and handed it to him.

He lifted it to his lips, but inhaled first. "Damn, that smells good. Thank you." He glanced at Lola in front of the stove. "Good morning. I didn't mean to sleep this late, but considering I was in Kabul less than a week ago, I figure it'll take me a while to get my hours turned right side up. I definitely have to tell your roommate she's got the most comfortable bed I've slept in in years."

"Kaz and Jake should be here in the next couple of hours. Sit down and I'll make you some breakfast. Mandy and I have already eaten."

As soon as Lola stuck a plate in front of him, Rico took up his station beside Ben's chair. Ben glanced at the mournful looking mutt and then at Lola.

"Don't you dare. He's not supposed to beg. You feed him, he's yours."

He made a sad face at the dog. "Sorry, Rico. I think she means it."

Rico finally gave up and wandered away. It was a lot easier to eat without the droopy-eyed basset laying a guilt trip on him with that uncompromising stare. Once Rico was gone, Ben thoroughly enjoyed his meal while Mandy told stories of some of her more eccentric customers at the coffee shop, and Lola talked about the different models working at Top End. Their easy camaraderie, the natural back-and-forth quips, comments, and even insults had him laughing at their stories, and missing RJ more than ever.

He and his brother had been the same way when they were kids—quick with the insults and the banter, the smart-ass comments. He missed that. In fact he hadn't realized how much he missed it until now, watching Lola and Mandy, listening to their easy conversation, the way they bounced comments and silly insults off one another.

He wondered if RJ would even talk to him.

He glanced at the clock. He was going to find out in the next couple of hours.

After he ate, Ben stood in front of the sink washing breakfast dishes while Lola dried. Mandy had just walked in from taking Rico out in back when she glanced toward the front door.

"I think I hear someone coming up the steps." She ran out of the kitchen.

Ben raised an eyebrow. "Did you hear anything?"

Lola just laughed. "No, but she's always right."

They both heard the sound of the door opening, and immediately, Mandy's shocked voice.

"Oh my God, Kaz! Your face! That bastard. I didn't realize how badly he'd hurt you."

Lola glanced at Ben and set the towel on the draining board.

Another voice. Sort of soft and husky, sexy. Had to be Kaz.

"It's okay. I'll heal and he's going to be in jail for a long time. Knowing that goes a long way toward making it all better."

Then Mandy shrieked. "Is that what I think it is? Lola! Get your skinny butt out here. These two are engaged!"

Lola was already headed out of the kitchen with Rico hot on her heels.

Ben just stood there. His heart pounded and it was hard to breathe, sort of the way he felt when he was on patrol and knew there were enemy insurgents nearby.

It's just RJ, you idiot.

He took a slow, deep breath and let it out just as slowly. Then he just stood there a moment, listening to the sound of laughter, of women talking a mile a minute, talking over each other the way they always seemed to do, and he knew that somewhere, in the midst of all that sound, was his brother.

He dried his hands on Lola's towel and walked quietly into the front room. He had a moment before anyone noticed him, a moment where he stood very still and stared at RJ. There was no doubt it was his kid brother—he still looked so much like Ben that it was like seeing a younger, taller, better looking version of himself.

He glanced at the three women sitting together on the couch. Kaz was in the middle between Mandy and Lola. One eye was badly bruised and she had more bruises on her face, but she was still beautiful. Gorgeous, in fact, but nowhere near as mesmerizing as Lola with her long, coal black hair, fair skin, and tall, slim body. Lola might not be a traditionally beautiful woman, but she was definitely fascinating.

He certainly found her fascinating, and had from the first moment he saw her.

He was going to have to think about that. For whatever reason, women had always been attracted to him. He'd never lacked for female companionship no matter where he was stationed, but none of them had ever drawn his interest like Lola.

He focused his attention on RJ once again, just as his brother turned and saw him for the first time. They stared at each other for a moment, and Ben couldn't help but wonder what he was feeling, what he was thinking. But then

RJ was coming across the room, his smile open and unguarded, an unexpected look of welcome in those dark brown eyes, wrapping Ben in a rib-cracking hug. Ben was shaking when he raised his arms and hugged RJ, and fighting tears when his brother finally let him go and stepped back.

"God, Ben. It's so damned good to see you. It's been too long."

Ben scrubbed at his eyes with the heels of both hands. "How can you say that, after what . . . ?" He took a deep breath. "Are you okay? They said you got shot, that . . ."

RJ shook his head. "I'm fine. Just grazed my shoulder, but the other? It happened, it's over, and one of these days we can talk about it, but right now I just want to enjoy the fact that you're here and alive, and that maybe I'll have you back in my life."

Ben stood still, watching him. "I didn't expect this. I thought you'd hate me."

RJ just shrugged it off. "I did. For a long time I hated you, but I got a lot older and a little bit smarter. I was an absolute jerk when I was a kid. So were you, but Kaz has really helped me see things through a different lens. I'm in a good place, now, but it's a pretty long story, how I got here."

RJ's softly spoken words gave Ben his first flicker of hope in a very long time. "I want to know it," he said. "I want to know all of it, because I would give anything to be in that kind of place." He sighed and glanced at the three women who sat close together, still talking nonstop.

"What I did was so wrong, and I was too much of a coward to admit it. I knew that if I didn't come back and beg your forgiveness, I'd be eating a bullet before long."

"That better not happen."

"Shit, man . . ." He shook his head. "Lola and Mandy

told me about your girlfriend, your fiancée now, I guess, and that she'd been kidnapped by that poor woman's husband, that you'd been shot. Everything I did that night—I didn't just kill two innocent people. I screwed up both our lives, and the lives of the ones who love us. I'm so sorry. I was a dumb shit, a selfish prick, and too many people have paid."

"For what it's worth, Ben, Kaz and I talked about that very thing last night. She asked me if I was still angry at you, because God knows, I was for a hell of a long time. But I realized I missed my brother more than I hated him, that my life now is pretty damned good, and if all that crap hadn't happened, I could have totally fucked myself up. The past is over. Kaz said we need to move forward. She makes a lot of sense. Can you do that?"

Slowly, Ben shook his head. "I don't know. I've been living with guilt for almost two decades. I don't know if I can leave it behind, but whatever you want, I'll try. Or if you want me to turn myself in, admit what happened, that you were innocent, I'll do that. It's your call."

"Juvenile records are sealed. Once I was released, that was no longer a part of my record. Besides, Ben, we were both in that car. I may have been the one locked up, but I imagine you've served as hard a sentence as I ever did. We can't undo what we did, but we can move forward."

"Okay. Yeah." He rubbed at the back of his head and stared at the girls again before turning to RJ. "There's something, though, that I want you to do."

RJ didn't say a word. Just stood patiently and waited for Ben to spit out what he had to say.

"Whether you go or not, I'm going to see the folks today. They need to know the truth. I went to them first when I got back, asked them where you were. I couldn't believe it when they told me they didn't know and didn't care, but they begged me to come home. I had no idea they'd written you off. I can't believe you never told them the whole story. Haven't you seen them at all since it happened?"

RJ shoved his hands in his back pockets and glanced away. Then he turned back to Ben. "The last time I saw our parents was when the bailiff led me out of the courtroom after the judge announced my sentence, which was to spend the next eight years at the California Youth Authority juvenile training center in Stockton."

Fuck. "Eight years? Aw, shit, man." He started forward without any idea where he was going. Eight fucking years. Spinning around, Ben turned and walked across the room. He slapped the wall hard and leaned his forehead against the back of his hand. He didn't know, but he should have. It should have been him. A minute later he turned and faced his brother. "Hell, RJ. I had no idea. None."

RJ was shaking his head. "I didn't do the whole eight, Ben. I was supposed to serve out the sentence until I was twenty-four, but I got out at twenty-one on good behavior. Mom and Dad didn't come see me once in all that time. I never got a phone call from them, not even a fucking Christmas or birthday card."

"I want you to come with me, RJ."

Jake laughed. "RJ's not going anywhere. RJ Cameron, aka Richie Lowell, went into lockup, but Jacob Lowell came out."

That made perfectly good sense to Ben. After everything RJ had been through, a new name was probably the best way to begin a new life. Ben shot him a cocky grin, feeling more lighthearted than he'd been in what felt like a lifetime.

"Is Jacob willing to face the parents? I know it's something I have to do. Maybe you, too." Ben glanced at his watch. "I think we need to set them straight, and then, personally, I don't care if I never see them again. I can't be-lieve they're our parents."

Jake chuckled. "Probably explains why we're both so screwed up."

Ben punched his shoulder, the way he used to, when Richie was still smaller than him. He was careful to aim for Jake's right arm—the uninjured one. "You're probably right. Will you follow me to the car rental place? I need to drop mine off. I'm actually going to buy a car, now that I'm back in the states."

"Are you here to stay?" He actually sounded hopeful.

Ben looked at him, at the little brother he'd treated like crap, at the smart-ass kid who had grown now into a pretty amazing man, and nodded. "Damn straight I am."

Lola watched the brothers leaving the house together—they looked so much alike, there was no denying their re-lationship, but the change in Ben's appearance, before and after seeing his brother, was nothing short of amazing.

He looked younger, more carefree, more *hopeful* than he'd been even an hour ago.

She'd been attracted to the man last night, even more so this morning. Right now, as the door closed behind Jake and Ben, she felt that attraction like a steady ache in her middle.

Had that kiss last night meant anything? She'd never been affected this deeply by any guy, not in any way, shape, or form. She wanted Ben Lowell with a visceral sense of need that left her feeling slightly stunned and definitely off-balance.

She was glad the brothers were taking off. She needed space, some time apart from Ben, time to think about the way she felt, the effect he had on her by merely smiling, saying a word, glancing her way. It was all new, it was ex-citing, and it scared the hell out of her.

Kaz said something, and she forced herself to pay attention. She really needed to quit thinking about the man, and focus on Kaz as she continued the story of her ordeal. However, try as she might, Lola realized Ben was too deeply embedded in her thoughts to disappear altogether.

"Well, if that's not closure, bro, I don't know what is."

Ben snapped his attention to Jake. He was still processing their parents' reaction to Jake's story, to Ben's admission of guilt. He should have guessed it would be all about them, about their sons' failure. At least he knew there was no reason to return. He and Jake talked for a moment, but then he interrupted the conversation.

"There's one more place I think we both need to go."

Jake stopped at a signal and turned to Ben. "The cemetery, right?"

Ben nodded. "Have you been there?"

Jake glanced away and slowly exhaled. "Once. I drove over but I couldn't make myself look for the graves. I sat in the car."

Someone behind them honked. The light had changed. Jake swung a left and headed the same way Ben had gone yesterday. "I've done the same thing," Ben said. "Twice." He gazed at the once familiar neighborhood as Jake negotiated the short drive to the cemetery.

This time, there were more cars in the parking lot, but Jake found a space and the two of them got out and stood beside the Escalade. Jake rubbed the back of his head and let out a deep breath. "Do you know where . . . ?"

Ben nodded and started walking. He'd made this short trip in his head so many times, but he'd never actually walked between the headstones. He'd made it part of the way the day the woman and her little boy were buried. He'd come wearing a hat pulled down over his eyes, and a leather jacket with the collar turned up to hide his face, and he'd stood in the shadows of an old bay tree while the mother and her son were laid to rest.

After that, on the two subsequent visits he'd made, he hadn't even had the balls to get out of the car. Today, though, with Jake beside him, the walk across the green lawn felt right. He led Jake directly to the markers, two engraved stones lying flat against the lawn.

He and Jake stood quietly. Ben remembered everything about that night with a clarity he'd not had in the twenty years since it had happened. He saw her face, the face of her child, and grief washed over him, almost knocked him to his knees.

He grabbed a handkerchief out of his pocket and wiped his eyes, blew his nose. Realized Jake was doing the same thing. "I wish there was something we could do," he said, "but it's too damned late."

"No, it's not." Jake turned to Ben. "C'mon. I want to tell you about a suggestion Kaz had on the way home today. Actually, I'll let her tell you about it."

It was late afternoon when Jake pulled up in front of the girls' house behind a dark gray Tesla. "Looks like Marc's already here. Kaz said she was going to invite him."

Ben nodded. "That's good. He's the only reason I found you, and even then he protected you. He wouldn't give me your phone number. He sent me to the girls instead."

Jake paused in the process of pulling the keys out of the ignition. "Marc's been like family all these years. I don't think I could have made it without him. He was the one who wrote to me when I was locked up, the only one to visit, to send me the occasional gift or letter. When I got out, I went straight to Marc's and stayed with him long enough to figure out where I wanted to go, what I wanted to do with my life. He's helped me get my photography business going. We're close. I . . ." He sighed and shook his head.

Ben felt like hitting something. He should have been there for Jake, but he wasn't. Instead, he looked at Jake, silently willing his brother to turn and face him.

After a moment, he did.

Ben grabbed his shoulder. He needed that contact. "I'm glad you had him as a friend, that you still have him. He's more your brother than I've been. I hope you'll let me earn my way back, Jake. But don't ever think I want to come between you and your friendship with Marc. At some point, I'm hoping I'll be included, but not until you know you can trust me."

Jake nodded slowly. "Thank you. For understanding." He glanced away, and then turned his focus back to Ben. "I never told him, you know. He thinks I was driving. I'm willing to let the story stay as is."

Ben laughed softly. "Ain't gonna happen, even if I wanted to keep living a lie, which I don't. I told Lola the whole ugly story last night, and I didn't ask her not to say anything. I don't see those three women keeping secrets from each other."

Jake frowned. "You did? But why?"

"It wasn't planned. She told me about Kaz's kidnapping, said it was the husband of the guy whose family you'd killed, and I realized it was all my fault. That the brother who'd lied for me, the woman he loved . . . both of them could have died because of something I did almost two decades ago."

"So you told her? Just . . ."

"Actually, it was after she chased me down in the back-yard and found me in the middle of a total meltdown." He glanced sideways at Jake. "Not one of my more manly moments."

Jake's laughter had Ben grinning back at him. "Unfortunately," Jake said, "I think we all have them once in a while. How'd she handle it?"

"Better than I did. She's a hell of a woman. I like her."

Jake grinned, moment over, at least for now. "C'mon. With any luck, Marc's brought some of the wine from Intimate. It's amazing stuff."

Marc, Lola, Mandy, and Kaz were in the front room sipping wine, eating crackers and cheese, and talking about the reception Jake and Kaz had missed Friday night, when Ben and Jake finally returned. Marc was on his feet in an instant.

"Jake. Damn it, you scared the crap out of me. Don't do that again."

Jake pulled him into a tight hug. "I have no intention of repeating the evening's activities, and neither, I might add, does Kaz."

Marc laughed. "I know. We've talked." He turned toward Ben, but his smile was guarded. "I see you found your way here."

Ben shook hands with him. "Thanks to you." He glanced at Jake, and Jake nodded and turned to the three women.

"Will you lovely ladies excuse us for a few minutes?" he said. "I need to talk to Marc." He turned to Ben. "You, too, bro." Jake grabbed a freshly opened bottle of wine off the coffee table. "Glasses full? Good. I'm taking this with me, too."

The girls laughed. Ben grabbed a couple of empty glasses, and while he noticed some curious glances, no one seemed to mind when the three of them went out through the kitchen and into the backyard. As Ben led the other two down the steps, he glanced behind him at Jake. "This is the scene of my infamous meltdown. Just thought I'd let you know I've already christened it."

Marc frowned, but didn't say anything.

"For what it's worth," Ben added, "It's a lot easier to navigate in daylight. There's a bench back here."

Jake and Marc sat side by side on the bench, while Ben stood in front of them. Jake refilled Marc's wine glass and then poured one each for Ben and himself.

Ben stared at the dark surface of the glass of wine in his hand. "There's a story you need to hear, Marc, about something that never should have been kept from you, about lies that have been allowed to stand much too long."

He'd thought it would be painful, standing here in front of his brother and his brother's best friend, but having already unloaded on Lola made it so much easier to tell Marc the truth. He didn't leave anything out, and he managed to get through the story without breaking down.

Marc stared at him for what felt like a very long time. Then, without raising his voice, he said, "I don't fucking believe it."

Jake chuckled. "I don't think I've ever heard you say 'fuck' before."

"Fuck." He stared at Jake and quietly said, "There. Is that better?" Then he took a deep breath and slowly shook his head. "It's hard to believe. You never said a word? You served all those years at the CYA on a lie? Either you're really stupid or really brave. Forget that. I know you're not stupid. That took a lot of courage."

"A hell of a lot more than I had." Ben squatted down in front of Marc, looked up at him. "I owe you an apology, Marc. As much as I owe Jake. He lied to protect me, but I know he hated like hell that he had to lie to you, too. He should never have done that. It's all on me, and I hope you won't hold it against Jake."

Marc merely shrugged, sort of pulled back into himself. "You do what you have to do. You're his brother, Ben. It's only right you'd have things between you."

Ben glanced at Jake and then focused on Marc. "You're his brother, too, Marc. In every way but blood. Don't ever forget that."

Jake chuckled. "Actually, blood, too. Remember that summer we slit our thumbs and did the blood brother thing?"

Marc's smile lit up his entire face. "I've never forgotten. I just figured it meant more to me than it did to you. You had Ben. I only had you."

"Not true. There was a long time when I only had you, Marc. You kept me going in every way possible. I doubt I'd have come out of that experience in as good of shape as I did if you hadn't been there for me." Jake grinned at Ben. "And now that Ben's back, I assume we've both got him. He's still a pain in the ass, but he's our pain in the ass. Our family's growing."

"You know how that works," Marc said. "Family isn't always the one you're born with. Some of us have learned to pull in extras just to round things out."

Ben glanced at Marc and, brushing nonexistent dust from his tan chinos, said, "You need to be more selective. You'll end up with more jerks like me."

Marc loosened up enough to punch him in the shoulder, and they were laughing when they went back inside. Mandy was the only one who didn't know the truth, and the laughter ended when Ben told her about the lie Jake had carried all those years, the same lie Ben had walked away from. Surprisingly, it got easier with each telling. Kaz and Lola already knew, and Mandy listened without judging.

He'd never expected anything like this; all of them accepting, forgiving. Then Jake joined the conversation and told everyone about their trip to see the parents. There'd been no forgiveness from them, no interest in reconnecting with either son. Once they discovered Ben had been driving, they wrote him off as easily as they had Jake, who was still guilty of, in their words, having thrown away the Olympic success they'd given him.

At the very least, it had offered closure to both brothers.

Mandy was furious, but she nailed it. "Don't feel badly, Ben. Those people you went to see today aren't parents. They're nothing more than sperm and egg donors."

Ben glanced at Jake and they both laughed. So did Marc. His family hadn't been any better, but Mandy was adamant. "Real parents love unconditionally. They don't force their children into molds to benefit their own needs. They help guide their children to find out who and what they're meant to be."

Ben wondered if Mandy and Lola also had huge issues with their own parents.

Kaz stood, wine glass raised. "Hear, hear! I agree, but I be hungry. Let's go eat."

Laughing and teasing Kaz about her flat, grumbling tummy, they all loaded into Jake's Escalade. He waited for a car to pass before pulling out. Ben didn't get a very good look at the two men inside, but he was almost sure it was the same dark sedan he'd seen last night.

He made a note of the license plate on his cell phone, just in case.

CHAPTER 5

Jake was the one to bring up the idea of the memorial at dinner, but then he turned it over to Kaz. "It was your idea, and it's terrific. Ben and I want to do it."

Ben picked up the thread, the way he and Jake used to finish each other's sentences when they were kids. "Jake told me what you'd suggested, Kaz. We don't want to re-invent the wheel, but if any of you know of a shelter for abused women, one that helps the kids deal with abuse as well, we'd like to set up a memorial in their names that would help with funding."

Jake shook his head. "She was Mary. Her little boy was Russell, Jr., but I don't want to have that bastard's name in any memorial to his wife and son."

"Agreed."

Marc interrupted. "The little boy's nickname was Rusty."

"How do you know that?" Jake frowned and glanced at Ben. "I didn't even know."

"I was at the trial. I sat in the back, but I was there every day."

"Shit, Marc." Jake reached across the table and grabbed his hand. "I never knew. I was so focused on holding it together, at not looking at my parents and seeing the obvious disappointment on their faces. I wish I'd known."

"I had to be there. Not just for you. For me, too."

Before Marc explained that enigmatic comment, the waiter arrived to take their orders. Lola assured Ben that they'd find out which shelter sounded like a good one to help support, but Ben couldn't stop thinking about Marc, about the fact he'd been there for Jake.

He wondered if anyone besides Jake had ever been there for Marc.

It was a good three hours later when Jake pulled up in front of the girls' house after a terrific meal. For Ben, it was more fun than he could remember having at any social occasion in his life. In spite of the brief discussion about the memorial, he'd discovered that no one could stay down when Kaz was on a roll. She was the perfect foil for Jake, and they'd had everyone laughing throughout the meal. But now, as they all piled out of the big SUV, Ben put a hand on Marc's shoulder as he started to head toward his car. "Hold up a minute, will you?"

"Sure. What's up?"

"In a minute."

After Jake helped Kaz out of the passenger side, Ben drew him aside. "Kaz? Mind if I snag your guy for a minute?"

She smiled, laughing at something Mandy had said. "Not a problem. It'll give me more time to grab some of my stuff."

The three men waited, watching as the women went up the stairs and into the house. Once the door closed, Jake and Marc both turned toward Ben.

He didn't waste any words. "For whatever reason, someone's following me."

"What?" Jake glanced at Marc, who calmly asked, "What's going on?"

Ben told him about the dark sedan he'd seen at the cemetery after he'd left the parents' house, then again here in front of the girls' place. And tonight, driving past as they had all piled into the Escalade.

"Marc, what's your phone number? I'll send you the license plate, make, and model. I figure with all your security you might have someone who can run the plates for me."

Marc smiled and gave him the number. "That I do. I probably can't get anything on a Sunday night, but I'll have my guy get on it first thing tomorrow."

"Thank you. I've been trying to figure out why anyone would be curious enough about me to warrant following me. My last couple of years in Afghanistan were actually pretty boring. I did some work down in Spin Boldak, an area on one of the main trade routes from Kabul that was a little out of the ordinary, but other than that, I've mostly just run security wherever I've been stationed. I probably wouldn't worry about this too much, but I don't want anything to come back on the girls. I appreciate your checking on this, Marc."

"Not a problem. I need to get going. Unlike some of you guys without a job at the moment, I've got an office where I'm expected at eight in the morning." Laughing, he shook his head. "I may need to change that. Nine sounds a lot more civilized."

He turned toward his car, and then paused and glanced at Jake. "Tell Kaz I really appreciate her invitation to dinner. That was a lot of fun tonight. She's amazing—I can see why you fell so hard—but her roommates are a lot of fun, too."

"I'll let her know. And you're right. It was and they are. We'll do this more often, I promise."

Ben followed Jake up the front steps. He paused on the porch and looked both ways along the wide street. No sign of the dark sedan. Shrugging off the sense he was being watched, he went inside.

A large tote bag filled with makeup, a hair dryer, and other female trappings, sat on the floor in the middle of the front room. Kaz was heading back down the hallway, but she paused and glanced at the guys. "Hey Ben! I forgot to tell you, you're welcome to my bed." Laughing, she added, "I, of course, will not be in it. I'm grabbing a bunch of my stuff so I can stay with Jake. You can keep my room for as long as you want it, or at least as long as Mandy and Lola can put up with you."

"You're sure?" He hadn't expected that; in fact, he'd been ready to ask Jake if he had an extra room where he could stay tonight. When Kaz nodded and disappeared inside her room, he glanced at Mandy and Lola.

"Works for me," Mandy said. "What would be really terrific is if you just picked up Kaz's part of the lease." She rolled her eyes at Jake. "It's not like we expect to get her back anytime soon."

Until this moment, he hadn't considered anything like that. But it did make sense. He would need a place to stay when he wanted to get away from the base, and it wasn't like money was a problem. He hadn't had many places to spend his pay since he'd enlisted. But he wanted to be sure both Mandy and Lola were okay with him as an occasional roommate. Especially Lola. He loved how she'd made him forget all the crap, made everything about now. He shot her a quick glance, eyebrow raised.

She merely shrugged, and said, "Works for me." At least she smiled when she said it.

Kaz came back into the living room with another loaded tote bag and a clear zippered garment bag bulging with dresses. "I'll get the rest of my stuff tomorrow. You can keep the bed and furnishings." She tilted her head back and kissed Jake's chin. He'd stepped close behind and wrapped his arms around her waist. Still looking at him upside down, she added, "Hey, it's all in the family, right?"

Jake laughed, but Ben felt the warmth of Kaz's teasing deep in his gut. Family. He'd gone without family for much too long, but now it almost felt like too much, too fast. Too many good things—how the hell could it possibly last?

"G'night, all." Kaz yawned. "Damn. I'm exhausted."

Mandy giggled. "Gee, I wonder why? You're coming off three weeks of back-to-back jobs, during which time you had to deal with the trauma of falling in love . . ."

"Trauma?"

Mandy continued as if Jake hadn't interrupted. ". . . and then Friday you had an attempt on your life, you were kidnapped, beat up, rescued, got engaged, and discovered a new future brother-in-law—and it's only Sunday. Busy, much?"

"Take me home, Jacob. Mandy's picking on me." Laughing, tossing insults, and lugging a lot of clothes, Jake and Kaz took off.

As soon as the door closed behind them, the room seemed terribly quiet. Rico, who'd not moved from the sofa since they'd come in from dinner, let out a soft woof and then went back to sleep.

"I need to get out of these clothes." Mandy headed toward her bedroom to change. Lola picked up the wine glasses they'd left in the front room earlier, remnants of their impromptu party. Ben carried an empty wine bottle, plates, and napkins, and followed Lola into the kitchen.

She washed the few dishes and glasses while Ben dried things and stacked them next to the rack since he had no idea where stuff went. Lola finished washing.

Ben folded the towel and set it aside, and then propped one hip against the kitchen counter. "Are you sure you're okay with me keeping Kaz's room? I mean, it's been a pretty feminine domain with the three of you here. I hate to mess with your dynamics." He smiled when he said it, but he knew Lola didn't have a clue how important is was to him, knowing they were really okay that he stayed.

She crossed her arms and got really serious. "There's only one thing, Ben, before you agree to anything. We have one rule that may keep you from wanting to stay. We never, ever bring overnight guests home. That's why Kaz was anxious to go to Jake's place. She knew he couldn't stay here. Are you okay with that?"

He didn't even have to think about that one. The only guest he wanted already lived here. "I am. How about we give it a month? I'll pay my share of the rent in advance, and we'll see how it works. If it doesn't, if you guys are at all uncomfortable with me here, I'll go, but I'll continue to pay Kaz's portion for the duration of the lease you've signed. The final decision will be up to you and Mandy."

"More than fair." She held out her hand. Her fingers were long and slim, her nails polished a soft pink. Feminine hands, fine boned, and almost fragile looking, but when he and Lola shook hands, there was nothing fragile about her firm grasp, or the shock of awareness that had him staring into green eyes that appeared every bit as startled as his must be.

He heard Mandy talking to Rico in the other room and let go of Lola's hand. She quickly turned away and went back to wiping down the counters, while Ben began putting away the dry dishes from the rack, with instructions from Lola. Mandy wandered into the kitchen with her face scrubbed clear of the small amount of makeup she'd worn out to dinner, hair clipped into a sloppy knot on top of her head, wearing a ratty green bathrobe and pink bunny slippers.

"Go get something comfy on, Lola. I'll finish up here. You, too, Ben."

He glanced down at his white oxford shirt with the sleeves rolled up his forearms, tan chinos and leather top-siders, and spread his hands wide. "This is comfy, isn't it?"

Mandy snorted, and covered her mouth with both hands.

"What's that for?"

Lola grabbed his arm and tugged him toward the door. "She doesn't want to be the only one in jammies and a ratty bathrobe. I know you've got sweats. C'mon."

"Sheesh," he mumbled. "I didn't know there was a dress code when I signed on." But he was laughing and having the time of his life, and there was no way in hell he wanted to do anything to screw this up.

Later in the evening, Lola glanced up from her book when Mandy stood and said, "I'm opening the coffee shop at five tomorrow. Have to be up before four. G'night, all." She tucked her book under her arm, grabbed her glass of wine and went down the hallway leading to all three bedrooms.

Lola held her book up. "I'm going to try and finish my book, Hon. Sleep well."

"Good night, Mandy." Ben smiled as Mandy left the room, and then went back to his laptop.

"What are you doing?"

Ben was sitting in the stuffed chair across the room, and had barely looked up from his laptop all evening. He raised his head and grinned. "I'm not surfing porn sites, if that's what you're thinking."

Lola cracked up. "Well, of course that's what I was thinking. You're a guy, right?"

"That is such a sexist statement." He slapped a hand over his heart. "I'm crushed! Honestly, Lola . . . do you have any idea how much malware you can pick up at those sites?"

"No. Not really."

His expression was all innocence and purity. "I only know what I've heard from others."

"Yeah, right."

He chuckled. "Hate to disappoint you, but I'm researching cars. Jake said he'd take me into San Rafael to check out some dealerships tomorrow. They're having a lot of sales right now."

"Any idea what you want?"

"Something with four wheels that goes where I want it to, and preferably one that doesn't use a whole lot of gas. I actually thought about a motorcycle, but the roads are just too crowded, and I haven't ridden one for years, so car it is."

"Go electric."

"I might." He shot her a quick grin. "I like the looks of Marc's Tesla. Unfortunately, I think it cost more than my parents' first house. But it's definitely hot." He went back to studying the screen.

Lola went back to studying him. He was quiet and polite in so many ways, and yet she sensed something coiled beneath the surface, almost as if another person waited inside, testing boundaries, biding time until there was a chance to break free.

She almost laughed when the errant thought entered her mind that maybe her inner person and Ben's inner person would like to get together. He was absolutely beautiful, his build and height close to perfect, his smile reserved but still over-the-top sexy. And his laughter? She loved his laugh. It sent shivers up her spine and made her want him even more.

Where Jake was quick to jump in with a quip or a tease, Ben watched, almost as if he were studying the human dynamics around him, trying to learn what made people tick. Yet all the while, there was a sense of energy, deep inside, that couldn't be ignored.

So why in the hell was she trying so hard to ignore it?

Lola set her book aside and walked around the coffee table to sit on the arm of Ben's chair. "Show me," she said.

He glanced over his left shoulder and caught her watching him so closely that she should have been embarrassed, but it wasn't like he hadn't kissed her just last night. She knew the attraction was there, had thought about it—about him—for most of the day.

She'd thought of hot sex and warm kisses, of laughing with him and arguing about whatever came to mind. She'd thought of change—specifically her own.

Yesterday, she'd been pissed off at the entire male gender. Today she was trying to figure how to get one of that demographic into her bed. If that wasn't change . . .

"I've got a better idea." Ben shut down the laptop leaned over carefully, and set it on the floor. Then, without warning, he slipped his left arm around her waist and dragged her into his lap.

She snuggled against his broad chest as if they'd known each other for years. Ben brushed his fingers through her hair and rested his chin on top of her head. Then he sighed.

"I have no idea what kind of car I want," he said. "I figure I'll know it when I see it. I'll need it for the commute to Camp Parks if I stay here on my nights off, though I'll be staying on base most nights during the week." He nuzzled the side of her neck. "While the company here is amazing, a forty-mile commute in Bay Area traffic isn't something I want to face every morning and night."

Holding his shoulders, she leaned back so she could look into those beautiful gray eyes of his. "Are you thinking of small and sporty? Big, honkin' truck with mega-tread tires? Sedan?"

He laughed. "What do you like?"

She shrugged. "Ours isn't fancy. Mandy and I share an old garage queen because we both walk to work most days. But then Mandy and I aren't worried about picking up chicks."

He bounced her on his knees. "I'm holding the only chick I'm interested in picking up."

She hadn't expected that. Not really. She didn't have a quick reply for him. Not a word.

"You and Mandy are really close, aren't you?"

This she could answer, plus he seemed honestly interested. "We are. Our mom is a total flake, we have different fathers, neither of whom is in the picture, and we learned to count on each other when we were really young."

"None of us wins the award for the perfect family, do we?"

Lola just shook her head. There really wasn't an answer for that one.

He was paying attention, but the conversation was secondary to the feel of Lola in his arms. "Totally off topic, but I'm discovering that I really like holding you in my lap."

She laughed. He hugged her closer and she rested her head on his shoulder. "I think I like being held." Then she stroked the side of his face, running her fingers over the stubble along his jawline. "Are you really okay, Ben? It's been a pretty traumatic few days for you."

"Actually, the past two decades have been traumatic. The past two days have been sort of cathartic." He chuckled, turned toward her, and placed a chaste kiss on her forehead. "I'm amazed you haven't run me off yet."

"Why would I want to do that?"

"Self-preservation, maybe? Common sense? Way too many reasons." He lifted and turned her so that she straddled his lap. "I want you, Lola. Badly."

Glancing at the erection tenting his sweats, she leaned close until their foreheads touched, and whispered, "I'd noticed, but I was trying to be polite."

"Polite isn't going to make it go away." He let out a long, slow breath. "I should probably let you go back to your book and head for bed."

She frowned. "Are you tired, or just trying to get away from me?"

"Far from it." He shook his head. "Not tired. It's early, and you are the sexiest woman I have ever met. At the same time, I've never opened up to anyone the way I did with you. That means an awful lot to me. I don't want to ruin that, ruin the friendship we've started."

She tilted her head and gazed at him. "Interesting. I'm straddling the lap of an obviously aroused male, and he's talking friendship. I must be losing my touch."

He studied her for a moment, concentrating on the mesmerizing green of her eyes, the coal black hair and fair skin. She was stunning, but he knew there was more to her than her appearance. "How come there's no guy in your life, Lola? You're sexy as hell." He cupped her shoulders, ran his fingers along her arms and forced her to look him in the eye when he sensed her turning away.

She sighed. "A couple of years ago, I got serious with a guy, first time in forever. Paul was really nice, very good-looking, had a great job. He got along with Mandy and Kaz and everything was perfect. Then he started to change. You'd think, living in the city, I'd know what to look for, but I had no idea he was using drugs. His personality got more and more erratic until I never knew what to expect. I finally realized any feelings I might have had for him were long gone, so I told him the relationship wasn't working, that we needed to end it."

Ben watched her as she talked, noticed when she quit meeting his eyes. This time he pressed his fingertips gently against her chin to force her to look at him. "I take it that didn't go well?"

She shook her head. "He showed up with a gun, said I owed him, that I was his. Kaz wasn't here, but Mandy was in her room and heard what was going on. She called 911, came out holding the phone, still talking to the dispatcher, and talked to Paul. She was absolutely amazing." Shaking her head, Lola laughed. "Damn, that girl has balls. She got him to put the gun down before the cops showed up."

"What happened after that?"

She closed her eyes and shook her head. "It was bad. Turned out he had priors, other situations where he'd gotten violent with his girlfriends, even beat one up, but this was his first weapons charge. He never hit me, but he would have killed me. He's in prison for the next nine years, though I imagine he'll get out sooner. Overcrowding in the prisons and all that."

"Are you afraid of him?" He brushed her hair back from her face, fought an almost overpowering need to kiss her. He imagined he could still taste her lips from that one kiss last night.

"No. I probably should be, but mostly I just feel sorry for him. He had so much going for him, but he got caught up in the drugs and the whole idea of using them to make him more than he thought he was."

Ben just shook his head. What was there to say to something like that?

"He didn't think I was serious when I told him I wanted to break up." She shot him a sassy grin. "Showing up with a loaded gun was pretty much a deal breaker."

"A girl's gotta have her standards, right?"

"Exactly."

"I'm not him and I really want to kiss you again." Probably not the most romantic approach, but it had been a long time since he'd had a girl in his lap, one he really liked.

Like maybe never, and wasn't that pathetic?

"I think that would be okay."

"You're not going to try and talk me out of it?"

Her smile lit up her whole face. "If I didn't want a kiss, would I be straddling your lap in my comfy old bathrobe with nothing on underneath?"

He knew his eyes had to be as big as saucers. "Nothing? As in, you're naked under that robe?"

"I am. What about you? I've heard a lot of guys go commando in sweats."

He swallowed, and he could have sworn the sound echoed. "That would be correct."

She scooted forward on his lap, untied the belt on her robe, and leaned over to kiss him as the soft fabric parted. He caught a glimpse of perfect breasts, her nipples still hidden by the fabric, and then her mouth was on his, her hands were in his hair, and he forget anything and everything else he'd been planning to say.

CHAPTER 6

With the tiny part of her brain still functioning on an intellectual level, Lola realized there was a damned good reason she hadn't been able to put Ben's kiss out of her mind. The man could kiss. She might have been the one to start this, but he'd taken over from the very first touch of their lips.

He cupped her face in his big hands and held her steady as he carefully and yet quite thoroughly devoured her. There was no awkward bumping of noses or clicking of teeth, and yet his tongue swept past her defenses, his mouth covered hers until all she could feel, the air she breathed, the tastes on her tongue—all of it was Ben.

She clasped his shoulders, hanging on for some semblance of balance, though he held her securely and she had no fear of falling. Except that wasn't really true, was it? Not entirely. It was much too soon, she hardly knew him, she had a horrible history with her ex, but she was terrified she was falling for Ben. He was a beautiful, wounded, wonderful man, and she couldn't have walked away from him if she'd wanted.

She didn't want to walk away at all.

His arousal was impossible to ignore, from the hard thrust of his cock only marginally hidden within his soft sweatpants, yet riding deliciously against the wet and swollen juncture of her thighs, to the thundering of his heart against her chest.

Or was that her heart, pounding away as if trying to escape?

But it was too late for escape. Not when their lips fit so perfectly together, when his tongue danced with hers as if they'd moved to the same music forever. She hardly knew him, and yet she felt that in many ways, she knew Ben Lowell better than any man who'd ever held her. He'd fallen apart in her arms, had told her things she knew he'd never told another.

He'd trusted her.

And for that reason, Lola trusted him.

When he finally broke the kiss, he didn't say a word. Instead, he merely rose to his feet with Lola clinging to him, her legs wrapped around his waist, hands still grasping his shoulders, her lips buried against his throat. Wrapping his arms around her body, big hands beneath her butt and holding her close, he walked straight down the hallway to Kaz's room.

Ben's room, now. She decided she liked that. A lot.

Without putting her down, he turned and quietly closed the door. Lola reached behind her and flipped the lock. Ben raised an eyebrow. Lola put a finger to her lips.

"I'd hate for Mandy to hear anything, think you were having a nightmare, and come to check."

"Are you saying I'll make nightmare noises during sex?" He kissed her again, quite thoroughly.

Whimpering against his lips, wanting so much more, Lola realized she was the one making the noises. Whispering into his kiss, she said, "Uh, you know. Moans, cries of ecstasy, the usual." She felt the arch of his lips as he smiled against her mouth.

"Excellent point." His whisper a rough growl. "I'll

remember that. I had no idea there were standard sex noises." Walking across the room to the big bed with Lola held firmly against his chest, he slowly lowered her back and shoulders to the comforter, leaned over her, hands planted beside her head. "I promise to keep the volume down."

"Excellent." She smiled brightly. "Though not entirely. We don't want to interfere with the experience. Besides, the door's locked. It's all good."

"I agree. Definitely good." He laughed, a deep, sexy rumble that sent shivers across her breasts. Lola kept her legs linked around his waist, but when she stretched her arms over her head, twisting her body to grab the headboard, her robe fell open, baring her to his gaze.

Ben's heartfelt groan vibrated deep inside Lola. Her nipples, already tightly beaded with arousal, tightened even more. He eased her to the center of the bed. Kneeling between her thighs, staring at her for what felt like forever, he finally ran his hands from her waist, up over her ribs, and cupped her breasts in his warm palms.

She watched his face, the way his eyes tracked the motion of his hands, saw his pupils flare and then tighten as he rolled her sensitive nipples between his thumbs and forefingers.

She arched into his touch, the perfect pain a shock of heat that shot straight between her legs; crossing her ankles at the small of his back, she pulled herself close against his belly. His erect cock rode in the cleft between her legs, and she twisted her hips, wanting him close against those sensitive tissues, needing the thick length of him filling her, not teasing her.

He eased himself down, resting his weight on his forearms, touching his forehead to hers. "This will change things, you know. I could be a horrible lover. You might want me gone by morning, and then you've lost a renter. Is it worth the risk?"

As silly as the words sounded, she knew he asked a whole lot more. Was she really willing to take the risk? Looking into his stormy gray eyes, she gave the only answer she could.

"I have to, Ben. For whatever reason, I knew from the first time I saw you that this was going to happen. I'm never this forward with a man, especially one I hardly know."

He kissed her so sweetly. "Yeah, though you already know me better than any woman ever has. And as strange as it sounds, I understand. I had the same feeling when I first stepped into your house and saw you."

He pushed himself away, sat on the side of the bed and grinned at her. "Okay. Here's your last chance. I have protection, but it's in my overnight kit in the bathroom. I'll be back in a minute. Is that long enough for you to give this a second thought?"

"Oh, yeah." And then she winked.

He'd never thought of a wink as a tactile move before now, but this one had the same effect as if she'd wrapped her fingers around his dick and squeezed. Amazing. He left the room, thankful he was wearing loose sweats instead of his jeans, walked down to the bathroom, rummaged through his kit until he found the small box of condoms. He checked the expiration date—he'd bought them almost two years ago on a short leave to England. Thankfully, they still had plenty of time left. The woman he'd met in London was traveling through on business. They'd had one okay night together and parted without even exchanging last names.

Not the most satisfactory of hookups, but it had helped to scratch an itch.

He chuckled—he still had four of the original six left.

If Lola expected a guy with experience, she'd made a big mistake with him. It wasn't like there were a lot of dating opportunities in Kabul, and he'd never been one to pay for feminine companionship.

That had been one of the darkest jokes, the fact that guys worried more about losing a hand to an IED than a leg. You couldn't jack off with your foot, and God, was that pathetic or what? He grabbed a couple of foil packs and went back to his room, amazed how his cock was still standing high and hard—it didn't appear to have any issues with his lack of a sex life over the past few years. Just the opposite.

When he was younger, it had been a lot different, back in the time before he learned to actually consider the consequences of his actions. He wasn't sure when that had changed, but he was almost certain it started with the nightmares.

Dreams . . . nightmares, had a way of changing a man. Lola? Now Lola was a good dream. Probably much too good for a guy like him, but that's what dreams were about, right? Hope, something to aim for, to aspire to.

He was grinning when he stepped back into the bedroom and carefully locked the door. Lola lay just the way he'd left her, legs bent at the knees, robe barely hiding the tips of her breasts, soft fabric covering the juncture of her thighs.

He paused beside the bed, took a few moments to stand there and just take in the beauty of her, the fair skin and long legs, muscles toned, probably from that daily walk to work. She stared at him, a slight, teasing smile on her lips that turned him on like nothing else. What was she thinking? What did she think of him? It should be unsettling, that steady, assessing look, but if anything, it made him hot. He stood there, gazing right back at her, clenching his hands to keep from reaching out and tearing that robe off of her.

Which, obviously, wasn't an acceptable approach, but as he drew in another deep breath, one that expanded his chest, tightened his muscles, and pumped up the rate of his already pounding heart, he decided acceptable really didn't matter.

Not at this point.

He tossed the condoms on the table beside the bed, ripped his T-shirt over his head and lobbed it halfway across the room, and then shoved his sweats to the floor. Lola didn't move, though her green eyes went wide and her pupils dilated. He crawled across the bed and knelt once again between her thighs. Capturing the open edges of her robe in both hands, he slowly pulled it fully open.

"I knew it." His laugh, a short, sharp bark probably had her thinking he was nuts.

"What?"

He could tell she was fighting a grin. He didn't even try to control his.

"I wondered if you dyed your hair. It's so perfectly black." He pointed at the neatly trimmed, dark blonde curls between her thighs. "This is proof." He slipped his hands beneath the firm globes of her butt and lifted her. "And, for what it's worth, I like the look." He dipped his head and swiftly ran his tongue between the plump folds of her sex before twirling the tip through the short, wiry curls.

Lola gasped, thrusting her hips high, pressing herself against his mouth. Her body was wet for him, her taste tart on his tongue.

He wanted more.

She wanted more. Lola tightened her fingers around the spooled posts of the headboard, grabbing the knobby surface for emotional balance as much as to keep from curling her entire body around Ben's amazing mouth. Paul had never done this, the bastard. He'd left her hanging, her body ripe for orgasm but unfulfilled so many times she'd given up on ever coming with a man inside her. He'd wanted her to take him in her mouth, but thought the whole idea of going down on a woman was disgusting.

Ben didn't seem to have any issues at all. His tongue made delicious swipes between her labia, licked deep, and then teased with the lightest of touches over her clit.

Damn, she really wanted more!

He couldn't possibly read her mind, she knew that, but the moment the thought entered her mind, he thrust two fingers deep inside her and wrapped his lips around her engorged clitoris, sucking with almost perfect pressure.

The climax hit so hard and fast it shocked a short, sharp scream right out of her, one she blocked by burying her face against her shoulder so Mandy wouldn't come to check. Ben reared back on his heels; one hand supported her bottom and he lifted her entire lower half up to his mouth, licking and nipping, fingers still thrusting in and out in time with the rolling contractions of her body. A second spasm rocked her as Ben slowly brought her down, both physically and emotionally, planting opened-mouthed kisses against her sex, licking slowly, finally pulling his fingers free and laying her back on the bed.

He crawled up her body, kissing her as he went, the burning heat from his lips searing her from hipbone, to belly, along her ribs to the nipple on her left and then on her right. When he reached her mouth, she was ready for him, taking his tongue deep, tasting Ben, tasting herself.

Another first, and contrary to what Paul the bastard thought, there was nothing at all disgusting about tasting herself on a man's lips. It was absolutely empowering, but at the same time, it scared the crap out of her.

What was Ben becoming to her? How had he rocked her world so quickly?

One mind-blowing orgasm followed by another was certainly an excellent way to begin.

He cupped her face in his hands and held his weight off of her, lifting himself on his strong forearms. The muscles in his shoulders, biceps, and chest glistened with sweat, and the dark hair that dusted his pecs and followed a perfect trail to his navel and beyond was damp.

"Are you okay?"

All she could do was nod. How could she not be okay? Two orgasms in the space of a couple of minutes?

"I want you, Lola. I don't want you to agree because your body's making the decision. I want your head involved, too."

It took a few long seconds, but she found her voice. "I think I can honestly say you've got all of me involved, Ben." She almost laughed at the understatement. Instead, she ran her fingers through the hair on his chest, and realized what it was about the look of male models that she'd always found so unappealing—besides the fact that most of the guys at Top End were openly gay and out of her dating pool. Their chests were uniformly smooth—either naturally so or else they waxed or shaved. There was never any shadow of dark hair defining their perfect bodies, no happy trail leading from their navels southward.

Ben was really lean with well-defined muscles and a six-pack any of the Top End guys would envy. He still looked like he could use a few good meals, and his body was covered with numerous scars and even some spots that weren't through healing, but there was a sense of power about him, rough edges, and an inner strength she found terribly appealing. She grinned at this totally irresistible man, and said, "I want you inside me now. Okay?"

"Definitely okay." He reached across her and grabbed one of the packets off the bedside table, sat back on his heels, and sheathed himself.

There was something about Ben that made her feel comfortable lying here this way, with her legs spread wide, her body still flushed from her climaxes and yet so aroused she knew there were more inside, waiting. At the same time, she felt more naked with her arms still in the wide sleeves of her robe because it seemed to emphasize how much of her was uncovered, open to his view.

And how he viewed! She had to bite back her laughter, but the look in his eyes was enough to make her glow. No man had ever stared at her this way, had ever focused so intently on her face, her breasts, the dark blonde curls hiding her sex—curls now wet from his mouth, from her orgasms.

He moved like a man in a trance, leaning forward, the thick head of his cock testing her swollen, needy flesh. He was big and it had been a long time for her. There was a moment when he first pressed between her folds, the broad tip pushing against the slick heat of her, and she felt the burn of tissues stretching, wondered if this was going to hurt more than it pleasured.

Her body adjusted. She closed her eyes and sighed as he gently filled her—and filled her even more.

"You're so tight." He kissed her every bit as gently as he'd entered her. "Are you okay? I don't want to hurt you."

This time Lola cupped his face in her hands and shook her head. "Pain is the last thing I'm feeling, Ben. I'm not fragile. You won't hurt me." She rotated her hips and he closed his eyes and groaned.

"If you want to enjoy this for more than a few seconds, I'd suggest you curtail the extra booty moves. Maybe the next time around, okay?"

Laughing, she grabbed his tautly muscled butt and pulled him close. "More, Ben. I want more."

"Yes, ma'am."

He grinned as he said it, but then he slowly withdrew, and then thrust deep, pulled out again and thrust hard and fast and it was absolutely right. He found his rhythm and took Lola along for the ride.

Her fingers dug into his ass and her eyes closed as he slipped into a hard, fast cadence that was so perfect he knew he wouldn't last. But her breasts were sensitive—he'd learned that right away—and holding himself on his elbows left both hands free to cup her breasts, to roll her nipples between his fingers.

She gasped, a sound of both surprise and pleasure, and he knew he had to hold on, had no other choice but to take her with him. He shifted just enough to bring her nipple within reach, drew the tightly furled peak between his lips and held it against the roof of his mouth with his tongue.

Her cry was a soft, breathy sound, and it was all so damned good. She was sweet, so damned sweet and this was all way too perfect to last much longer. He switched to her right breast, working that nipple as carefully as he had the left, and he felt her inner muscles clench against him, knew she was right on the edge.

So was he.

A slight shift of his hips and she cried out, and he knew he'd hit the sweet spot, knew he wasn't going off this ledge alone.

Her legs wrapped tightly around his waist, her heels dug into his butt and she rocked hard against him. He kissed the cry from her lips, silenced her before the ever-attentive Mandy came running, but it was impossible to quiet his own deep groan of pleasure, the curse he'd not intended when the coil of blinding lust rolled from his spine to his balls to the hopefully strong condom, because he knew he'd just come harder and longer than he'd ever come before.

Panting, gasping for air and hoping he wouldn't pass out on this amazing woman, Ben struggled to keep his weight off her slight frame.

Struggled and lost, but she was pulling him down on her, wrapping her arms tightly around his back and holding him close.

He gave up the fight, settled his weight to one side and held her while he struggled to catch his breath.

It wasn't until his breathing settled down that he realized she was crying, but when he lifted his upper body away to see what was wrong, she turned away and sobbed even harder.

He held her and let her cry herself out, thankful it was only a minute or so before she was reaching blindly for the box of tissues on the bedside table. He grabbed a handful of tissues and handed them to her. She sniffed, wiped her eyes, turned away to blow her nose.

He took that opportunity to grab hold of the base of the condom and pull out of her tight sheath. He used more of the tissues to wrap it up and toss it in the wastebasket beside the bed. He'd deal with it later, but right now Lola needed him.

He turned and scooted up against the headboard, dragging a pillow to lean against and then pulled Lola into his lap. "You gonna tell me what's wrong?"

Shaking her head, she kept her eyes turned away from him. "Nothing's wrong. I feel so silly." She sniffed and muttered, "Everything's wonderful. Better than wonderful. I don't know why I started crying."

She snuggled against him and petted his chest, her fingers stroking him so perfectly, but he wondered if she was even aware of what she was doing. Maybe she was using him as a stand-in for Rico—something warm to pet.

No matter. He tightened his arms around her. There was no way he could hold her close enough. Only when he was inside her—that worked. Of course, it would make it tough to ever leave the bedroom, but . . . Reining in his idiotic thoughts, he kissed the top of her head and said, "I thought maybe I hurt you. You're sure you're okay?"

She took a deep breath. "Happy tears are okay. They took me by surprise. You took me by surprise . . . I'm not normally the kind to fall apart like that."

"I understand happy tears. Not that I've ever been the recipient until now. You make me feel like a sex god. I think I like it." He kissed her again. "You know, all manly, like I should thump my chest and roar."

She snorted. That fit. She didn't strike him as a giggler. "That's a visual I'm having trouble with. You might have to demonstrate."

He shook his head. "Nah. Don't want to wake Mandy."

Lola's shoulders started shaking.

He tilted her chin up. "I hope you're not crying again."

"No, doofus. I'm trying not to laugh."

He sighed. "From sex god to doofus? I don't know if I can take this lack of respect."

"It happens. Of course, if you were willing to provide another demonstration of your sex godliness . . ."

"Sex godliness? Is that a word?"

"It could be, but only if you earn it." She glanced at him out of the corner of one eye—an eye that was definitely twinkling.

He'd had his meltdown; Lola'd just had hers. He liked hers a whole lot better.

He reached for the second condom.

CHAPTER 7

It was still dark the next morning when Ben rolled over and reached for Lola, but her side of the bed was empty, the sheets cool. Her scent lingered, a citrusy aroma that tickled his senses, but there was no sign of the woman who'd definitely blown his mind, among other things, last night. The memory of her blush-red lips stretched around his cock crowded out all other thoughts, had him hard and wanting her, but she was gone.

He lay there in that half-awake, half-asleep state and wondered where she was, why she'd left, and then decided she couldn't have gone too far. He glanced at the clock, saw that it was just a little after four-thirty, and closed his eyes again.

The visual of her was clearer against closed lids. Naked and kneeling between his knees, her perfect lips wrapped around an erection that was so hard it was painful, even after he'd already come twice. They'd laughed about being too exhausted to go back to the bathroom for more condoms, and Lola had decided to improvise.

Damn. Had she ever.

Maybe if he wished hard enough, she'd come back. He was really not good with the morning-after rules, if there were any. Half his life had been spent in the military with hookups happening or not, usually on leave where he'd meet up with women who, like him, had no desire to go home.

It was truly amazing how many people lived that way, for whatever reason. The army was their home, their fellow soldiers the closest thing to family they had.

And yet, he felt closer to Lola—and even her sister— after only two days. Closer than he'd ever felt to anyone other than Jake. He lay there, drifting, thinking about that for a bit. Wondering how it could be that one pushy woman had somehow managed to push all the right buttons.

Lola was dressed and waiting in the kitchen with the coffee already made when Mandy walked in.

"What are you doing up so early?" Mandy went straight to the pot and poured herself a cup.

"I thought I'd give you a ride to work. I don't like you walking down there in the dark. It's too dangerous."

Mandy turned and leaned against the counter. Sipping her coffee, she stared at Lola. Lola held her cup to her lips and smiled at Mandy. She knew what was coming, but it was more fun if she made her sister work for it.

After a very long moment, Mandy raised one eyebrow. "I'm really glad you made coffee, and I appreciate the offer of a ride, but we both know there are more important things to discuss. Dish, girl. What's he like? As hot as he looks and as sexy as he sounds?"

Lola buried her face in her hands, then peeked at Mandy between her fingers. "You weren't supposed to hear us."

Laughing, Mandy took her regular chair across from her sister. "Didn't have to. I got up to pee around two and your bedroom door was open. I peeked in . . ." She shrugged and took another sip, "And your bed wasn't just empty, it was still made up. And the door to Kaz's room was shut tight. So, dear big sister, how was your night?"

Lola sighed and gave up. She'd come out here expecting the third degree. There was no point in trying to keep secrets from Mandy. Besides, she had no doubt Mandy would bug Ben if she didn't answer, but wasn't that why she was out here in the first place? Why she'd crawled out of bed and left the best thing that had happened to her, ever, so she could talk to her sister?

"So good it's still not real. Scary good." Lola sat back and took a swallow of her coffee. "I wanted to let you know we'd spent the night together. I have to be sure you're okay with it. Sleeping with the new roommate? That's not something I wanted to spring on you." They may not have had good parents, but she and Mandy had always had each other, and there was no way anyone was going to come between them. Not ever.

Mandy reached across the table and grabbed Lola's hand. "Hon, don't worry. I could see there was something between you two from the moment he walked through the door. He was polite to me, but he was a hundred percent focused on you." She got up and grabbed a container of yogurt out of the refrigerator. "Want one?"

Lola shook her head. Food was the last thing on her mind. What she really wanted to do was crawl back into bed before Ben realized she was gone. She still had a few hours before she had to get ready for work.

Mandy sat down again and dipped her spoon into the yogurt. "Besides, Lola. You already called dibs, remember?"

Frowning, Lola shook her head.

Mandy gave her a totally condescending look, as if she was the biggest idiot on the planet.

"When we were talking just before Ben showed up, you said if any nice, good-looking single guy walked through the door, you got dibs and he was yours because you're the oldest." She laughed. "And since you will always be older than me, he's all yours."

Lola was still grinning when they pulled out of the garage in the old Nissan. Mandy was staring out the window as they started down 23rd toward Irving.

"Slow down . . . see that car?"

Lola glanced to her right, at the dark sedan parked across the street and a couple of doors north of their place. She noticed shadows moving. "Yeah. Looks like a couple of guys inside. Wonder what they're doing?"

They drove slowly by, but the sedan windows reflected the newly replaced streetlight nearby, and Lola couldn't make out any details.

Mandy turned back to Lola. "They've been there off and on for at least the past couple of days. I thought at first it was a stakeout, that they were watching Jasper and Abdul's place, but I think they're watching ours."

Jasper and Abdul were a couple of forty-something guys who'd been partners as long as Mandy and Lola had lived here, but it was no secret they grew a little pot in the backyard to help make rent, as well as for a parent dealing with cancer. "I can't imagine a stakeout for the little grow that the guys have going. Most of it goes to Abdul's mom to help her handle her chemo, but why would they watch us?"

"I dunno, but you might want to let the guys know."

"Yeah. We probably should." Lola shivered, but it wasn't the cold. It was the sudden realization how very little she knew about Ben Lowell. She barely even knew his brother, and Kaz was already engaged to the man. What if they weren't what they seemed? What if that suspiciously official-looking gray car was here because of something Ben had done?

She knew it was going to bug her until she talked to

Ben, and once she'd made that decision, she put it out of her mind. For now, anyway. A couple minutes later, she pulled up in front of the coffee shop. Mandy got out and made a point of looking at her watch. "Looks like you've got time to crawl back into bed with a very hot guy. Thanks for the ride, Sis! I still want details."

"In your dreams, sweetheart."

She was still laughing as she watched Mandy unlock the door and head inside the coffee shop. But when she drove by the dark sedan still parked in the driveway of the empty house across the street, she made a point of looking during the brief moment when the light from her head-lights illuminated the interior of the car.

Two men, the one in the passenger seat holding binoculars. And he appeared to be focused directly on her house.

Ben dozed a while, more asleep than awake until he realized he was actually awake, and there was no point in just lying here, thinking. Thinking too much could get a guy in deep shit.

With that thought in mind, he got up and headed for the bathroom and a quick shower.

It was almost five, the house was quiet, the door to Lola's room closed. Mandy's door was open, her bed already made with Rico asleep in his bed, and he remembered Mandy saying she had to open the coffee shop at five, which meant Lola must have gone back to her own bed.

Ben thought about that as he adjusted the controls on the shower, about how he'd felt when he awakened and realized she hadn't stayed, that he'd missed her, and that made him think of his brother and Kaz. Damn, but his thoughts were spinning in such odd directions this morning. But seeing RJ—no, dammit, his name was Jake now—and his new love together had hit him even harder than seeing his baby brother all grown up and taller than him.

Ben had watched the way Jake looked at Kaz, and realized it wasn't lust or mere appreciation of her beauty. It
was something entirely different, a place Ben hadn't ever
actually considered for either his brother or himself.

Jake looked at Kaz as if she was everything he'd ever
wanted, every wish he'd ever made, every wonderful dream
he'd ever dreamed. He looked at her as if all those needs,
those desires, had been met in his woman.

And why, Ben wondered, was he thinking like that
about Jake, and picturing Lola?

Why had she left his bed?

Maybe she wasn't ready for Mandy to know about them.

That stopped him. He wondered if there was a *them*.
He'd hate to think that Lola wasn't interested in seeing
where this . . . well, it wasn't really a relationship yet, but
whatever it was, he hoped she wanted to see where it led.
Because if he was being honest with himself, he was already starting to think of it as a relationship, as opposed
to just another hookup.

He lifted his face into the streaming shower, then turned
and washed and rinsed his hair. Hell, he was thirty-eight
years old and thinking like a teenager, but he was sick and
tired of one-night stands with women who made him feel
absolutely nothing.

He turned off the water and wished he could turn his
brain off as easily, grabbed a clean towel off the rack and
dried himself. There was no denying it, though. This whole
thing with Lola? It felt like a lot more than a hookup to
him. A hell of a lot more.

Grabbing a can of shaving cream and the razor Mandy
had left for him, he went to work on the stubble. He'd been
so scruffy last night, he was sure Lola had razor burn. And
then he thought of where he might have scraped her sensitive skin and left it just a bit reddened, and once again
he was hard as a rock.

"Damn." If he got hard every time he thought of her, this was going to prove to be a rather uncomfortable place to stay. After a couple minutes of dedicated scraping away at his beard, Ben tightened the towel he'd wrapped around his hips and finished wiping the shaving cream off his face.

He wondered if Lola was still asleep. Her door was closed. Would it be impolite to knock?

"Yeah, jackass. Wearing nothing but a towel?"

He really needed to get his head screwed on straight. Of course, if he knocked wearing a towel with a box of condoms in his hand . . .

He'd just stepped inside his room when an unexpected sound stopped him. He was almost sure it was the front door clicking shut. Quietly, as if someone was trying to sneak inside.

Setting the box with the last two condoms on the bedside table, he tightened the towel around his waist again and slipped quietly down the hallway.

As he paused against the wall, Lola turned the corner and slammed into him. Cursing, he caught her by her arms to steady her. She screamed, a short, sharp cry of absolute terror.

Hugging her against his chest, he rocked her and tried not to laugh, except his heart was thudding inside his chest, pounding a mile a minute.

"I hope you appreciate the fact you just scared the crap out of me."

He kissed the top of her head. "I thought you were asleep in your bedroom."

She leaned back and looked at him. "Why would I be in there? I was sleeping with you."

He shrugged. "Well, if you didn't want Mandy to know—I just thought you'd gone back to your room. I was planning to hunt you down after your shower. Just in case . . ." He raised one eyebrow.

Laughing, she said, "I got up early so I could tell Mandy." Then she leaned back in his embrace and smiled broadly. "We're close. I didn't want to blindside her with the fact you and I spent the night together."

"So, what did she say?"

Lola rolled her eyes. "She already knew. Noticed my room was empty, your door was closed, put two and two together."

He watched her face, looking for clues, not at all sure if that was a good thing or a bad thing. "And?"

"And she wanted details. Which I refused to provide." Definitely a smirk.

"Oh. That bad, huh?"

"No, idiot." She rose on her toes and kissed him. "Ben, last night was so good it was scary. I'm not ready to talk about it. Not yet. Not even to my sister." Then she laughed. "Not even to you!"

He tangled his fingers in that long, black, hair, and tugged, tilting her mouth up to his. When he kissed her, it felt as if a few more pieces of his scattered life realigned themselves. Not that any of this made all that much sense, but he was kissing Lola, and she was kissing him right back, and obviously this was one thing that was absolutely right in his world. "How about coming back to bed with me, maybe working on the details. Get a little better at them, and then you'll have something interesting to tell Mandy."

He felt her smile into his kiss, the soft curve of even softer lips. "I think that's an excellent idea."

"Good," he said, grabbing her hand and tugging her down the hallway. "We're doing great. See how well we agree on stuff?"

He loved the sound of her laughter. When they reached the bedroom, he grabbed her around the waist and lifted her bodily onto the bed. And then he discovered even more things to love about Lola Monroe that should be scaring the shit out of him.

Except he was enjoying himself way too much.

A couple of hours later after some of the best sex he could recall, Ben stood at the stove fixing breakfast. The fried potatoes were warming in the oven with the bacon, and mushrooms and garlic cooked slowly in butter. He heard a knock on the door, but before he could answer it, Kaz called out.

"We're here. Hope you're all decent."

He heard Lola's laughter, which meant she was out of the shower and dressed, and then Jake said something, but Ben couldn't make out the words.

A moment later, Jake stepped into the kitchen.

"Hey, bro! I had no idea you could cook."

Ben turned away from the stove, grinning broadly. "One of my very few talents. Got room for breakfast?"

"Always. But give me a couple of minutes. Just wanted to let you know we were here. Be right back."

Ben added more eggs to the bowl and whipped them up. Threw a handful of fresh chopped spinach into the pan with the mushrooms and garlic, cooked it long enough to wilt, and added the eggs. He was putting the serving plates on the table when Jake, Kaz, and Lola walked in.

Kaz grabbed plates out of the overhead cupboard, Lola put out the silverware and napkins, and she, Ben, and Kaz took their seats. They waited until Jake put his big camera on the counter and joined them before they started passing the plates.

"What's the camera for? You and Kaz doing some work today?"

Jake looked up from the eggs he was scooping onto his plate. "I saw that gray sedan outside and got a picture of the license plate from the front porch. Marc's security guy couldn't find a match to the number you gave him, but I think they've covered part of an eight to make a three, and have maybe done the same to turn a four into a one. I took some high resolution shots that'll let me blow them way up—should show if there's tape covering anything or if the numbers have been doctored."

"They were there when I took Mandy to work this morning a little before five. She said she's seen them out there the past couple of days." Lola used the piece of bacon she was holding to make her point. "There were two guys in the front seat with binoculars trained on this house." She frowned and took a bite of the bacon. "Any idea why they're out there?"

Crap. He really hadn't wanted the girls involved, but obviously they needed to know the truth. "I think they're following me." Ben glanced at Jake, but then he focused on Lola. "I saw them near my parents' house the first day I got here. Then, later in the day, I noticed them here. They drove by last night when we were leaving to go out to dinner, but I didn't realize they were back. I'm not positive, but I'm almost sure they're the same guys." He laughed, a short, sharp bark devoid of humor. "I mean, how many guys could be following me?"

Lola's fingers curled around his wrist. "But why?"

He covered her hand with his and shook his head. "I don't know. Possibly something I saw in Kabul? I worked security at the embassy the past couple of years, and other than a temporary job in a place called Spin Boldak, that was it. A lot of politicians came through on their little junkets—you know, the kind of trips to make the voters think they're actually working."

Jake frowned at him.

"What?" Ben took another bit of potatoes. "You're looking at me like you used to, when you were absolutely sure I was hiding something from you."

"And were you?" Kaz grinned at him, and Ben laughed.

"Of course," he said, glancing at her. Then he focused on Jake. "So why the look, little brother?"

"What, exactly were you doing in Spin Boldak? It was in the news a while back. A suicide bombing and an attack against NATO troops by what appeared to be an Afghani policeman. A bunch of Americans were injured, too. The reporter said there'd been some talk it was tied into the drug trade, not so much the Taliban or the fight against ISIS."

Damn. He really hated to ruin such a nice morning. "The reporter got it right. I was there. That's how I ended up with all the shrapnel. About six months ago I got sent down there to help a security contractor meet the people he'd be working with. Then, six weeks ago he said he wanted me back, needed to meet with me in person, though I have no idea what for. I got there late in the day, headed to the command post to meet up with him. Unfortunately, about the same time I got there, a suicide bomber wearing a police uniform decided to blow himself up. He killed some NATO troops, but he also killed the contractor I was there to meet along with a guy he was talking with. Half a dozen other soldiers and a couple of civilians were also injured."

"And you?"

Jake's softly spoken question had Ben nodding his head. "Yeah. Me, too, though I wasn't all that close to the bomber. Caught some shrapnel, but I was lucky." In more ways than one. If not for that attack, would he have found the courage to search for his brother? It had been that fear, that he might have been killed before he could apologize, that had finally forced him to make such a long overdue decision.

Lola's gray eyes were troubled. "You could have been killed."

Ben wrapped his fingers around her hand and squeezed. "But I wasn't. I've been in war zones for most of my career.

I've had a lot of near misses, but I figure if a little shrapnel is all I took, I've been damned lucky."

Lola shook her head. "I'm not sure I'd call getting shot full of metal lucky, but I'm really glad you're okay."

"Thanks," he said. "Me, too. But that doesn't explain why I'm being followed."

CHAPTER 8

"No, Jake, I really don't think shopping for a new car for Ben sounds like fun," Laughing, she shoved Ben and his brother out the door. "Go. Spend Ben's money. Buy something sporty and sexy and totally impractical. I'll be here clearing out the rest of my girly stuff so Ben doesn't have to worry about any gender identity issues. You know, like grabbing a cute little lacy pink thong out of the dresser and wondering how it'll go with his army duds?"

"She's got an excellent point, bro." Ben grabbed Jake's arm and dragged him down the front steps, with Jake mumbling 'sexy pink thong' the whole way. "Let her stay and cleanse the premises of girly stuff."

Lola followed behind them, shaking her head. "Kaz, we may have to renegotiate the subletting of your room," she said, glancing over her shoulder. "These two concern me. Especially the older one."

They were still laughing when Jake pulled away from the curb. Ben checked but didn't see the gray sedan. He was still keeping an eye out when they parked in front of Top End to drop Lola off for work.

Of course, that didn't mean the men weren't still following him. He hated thinking that way, hated letting what felt like pure paranoia take root in his mind.

Jake left the motor running as Lola got out of the back seat, but Ben was right beside her, walking her up to the front door of the business. He stood beside her while she unlocked the door. Then he followed her inside and waited for her to turn on the lights and check her answering machine.

"Do you want me to pick you up when you get off?"

She glanced up from the mail on her desk, and smiled at him. Damn, she had such a beautiful smile.

"Thanks, but I need the exercise. I get off at five. It only takes me about fifteen minutes to walk home." She came back around her desk and looped her arms over his shoulders. "I have to admit, though, that I really enjoyed my morning in bed."

"You weren't the only one. That's exercise, too." He kissed her. "If I get a new car, is it okay if I bring it by to show you?"

"You'd better! We're usually not that busy on Mondays. I hope you find something absolutely perfect. Have fun." She kissed him this time, short and too fast, but that was probably for the best. "I'll see you later," she said. Then the phone rang and she grabbed her notepad and the phone, mouthing another good-bye as Ben headed for the door.

He didn't want to leave her, which was something that had never happened with another woman, but Jake was waiting, and Lola was focused on her phone call.

Ben climbed into Jake's big Escalade, and they headed out.

"Looks like things between you and Lola have changed a bit."

Ben chuckled. "You could say that." He shot a grin at Jake. "She's really pretty amazing."

"How's Mandy feel about you sleeping with her sister?"

Ben raised one eyebrow. "Is it that obvious?"

"Yeah. It is." Jake nodded, but he kept his eyes focused on the traffic.

Ben still wasn't sure how his brother felt about him, and especially about him with Lola, and he realized he really didn't know this older version of Jake at all. Hopefully, spending time together would fix that. "It appears that Mandy expected it. This morning, she told Lola she could see a connection between the two of us as soon as I walked in the door Saturday night. Lola said she felt it, and as freaky as it sounds, so did I." He turned in his seat so he could better see Jake. "Nothing's ever happened to me like that. Ever."

Jake was grinning when they stopped at a light on Nineteenth. "I know exactly what you're saying. That's what happened with Kaz. Instant attraction. I wasn't about to let her go."

This time Ben was the one laughing. "And look where that got you!"

"That it did, Ben." Jake's calm smile was almost shattering, a look of such utter certainty that it left Ben shaken. Then he winked at Ben. "My advice? If it feels right, don't fight it."

Ben was still thinking about that as they headed out of the city. Good things like Lola didn't happen to him. Not ever. He didn't want to do anything at all to screw this up.

By lunchtime—if you didn't mind eating after one o'clock—he was the owner of a brand-new Subaru Forester. He had seriously been thinking of a sporty little two-seater, at least until Jake reminded him that their women tended to travel in a pack.

The SUV he purchased could hold five adults. Jake's Escalade would have to handle larger groups, but that was the nice thing about having a brother nearby. Something he told Jake when they met up at a Mexican restaurant after leaving the dealership.

"I think it's something I'll have to get used to," he said.

"What? Paying over four bucks a gallon for gas?"

Ben dipped his chip in salsa and used it to point at his brother. "Well, that, too, but it's the idea of being near family. Having someone to call when I need help with something or just want to hang out."

"We used to have a lot of fun when we were kids." Jake leaned back so the waiter could set their plates on the table. "Then it all got so crazy with the swimming and the pressure. I didn't handle it well at all."

"Jake, you won three gold medals at the Atlanta Olympics. Hard to handle it any better."

Jake shook his head. "Yeah, but I totally screwed up my perspective, lost track of what was important. I let Mom turn me into her little media star." He paused with his taco halfway to his mouth. "I was a total jerk, and Mom encouraged all that attitude. Ya know, I've thought about that a lot lately, since meeting Kaz and getting my life in order, and I wonder what would have happened if we didn't have that wreck, if I hadn't gotten locked up."

Ben stared at him, waiting for the punch line, because Jake couldn't actually mean what he'd said, but he just calmly took a bite of his taco and went on eating.

Finally, Ben couldn't stand it. "Hell, Jake. How can you even wonder? You'd probably be making movies in Hollywood, that's what you'd be doing. Good God, you had so much going for you before I fucked it all up. I ruined everything."

Jake shook his head and started in on the second taco. "Eat. I have to get back to work. We're not all on vacation." He spoke softly. "Ben, the truth is, we did ruin the lives of two people, and we also ruined our mother's big plans. Yes, it was horrible, and I will live with the guilt the rest of my life."

"Whoa, Jake. Guilt? Are you believing your own lies

now? I was the drunk and I was driving. There is no *we* here. I'm to blame. You were as much a victim as that woman and her son."

"I'm as guilty as you, Ben. I knew it that night and I still believe it now. But the only thing I would change now would be for those two people to still be alive. I never wanted the fame, and Mom's got the gold medals. Unless she sold them. I've never gotten them back from her. Yeah, I wanted to win in Atlanta because I'm pretty damned competitive, but I was so caught up in the glitz and glamour that I'd lost all sense of what was important. What I've got now is what counts, a career and a woman I love, a woman who loves me, and something I'd pretty much given up on—I've got you back. That's what counts. You need to get past it. I think you've spent the last nineteen years beating yourself up over what happened that night, while I've moved on."

Ben's first reaction was anger, but then he realized Jake was spot on. He bit into his taco, and chewed long enough to get a little perspective on what his brother had just said. It wasn't all that hard. "I've really turned into a neurotic dick, haven't I?"

Jake just about choked, laughing with a mouthful. It took him a minute and half a glass of water to get it together. "Yeah, bro, you have. Now get over it."

He doubted he'd ever get over it entirely, but Ben sat back and enjoyed his meal and the easy conversation with Jake. They were both finishing up their lunches when Jake went totally still. "Gray sedan, two men. Just pulled into the parking lot. Far side, under the tree, and they're not making any move to get out."

"I see 'em." Ben started to rise.

Jake shook his head. "Nope. Let me. You get to pick up the check. I'm going out there to have a little conversation with our gentlemen friends."

"I don't know if that's such a . . ."

"Trust me?"

It was the question behind the statement that had Ben reaching for his wallet. "Be careful," he said.

The waiter saw them rising and hurried over with their bill. Jake smiled at him, pointed at Ben, and headed outside. Ben paid the bill and left a hefty tip, but he kept an eye on the car, and on Jake's progress across the parking lot.

He thought for sure the driver of the sedan would pull out as soon as Jake headed their way, but instead he rolled down the window. Ben moved a little faster and was right behind Jake when he stopped by the driver's side. Jake glanced over his shoulder at Ben.

"You want to take this?"

"Yeah. I do." He looked at the two men. The driver was older, at least late forties, early fifties, Caucasian, dark hair with a little gray showing. His partner was younger, either Hispanic or Native American, or maybe a little of both. The men wore almost identical dark suits and dark glasses, their appearance almost a caricature of an FBI or Secret Service agent.

Ben planted his palms on the frame of the open window. "Do you mind telling me why you're following me?"

The men looked at each other. The driver lifted his shades and frowned at Ben. "You've seen someone tailing you?"

Ben glanced at Jake, then back at the driver. "Yes, but first, I'd like to see an ID."

"Fair enough." The driver reached for an ID badge clipped to the sun visor. "You are Master Sergeant Benjamin Lowell, are you not?"

"I am." Ben took the badge. "FBI? Okay, Agent Theodore Robinson, what the hell is going on?"

"You've had someone tailing you. Where and when?"

"Gray sedan, similar make and model to this near my parents' house in Marin. Then again, parked across the street from the house where I'm staying on 23rd in San Francisco, most of yesterday, early this morning. And you. Here." He handed the agent's badge back to him.

"We just got the assignment this morning."

"To do what?"

Again, the men exchanged glances. The one on the passenger side nodded. The older man said, "We're supposed to keep you alive long enough to testify."

"What?" Ben shot a quick glance at Jake. "Testify to what? Where? I have no idea what you're talking about."

Jake interrupted. "Was that you across the street from the house this morning? Car was a late model dark gray Buick."

The driver glanced at his passenger and then looked steadily at Jake. "Not us. Did you get a look at them?"

"No. Windows were tinted, but I got a high-res shot of the license plate. It appeared that the numbers might have been altered with tape."

The guy in the passenger seat reached across his partner and handed two business cards to Jake, who passed one to Ben.

The driver said, "If you could send us a copy of the photo of the plate, we might be able to get some intel on the vehicle and, with any luck, find out who's driving it, and who's behind the tail. In the meantime, you could make our job a little easier." He smiled at them and shrugged as if he didn't expect an answer. "Do you mind telling us where you're headed?"

Jake once again glanced at Ben. This whole thing was so bizarre, Ben was afraid he'd start laughing, which probably wasn't the smartest move. Instead he asked Jake, "What's the address for Marc's office?"

Jake rattled off the street and number.

Ben focused once again on the agents. "How do I find out what this is all about? I've been back from Kabul for less than a week, so it's got to be something that happened there, but for the life of me, I don't know what it could be."

Agent Robinson glanced at his partner and then turned to Ben and said, "Once you report for duty at Camp Parks, I'm sure they'll fill you in on as much as they can. We're not free to discuss the investigation at this point."

"Understood. So what about these other guys who also appear to be tailing me? I don't see them around right now, but they certainly managed to find me as soon as I got into SFO."

"Rental car?" Agent Robinson glanced at his partner, then at Ben.

Ben nodded.

"They might have a GPS locator on the car."

"Makes sense." Ben turned to Jake, who'd been scanning the surrounding parking lot. "See anyone familiar?"

"No, but I've got that crawly hair-standing-on-the-back-of-the-neck feel, like someone's watching us."

"Now that you mention it . . ." Ben glanced toward Jake's Escalade and his new little Subaru. "Let's get going. I want to catch Marc before it's too late." He held out his right hand and the driver reached out, shook his hand. "In the spirit of simplifying your lives, gentlemen, after we leave Marc Reed's office, I'm headed to the house on 23rd." He flashed a quick grin at his brother. "I'd say it's been interesting," Ben said, "but that doesn't even come close. I'll do my best not to get killed. I'd appreciate your backing me up on that."

Robinson chuckled. "That would fit with our plans, as well." Then he stared straight ahead for a brief moment. "Watch your back, Sergeant. You're tangled up in some pretty nasty stuff, and I wish I could tell you more, but I can't. Just . . ." He let out a deep breath. "Be careful."

"Thanks for the advice." Ben turned away and walked with Jake back to their vehicles. "I'll follow you to Marc's."

"Yeah." Jake glanced his way. "Then we need to figure out what the fuck you know that could get you killed."

It was almost five o'clock by the time they left Marc's office over on Battery. They'd decided to fill him in on their meeting with the FBI agents, but then Marc's head of security, Bill Locke, arrived, and Ben wasn't comfortable telling his story to anyone other than Marc.

Locke was a big man, soft-spoken but intimidating all the same. He took the photos Jake had gotten of the license plate and disappeared into a small office. While they waited for Marc to get off a call, Jake transferred copies of the license plate photos to his phone and e-mailed them to Agent Robinson.

Marc finished his call, and then took a couple of minutes with Jake to catch up on some of the details regarding the photo shoot Jake and Kaz had done for the new jewelry line, which was already getting orders. Then he had to take another call. Locke was still researching variations of the plates, and Marc looked like he was going to be tied up for a while, so Ben and Jake took off.

Ben stopped beside Jake's Escalade after they left the building. His own car was about half a block down the street. "I still want to tell Marc what's going on, or you can tell him when you see him next, but I'd rather not involve the security guy."

"I figured that's why you clammed up in there. How come? Marc obviously trusts him."

"I don't know him, and until we know what's going on, I'd rather not let anyone know we talked to those FBI agents today. Private security guys are usually familiar with each other—they trade jobs, back each other up, move around a lot, and keep their connections. I have no idea who's interested in me being dead or otherwise incapacitated, and until I do, I want to keep this quiet."

Jake grinned. "I keep forgetting you're in security."

"Yeah, and generally in uniform. I'm getting way too used to civilian clothes."

"They look good on you. You've almost got twenty years—do you plan to stay in?"

"Not if I can find a decent job. I'll finish out my twenty, but I need to find out if there's life after the Army." Ben stared at the building they'd just left, thought of the man who was so close to his brother. "When you and Marc were kids together, did you ever imagine him the way he is now? I mean, I remember him as such a twerpy little kid."

"He was, and no, never." Jake glanced at the third floor where Marc's offices took up the entire level. "Except he was always focused on what he called 'important stuff.' He still is."

"Which was?"

"Our friendship, mostly. He always said that came first, because I was there for him when his parents weren't, but he was there for me in the same way. I told you, when I went to the CYA, he wrote to me, sent me cookies and books and stuff. Even when he was in college, he never forgot to write, and he'd call when he could. I had no idea he'd been to the trial every day. I still can't get over that."

Ben sucked in a deep breath. Hearing the small stuff, the details about the trial, about Jake's time locked up, made him physically hurt. Damn, he owed Marc.

Jake punched his shoulder.

"What the hell was that for?" Rubbing his shoulder, Ben glared at his brother.

Jake just grinned back. Infuriating as hell, exactly how he used to be. "You're doing it again," he said. "Whenever I mention my time locked up, you get all quiet and depressed and I know what you're thinking. Stop obsessing.

I want you to know about that time in my life, but I can't tell you if you're going to get all pissy."

It was hard to argue with him when he put it like that. Ben let out an irritated huff. "Jake, you are still such a pain in the ass. Do you know that?"

Jake's smile was angelic. "Of course. I've learned to work it. C'mon. I need to go pick up Kaz. She's texted me a couple of times to let me know she wants me back."

Ben was chuckling as he turned away. "See? It's already started. You're pussy-whipped. She calls, you run to answer."

"Damned right." He shot a grin at Ben. "And loving every minute."

Jake headed for the house while Ben stopped at Top End. He found a parking place across the street and jaywalked over to the building where Lola worked, but when he reached for the door, he stopped just outside. Lola was behind her desk, sitting with her arms folded across her chest and a very stubborn look on her face while a pudgy little man leaned into her space.

He was obviously berating her about something. Ben quietly pushed the door open and put his finger to his lips at the same time. Lola blinked, but remained focused on the man. Ben stopped behind him and loudly cleared his throat.

"Excuse me?"

The man whirled around, still sputtering. There were little bubbles of spit at the corners of his mouth, almost lost in his flabby jowls. He gave Ben a speculative up and down glance and then turned to Lola. "Please take note of what I said, Ms. Monroe, and help this gentleman, now." Then he stalked into the office behind Lola's desk and shut the door behind him.

Ben watched him walk away, turned and grinned at Lola, and said, "Well, he's certainly an asshole."

"That he is." She stood and glanced over his shoulder. "Did you buy a car? What'd you get?"

"Can you come see?"

"Yes." She glanced at the door behind her, where the guy who was obviously her boss had disappeared. "I haven't even gotten lunch yet, and it's after four."

"Come see my new car, and then I'll take you over to Mandy's place for something to eat."

"Perfect. I think she's already gone home, but the food's good." She turned to the manager's closed door, rapped on it, and then opened it. "I'm leaving for half an hour. I haven't taken a lunch break yet."

He actually snarled. "Who's going to cover the phones?"

"Looks like you, General."

She didn't wait for him to answer, and when she shut the door behind her and smiled at Ben, it felt as if the entire room lit up. He instinctively reached for her hand, and when her fingers closed around his, it felt like he was a kid again, back in high school and the prettiest girl in class had just agreed to go out with him.

Except that had never happened—he'd been too big a jerk.

When Ben's fingers wrapped around hers, Lola felt the connection everywhere, a ripple of heat from fingers to nipples and beyond. She pushed the sensation aside. Later. They had all night, but that thought had her feeling it even stronger. She'd never reacted to any man this way, but she glanced at Ben and grinned as if he hadn't just rocked her world.

"So, did you get a sporty little go-fast two-seater?"

He laughed. She loved his laugh. Sometimes he almost sounded surprised by the sound he made, but it was deep and sexy and sent shivers down her spine in a very good way.

"Actually, it's just a few steps short of a minivan, but Jake assured me that you ladies tend to travel as a pack. Where would we put Mandy in a two-seater? Or Rico?"

She stopped. Dead stop, right there on the sidewalk. "You bought a car with Mandy and Rico in mind?"

He frowned. "You mean I shouldn't have?"

She couldn't have stopped smiling if she'd tried. "Oh, no. It's the coolest thing ever, that you'd even think of them. Of us. Thank you."

He turned and stared at her, smiling that really sexy smile and slowly shaking his head. "Lola, of course I'm going to think of you and Mandy." He rubbed the back of his neck, uncertain, almost vulnerable, like he wasn't sure what to say, and Lola knew that if she hadn't been falling for him already, she would have tumbled at this very moment. "I mean, you're the best thing that's ever happened to me, and I hardly even know you. I can only imagine what the future might hold for us, except . . ."

He glanced away, almost as if he might be regretting what he'd said.

She hoped not. "Except what?"

He shrugged and took both her hands in his. "Except I'm not sure you're even thinking like I am. You hardly know me, and let's face it, what you know of my history sucks."

"What I know of your history is that you screwed up big-time, and you regret it, and you're trying to make that better. That's not a bad thing, Ben, as long as you're sincere about changing, about moving forward."

He let out a deep breath and nodded. "Yeah. I'm doing my best." He dropped her right hand, tugged the left, and they jaywalked, headed toward a sea-green SUV on the opposite side of the street.

He led her around to the sidewalk and cupped her shoulders with his palms. "Well?"

It wasn't at all what she'd expected. "This?" Oh, crap.

Her voice actually squeaked. "It's beautiful. I didn't know you were getting a *new* car, I mean, I figured you for a late model used something, I dunno, but . . . wow."

He clicked the remote, unlocked and opened the door for her. She stuck her head in and laughed. "Ah . . . new car smell. I love it!"

"Good. As long as you approve. Color okay?"

"Yes. It's really pretty." She put her hands on her hips and cocked her head. "But what if I didn't approve? What if I hated it? Then what?"

He gave her sort of a ballsy grin that was every bit as attractive as all the other looks he'd given her. "I have it in writing from the manager that I can return it for the color of your choice. This, however, appealed to me because it's the same color as your eyes. Now, let's get you something to eat."

She really didn't have an answer to that. Which was okay. Definitely okay.

CHAPTER 9

Since Mandy had gone into work so early, she'd gone home around two. Eddy, the kid who'd been the weekend dishwasher, had been promoted as of yesterday. He was running the place on his own this afternoon, and he seemed to have it all under control. According to Lola, the promotion was a reward for his quick thinking—he'd written down a partial license plate of the guy who shot at Kaz, information that had helped lead to the man's identity and arrest.

The place was almost empty when Eddy took their order at the counter. Lola chose a slice of mushroom quiche and a caffè mocha. Ben decided on a black coffee, and they took a table near the window to wait for their order.

Lola pointed out the new wood and obvious repairs. "This is where a pickup truck almost got Kaz a couple weeks ago. She was walking out in front when the truck came flying toward her. She didn't even see it, but luckily she stepped inside seconds ahead of the crash. The guy who eventually kidnapped her had hired a kid to run her down, to make it look like an accident. Luckily no one was hurt, but it was a huge mess, and Mandy said it was pretty scary. Then it got worse—he took a couple of shots at her last Friday. There are still bullet holes in the wall outside.

That's why Eddy got promoted—he was the only one who thought to write down as much of the license plate as he could remember."

Ben knew he was going to have to get used to hearing this stuff, the constant reminders that he'd failed his brother. His only consolation was that no one else seemed to be holding a grudge, least of all, Jake. Ben was going to have to accept that, and, as Jake said, man up and get past it.

It wasn't easy.

"Yeah. Jake told me what happened. The guy was nuts. I didn't know anything about him because I got the hell out of Dodge as soon as the judge cleared me. Kaz must have been terrified."

"Not terrified enough." Lola's grin was pure mischief. "She was more pissed than anything. You heard she punched the bastard, didn't you? Broke his nose and gave him a black eye."

"Good for her!" Ben sipped his coffee while Lola told him more stories about the woman who was going to marry his brother. He'd felt really comfortable around her from the beginning, but seeing her through Lola's eyes gave him a new respect for Kaz. She was obviously a whole lot more than a pretty face.

Lola glanced at her watch and grimaced. "My half hour's up. I need to get back before the General has a heart attack."

"General? I heard you call him that earlier. That little weasel can't have been a general."

"You're right." Lola gathered up her waste and carried it to the trash container by the counter. "Bye, Eddy. See you later."

The kid waved and Ben opened the door for Lola. She nodded toward her office, across the street and down a bit. "He wasn't a real general, but his last name's MacArthur, and I guess the kids in school called him General. I imagine they were making fun of him, but he's such an idiot, he actually thinks it's a compliment. What a jerk."

"Does he own the business?"

"Lord, no!" She laughed. "He's supposed to be the manager, but he sits in his office and watches porn online all day. I think his sister owns it. She's actually pretty nice. I think she got all the brains in the family."

They paused just outside the front door to Top End. Ben cupped her shoulders. He had to tell her what was going on, at least a little of it. "Before you go in . . . Jake and I learned some stuff today that ties into that sedan that's been parked across the street, the guys watching the house, and it's not good. Tonight, at least, I'm going to pick you up. I know you said you like to walk home, but humor me this once, would you? Jake's at the house now and we've invited Marc over when he can get away from the office, so we can talk about it with all of you. Are you okay with me coming back for you?"

"Of course. I can leave at five. That's only half an hour away."

"I'll be here. And don't worry about dinner. Marc's picking up Chinese."

"Yum. I think our quality of takeout is improving dramatically with Marc supplying. He's got excellent taste."

"Yeah, and the money to pay for it." He gave her a quick kiss. "See you in half an hour."

Lola turned to go inside, paused, and said, "You know, Marc may have the money, but he doesn't have the attitude. I actually like him. I didn't think I would."

"I know. It's hard to find fault with the guy. I'm glad he's been there for Jake."

Again, she paused and leveled that sea-green gaze on him. "Ben? Don't forget that you're there for Jake, too. And he's there for you. We all are." She closed the door, but he thought about what she said all the way back to the house. So many unexpected changes in his life over the past few days. Really good changes, at least most of them.

The gray sedan was no longer parked down the street, and for some reason that made him uncomfortable.

He realized he preferred knowing where the enemy was, even if it was too damned close.

Lola was finishing up her paperwork and straightening up her desk just before five when her boss stormed out of his office, waving a folded magazine.

"Who the hell hired this bitch? She's under contract to us." He threw the glossy magazine down on her desk, scattering everything Lola had just organized.

She'd been waiting for this, and it wasn't easy to keep from smirking when she opened to a full-page ad in *People* of Kaz in the vineyard in Dry Creek Valley. Sunlight was shining through new leaves still pale green against the dark vines, but the focus was on the jewelry, ruby studs in her ears, the one in the left connected by golden chains to another in her nostril. She held a glass of wine the same shade of red as the stones, and the look on her face was exquisite—a combination of seductive minx and innocent ingénue.

Lola raised her head and smiled serenely. "After you fired her, Kaz went to work for R. Jacob Lowell as the model for Marcus Reed's new line of intimate body jewelry. She's also shot a commercial with Fletcher Arnold for Lucullan Cellars. You know the one . . . Tim was on the same shoot."

"And why the fuck didn't anyone think to tell me? Kaz Kazanov works for me. That bitch can't sign a contract with anyone else. We own twenty percent of whatever she earned."

"Actually, Milton, you fired her and I hired her."

Lola spun around and smiled. "Oh . . . hi, Jake. I thought Ben was going to pick me up. I'll be ready to go here in a minute. I was just getting ready to remind Mr. MacArthur of that very same thing." She turned around and smiled at the slimy little bastard. "I heard you fire her and Jake heard you as well. Now, I have to leave. Was there anything else?"

"You might want to think about how much you want this job, little girl."

"Actually, not that much. Are you firing me, too?" She turned to Jake. "If I've been fired, I need to grab my things. Do you mind waiting a moment longer, Jake?"

Jake shook his head. "Not at all. Take your time." He towered over MacArthur, and the little man took a step back and glared at Jake. "Well? Does Ms. Monroe have a job or not?"

He puffed up like a little rooster and practically shouted, "No. She does not. Empty your desk and get of here."

"Works for me. Jake, do you still have that empty box in the back of your car?"

"Yep. I have a couple."

He was back in a minute, and in less than five, Lola had packed the few things she'd brought to the office. It wasn't until she got into the car next to Jake that she realized her hands were shaking.

"Crap. It felt really good to walk out of there, but what am I going to do now? I need to find a job, and fast."

"I can put you to work for a while if you can't find anything, but I wouldn't worry about it. You're smart and personable, and I imagine you'll find something else really fast. Whatever it is, it's bound to be better than working for that little dipshit."

Laughing, Lola leaned her head back against the seat and realized she felt pretty good, considering. "You're so right. Thank you for putting this into perspective. Two of the models, Marty and Tim, have both left, and I think a new guy we just hired, Steve, is on his way out, too. They're the ones who've made the job fun for me, but they've all had it with that jerk. The only ones left are mostly part-timers who do on-call work, not our regulars. They've all moved on. I've got a check due, though I have no idea how I'll get it, since I'm the one who's always made them out. Which reminds me . . . where's Ben?"

"He got a call from someone at the base just as he was getting ready to come pick you up. I told him I'd get you. He's going to be disappointed he missed the drama."

"I'm glad you were there as a witness to back me up. Can you believe that idiot? After firing Kaz the way he did, thinking he can get twenty percent of her income?"

"You're better off without him, you know."

"I certainly hope so." But she really needed a job, and fast.

Ben was watching for Jake's Escalade. He started down the steps the minute his brother pulled up and parked in front of the house. Lola got out, said a quick hello, and then opened the door to the back seat and grabbed a box full of stuff. The plant from the bookcase behind her desk at work was poking out of the top.

"What's this?"

"Let me get inside. Can you take this? It's heavy."

He was already reaching for it when Jake walked around the back of the car with another box in his arms. "What's going on?"

"Her jackass of a boss fired her."

Ben stopped and took a better look at Lola. "Are you okay? What happened?"

"Long story, and yes, I'm surprisingly okay. I need to find a job, but I'm not going to miss the General."

"C'mon in so you can tell me about it." He followed her

up the steps, but Lola went straight to the kitchen where Mandy and Kaz were having a glass of wine. Ben paused for a moment with his arms full, and then headed down the hall to Lola's room with her stuff. Jake followed close behind, and closed the door as soon as they carried the boxes inside.

"What was the call?"

"My commander at the base. He wants me to report first thing tomorrow. There's some really ugly shit going down, but he couldn't give me too many details. However, it appears that suicide bombing I got caught in down at Spin Boldak wasn't a random insurgent out for glory and virgins in the afterlife at all. It was a hit, pure and simple."

"Good God! On who?"

"The contractor I was showing around, and me."

"Holy shit."

"Yeah. My thoughts exactly." Ben turned and grabbed the door handle. "I need to get away from the girls before I put them in danger, but I'm not sure if I should tell them why or not."

"Tell them."

Jake's immediate response made Ben turn away from the door. "Wouldn't it put them in more danger, or at the very least, scare them?"

"The truth, Ben. Kaz and I learned that the hard way. The truth, and not just part of it. All of it. Let them make the decision about how dangerous it is, but for what it's worth, all of us are involved whether you want us to be or not."

"No." He shook his head, denying what Jake said with everything in him. "No. I can't involve you or the girls. Not Marc either. This is all on me, Jake. I just need to get out of here and . . ."

"Run?" Jake's smile took the sting out of it—a little.

"You did that almost twenty years ago, Ben, and look what it got you. Report tomorrow as planned, but keep us in the loop as much as you're able. Those guys already know where Lola and Mandy live. I'll do my best to keep an eye on things here, and if the girls know to stay alert, they'll be better off than if they don't know what's going on."

"Okay." He stared at his feet for a moment, then the wall. Anywhere but at Jake. Damn, how he hated that his brother was right. Hated that his own first reaction had been to pull essentially the same stunt he'd pulled so long ago. "I don't like it, Jake, but you're right."

The door flew open, and Lola barged in. "What are you two doing in here?" Laughing, she walked right up to Ben and planted a big kiss on his mouth. "How can I celebrate my new unemployed status if you and Jake are hiding out in my bedroom?"

"I'll have you know we were carrying those massively heavy boxes of your stuff to your room, Ms. Monroe." He swept his arm over the two medium sized boxes now sitting in the middle of her bed. "What's in those things? Bricks?"

She pinched his biceps. "Wimp. C'mon. Marc just showed up with enough Chinese food to feed an army, and Mandy and Kaz are putting it out on the counter now."

"Coming, dear." He chucked her under the chin and ducked when she took a swing. But when he glanced over his shoulder at Jake, his brother wasn't smiling.

Ben shot a grin his way. "I am admitting, in front of witnesses, that you're right, Jake. Thank you for the reminder."

"About what?" Lola's gaze went from Ben to Jake and back to Ben.

"You'll find out later, though you might have to bear witness to the fact that I've told my baby brother he was right about something." To Jake on the way out, he added, "Don't get used to it."

Ben loaded up his plate at the counter where Kaz and Mandy had lined up more Chinese food than the six of them could eat in a week, and grabbed a tall glass of ice water. An extra leaf had been added to the table, making it oblong instead of round, and perfectly comfortable for all of them to find a seat.

Rico wandered around the table twice before he finally plopped his butt on the floor next to Ben. Lola rolled her eyes. "I told you he was yours when you fed him bacon this morning. Hope you have room for him in the barracks, or wherever it is you'll be sleeping at Camp Parks."

Ben looked at the dog. "Rico? Go away. You're getting both of us in trouble."

"Forget Rico."

Mandy so rarely spoke up that everyone immediately stopped talking and turned her way. She looked absolutely surprised that her soft exclamation had actually caught their attention.

Marc was the first to start laughing. "Hey, you don't say much, but when you do, it appears we all listen. Good job."

Mandy took a deep breath, exhaled, and continued. "Okay, I wanna know why Lola got fired, and she said she wouldn't talk until we were all together."

Marc's head swung her way. "You got fired? That little turd fired you?"

"He did." And then she proceeded to tell everyone the details, up to and including his claim that Kaz owed the General twenty percent of her earnings.

"Like hell." Kaz turned to Jake. "You heard him fire me, and Lola heard him, too. He can't do that, can he?"

"He can try," Marcus said. "But he won't get anywhere. Not with witnesses and the fact that he didn't try to contact you to tell you it was all a big mistake. Firing you voids your contract." Then he turned to Lola. "So, you're looking for a job?"

She shrugged. "I guess. I still haven't wrapped my head around the idea I'm not going back in tomorrow."

"I might have something for you if you're interested. My office manager gave final notice last week. She's pregnant, and she's having twins. She's actually been giving me notice for the past few months, but I've been ignoring her because I hate hiring people I don't know." He shook his head, obviously irritated with himself for not dealing with the issue.

"Anyway, she doesn't really need the job, and since this is her first pregnancy, she knows she's going to have her hands full once the babies are born. Her husband would rather she wasn't working, at least for now, and I honestly don't think she's coming back. Are you interested? It's five days a week, though I let Mary telecommute when she doesn't feel like coming in, and it's worked out well. She handled the books for both the winery and the new jewelry line, along with my scheduling. I've got a business manager for my investments and such and actually making the payments, so you'd need to work closely with Theo on occasion. Mostly it's just answering the phone and keeping track of my schedule."

"I'm definitely interested. Is Mary still there? Would she be able to train me?"

"She is, and yes on the training. Mary's husband Michael and I were on the same software team for some of my earlier developments, so I already knew her. He took the money and ran a few years too early, but he's still doing well enough that his wife can afford not to work while their babies need her at home."

Jake laughed. "Doing well by Marc's standards must mean that Mike's only a gazillionaire, not a bazillionaire . . . or is it the other way around?"

Marc pointed his chopsticks at Jake. "Neither, you jerk. Now be nice or you'll scare her off." He grinned at Lola. "I'm perfectly harmless. Don't let Jake sway your consideration of my offer. I can promise you will earn more and have better benefits than General Dipshit gave you."

Lola laughed, but Ben liked the way she shot him a quick glance before replying to Marc, as if maybe his opinion mattered? He wasn't quite certain how to read her yet, though he thought he was getting better at it.

While Marc and Lola worked out the details, Mandy and Kaz traded stories about their day, and Ben put off telling them his news. Finally, there was a lull in the conversation. Lola turned to him with a raised eyebrow, and he realized he knew exactly what she was asking.

The thought warmed him, made him feel that connection he'd been searching for since she'd gotten home.

"I'm glad that Lola has had some good news to offset mine." That certainly got everyone's attention. "You know about the FBI agents tailing us, right?" When everyone nodded, he took a sip of his wine, and said, "I heard from my CO today, my commander at Camp Parks. He wants me to come in tomorrow, to report early for my new assignment, but he didn't say why. So I asked him about the FBI agents, and I told him they said their job was to keep me alive to testify, but that I had no idea what I'd have to testify about."

"Did you tell him about the other guys, the ones that have been out here?"

"I did, and he'd already heard about it from the FBI agents. I think it's part of the reason they want me on base, since it's a more protected environment. Anyway, I asked if he knew anything and he said all he could tell me was that the suicide bomber down in Spin Boldak wasn't a random attack, that it was a planned hit. The contractor

I was supposed to meet was one of the targets. I was the other one."

"No!" Lola grabbed his hand.

"Unfortunately, yes." He squeezed her fingers, so intensely aware of their connection, the sense that maybe Lola needed him almost as much as he needed her. "The pair that have been watching me here are obviously not on the same team as the guys Jake and I talked to today, though I'm not sure what they're hoping to accomplish by following me. The problem is, no one seems to know who's behind the bombing in Spin B, although they think I'm still alive because I was late for the appointment with the contractor. Turns out he was talking to another man who looked similar to me—same approximate size and coloring— around the time I should have been there. He was a civilian contractor wearing army fatigues. The bomber might have thought it was me."

"That poor man," Mandy said. "I mean, I'm so glad it wasn't you, Ben, but to die just because you're in the wrong place at the wrong time. It's horrible."

"I agree, Mandy. It's one of those things that doesn't make any sense." He turned to Lola. "That's when I knew I had to come home and see Jake. I could have died so easily—there was too much between us that was unresolved." He raised his head and met Jake's unwavering gaze. "I wanted him to know how sorry I was before I died and it was too late to tell him."

Jake nodded at Ben. "Jake knows," he said.

Lola was still hanging on to Ben's hand. "So what now?"

If he had it his way, he realized he'd just ask everyone else to leave so he could take her to bed, but that wasn't going to happen. It was only a little after seven. "I report tomorrow at 0800. I'll get checked into a furnished studio apartment since this is considered a temporary assignment, which I wasn't aware of, but it appears that the senator who pulled some strings to get me based here is under some sort of legal indictment and it's not certain that his recommendations carry much weight."

He focused on Lola. "For now, anyway, I'm mostly five on, two off, but there's no set schedule at this point. I'll let you know when I can get away and spend a night or two here, but for now I hesitate to hang around here too much. I don't know why somebody wants me dead, but I certainly don't want that threat affecting you."

"Don't stay away because of that. It's already affecting us, Ben."

"I know, Lola. I'm so sorry. I never would have stayed here if I'd had any idea there was someone after me. I . . ."

"No. You don't get it." Lola took both his hands in hers. "It's affecting us because we care about you, because you're Jake's brother and our friend. You are always welcome here. So far, all those jerks have done is watch the place. We'll let you know if they come back once you're at the base."

"Thank you." He leaned over and kissed her, and no one—especially Lola —seemed to mind. He pulled back, and she was smiling at him. He liked that a lot. This was all so new, having people who cared about him, about his safety. A woman who cared about him. He dragged himself back to the business at hand. "Do I have everyone's number?" He checked his cell phone. Lola had added Mandy's number to his contacts, but he was missing Marc's, so Ben added his number.

This whole process, the fact they had to worry about this crap, brought him back to earth; actually, it flat-out infuriated him, but he couldn't say that. Couldn't let go of the anger that was the only thing keeping him from getting in his car and leaving. Jake was so right when he'd accused

Ben of taking the easy way out, of not wanting to tell anyone what was going on. Who was he kidding? He hadn't been thinking of protecting them. His first thought had been of saving his own ass, of leaving so he wouldn't have to talk about something that confused the hell out of him and made him angry. Something that scared him, as much for Lola and Mandy, as for himself.

He'd gone almost two decades not worrying about anyone but himself, and suddenly he had this . . . oh, hell. He had a family to worry about. People who worried about him, and as much as he loved that they cared, he didn't know how to deal with the pressure. The sense they expected him to do the right thing. He wanted to. He wanted to be that guy, but how could he be sure he had it in him?

What the fuck had he gotten himself into?

He set his phone down and focused on Lola, but he was talking to all of them. "This wasn't how I wanted to spend my last evening with you guys. You shouldn't have to deal with my mess. I'm sorry."

"Quit apologizing!" Jake slapped his hand down on the table, rattling the dishes. All eyes turned to him. "You're my brother, which means I deal whether you want me to or not, but you're their friend. Damn it, Ben, you're important to all of us. You obviously have no idea how important you are to me. You are my brother, Ben, so deal with it. Yes, it's crap, but face it, bud, this time, it really isn't your fault!"

Jake saying it like that—clearly, forcefully—had an impact on him he'd not expected, made him feel even more guilty. He took a deep breath, exhaled. "I know. But, Jake, I've already screwed you over in so many ways. Not again. I hate that you're all caught up in what's still my mess, no matter how you look at it."

"Okay. I'll grant that." Still furious, Jake's eyes flashed.

"It's bullshit, but we need to concentrate on what the hell's going on, not waste time apologizing for something over which you have no control."

Ben let out a pent-up breath. "See, that's what pisses me off. I want to know who's after me and why, and I don't want any of you in danger because of me. You shouldn't be part of this."

"But we are, Ben, and hating it won't make it go away." Lola held both his hands in hers, and stared at him in that way she had, so calm and contained when he was seething inside. "You didn't cause this and you can't control it. So deal with it."

And that was the crux of the matter, wasn't it?

Someone he didn't know wanted him dead, but Jake was right—it was absolute bullshit, putting the only people he cared about in danger. So wrong.

Damned wrong.

But Lola was right, too. It wasn't going to go away. He was just going to have to deal with it. And for the first time in longer than he could recall, he didn't have to deal with it alone.

CHAPTER 10

Marc took off before nine with a big bag of plastic containers filled with leftover Chinese food that Mandy, Lola, and Kaz had put together for him. Ben left the kitchen while they were packing it up so he wouldn't laugh out loud; the way the women fussed over the guy. The fact Marc lived alone meant he was obviously starving, or at least that's what the girls appeared to think.

Ben had spent the evening trying to fit Marc into a category that made sense. He was a quiet guy, one who spent more time observing than talking, yet it was obvious he was enjoying the attention. He'd actually teased Mandy a little, which was a first. Ben had pegged Marc as one of those types who usually stayed in the background, but his soft-spoken manner hid a lot of strength.

He was beginning to see what drew his outgoing younger brother to a man like Marcus Reed. Marc's quiet personality complemented the exuberant Jake, while Jake probably craved Marc's steady, calming influence.

Ben had provided that for Jake at one time.

He was working on regaining at least part of that role, though in many ways, Jake was now the one providing the stability Ben had lacked for so long. But as far as Jake and Marc? It was a perfect friendship, one that was open now to Ben, drawing him back into what he thought of as that elusive normal he'd missed for so long. Where the army had given him structure, Marc and Jake were helping him reclaim his soul.

Sort of how Marc was reclaiming a lot of the Chinese takeout he'd brought over. He'd apparently figured out that he wouldn't be leaving without enough to eat for at least the next couple of days, and he took Mandy and Lola's fussing with good grace. It was obvious he loved hanging out here with all of them, and Ben wondered why it was that a guy as successful and personable as Marcus Reed was still single well into his thirties.

He'd asked Jake the same question, and he had said that no, Marc wasn't gay.

But it also appeared he wasn't interested in hooking up with any of the girls, which was probably just as well, since Mandy didn't seem interested, and both Lola and Kaz were taken.

Ben caught himself on that thought. Was Lola taken? He'd known her now for what, barely forty-eight hours? Yet somehow their short time together felt like a lifetime compressed. Probably because he'd kept so much bottled up for so long. Once you opened the lid, it felt as if the damned emotions wanted to take over, but there was no point in fighting it. Not now.

So yes, Lola was definitely taken. She might not know it yet, but she was his.

After Marc left, Mandy announced she had another five A.M. start time at the coffee shop, took Rico with her, and went to bed. Shortly after, Jake dragged Kaz out the door with a reminder that they had an early photo shoot for a spread in *Vanity Fair*—a coup for both Jake and Kaz, since he was doing the photos and she, of course, was on her way to becoming the hottest new star around and wasn't allowed to show up with bags under her eyes.

Kaz was laughing hysterically when Jake led her down the front steps, but he managed to turn around and tell Ben there was no sign of the dark sedan in the usual spot across the street and a couple doors down.

Somewhat mollified though not entirely relieved, Ben went into the kitchen to start the dishes. When Lola followed him, he stopped her in the doorway. "Go. Get a shower, put on something comfortable. Relax. You've had a long day. I'll clean up in here."

"But . . ."

He kissed her to shut her up. It worked perfectly, and he loved the dazed expression in those expressive green eyes of hers when he finally ended the kiss and pulled away far enough to actually see her. "Go."

She went.

He loaded the dishwasher, wiped down the counters, and took the extra leaf out of the table so the kitchen wouldn't feel so cramped. By the time Lola wandered back out wearing her robe and slippers, he was turning on the dishwasher and hanging the damp towel on the oven door handle to dry.

"Wow. I could get used to this." She walked across the kitchen, wrapped her fingers behind his head and dragged him down for a kiss. "Thank you for cleaning up."

"My pleasure. But so's this." He took control of her mouth, his fingers threading through her thick, black hair. His tongue tangled with hers; the taste of Lola was on his lips, on his tongue, and her scent filled his head. He loved the way she melted against him, following his lead without hesitation.

After a lifetime of living alone, of not needing or wanting anyone in his life, he already hated to think of sleeping without Lola beside him.

But he was leaving in the morning, and he had no idea when it would be safe for them, should he come back here.

Damn, he was going to miss her. He caught her whimper and breathed it in, lifted her against him, holding her body against his, her feet off the ground, her arms wrapped tightly around his neck. It was a simple thing to lift her fully in his arms, hold her tightly against his chest, and carry her out of the kitchen.

Laughing, she flicked off the light when he paused at the kitchen door, and when he moved on to the front door, she turned the latch and locked it, and then turned off the porch light. Ben slowed again, this time by the switch beside the hallway, and she turned off the lights in the front room.

Everything went dark, but Ben's room was the first door on the right, and he carried her through the open door. She turned this light on when he paused, and he tilted her back so she could close the door and lock it.

And then she lifted herself in his arms, brought her mouth to his, and kissed him.

Everything else fell away.

She really didn't want to think of the fact Ben was leaving in the morning. She'd thought they'd have the week together before he had to report, a week when she'd have a chance to get to know him better, to find out the little things that only came with time and intimacy.

But Ben was in danger, and worried about bringing that danger into their lives. He was leaving, and while he'd only be across the bay, he had no idea when he'd be able to come back to San Francisco.

Back to Lola.

He lay her down on the bed and slowly unbuttoned his shirt. She propped herself up on one elbow, watching Ben with the sense he was unwrapping a package just for her. He was so beautifully built—lean and strong, his muscle definition absolutely perfect.

She rose up on her knees and ran her hands inside the front of his shirt. He dropped his hands to his sides and cocked one very expressive eyebrow at her.

"Going to help me undress?"

"Thought about it." She smiled at him and went back to exploring his chest, tracing scars both old and new with her tongue and lips. One particular puckered scar looked as if it had barely healed. "Shrapnel?"

"Yeah. That was a big enough piece they had to cut it out."

She swallowed back a curse. He was so matter-of-fact about his injuries. She didn't want to let him know how much it hurt her to know he'd been hurt. "What about this one?"

He shrugged. "I'm not sure. It happened a long time ago. Shrapnel, bullet fragments. It's hard to keep track." He slipped his shirt off and threw it on the chair by the bed, turned, and traced a long curved scar that crossed his ribs. "I remember this one. A guy came at me with a knife. I zigged when I should have zagged."

"Oh, Ben." She covered her mouth with her hand. "I shouldn't laugh, but I swear it's like you're talking about an alternate reality. Mandy and I have lived in San Francisco all our lives. It's been a pretty mundane existence."

"An ex-boyfriend coming after you with a gun?" He bunched her hair in his hands, pulled her close and gently kissed her. He was smiling when he ended the kiss. "Doesn't sound at all mundane."

She licked her lips. "I guess that sort of violence is so common anymore." Then she walked closer on her knees and threw her arms over his shoulders. "Mandy and I spent enough time in homeless shelters that we learned to ignore a lot of the violence. Either that or we'd all live with one of Mom's boyfriends. They changed faster than the seasons, and she spent a lot of time out finding herself and just left us with the friend of the moment."

"And did she?"

Lola didn't even try not to laugh. "What? Find herself? We figured long ago that Mary Louise Monroe will still be looking for herself until the day she dies. She's certainly made a thorough search. It's taken her all over the world. Mandy and I are just the opposite. We stick close to home, wherever home at the moment is."

He kissed her, but then he broke away before Lola was ready to end it. "Yet you're both well-educated, intelligent women. You've built successful lives."

"I guess." She glanced aside, rather than tell him the truth, which was that neither of them had taken the time to look for love. It was much too easy to believe it didn't really exist. At least, until Kaz met Jake. Until he risked his life and his career to save her and proved to her roommates that yes, love just might exist, but it wasn't easy.

Which made this thing, whatever it was, that she had with Ben so utterly terrifying while at the same time absolutely thrilling. She had no idea where it was going to go, but she didn't want it to end. She didn't want to lose him. He was just going across the bay, not to the other end of the world, but they were still so new, and she was terribly afraid he was much too good for her to keep.

He'd kicked off his shoes earlier in the evening, and she'd grown inordinately fond of his long, narrow feet with the dusting of dark hair across the tops. Now, though, her attention shifted from feet to muscled abdomen and rock hard thighs as he shoved his jeans down over his lean hips. His underwear went with them.

She rolled around to her knees and sat back on her heels, just gazing at his body. When he lifted a quizzical eyebrow, she slowly shook her head. "Do you have any idea how sexy you are? How much just looking at you turns me on?" Before he could answer, even if he'd intended to, she reached out and stroked him. He sucked in a breath and his firm muscles quivered beneath her touch; his erection grew harder, more insistent.

It was such a simple thing to lean forward, to slide her lips over the velvety tip. He jerked, just the slightest thrust forward and she opened for him in spite of his whispered apology. She loved the sound of his deep groan of pleasure when she sucked harder, the growing tension in his muscles when she used her tongue on him, loved the taste of him in her mouth, his scent. She was transformed by the intimacy of the act, the sense of power, the fact she was the reason behind that quivering sense of urgency radiating from a warrior's body.

At least it was fun while it lasted.

She should have known he wouldn't let her hang on to so much control. He pulled free of her mouth and took a few deep breaths. Then he stretched out beside her on the bed. "You really have to stop that, at least until we have a chance to explore what you want."

"I want you. Now."

She couldn't believe she'd actually said it out loud.

"Not as much as I want you." He rolled over her, propped himself on his elbows and rested his thick length between her legs. "You're sure?"

"Oh, yeah . . ." She tilted her hips, rolling against him, wanting him.

He reached over her, grabbed the drawer on the bedside table and pulled out a handful of condoms. "I went shopping after I saw you this afternoon."

"Excellent planning." She frowned at the pile of at least a dozen packets he'd dropped on top of the table. Biting back a grin, she asked him, quite seriously, "Think you have enough?"

"For tonight," he said, kissing the smile right off her face.

And then he did his best to work his way through that pile of foil packets.

It was after the third, maybe the fourth time they'd both come, when Ben turned to her, ran his fingers through her hair, and whispered, "You're much too good for me, Lola. I don't get it, but I'm not stupid. I have no intention of asking you to reconsider getting involved with a bastard like me."

She sighed and snuggled against his chest. They were both damp with perspiration, their hearts still pounding away. "You really are awful, Ben." She licked salt from his collarbone, ran the tip of her tongue along the line of his jaw. Didn't he realize that everything about him appealed to her? "You are definitely a horrible man. Think about all the terrible things you do. I really don't understand why you're so willing to listen to me as if I matter, and the fact you obviously love your brother enough to come back here and apologize and then do your best to fix all the stuff you screwed up. Unforgivable."

She rolled over and straddled him, holding him in place with both her hands on his shoulders. "Sounds stupid like that, doesn't it? You know why? Because you, Ben Lowell, are the strongest man I've ever known. Strong enough to admit your mistakes. Strong enough to try and fix what you've broken. Don't you ever forget that it takes courage to do what you've done. What you're still doing."

Lola awoke a number of times during the night, and each time it was to smooth, sensual strokes, Ben's warm hand coasting slowly over her shoulders, along the line of her back, over the curve of her bottom. And each time she turned to him for more.

He was leaving in the morning. She'd never had another man in her bed overnight.

She already missed him.

The smell got to him first, the stench of dirt and motor oil, unwashed bodies. He spotted the contractor on the far side of the road talking to someone Ben didn't recognize, but since he was running late, he figured it was okay to interrupt the conversation. He took a step toward the guy he was supposed to meet.

The blast came out of nowhere. Usually the pain woke him. This time it was the echoing reverberation, the explosive concussion as one more militant blew himself—and Ben's afternoon appointment—to pieces.

He awakened just before the alarm was set to go off, mildly surprised at the dream. It had been a few weeks since he'd had that one. He shut off the alarm, forced himself not to touch Lola again, and headed for the shower.

Long before five he was showered, shaved, and dressed in his ACUs, his army combat uniform, which was standard gear for the type of work he did in the Middle East and here in California. As he left the bathroom with his overnight kit, he noticed the door to Mandy's room was open, her bed made up, and Rico still sound asleep in his bed on the floor. She'd said she was opening the coffee shop at five this morning. He'd thought about putting on a pot of coffee here, but decided to see if Mandy needed a ride in. It would be a lot easier to take her to work and just buy a cup of coffee there.

She was in the kitchen, leaning against the counter, eating a cup of yogurt. "I'm leaving in a few minutes," he said, keeping his voice low. Can I give you a ride in?"

"Good morning, and yes. I was planning to leave now and walk, but if you're going to drive, I'll wait."

"I'll be right back. I need to tell Lola I'm leaving, and grab my gear."

He wasn't looking forward to leaving her. Not at all.

He'd lost track of how many times they'd made love during the night, lost track of the moment he'd stopped thinking of what they were doing as having sex. No, they'd made love, and it was the most amazing, heart-stopping, terrifying thing he'd ever done in his life. Making love with Lola Monroe meant putting his life in her hands. It meant trusting her.

Asking Lola to trust him.

He'd never trusted anyone other than his brother, but he hadn't been worthy of Jake's trust. He would be worthy of Lola's. There was no other option.

He went back into their room and watched her for a moment, sleeping so soundly. He'd probably worn her out last night. He hadn't been able to sleep, hadn't been able to keep his hands to himself, and each time she'd awakened to his touch, she'd reached for him. Welcomed him.

There weren't very many condoms left on the bedside table this morning. He quietly opened the top drawer, brushed the unopened packets inside, and then closed it. Smiling, he knelt beside the bed, leaned close and kissed her cheek. She didn't open her eyes, but her hand found the side of his face and she turned and kissed him.

"I have to go," he whispered. "Don't get up. I'll call you tonight, but you don't have to go to work, and I imagine you're really tired this morning."

She blinked, all soft and sleepy-eyed. "And you're not?" Even half asleep she managed to arch an eyebrow.

"Energized, sweetheart. You're good for me." He kissed her again and stood, shoved his overnight kit into his duffel and swung the heavy bag up over his shoulder.

She was already falling back to sleep. He paused in the doorway and felt something tighten around his chest, and he wanted to tell her how much she meant to him, that she was already changing his life. Wanted to say that she was his and no one else's, but he didn't have that right. Not yet.

Quietly, he closed the door, leaving just a crack so she could hear Rico if he wanted out. Mandy was waiting in the front room. "Ready?"

"I am," she said, and then she laughed. "I get to ride in the new car before Lola. She's going to be so jealous!"

Ben smiled as he held the door for her. "Is that going to be a problem?"

"Not for me, and I'm sure Lola will get over it. Besides . . ." she hesitated, midsentence. "Crap, Ben. Your buddies are back."

The dark sedan was parked right where it had been off and on over the past couple of days.

"Here." He handed her the key. "Get in and lock the doors. I'm going to go have a very quick chat with our friends." He checked his watch. "I can still have you at the shop before five."

The laughter was gone. "Be careful, Ben."

"Always."

He threw his duffel in the back of the SUV as soon as Mandy had it unlocked, and then waited until she was safely in the car before walking diagonally across the street to the driveway where the gray sedan was parked. He was ready to knock on the driver's side window when he realized there was something on the glass. It was too dark to tell what, so he grabbed the penlight out of his pocket and aimed the beam at the window.

There was too much reflection on the tinted glass to see inside, but the light was shining through something dark red. He raced around to the passenger window. It was almost entirely blown out. The man on this side was missing most of his face and half of his skull. The driver was alive, but barely, gasping for breath. Blood ran slowly from a wound in his chest.

Ben grabbed his cell phone, punched in 911, and gave the dispatcher the address, and described the scene. She asked him a few questions and told him to stay on the line. He walked back to his car, still talking, but he had to tell Mandy what was going on.

She unlocked the door and he opened it and leaned in. "Two men. They've both been shot." She gasped and covered her mouth with her hand, but he kept talking, and realized the voice he was using was the same voice in which he'd reported the bombing at Spin Boldak. Professional, absolutely emotionless. It was the only way he knew to stay in control, if not of the situation, at least of himself.

"I've got the 911 dispatcher on the line. Do you want me to get Lola to take you in to work? The dispatcher asked me to wait here."

"No. I'm going to call my boss. She can open up a few minutes late. I know she's up." Mandy hit a number on speed dial as two police cars rolled up across the street. They came in quietly, without lights or sirens.

"You okay? I need to go talk to the cops."

Mandy nodded, talking to whomever had answered. Ben told the dispatcher the police had arrived, ended the call and went back across the street. One of the policemen was already checking the man who was still breathing. His partner turned toward Ben as he approached.

"I'm Officer Macias. José Macias. How'd you find them? Did you see the shooting?"

"Master Sergeant Benjamin Lowell. I'm the one who called this in. No, I didn't see or hear anything, but they or someone who looked just like them have been tailing me since I got back in the states early Saturday. I was getting ready to take my girlfriend's sister into work, saw the car, and decided to ask them why they appeared to find me so interesting. I had Mandy wait in my car, and walked over here. I went to the driver's side first, but something didn't look right, and no one acknowledged me standing here, so I used my penlight and saw the blood on the glass. I didn't try the door. Just went around to the passenger side. That's when I realized both men had been shot. Looks like they used a shotgun."

The ambulance rolled in just then, with lights flashing and siren blaring. Ben noticed the light go on in his bedroom, which meant Lola'd be out here any minute. Other lights were going on up and down the normally quiet street. "I need to call my girlfriend," he said, pointing toward the window across the street. "Looks like she just woke up. Then I better get in touch with my boss. I have a feeling I'll be reporting late."

Macias glanced at the dark sedan. "I can just about guarantee that."

Ben called Lola to tell her what had happened, but Mandy was already with her, so he got off the phone and dialed his CO's office at Camp Parks. Captain Booker was already at his desk. Ben filled him in on the situation.

"These are the two who've been following you, the ones who aren't FBI?"

"As far as I know. I've never actually gotten a good look at either one of them, but according to the FBI agents Jake and I talked to, they hadn't been assigned to follow me until yesterday. These two were parked in the same place as the other unknown tails, but . . . just a minute."

He walked over to where he could see the license plate. "The license plate is different, though I think the model and make of car is the same. Hell, these two could be FBI. I don't know, sir. The police are going to want me here, I imagine. If it's okay, I'll answer what questions I'm able to, and then get to the base as soon as I can. Which reminds me—is any of this classified? Can I answer them?"

"As far as I know it's not, though with the FBI involved, it's hard to tell. Paranoia seems to be a big part of their system. I'm going to call the number I've got for the local guys and find out if they had anyone on you at that location. Keep me apprised of the situation, and report in as soon as you can."

He'd never met the man, but already Ben had a good feel for his new captain. He sounded level-headed and entirely logical, something that wasn't a given with Army officers. Ben ended the call and walked back to the police officer. Paramedics had strapped the wounded man onto a gurney and quickly loaded him into the ambulance. There was a blanket covering the head and shoulders of the man who'd died. They'd left his body in the vehicle.

The ambulance pulled away with lights flashing and sirens wailing. More lights up and down the street went on, doors opened.

Officer Macias turned off his phone and approached Ben. "Sergeant, what can you tell me about this situation you found?"

"I honestly don't know, but I just checked in with my CO and asked if any of this was classified, and he said not to his knowledge. With that in mind, it might be, shortly, so I'd better tell you what I can while I can." He rubbed the back of his neck and glanced toward the house. Both Mandy and Lola were coming across the street.

"Good morning, José." Mandy walked up to the officer and slipped her left arm around his waist. "I didn't realize it was you."

Officer Macias nodded to her and returned her quick hug, but he was shaking his head. "When I heard the sergeant, here, mention Mandy, I wondered if it might be you. I knew you guys lived in the area. I'm glad you weren't hurt. Good morning, Lola."

"G'morning, José."

She moved close to Ben and he wrapped his arm around her, well aware his inner caveman was actively staking a claim. He wondered if he seemed that obvious to Lola.

Mandy stepped away from the officer. She stood next to her sister and glanced at Ben. "José is the one who came when Kaz almost got hit by the truck and again when the guy shot at her." She smiled at the officer. "I feel like we're old friends."

"And she makes great coffee."

"If that was a hint, José, be patient. I just put a pot on, and Lola stuck some cinnamon rolls in the oven. You'll get your caffeine and sugar fix. Any idea what's going on?"

Immediately, he was all business. "I was just getting ready to talk to the sergeant, and see what we can find out."

CHAPTER 11

Ben carefully and methodically explained what little he knew. Officer Macias took notes, but, with Ben's permission, also used the recording app on his cell phone.

"So, that's all I know." Ben had told the officer everything that had happened to date, but realized it wasn't much for the man to go on. He had a feeling that this particular hit might be well beyond the scope of the local police force. "I imagine you'll hear from the two FBI agents my brother and I met yesterday. My CO said he was going to contact them after we spoke earlier this morning. I wish there was more I could tell you, but at this point I can only guess that it must involve someone either politically or financially connected enough to be able to afford the kind of interest I've acquired. Private detectives or whatever these two are don't come cheap. And, it has to be tied to my time in the Middle East. I haven't lived stateside for almost twenty years."

"Thanks, Sergeant. Can you hang around a few minutes longer? We're waiting for the medical examiner's office to get here, and I've got a call into the precinct captain to see if they have any idea why someone would be following you. Sometimes they're in the loop on special operations in the area. You never know. And obviously we'd appreciate anything your commander might come up with in the course of his investigation that . . ."

"Just a moment, officer." Ben watched a familiar dark sedan pull in behind Macias's patrol car. Two men got out and walked over. Ben stepped forward and held out his hand. "Agents Robinson, Renteria." He shook hands with both men and introduced them to Officer Macias, who immediately asked if the two men who'd been shot were with the FBI.

Robinson answered. "Not as far as we know. Dead?"

Macias shook his head. "One's still alive, though he looked pretty bad. He's been transported. There's still a body in the passenger side, but I don't know if there's enough left for a visual ID. Whoever pulled the hit appears to have used a shotgun. We're waiting on the medical examiner's office."

Robinson sighed. "Renteria, this one's yours."

"Thanks loads." Grumbling, the younger agent reached into his back pocket for a pair of latex gloves. He pulled them on as he walked over to the sedan, and was back within a couple of minutes. "He doesn't look familiar, but there's not much left to go on. We'll probably have to rely on fingerprints or DNA to get a positive ID. How long before your forensics team gets finished?"

Macias checked his watch. "Lord only knows. I called this in as a priority almost forty minutes ago. I expected someone from the medical examiner's office by now. You can probably take off if . . ."

Robinson interrupted. "Actually, Lowell, we'd like for you to hang around a bit longer. I can call your CO and clear it for you, if you like."

Ben shook his head. "It's not necessary. He said to come in when I can."

They all turned as a dark SUV pulled in across the street and parked behind Ben's vehicle. Macias was the first to speak. "Good. Here's the ME." He quickly got Ben's phone number and handed him a card with his information on it, and then stepped away to meet with the man and woman who had just arrived.

Ben hugged Lola close against his side. "You two going to be okay?"

"Yeah. We'll be fine," she said. "What a horrible way to start a morning. Those poor men. I mean, even if they were the creeps following you, they didn't deserve this."

Macias walked back to the small group. "If you've got the time, Sergeant, I do have a few more questions."

"Would you be more comfortable in the house?" Lola glanced at Ben. "Mandy's got a pot of coffee on, and I have to check on the cinnamon rolls."

Agent Robinson surprised Ben when he actually smiled at Lola. "That would sure work for me, if you don't mind. It's been a long night." He glanced at his partner. "We could both use a cup of coffee."

Officer Macias stayed to speak with his partner while Mandy and Lola went on ahead. Ben and the three men followed a couple of minutes later. He led them up the stairs to the place he was already thinking of as home. Walking into the bright kitchen filled with the scent of cinnamon, the sight of Mandy pouring cups of coffee, and Lola pulling a tray of steaming hot rolls out of the oven definitely reinforced the feeling.

He stopped behind Lola and rested his hands on her shoulders. "How'd you find time for this?"

She blushed. "I cook when I'm stressed out. I had these in the freezer and thawed them overnight so I could make them before you left today. And then I overslept. I stuck them in to bake before I went out to meet you."

Ben leaned over and kissed her. "Works for me."

"I'm not complaining, either. Thank you." Robinson

took the cup of coffee Mandy handed to him and sat at the table.

Ben grabbed a cup and carried the tray of rolls for Lola, and she and Mandy sat on stools at the small bar at the end of the counter. Once everyone was seated, Robinson took the lead. He glanced at his partner and then addressed Ben. "First of all, I apologize for not giving you more information when we spoke yesterday. I needed clearance, and I've got it. The story's about to break nationally, though we still don't have all the answers. He glanced around the table and then at Lola and Mandy.

"I do have to ask you all, though, to bear with me. Anything we discuss here today can't leave this room, at least until the story hits the papers. We figure we've got less than a week before the news agencies feel they have enough to run with, though obviously it could come sooner rather than later. Or, threats of legal action may make them hold off for a while. It's hard to say, though my office would prefer that it stays quiet for as long as possible. Officer Macias, I'll meet with you later and let you know what's available for your report at this point. Everyone okay with that?"

He waited until they'd all agreed and then turned his attention to Ben. "If you don't mind, I want to know what you remember of the contractor in Afghanistan at the time you were assigned to him."

"Other than the fact he was a class A dick?" Ben shook his head, remembering the man who'd made him seriously hate his job. "How his company got the contract for security never made any sense. The man was arrogant and stupid, which is a bad combination at any time, but in the middle of a war it can get you killed. Which, obviously, is what happened to him and the poor guy he was talking to, along with a few other innocent bystanders. He had no idea how security should be run in the field, and not a clue how to work with the Afghani people.

"Our soldiers had spent a lot of time in Spin Boldak developing a fairly decent relationship with the locals, and then Hendrickson came along and undid months of work with a few idiotic moves. He seemed to have an awful lot of ready cash—part of my job was to follow him around with bags of money for cementing certain deals I was never privy to."

Robinson had been taking notes while Ben talked. He glanced up then, and asked, "Do you have any idea where the money came from? Who was supplying it?"

Ben shook his head. "I know it came in on the weekly transport of goods that we got out of Kabul while I was there. I discovered that by accident when one of the soldiers delivered a package to me because he couldn't find Hendrickson. The corner of the box was ripped open and I could see what looked like stacks of bills. I don't know what denominations they were, but there was a lot of cash in that box, and it appeared to be American currency."

Renteria spoke up. "Obviously, Hendrickson wasn't doing this on his own, then. But why the hit? Do you have any idea why someone would have wanted to kill him? And you, as well?"

"I have my theories, though there's nothing I can prove."

"I'm all ears." Robinson took a sip of his coffee and sighed. "Absolutely wonderful." Then he grinned at Mandy and gave her a thumbs up.

The man was looking more human all the time.

"Let me give you a little background, first," Ben said. "Local government in Afghanistan is so entirely different from the way things are done here in the states." He gave a quick rundown of the opium trade in Kandahar Province, and Spin Boldak's importance near the border of Pakistan on a major trade route, as well as the different levels of political and religious control. "There are village councils and representatives who are links between the village and the government, and then you've got the mullahs," he said. "They're the religious leaders who are the heart of most villages. They're also the ones with the power and access to village funds."

"And I imagine that adding to those funds helps them build more power?"

Ben grinned at Agent Renteria. "Give the man a prize. Exactly. While I was in Spin B, I traveled a lot with Hendrickson. My job was to keep him alive so he could do whatever it was he was doing. The thing is, he mostly visited the mullahs in the various villages, and he left them with large sums of money. At least the briefcases I carried to those meetings were pretty heavy when I got there and very light when I left. I was never in the rooms with them during any of their transactions. On occasion, I'd hear arguments, but most of the visits were pretty low key."

"Did you ever see any opium?"

Ben shook his head. "Never. Processed or otherwise. Nor did I see anything at all that could tie anyone to the drug trade, but there was too much cash, and too many mullahs willing to do business with Hendrickson. He spoke the language, which put him at an advantage. I understand a little, but not enough to follow any major discussions. But if not drugs, what else?"

Ben took a sip of his coffee and continued. "And personally, I don't think Hendrickson was anything more than a supervisor or manager of some kind. There was a younger man who showed up very early in my assignment, and Hendrickson just about had his lips fused to the kid's ass, he was trying so hard to please him. I probably have his name somewhere in my notes, but at the time I assumed he was the one actually running the so-called security company. In fact, I would suggest you look into the contract his company got to run security in areas that didn't use security forces. Not once did I see any of the people over there who were associated with that outfit doing any actual security work. And even with all the cash Hendrickson was spreading around, the man was pretty much hated. That hit could have come from anyone, including the politician or the money behind a politician in this country who got him stationed over there."

Robinson exchanged a quick glance with his partner. "You have good instincts, Lowell. What you're saying fits with our investigation." He tapped his pen on the table a few times, and then took another swallow of coffee, a bite of the cinnamon roll. "Aw, jeez. That is so good." He smiled at both Lola and Mandy.

Officer Macias set his cup down and stared at Robinson for a moment. "Can you tell us the name of the senator you suspect might be linked to this investigation?"

Robinson's head shot up. "What makes you think it's a senator?"

Macias smiled, shrugged. "Just a hunch. Something that might tie into a fairly local story, one that I was reading about a while back."

"The politician isn't local." Robinson's stare held a laser-sharp lock on Macias.

The officer merely smiled. "No, but his story is. I'm a news junkie. I love finding connections between people I know and people in the news." He glanced at Ben. "Ask your brother about the winemaker at Tangled Vines, the winery where he rescued Kaz. About the winemaker's father's story. His name was Colonel Mac Phillips, retired US Army, FBI, and then Secret Service. He investigated a US senator of questionable ethics back in the 1980s, but the report was buried and Colonel Mac was forced to retire. He bought the land in Dry Creek Valley and made really good wines until he died last year."

Ben noticed that Robinson hadn't taken his eyes off Macias, but he didn't stop him, either.

"The old man had dementia at the end, and lost the winery. Your friend Marcus Reed bought it, renamed it Intimate, but that's not what's important. The thing is, Colonel Mac had kept copious notes of his investigations of the senator, and he hid them in the wine cave across from the family home. There was quite a story about an attempt by a man hired by this particular senator who tried to recover that material. The old man, dementia and all, stopped him. When Colonel Mac died, his daughter turned her father's briefcase filled with all of those notes and tapes over to the Secret Service, since that's the organization that had ordered the original investigation." He gazed steadily at Ben. "That would be the investigation that was stopped, the one that got Colonel Mac fired."

"I read about that," Mandy added. "The investigation was of Senator Ewing. Burl Ewing." She glanced at Ben. "But the winemaker, Cassie Phillips, also gave complete copies of the papers and tapes to a reporter for our local newspaper first, before giving the originals to the Secret Service. The paper did a big spread on how the colonel's long-buried notes had led to a huge investigation that's still going on, but they didn't go into the details of that investigation."

Robinson glanced at each of them. "The senator in question is an extremely powerful man. A very dangerous man with dangerous friends, and we still don't know if he's pulling the strings, or if there's someone pulling his, but something is holding up that story. The FBI is working in conjunction with the Secret Service on this one, but I'd prefer that you didn't discuss any of this—like I said, a lot of this is old news and the rest is due to be made public shortly—but it could still be dangerous for you. We don't know if those men who were shot worked for the senator or for someone with an ax to grind against the senator. Point being, the longer we can keep this quiet and your role out of the news, the safer you'll be, and the more we're apt to find out. And Sergeant Lowell, while you don't think you have anything of value to testify to in court, I believe you do. Especially since you said you've kept records of the dates and the deliveries, and the people you and Hendrickson saw. I hope those records are in a safe place." He looked at Ben, as if waiting for him to reveal where he'd stashed the information.

Ben, however, replied with a simple, "They are." He'd turned them over to Marcus Reed the day he'd gone to see him when he was trying to find Jake. Marc had promised not to let anyone—including his chief of security—know he had the briefcase stuffed with notes. The security guy put off a vibe Ben didn't like, but he trusted Marc completely. Still, he wasn't about to tell Robinson where the information was. If nothing else, he didn't want Marc in any danger or legal trouble for helping him.

Robinson and Renteria stood. So did Ben and Officer Macias. Macias shook hands with both agents. "Thank you, gentlemen. I've got your contact information, and I'll get the ME's report and identification of the two victims to you as soon as we have them."

Then he turned to Mandy and Lola. "Thank you for your hospitality, ladies. This was an unexpected but very welcome break."

Mandy handed him the last cinnamon roll wrapped in a napkin and a travel mug of coffee. She gave him a snarky grin and said, "This is not for you, José. It's for the poor man you left out there with the body. Just have him drop the cup off at the coffee shop."

"You are a cruel woman, Mandy, but my partner will thank you."

Robinson paused at the front door. "Lowell, feel free to

discuss all this with your captain. I'll get in touch with him as soon as I have some facts to share, but I'd suggest you be overly cautious, at least until the issue in Washington is resolved. I have a feeling a lot of people will rest a lot easier once Ewing is behind bars, but knowing how Washington works, that could be a while. Like I said earlier, he could merely be a puppet in all of this, though from what I know of Ewing, I'd suggest you watch your back."

He and Renteria left. Ben glanced at the clock. It was almost eight o'clock. "I need to get going. Mandy, do you want me to drop you off at the coffee shop?"

"If you don't mind. My boss has a bunch of stuff she was planning to get done today. I really should get down there so she can take off."

He leaned close and kissed Lola. "Will you be okay here?"

"Yes. I was thinking of taking the Muni bus over to Marc's office, but I think I'll just hang out and be a bum today."

Mandy left the room. Ben wrapped his arms around Lola and held her close. "I'm going to miss you. A lot more than I have a right to." He kissed her again.

When they finally came up for air, Lola smoothed his hair back with her hands and said, "I think you have every right. I'm going to miss you, too." She shot him a cheeky grin. "Ya know, I bet they make you get a haircut." She ruffled his long hair with her fingers. It made him feel like purring, but he was still smiling when Mandy returned.

"You're probably right. It's too long." Ben touched the side of Lola's face, whispered good-bye, and followed Mandy out to his car. Officer Macias was just getting ready to leave. Two men were loading the bagged body from the sedan into the back of a large van. The woman from the ME's waved to Ben.

"Excuse me." She walked quickly across the street. "You're Ben Lowell?"

"I am. What can I help you with?"

"One quick question—what time exactly did you find the body?"

"Less than a minute before I called 911." He glanced at Mandy. "It was about ten minutes to five, right?"

She nodded. "If the clock on the car is right, it was 4:51 when I got in and you walked over there."

"Nine to five, then." He grinned at Mandy when the song title popped into his head.

Mandy winked. "Another old-movie fan, eh? Sorry. It's already been a long day, and it's barely eight in the morning."

The forensics specialist smiled. "Thank you, though. Me, too. I needed that. I've been going since ten o'clock last night. Officer Macias has your contact information?"

"He does. Please feel free to call me any time. I'm reporting to Camp Parks this morning, but I'll have my cell phone."

"Thank you."

Ben and Mandy got into the SUV; he made a U-turn and headed back down the street toward Irving. Mandy turned toward him, grinning. "She was hittin' on you, ya know."

"Who?" He had no idea who Mandy was talking about.

"That forensics woman. She headed for you the minute she saw you coming down the steps. I don't think she saw me at first."

He just laughed. "Guess I missed the signal." Then he shrugged. "Besides, she's not Lola."

Mandy patted his arm. "I really do like you a lot, Ben."

Ben smiled and kept driving. A couple minutes later, he'd dropped her off and was headed across the bay toward Dublin. It was a little after eight. With any luck, maybe the worst of the commuter traffic would have gotten where they were supposed to be this early on a Tuesday morning.

He stopped for a breakfast burrito in Oakland when the traffic slowed to a crawl, and by the time he pulled back onto the freeway, it was moving once again. He found Camp Parks without any trouble, and got directions to headquarters. When he finally walked into Captain Booker's office and saluted his new CO, it was a little after nine-thirty.

He liked Booker right off the bat. He was a big man, at least as tall as Jake and probably forty or fifty pounds heavier—none of it from fat. His skin was dark, his look as much Hispanic as African American, and he carried himself like a man well aware of his strength.

After they got all the paperwork taken care of and officially transferred Ben to the base, Booker walked him around the area, showed him where his office was. Available housing was off base, but by the end of the day, Ben had a furnished studio apartment that was at least clean, close, and affordable.

His CO invited him for dinner. Ben had a few minutes to call Lola and catch her up on his day and his new digs, which, he told her, really made him miss the house on 23rd Avenue almost as much as he missed her.

Booker lived off base in a neat little ranch-style house near the base, not far from Ben's apartment. His wife, Jia, was petite and lovely, and their three boys, ranging in age from eight to twelve, stayed in constant motion, while managing to remain unfailingly polite.

After dinner, Booker and Ben cleaned up the dishes and then took their iced tea out on the back patio while Jia helped the boys with homework.

They sat there for a bit, sipping their drinks, before the

captain spoke. "I've got a rule when I invite men or women home from the base. When you're at my house, when it's just the two of us, we're not military, I'm not your CO, and you can relax. I don't have any ulterior motives, but I think all of us need to touch base with our civilian side once in a while."

"Good luck with that, sir." Ben set his glass on the arm of his redwood chair. "I don't know if you've read my service history, but this is the first time I've been back in the states for years. I've taken some classes, done short temp assignments, but half my life has been military without many forays into the civilian side of life."

"I actually read the whole thing, Ben. In almost two decades, almost all of it spent on foreign soil, you've got a Bronze Star with V device, a couple of Purple Hearts, and very few negative comments. Other than turning down any and all offers to attend OCS, you've managed to complete a college degree, including your masters, and have had an exemplary career."

He chuckled, but Ben sensed the captain's question before he asked. "I'm curious, Ben. What the fuck have you been hiding from?"

He laughed. "Well, that's not what I expected. Pretty damned perceptive, though. It's a long story for another time. I can tell you, though, that the reason for this trip home was to fix something I screwed up almost two decades ago. That's been done, to the best of my ability. I'm planning to stay here, finish out my twenty years, and find out what else life has to offer. The reason I've turned down OCS is that I'm not officer material, sir. I'll leave that to younger guys who are smarter than me and not quite as jaded."

And that Bronze Star with the V device for valor? He'd been scared shitless during that operation. It was enough to get out of it alive. It almost felt wrong, getting a commendation for pissing his pants.

"Unfortunately, I understand all too well." Booker paused, glanced away, and then said, "I got a call from the FBI agent, Robinson, this afternoon. He said they got positive IDs on both men. The driver died in surgery, so they weren't able to question him, but he wanted me to tell you he doesn't think they worked for Ewing."

"Really? Interesting. Has Robinson filled you in on the story yet?"

Booker shook his head. "Not enough. Can you give me what you know?"

"I can. It's not classified, mainly, I guess, because the story's supposed to break in the media over the next week or so. I'm still not sure why I'm an important enough target to generate this much interest, but obviously someone thinks I know something. I have a feeling it's going to get pretty exciting before it all settles down."

He told his CO everything, including the link to the winery in Dry Creek Valley, and the fact that there were so many strange connections, but they all appeared to lead back to one very powerful senator. One his testimony might be able to connect to illegal activities in Afghanistan.

It was growing late by the time he finished the story. Booker didn't have much to say, though he agreed that it was a messy situation. Ben got up, carried his glass into the kitchen, and set it in the sink. Jia was still at the kitchen table with the boys, and he thanked her for dinner. The captain walked him to the door.

His studio apartment was only a couple of blocks away, so he was there within minutes. And after sending a quick text to Lola, he crawled into his very lonely bed.

It took him a long time to fall asleep. Enough time to

imagine all kinds of scenarios with one lovely, smart, sexy as hell woman.

He had the weekend off. Friday night wasn't going to get here soon enough.

CHAPTER 12

She'd always liked being home alone, just Rico for company and no one bugging her, but after all the crazy stuff this morning, Lola couldn't settle down and relax. Even though she was currently unemployed, she wasn't one to sit around. She'd taken a shower, dusted, and picked up around the house. She'd even tried reading, but the book couldn't hold her attention. She didn't feel like working in the yard, the laundry was done, and the dog fed and walked.

She missed Ben. It was that simple. She hardly knew the man—well, obviously they knew each other, and didn't that thought make her blush—but he'd not been part of her life for long at all, so how could she miss him so much?

Easy, a little voice in her head kept muttering. Way too easy.

Her cell rang. Marcus Reed wondered if he sent a car for her, would she be able to come in today? She might not have as much time with Mary as he'd hoped. Lola said she'd be ready when the car arrived.

It was barely fifteen minutes later—she'd just finished dressing and made sure Rico's water dish was freshly filled and his doggy door to the backyard unlatched—when

Marc's Tesla pulled up in front. Grabbing her purse, Lola locked the front door and went down the steps.

He'd already gotten out of the car and had the passenger door open for her.

"What? No chauffeur's cap?"

Marc grinned and made a deep bow, one arm behind his back. He really was cute. "At m'lady's service."

"Oh, I like this. The boss himself picking me up. I thought you were sending a driver." She got into the car.

Marc went around to the driver's side and climbed in, but then he smiled at her. "That was the plan, though I didn't expect the driver to be me. My regular driver was at lunch. I didn't want to bother him, and I know Ben doesn't care for my security guy, so I wasn't comfortable sending him to come get you."

"Thank you. I'm not sure why Ben feels that way, but I appreciate you considering his opinion."

Marc glanced her way. "Doesn't matter. He's obviously got his reasons." He turned his attention to his driving.

After a couple of blocks, she realized he probably didn't know about the shooting. "We had some excitement this morning," she said, and then she told him as much as she could without going into too much detail.

"I'm glad you're all okay. My guy never did find out anything about who was following Ben. I imagine the FBI will figure it out."

Their conversation drifted from the killing to Lola's duties at Marc's office, and then ended altogether. He was very businesslike with her, though he'd been a more light-hearted man when he was at their house. He wasn't at all like Ben or Jake, but he was a nice guy. Quiet, really thoughtful.

And not her problem. She was having enough trouble just trying to figure out what made Ben tick. She realized she was grinning as they drove down the street, neither of them talking. Marc's electric car was just like him—it barely made a sound, either.

At a little before five o'clock, Marc poked his head out of his office. "Ready for your ride home?"

"I am. Just let me put these things away." She'd been going through records and receipts for Marc's winery in Sonoma County. Everything was well organized, and she'd needed very little help from Mary to get started, though all the government regulations covering wine production were enough to give her a headache. At least Lola had Mary's home phone number with instructions to call if she had any questions.

She'd started a list. It was already a long one, but that could wait until tomorrow.

Finishing up, she closed the desk drawer and grabbed her handbag. "You didn't tell me Mary was ready to pop."

Marc stood there looking sheepish. "Yeah, well I thought she was just big because there are two. I didn't realize she was due next month."

"Three weeks, Marc. And twins often come early. That poor woman is exhausted, and so ready to have those babies! I think you barely dodged a bullet with this one."

She teased him about how close he'd come to delivering his office manager's babies, and they were both laughing when she followed him downstairs to the private parking lot dedicated to his building. She'd just discovered it was his building. When he'd needed office space, he said it was cheaper to buy the building and rent out the two lower floors he didn't need than to try and find a good location with parking.

They were less than a block from Marc's office, heading through an intersection, when Lola glanced up and to the right, and screamed. A small red car was racing toward them, accelerating through the red light. It slammed into the right rear panel, spinning the Tesla in a half circle. Lola's scream was cut off by the air bags deploying from all directions. The driver of the Toyota climbed out on the passenger side and took off running, while Lola stared at the airbags deflating all around her. Still a bit loopy from the impact, she raised her head.

Marc looked just as rattled, but he shot a quick look her way. "Are you okay?"

"Other than possible death by airbag?" She shoved the deflated one beside her out of the way. "Yeah. Just shaken. How'd your car fare?"

"Better than the other guy's. My door's okay, but yours might be jammed. You're sure you're all right?" He unfastened his seatbelt, got out, and came around to her side. People were gathering, drivers going around the crunched Tesla and a badly damaged Toyota.

It took some jiggling and a kick to the bottom side of the mashed door, but he helped Lola out just as a policeman arrived.

"Are you folks okay?"

"I am, thank you." Marc glanced at Lola. "You're sure you're not hurt?"

"I'm fine. Marc, did you see where he came from?"

"The guy who hit us? He ran the red."

"I know, but he was stopped at the light until we started through. Then he gunned the car. He was still accelerating when he hit the back panel."

The officer focused on Lola while another man in uniform directed traffic around the two cars. "You're saying he ran into you on purpose?"

"It certainly looked like it to me." She shot a loopy grin at Marc. "On the other hand, after the day I've had, I might just be paranoid."

But Marc was staring in the direction the driver had run. "Marc? What's the matter?"

"I don't know, but . . ." He shrugged. "I just realized he looked familiar. I'm not sure why, but . . ." He let out a frustrated breath. "Doesn't matter. It'll come to me when I'm not thinking about it, and not before."

Even the cop grinned at that one. "Happens to all of us, but let me know if you come up with a connection."

His partner joined them a moment later. "I just called it in. The car was reported stolen about two hours ago from a parking garage near Pier 39." He gazed at the mangled wreckage, what was left of the older car. "Not much left to recover, is there?"

It was a full half hour before Marc had arrangements made to tow his car. They retrieved their belongings, and he and Lola took a cab to her house. "C'mon in, Marc. If you don't have plans, why don't you at least grab a bite of dinner with us?"

"You're sure you don't mind?"

She smiled as he closed her door behind her. "Of course not. It's going to seem really empty without anyone here but Mandy and me."

They fixed soup and sandwiches for dinner. Afterward, Marc and Mandy were watching some dumb show on TV and laughing hysterically when Lola got a call from Ben. She took the phone with her and closed her bedroom door, but she'd already decided not to tell him about the wreck. He had enough on his plate right now. The last thing she needed to do was give him something else to worry about.

He said he was going to his commander's house for dinner, and then back to his studio apartment. She said she missed him. He said he missed her.

Lola had a feeling there'd be a lot of calls like this, but did they have enough to make this work, to build a real relationship while living apart? Granted, he was only forty-odd miles away, but their lives were so different and she wasn't sure if he felt as much for her as she felt for him. She just wished he'd come home.

On Friday morning, the captain popped into Ben's office. Ben was just coming off an all-night training event, finishing up his paperwork, and considering starting his weekend early with Lola. It felt like forever since he'd made it back across the bay.

It had only been three days.

"G'morning, Sergeant." Booker sat heavily in one of the chairs in front of Ben's desk. "How'd last night's class go?"

"Really well, sir. I swear, though, they're way too energetic." Ben shook his head. "I mean, I'm not old. I'm not even forty yet, but I realized I could have kids the age of some of these soldiers coming through."

"I take it someone beat your time on the obstacle course."

Ben laughed. "Not quite, but I don't remember working that hard to stay ahead. Any word on the investigation?" The second man had never regained consciousness. He'd died in surgery with no one any closer to figuring out who had hired them and why.

Ben hadn't had time to dwell on any of it. The past few days had been crazy busy, but the good thing about working steadily was that time flew by.

He missed Lola, though. Missed her a lot. On the upside, in a very brief time, they'd certainly developed some wicked phone sex skills. Probably not something he needed to be thinking about with his CO sitting in the chair across from his desk.

"That's why I'm here," Booker said. "I just got a call from Agent Robinson. He said some new details are coming up in the course of the investigation. He asked me if you'd noticed a high number of Hispanic employees with Hendrickson's crew?"

Ben thought about that a while and finally shook his head. "Some, but no more than the numbers among our regular soldiers. His crew, at least the people I saw, seemed about as racially mixed as the Army, but it's hard to say. Face it, a lot of us are nothing but mutts."

Booker laughed at that. "I know. As dark as I am, my grandmother was white. She was a blue-eyed blonde when she was young. I remember that peaches and cream skin and snow-white hair. And Jia's ancestors are from all over the map, quite literally."

"It works for her." Ben laughed. "Your wife is a beautiful woman, and I like the way she keeps all her men under control."

"You noticed that, eh?" Booker chuckled. "She says jump, we don't even ask how high. We just know to do it."

"See? That's the kind of response I want from my soldiers. Maybe your wife should be the one running leadership classes."

Booker shoved himself out of his chair and turned to leave. "I am not going to tell her you said that."

"You going to tell me why you wanted to know the racial demographic of the contractor's crew?"

Booker paused in the doorway. "You ever hear of Nuestra Familia?"

Frowning, Ben shook his head. "I'm not sure. I think so. It's a gang, isn't it?"

Booker nodded. "Prison gang, with members on the outside as well. They run a lot of the prison drug supply across the country, though the gang originated here in California. Has roughly around seven, eight thousand members. Agent Robinson said they've found some interesting links between Nuestra Familia and a certain senator we discussed a while back."

"Really? What about the men who were following me?"

"Both men who died were white. No connection to the gangs, but Robinson said there could be a gang link to their killer."

"With drugs the common denominator?"

"In a convoluted, roundabout manner, yes. Drugs, power, secrets. There's a lot of power in secrets."

"You don't have to convince me." A couple of days earlier, uncomfortable with his secrets, and even though he was still pretty new here, Ben had come to the conclusion that he respected and trusted his CO enough to confide in him, to tell him the whole, sordid story about his lies as a young man and the damage they'd done. His CO had listened, and he'd surprised Ben with his response. Captain Booker had reminded Ben that he wasn't that irresponsible kid anymore, that he'd already started the process of redeeming himself on the battlefield with the lives he'd saved. Then, after essentially absolving Ben of so much of the guilt he'd carried with him, Booker had calmly turned away and they'd both gone back to work.

It had been a spectacularly freeing moment for Ben.

"So who's out to get me?" he asked. "The senator? Nuestra Familia? The FBI?"

"Hopefully not the FBI. That could be awkward." Booker laughed. "My guess is the guys who were killed worked for the senator, or they worked for someone who works for him. I imagine Nuestra Familia used the hit as a warning, whether to the senator or the newspapers working on the story. The reports have suddenly dried up, and the story has been put on hold, again. At least for now."

"That's scary." Ben stared at the reports he'd almost finished. "Any chance of my breaking away a little early today? I'm almost done here, and I haven't seen my girlfriend since I reported for duty."

"You afraid she'll forget who you are?"

He grinned. "There is that. Actually, I miss her cooking. Among other things."

"Go. You worked all last night. I don't think anyone will have a problem with you slipping out early, least of all me." He laughed. "After you finish those reports."

Ben was in his civvies and on the road by two in the afternoon. Jeans and a crewneck sweater felt really good after almost a week in his ACUs.

Traffic was a mess, and there'd been a big wreck on the Bay Bridge, but Ben finally stopped at Marc's building on Battery just before five to pick up Lola. They'd talked every day, usually more than once, but he needed to see her. Touch her. Make sure the connection they'd made hadn't disappeared over their few days apart.

It was almost impossible to tell from a phone call. Hell, he'd known guys in country who'd gotten Skype calls regularly from their wives, only to find out the woman had moved some other guy in during his absence. He couldn't envision Lola doing anything like that, but did he know her enough to trust her? Besides, she was working with Marc Reed, now, a man who was good-looking and rich.

What if being with Marc all day had her looking at him the same way she'd looked at Ben? No. He was not going to go there. Either he trusted her or he walked away and let her make her own choices.

But what if she didn't choose him? Shit, he was driving himself crazy! His head was practically spinning by the time he lucked into a parking place in front of Marc's building and headed up the stairs to the third floor. There was an elevator, but he was too wired to wait.

What if she'd gone home already? He should have called ahead, let her know he was coming early. Last time they'd talked, he'd said he might be home by dinnertime.

He heard laughter coming from the main office, and paused just outside the door. Marc said something and Lola laughed. Ben stepped through the door.

She stopped in mid-sentence and was across the room and in his arms before he had time to register the fact both Jake and Marc were in the front office.

But when Lola wrapped her arms around his neck and kissed him, he didn't care who was there. All he cared about was the light in her eyes, the joy in her greeting, the taste of her mouth.

Jake's laughter and words finally registered. "Maybe you two oughta get a room."

Lola broke the kiss, leaned back in Ben's embrace and said, "You're just jealous because Kaz is having dinner with her dad."

Marc spoke up. "I'm just jealous, period. No one's greeting me like that."

A phone rang. "Put me down," Lola said. "I'm still on the clock." She reached for the phone on her desk and answered. "Thanks. I'll let Mr. Reed know. You're open until six? Good."

Hanging on to the phone, she turned to Marc. "The Tesla's all fixed. If you can get over there by six, you can pick it up tonight, or they'll be there at eight tomorrow."

"Tell him if I can't pick it up tonight, I'll come by in the morning."

"Okay." Lola went back to the call.

"What happened to the Tesla?" Ben sat on the edge of Lola's desk. He notice Marc's glance in Lola's direction, but she was still on the phone, writing something on a pad.

"Uh, Lola and I got broadsided Tuesday evening. Put a dent in the right rear quarter-panel on the Tesla. Didn't hurt it too bad, though we discovered there are a lot of airbags in that sucker."

Why hadn't she said anything? Ben glanced at Lola, who'd just hung up the phone. Her expression had guilt written all over it. Before he could say anything, she held up her hand.

"Now don't get upset. I didn't want to worry you and I asked Marc not to say anything." She walked around the desk and wrapped her arms around his waist. "It was your first day reporting to Camp Parks, and we weren't hurt."

Ben leaned close, touching his forehead to hers. "Please don't hide things from me. If I think you're not telling me everything, I'll make stuff up to worry about."

Lola rolled her eyes. "Okay. Then I'll tell you the rest of it. The guy was driving a stolen car, and I think he was waiting for us. He came flying through a red light, but he was gunning it out of a parking place. He didn't run the light until we were in the intersection. I think he misjudged, and that's why he only clipped the back of Marc's car and didn't do more damage than he did."

"Shit."

Marc nodded. "My feeling as well, Ben. The guy was out of the car and gone as soon as we stopped moving. Cops were there almost immediately. The Tesla wasn't badly damaged, but the older Toyota he was driving was pretty much totaled. We gave the info to the police, but they couldn't get any prints off it. It had been stolen just a few hours earlier."

"Well, crap." Ben rubbed the back of his neck, suddenly sympathizing with Lola's desire not to tell him everything, because now he was having the same sort of misgivings. But Jake had nailed him on telling the truth, and he wasn't going to screw it up at this point.

"This may or may not tie into some news I got from my CO earlier this morning, that one of the players might be

Nuestra Familia. I'm not sure how the link works, whether they're working for the senator or they're after him, but the last thing we need is to get caught in a pissing contest between a politician and members of a notorious prison gang."

Jake just leaned against the wall and laughed. "Damn it all, Ben. Don't you do anything the easy way?"

Sighing, Ben shook his head. "It doesn't look like it." He grabbed his cell phone. "Marc, do you mind if I let the FBI agents know about this? They've been pretty good about keeping me and my CO in the loop on everything. I'd hate to think we missed something important."

Marc shot a quick glance at Lola at the same time Ben looked at her. She threw her hands in the air, and said, "What? It's your car, Marc."

"Yeah, but it's your name they're going to be interested in, not mine."

"You don't really think they were after me, do you?"

Marc folded his arms across his chest. "Are we sure they weren't?"

Her green eyes went wide, but she was looking at Ben, not Marc. He liked that she turned to him. Hated the reason for it. "Well, I'd like to think not," she said, "but obviously I don't read enough mysteries. It sounds way too convoluted to me."

Ben had already called. Robinson answered on the first ring. When Ben finally hung up, Lola was grinning at him. "I see you've invited him for dinner. Is he coming?"

"Yep. Renteria will be glad of that. He's a local boy. Robinson is here from Virginia and he's getting tired of eating by himself or following Renteria home."

"Well, it's after five, boys, and I'm ready to go home. Jake, why don't you and Marc join us? I've had a big pot roast with veggies in the Crock-Pot all day, and there's plenty for all of us."

"Count me in," Jake said. "Marc? I can give you a ride and drop you off later when I go pick up Kaz."

Marc nodded. "Thank you. Yes, I'd like that. Thanks for the invite, Lola."

Ben walked her down the stairs and out the front door to his SUV. As soon as they were inside, he leaned close and drew Lola into his arms. "If I don't get just a little taste of you, I feel like I'm going to explode."

She brushed her fingers over the side of his face. "Don't do that. You'd make such a mess in your nice new car."

"You're right," he said, nuzzling her palm. "It'd probably play hell with that new car smell you and Mandy seem so fond of."

He kissed her slowly, methodically. Tasted the sweet curve of her lips, the line of her jaw, the ticklish spot beneath her left ear. Then he whispered in her ear, "We're about to be interrupted."

The loud slap of a hand against the window next to Ben made Lola jump, even with the warning. Ben merely raised his head, turned the key and lowered the window. "Jake? Get your mitts off my car."

"Killjoy. Go home and get dinner going. Marc and I are hungry. We'll be a few minutes after you. I'm going to take Marc by to get his car, since he won't have anyone to haul his ass over there in the morning."

"Sounds good. See you in a bit."

Ben pulled out well ahead of Marc and Jake, taking the crosstown drive slowly in the evening traffic. Lola sat with her back turned slightly toward the door and just smiled at him as he drove.

"I'm glad you're back," she said. "I guess I got used to rolling over and finding you next to me at night."

"Yeah," he said. "That pillow I've been hanging on to isn't nearly as sexy." He glanced over quickly and caught her smiling. Then he looked forward so he could pay more attention to his driving, though his awareness of the woman sitting beside him definitely competed for his full attention.

He was hungry, but it wasn't pot roast he was thinking of. Not even the fact someone was out there, watching, possibly trying to hurt him, for whatever reason.

No, Lola was front and center, and he couldn't wait to get her alone.

CHAPTER 13

Ben added the leaf to the round oak table. Agent Robinson—who had finally relaxed enough to tell them to call him Ted—joined the rest of them at the table. Marc opened a couple of bottles of his wine, Lola put a big platter of pot roast and vegetables out, and Mandy set out a basket of rolls she'd brought home from the coffee shop.

Conversation ebbed and flowed as the food disappeared. It ranged from Marc's repaired Tesla and whether the wreck might be connected, to the investigation the FBI was pursuing, to Kaz and Jake's wedding plans and the fact they had chosen to be married at Marc's winery where they'd fallen in love. Jake glanced around the table, obviously missing his woman, and said, "It's where I found her. It's where I almost lost her. It's where she promised she'd be my wife."

Ted Robinson was the only one who missed the significance of Jake's comment, so Jake gave Ted an abbreviated version of Kaz's kidnapping and rescue. Ben caught Jake's eye and the two of them shared a look that left Ben shaken. His brother and Kaz had been tested, and their relationship had come through strengthened by what could so easily have been a tragedy. Did he and Lola have what they needed to survive as a couple, not only to grow but to flourish? Jake and Kaz had been together less than a month, and yet what they had was rock solid.

Ben wanted that, but what did Lola want? He glanced her way as she reached for her wine glass, caught her steady gaze over the rim of her glass.

She smiled and took a sip, and then Mandy brought up the memorial Ben and Jake wanted to set up in honor of the woman and child who'd been killed so long ago. She, Kaz, and Lola had started researching some of the local women's shelters and were narrowing down the list to a few that looked promising.

"We want to visit the top three and then we'll feel better about recommending one of them," Lola said. The discussion moved on until Ben raised his head, glanced at the huge amount of food disappearing from the table, and sent another glance at Lola.

"Lola, were you expecting a crowd tonight?"

"No." She smiled at him. "Just you."

"You cooked enough for an army."

This time the smile was pure seduction. "You're Army, aren't you? I wanted to make sure you were well fed. Lots of protein for . . . strength and endurance." She winked. "You'll need it later."

Ben glanced around the table and realized everyone was staring at the two of them. All of them smiling. "You may all leave at any time," he said. Then he turned to Mandy. "Except for you. You I can send to your room."

Ted Robinson shook his head. "This is the best pot roast I've had in years, and there is no way in hell I'm leaving." His gaze on Ben, along with his comment, were totally deadpan. "My apologies, Sergeant Lowell, Ms. Monroe, but you two could boink right here on the table as long as you didn't get between me and that serving bowl."

Ben turned to Lola, and said, just as seriously, "Needless to say, that ain't gonna happen."

It wasn't until later when the pot roast dinner was reduced to a small bowl sufficient for someone's lunch, and the dishes were done, that all of them moved to the front room.

Robinson grabbed his coat when the others settled in to talk. "I've intruded enough," he said. "I really appreciate the invitation. Dinner was wonderful and the company definitely not boring." He grinned at Jake. "You're sure you guys want to get married at that winery? I mean, the wine is excellent, but after what happened there . . ."

"Well . . ." Jake spread his hands wide, but he wasn't smiling. "Some of the best and worst things of our lives happened there. Kaz and I talked about it, figured a marriage is full of good things and sometimes bad things. We've been through about the worst we could imagine happening, and it happened there. We survived. I proposed to Kaz there, she accepted, and they make damned fine wine. It seemed like the good outweighed the bad."

"Well, when you put it that way . . ." Robinson took another quick look at all of them, and then folded his arms across his chest. "Be careful. All of you. Adding the gang connection to this case has changed the dynamics. Essentially, the rules are out the window, and we have no idea what any of the subjects involved are going to do next. Try not to be alone anywhere, keep your cell phones handy, and my number on speed dial. And if anything . . . anything at all looks suspicious, call me. You might think it's nothing but if it's enough to catch your attention? Call me. I can't emphasize that strongly enough."

He turned once again to thank Lola for dinner. She shoved a plastic-covered bowl into his hands. "You're in an extended-stay inn, right?"

When he nodded, she said, "Then stick this in the

refrigerator. It'll make a good lunch for you tomorrow. Just nuke it."

"Wow. Thank you, Lola. It was really delicious." He laughed. "I'll be dreaming of leftovers." Then as he turned to leave, once more he said, "Be careful, please. All of you."

Shortly after Robinson left, Marc and Jake took off as well. Ben checked the door, made certain it was locked, and checked the back door as well. He heard Lola's laughter and followed the sound to Mandy's room. It was only nine, but Mandy was sitting in bed, propped up with a stack of pillows, holding a book, wearing headphones.

She grinned at Ben as he stood in the doorway, and pulled one side of the headset aside. "I was just explaining to Ms. Lola Marie, here, that this insures complete privacy for whatever goes on in any other bedroom tonight." She tapped her headphones playfully.

Ben looped an arm around Lola's shoulder. "Your sister's a keeper. You know that, don't you?"

She walked over to Mandy, gave her a hug and then grabbed Ben. "C'mon. I want to work on some of the instructions you gave me this week."

Mandy ripped the earphones off. "Instructions? What instructions?"

"Keep the headset on, sweetie, and I might tell you tomorrow."

Ben slung his arm around her neck and hauled her down the hallway toward the bedroom, but Lola couldn't quit laughing. He pressed his lips against her ear and whispered, "That wasn't very nice, teasing poor Mandy like that."

She rolled her eyes. "She deserved it, picking on me tonight."

This time Ben was the one laughing. "If you think getting teased about the color you dye your hair is picking on you, you obviously didn't grow up with brothers. Jake and I got downright vicious at times, all in the name of brotherly love, of course."

They'd reached his room and Ben stopped in the doorway. "I didn't even ask you if you wanted to stay with me tonight. I guess I just assumed . . ."

She loved the serious look in his stormy gray eyes. "I think that, at this point, it's safe to assume I'll want to share your room."

He shook his head. "I don't want to assume anything, ever. You're too special to me, sweetheart. I don't ever want to take you for granted."

"I like that." She rested her forearms on his shoulders and looked into his eyes. "I like you, Ben. More than I've ever liked any man ever. It's scary and exciting. And good. Really, really good." She hoped she hadn't said too much. Sometimes it felt as if what they had—what they were building—was so fragile, so ethereal, it was almost dreamlike.

It was easier when they talked on the phone, though that first call on Monday night had been sort of stilted and awkward, as if neither one of them felt comfortable admitting how lonely they felt. Lola had felt as if part of her was just gone, which she knew sounded horribly melodramatic. But that second night, everything had changed. Ben had gotten to his apartment early and called her. Her cell had warbled shortly after Marc dropped her off. She knew Mandy was out with a couple of girlfriends and wouldn't be in for a few more hours, and she was looking forward to time by herself. Time to think about her complicated feelings, her need for a man she barely knew.

Her evening hadn't gone the way she'd planned.

The empty house and Ben's voice, the glass of wine she'd poured the moment she'd gotten home; any of those things—all of them—conspired to make for a very interesting evening. Somehow he'd caught her at exactly the right moment, standing in her bedroom in nothing but her panties, staring at her open dresser drawer and wondering which comfortable old pair of sweats to put on so she could kick back and relax.

When her phone rang, she saw it was Ben, so turned on the speaker, said "Hi," and set the phone on top of her dresser.

"Hi, yourself," he said. "How was your day?"

"Okay." She'd just started digging through her drawers, searching for an old pair of men's flannel pajama bottoms. She knew they were in here somewhere. "I'm getting the hang of Marc's office," she said, shoving heavier fleece aside. "Mary was really well-organized, so it shouldn't take me long at all to figure it all out."

"What're you doing?"

"Digging through my dresser drawer. I'm trying to figure out what to wear."

"Really?"

The suggestive pause after his question made her nipples tighten. She straightened and ran her right palm over her left breast, stroking the nipple to an even tighter peak. And then someone else—because it couldn't have been her—took over her voice. "Yeah," she said. "All I'm wearing now is a pair of bright red panties I think you'd like."

The long silence left her grinning. She took a sip of wine.

He cleared his throat. "And what else?"

"Nothing."

"Oh." His laugh sounded wonderfully strained. "Why don't you take off the panties, too. You'll be more comfortable, and I would . . . really like the visual."

"I dunno," she'd said, slipping her panties over her hips,

shoving them down her legs and stepping out of them. "Tell me what you're wearing first."

"My ACUs, but they're coming off."

There'd been the rustle of fabric, the sound of his boots hitting the floor, a clunk that might have been a belt. She'd pictured his warrior's body, the sleek muscles across his chest, and his thick biceps, the dusting of dark hair bridging the space between those perfect nipples and the happy trail that arrowed down to the darker hair at his groin.

She knew he had to be hard, the length of him thick and solid, that the mere thought of his erection had her mouth watering. But the oddest thing was realizing she'd been touching herself as she listened to the sound of his clothes coming off. Running her fingertip between her swollen folds, stroking over her engorged clit, doing it without thinking, because in her mind, it was Ben stroking her, his fingers, or maybe his tongue. And her breath was coming faster, her heart picking up its cadence, racing along with the rush of her breathing.

She moved the phone to the bedside table and stretched out on the bed.

"Is that the bed I just heard?"

"Yeah. I'm sitting up, though, with pillows behind me."

"Just sitting? What do your nipples look like?"

Her breath hitched in her throat. At the moment, she was teasing them, twisting the taut peaks, using both hands. So she told him.

He didn't even try to disguise his moan.

"I want you to touch between your legs. Not your clit. Go around it."

She sucked in a breath. "Okay. But stroke yourself." She laughed, embarrassed by the power of her need. "I'm not doing this alone. Set the phone aside and cup your balls in one hand and wrap your other hand around your cock. But you can't squeeze hard. Stroke it lightly and pretend it's me, teasing you.

"I don't have to pretend. You've been teasing me since you said you were wearing nothing but red panties. Which reminds me. Are they off, yet?"

"They are. What are you doing?"

"What you told me to do." His breath came out in a slow hiss. "I'm cupping my balls in my left hand and have my right fist wrapped around my dick."

"You're not squeezing too hard, are you?" Laughing, she said, "Remember, this is sweet, feminine little me stroking up and down, tracing that heavy vein along the bottom with my very sensitive fingertips, separating your testicles with my fingers and rolling each solid ball around inside your sac. Are you doing that?"

"Shit. Yeah. Just like that. Pinch your clit and one of your nipples. Exactly the same pressure so you can't tell them apart.

She did as he said. Her breath caught in her throat. "Ben? I really want to come. I am so ready. You can squeeze harder if you like. Move your fist up and down really fast and squeeze hard."

"Rub yourself. Fast and hard . . ."

He was panting harshly now; the sound coming from her phone next to the bed was so sexy. "I am," she said, and her breath caught the same as his.

"Put your fingers inside yourself, deep as you can, and rub your clit."

His instructions weren't easy to understand through his ragged breathing, but the sound of his straining voice and the graphic visual she held of Ben stroking himself was all it took.

In moments, she had brought herself to her own peak. She'd cried out, her fingers buried deep, her other hand flying over her swollen clit, and she'd come so hard, her body writhing on the bed, her muscles clenching at her fingers, the sound of Ben's muffled curse in her ears an aphrodisiac all its own.

It took Lola a minute to catch her breath enough to speak. "I've never done that before."

"What? Never jerked off?"

She'd laughed. Giggled so hard it was like an orgasm all on its own. "No, silly. That was the first time I've ever come with a guy on the phone giving me instructions."

"Same here. Wow."

She was thinking of that now, of how easy it had been to say exactly what she wanted because they'd been on the phone, which somehow made it both dirty but also acceptable. Why was it so hard to talk like this in person?

She stood there now, her body throbbing with need after thinking of the past two nights of phone sex with Ben. How she'd ended each call feeling satisfied and needy at the same time.

Now she just felt needy.

Resting her forearms on his shoulders, fingers creeping slowly across his back to the nape of his neck through hair clipped short above his collar, Lola sighed. She ran her fingers high, threading them through his short, thick hair, sliding over his skull. It was a little bit longer on the top and back. "I knew you'd have to get a haircut, but I'm going to miss running my fingers through your long hair."

"I'm going to miss that too, but I didn't want Captain Booker to have to ask me to get it cut. First impressions and all that."

"You made a really good first impression on me."

He snorted, and she laughed. "You snorted!"

"Well, yeah," he said. "You were impressed with my meltdown in your backyard? With the fact I was a fucking coward and let my brother do almost six years in lockup to save my sorry ass? I think really weird stuff turns you on."

"Idiot." She kissed him gently, and pulled away before he could hug her closer. "I was impressed that you actually told me what was upsetting you. I was impressed that something truly awful you did when you were a kid has haunted you for all these years. There are far too many men—and women for that matter—who'd just be glad they got away with it. You're not, and that tells me about the man you are now. Ben, I think you're hot, but knowing those things about your basic personality makes you even hotter. You're a good guy in spite of yourself."

She kissed him, hard and fast. "And did I say you're hot?"

He laughed. "Yeah, I think you mentioned that." Then he pressed his forehead against hers. "I'm trying, Lola, but it's damned hard. My first instinct is still to run when things get tough. Kick my ass if you see any indications of that, okay?"

"You got it. As long as you don't, we're good. You do? Butt gets kicked. Hard."

He laughed, and it was hard to remember the person he'd been just a week ago when they'd met. Had it only been a week since he'd stepped into their house and changed his life, and hers as well? He'd been a broken man, so close to the edge. Lola had been afraid for him that night in the garden. In just a week he looked healthier, happier, less like a man who wanted to be anywhere rather than where he was now.

No, Ben looked like he was exactly where he wanted to be. He raised his head, glanced over his shoulder, and the next thing she knew, he'd swung her into his arms, taken the few steps to get where he wanted to go, and dumped her on the bed.

"Got any plans for the weekend?" He lay over her, resting his weight on his forearms, his mouth hovering bare inches above hers.

"Not yet, though you look like a man with a plan."

"I am. And the first thing is to get you naked. Arms up."

She raised her arms and he slipped her sweater over her head. Her slacks came next and then her socks. She'd kicked her shoes off after dinner.

She was wearing her red bra and matching panties—not the same set she'd had on Tuesday night, but close. Ben didn't seem to care what color they were. He did, however, appear to approve.

"My visual the other night was nothing compared to the real thing" He licked her right nipple through the silk. It obediently rose to a taut point. He stared at it for a moment, and then sighed. "I like it better when they match." He licked the one on her left. "Much better." Then he released the plastic catch between her breasts and slipped the bra straps over her shoulders. She arched her back and he pulled the whole thing carefully off of her. Then, just as carefully, he covered both her breasts in his big hands, squeezing her nipples almost-but-not-quite painfully between his fingers.

She felt the exquisite flash of pleasure/pain from her nipples to that most sensitive place between her legs. Crying out, she arched into his touch. "You're still dressed," she said, but her breath caught. She reached for the hem of his sweater, tugged it frantically over his head. "Off. Now."

In moments, he'd stripped everything away—her panties, his clothing. His body was hot and heavy, but she pulled him close, held him against her with her legs clenched tightly at the small of his back until he laughed and moved far enough away to sheathe himself. When he rolled back over she was ready, and he slipped perfectly into place without any need to guide his heavy erection. He filled her so naturally, so perfectly, and the heat of his entry, the perfection of his strong body covering hers in that most primal fashion was all it took. She didn't want to come so quickly. She wanted it to last, but this was all she could take, all her heart and lungs could handle as her climax swept over her, through her, engulfing her in a pounding, clenching rush of pleasure so powerful, so personal, that it happened again.

Swamped by the emotions, the release, the way she felt about this man, Lola lost it altogether. By the time Ben's climax had eased enough to let him breathe, she was sobbing in his embrace.

This time he seemed to expect it. "Too much of that sex godliness? Sweetheart? Are you okay?" He turned her face to his and kissed her, kissed the tears and her laughter as she finally pulled herself back under control.

"Never too much, Ben. But oh, what you do to me." She didn't think he really had any idea what it was like when a man totally rocked a woman's world. Made her feel things she'd never thought she'd feel, gave her joy more profound than she'd ever expected.

She rolled into his embrace and lay there, surrounded in his warmth, and it was good. So damned good.

Ben wasn't sure what awakened him, but suddenly he was wide awake. He glanced at the clock beside the bed. Almost two thirty in the morning and he had a warm and wonderful woman beside him, sleeping all curled up against his chest.

But something had pulled him from sleep, and it wasn't Lola. Last time he'd come awake ahead of the alarm clock, he'd realized later it had probably been the sound of the shotgun blast when the men were shot across the street. Alert now, he easily called upon the instincts that had kept him alive for so many years in battle. Sliding carefully out of Lola's embrace, Ben slipped on his sweats and pocketed his cell phone after checking to make sure it was on vibrate. He thought about his boots, but then decided bare feet were quieter. He grabbed the bowie knife he'd stashed in his duffel, and went to investigate.

CHAPTER 14

He went to the front room and listened. There was not so much a sound, yet his sense that something was wrong was growing. Those same senses pointed him toward the front yard, but he went through the kitchen and took the back stairs down to the garage on the lower level.

Moving quietly in the darkness, he skirted the old Nissan Lola called their garage queen, and paused near the big aluminum garage door. He heard voices, soft whispers just outside. It was difficult to understand everything they said, but he recognized the soft hiss.

They were spray painting something on the garage door. He was almost sure of it.

Taggers? In this neighborhood? Quietly, he went back upstairs and slipped out the front door and into the night. Fog had blown in, muffling the voices below, and hopefully, the sound of his bare feet on the stone steps. He stopped behind a large green bush at the bottom of the steps and watched the two guys; they looked like kids, but that made them more dangerous. An adult might think of the consequences of attacking Ben—kids were all balls and no brains.

He brought up his cell phone and snapped a couple of pictures in quick succession. The flash went off and both kids freaked. One took off running, but the other pulled out a pistol and turned toward the bush where Ben had been hiding.

Except he wasn't there anymore. He'd slipped behind a shrub in the neighbor's yard with his camera on video now, no light, but recording the sound as the kid cursed and poked into the bushes.

The damn kid appeared to be holding a fucking M9. It looked identical to the Beretta he'd left locked up at his place in Dublin. Grabbing a rock out of the landscaping, Ben chucked it toward the kid. It landed behind him. He spun around and fired off three shots in quick succession. It was loud, but it sure didn't sound like the M9 Ben had.

Light shimmered across the front walk as the bedroom light overhead went on.

Curious now, Ben raced across the yard. Running behind the teen, he slipped around the front stairs, into the shadows. He needed to get this finished, now, before Lola came out to see what was going on.

Everything happened at once. The kid cursed and ran into the shadows as the porch light went on. Switching the knife to his left hand, Ben snagged the little bastard around the neck with his left arm, at the same time, grabbing the kid's gun hand with his right. "Drop the gun. I can break your neck and gut you before you even think about pulling the trigger."

He heard the satisfactory clatter of the weapon hitting the cement, adjusted his hold and put the blade of his knife to the kid's throat. "Do not even think of moving."

The kid was shaking like a leaf. Ben pulled his right arm behind him, still holding the knife against his throat. "Lola? That you?"

"Yes. Are you okay?"

"I'm fine. Call 911, tell them one kid got away—he's wearing dark clothing and might still be carrying a can of spray paint. Headed north on 23rd. Also, let them know I've disarmed a suspect and I have him in a stranglehold, that I could use a little help. Then call Ted. Tell him he might want to come over."

She didn't say a word, but he heard her make the first call and give precise directions to the dispatcher. Then she called Ted. A moment later, she came down the stairs with a handful of zip ties.

"I've been told these make pretty good handcuffs."

He shot her a grin. "They do. Thank you." He took the ties from her and quickly secured the kid's hands behind his back before dragging him out on the front walkway and restraining his ankles. Mandy came out with Rico on a leash, wearing her fluffy robe and bunny slippers.

"What's going on?"

Lola called to her. "Over here. Look at this mess. What's this they were tagging the garage with? I don't recognize what it's supposed to be."

Mandy laughed. "Maybe they're just lousy artists."

"It's not done, bitch."

Ben punched the kid in the face—not nearly as hard as he wanted to, but at least it shut him up. Then he checked the restraints and added extra ties to attach his ankles to his wrists, and left him on the front walk. He studied the almost completed graffiti. "This is a sombrero, and this line under it looks like a knife. Not good."

Lola frowned. "You're kidding. It looks like a soup bowl. And why is it not good? Other than the fact that it's really crappy art and we'll need to repaint the garage door."

Ben bit back a laugh. She was right, but he wasn't going to tell her that. Maybe later. "It's a stylized symbol of the Nuestra Familia gang. I want Ted to see it before you paint over it."

"Well . . ." She stared at the graffiti. "Damn. You're right. That's not what I wanted to hear." Then she teased,

"I'm beginning to wonder if you're more trouble than you're worth."

She was smiling when she said it, but Ben still recoiled, as if she'd slapped him. He almost wished she had. He hated bringing trouble like this her way. Damn.

A police car pulled up to the curb with lights flashing but, thankfully, no sirens. There was someone in the back seat, but it was too dark for Ben to get a good look at him. The officer climbed out of the car and glanced at the kid lying on the sidewalk in restraints. "I think I've got his partner in the back—caught him running down Irving a minute ago, hanging on to a can of black spray paint. What happened?"

Ben led him over to the garage door.

"Nuestra Familia?" He stared at Ben. "They're not usually in this area. How'd you get on their bad side?"

Ben laughed. "It's a long story, but I don't think these two are part of that particular gang. They just don't have that gangbanger vibe. I think they're just a couple of brainless kids." He shook his head. "I'm a witness in an FBI investigation, one that appears to have some ties to the group, but I'm wondering if these two were merely hired to do some decorating by someone else."

"What makes you think that?"

"Just a hunch." He glanced up as Ted Robinson's rented sedan pulled in behind the police officer. "This gentleman might be able to help clear some things up. In the meantime, you should probably secure the kid's weapon."

"He was armed? I didn't get that info from the dispatch."

"I didn't have Lola report it. I haven't had a chance to look, but I think it's just a very good replica." He pointed out the pistol lying on the ground near the front steps as Agent Robinson approached.

"Damn good. Looks real. Stupid kid." The officer

secured the gun in an evidence bag, and then read the kid his rights before cutting the ties and restraining him in regulation cuffs. Then he stuck him in the backseat with his buddy. The two obviously knew each other. They looked enough alike to be related, and more scared than defiant.

Ben took Ted aside while the officer answered a phone call.

"What do you want to bet, someone hired these two to make it look like a gang tag?"

"Why do you say that?"

"I listened to them through the garage door before I came outside, and it sounded like they were copying a drawing someone had given them. Oh, and I got a couple of pictures. Wonder how they came out?" He turned on his cell phone and checked the pictures. "Damn, I'm good." Laughing, he walked over to the officer, who was just ending his call.

"This the kid you have in the back?"

The officer looked at the first picture and laughed. "This is good. Nice and clear, and yep, that's the one I caught running down Irving and the other is the one you so generously packaged for me." He handed Ben his card with his e-mail address. "Send them to this address, okay?"

Ben sent them.

Another police car pulled in beside the first one. Two officers, a man and a woman, got out. The three of them chatted for a moment while Ben walked back over to speak with Ted, who was taking pictures of the graffiti on the garage door with his mobile phone camera.

Ted told him that Mandy and Lola had gone back inside.

Ben really wished he was following Lola.

"So tell me more about your hunch." Ted tucked his cell phone back in his pocket.

"I will, but some questions first, if you don't mind," Ben

said. "The guys who ended up dead—were you able to trace them?"

"Yes. Jake was right about the license plate. It had been changed using colored tape to alter the numbers. The vehicle came out of a government fleet and we were able to link it to a member of Senator Ewing's staff—not his office staff, his wife's household staff. Authorization came via a phone call, and didn't follow standard procedure."

"The household staff has permission to pull vehicles?"

"They must. Either that or the process is totally screwed, which could also be the case. We're checking. We've got a link to the car and his household staff, but we don't have a link between the men and the senator's office. They weren't on his official payroll."

"Were they local?"

Ted nodded. "They were, but as you know, Senator Ewing isn't. His wife was from San Francisco, but last I heard, she was in Washington. We're still searching for a connection."

"What about the killer? What made you think they were Nuestra Familia?"

"Chatter from informants, talk about the hit being gang related."

Ben thought about it for a moment. "What if someone just wanted to make it look like Nuestra Familia? Maybe it's something else altogether. Those two boys aren't gangsta types at all. The gun's an expensive looking replica. It's a pellet gun. Even so, when he fired the thing, I think it scared him. He wasn't planning to shoot it. He's playing it tough, but I'll bet he's sitting in that police car right now trying not to cry because he knows he's in deep shit when he gets home."

Ted glanced at Ben with one eyebrow raised and walked over to the patrol car.

The officer turned, frowning. "Is there a problem?"

"Just wondered if I could talk to the two in the back-seat for a moment."

The officer shrugged. "Without an attorney . . ."

"I think I might be able to help them out. You're welcome to listen."

The officer opened the front passenger door and talked to the two boys behind the wire cage. Ben stood back where he could watch them. He had a feeling he'd called this one right. They both looked scared to death.

Agent Robinson flipped out his badge and ID. "I'm with the FBI," he said. "And this gentleman behind me thinks you two might have been set up. Did someone hire you to paint that design on the garage door?"

The two looked at one another. Finally, the older of the two nodded. "Yeah. An older guy." The kid dug into his pocket. "He gave this to us, said he'd give us a hundred bucks to paint it on that garage door." He handed the agent a sheet of paper with a photocopied image of the well-known Nuestra Familia emblem—a Mexican sombrero with a large knife beneath it.

The younger kid spoke up. "He drove us by here, said it was a joke he was playing on a friend of his. We didn't expect . . ."

"Why the gun?" Ben leaned against the squad car. "I know it's not a real pistol, but I didn't know that when I went after you."

"What gun?" The younger kid stared at the other boy. "You dumb shit! You didn't take Dad's new pellet gun, did you?"

The older one's face crumpled. He looked at Ben, not his little brother. "Jimmy didn't know I had it." He glanced at his brother. "Dad's gonna kill me."

"If I don't do it first." His little brother was obviously furious. "Why'd ya do something stupid like that?"

The kid shrugged.

Ben glanced at Ted. It was obvious the agent was fighting a grin. "Okay," Ted said, "What can you tell me about the dude who asked you to paint the door? Did he pay you?"

Jimmy glanced at his brother. The older boy shook his head. "What? Jonah, you said he was paying you in advance. You mean he didn't?"

Again, Jonah shook his head.

Ben whispered to Ted, "It appears Jonah is not the brains of the operation." Then he stared at both boys long enough to make them uncomfortable. "Okay," Ben said. "Where did you meet up with this guy? What does he look like? What kind of car?"

"He has brown hair. Had an old dude's kinda car," Jimmy said. He pointed to Ted's rental car. "You know, boring? Gray, four doors, and he had another guy in the passenger seat, but you couldn't see him. Windows were tinted."

"So he just stops two kids on the street and offers them a hundred dollars if they'd paint a picture on a friend's garage door as a joke? And you believed him?" Ben shook his head. "There's an excellent lesson here, kid—don't believe every guy who comes along offering you money. When was this?"

"Last night." Jonah sighed. "I feel like an idiot."

"You should. It was a pretty idiotic move. Be right back." Ben moved away from the car and signaled the police officer and Ted to join him. "I think maybe I'd rather not press charges, though I do want these kids' parents to know what they were up to, and they definitely need to know about using the dad's pellet gun. Any way to make that happen? Maybe they can repaint the door. What do you think?"

Ted shrugged. The cop nodded. Ben had no idea how the legalities of such a move might work.

"It's okay with me," Ted said. "Mainly, I'm concerned the kids might end up on someone's radar if they go through the courts."

The officer glanced at the kids. "I think that if I take them home in the squad car at this hour and get their parents out of bed, it might make a good enough impression on everyone to keep them home and off the streets. Lowell, are you serious about making them repaint the garage door? Because that's an excellent idea. It'll teach 'em a lesson, and hopefully keep them out of the system for good. Kids learn too damned much of the wrong stuff once they get arrested."

"I'm sure my girlfriend and her sister will approve, but make sure the parents know what their kids could have gotten themselves involved in. Hell, I'm a soldier. I've been in war zones around the world for almost twenty years. I had the older kid disarmed and in a choke hold with a knife at his throat in seconds. If he'd been any bigger, or if he'd fought me, there's no telling how this might have ended. And another thing, these guys that have been tailing me are not anyone they want to deal with. Can I talk to them?"

"Be my guest." The cop was grinning at this point, probably because he wasn't going to have to book a couple of dumb kids.

"Here's the deal," he said. "Officer McGowan is going to take you two home. He's going to get your parents out of bed, and let them know what's happened here tonight. He's going to return the gun to your father, and he's going to tell your parents that I'm not going to press charges as long as you guys promise to come back over here and paint over the garage door and clean up the mess you made. Any questions?"

The kids looked at each other and then at Ben. "We're not going to jail?" The younger one definitely sounded relieved.

"Not at this point, but if you two don't get your butts over here to paint over that door, I have the option to have you charged—and that includes the gun. Even though it's not a real M9, it's a good enough replica to get you boys in a lot of trouble."

The officer handed Ben a tablet. "Give me your contact info and I'll pass it on to the boys' parents."

Ben wrote down his name and phone number, and made a point of identifying himself as Sergeant Benjamin Lowell. You never knew what might catch someone's attention, but obviously the boys' parents needed to keep better track of their sons. He glanced at his watch. It was getting close to four in the morning, but he was way too wired to sleep.

He wondered if Lola was still awake.

The officer left to take the boys home. They only lived about five blocks away. Ted thanked him for the call. "We all have a lot more to think about at this point," he said. "Though I imagine I'll think better after a few more hours' sleep."

"Agreed." Ben watched him pull away from the curb, and went back inside the house.

He locked the front door and went down the hall to the bathroom. Mandy's door was closed but Lola's was wide open, and her bed was still made up and empty.

He'd been afraid she might have gone back to her own bed. The fact she was in his had him feeling much better about the messed up evening. It could have been a whole lot worse.

He used the bathroom, washed his hands and face and headed back to his room. Slipping in quietly, he shut the door behind him and took off his sweats. His eyes were slowly adjusting to the dark, and he realized Lola was awake and watching him.

"Sorry to take so long." He crawled in beside her and pulled her close. She snuggled against him, all warm and sleepy. "I hope you don't mind, but I told the officer we wouldn't press charges as long as the boys come back and paint over the mess they left."

"Good. They looked like kids." She nuzzled his chest. He ran his fingers through her hair.

"They are. I'm guessing thirteen and sixteen, the same difference as Jake and me, and the older one is dumb as a stump. A lot like I was at that age." He closed his eyes and rolled his head against the pillow. "Damn, I hope I've gotten smarter. Anyway, he's the one who had his father's pellet gun, but the younger kid didn't know he'd taken it. Someone paid them to paint that design on the door. I don't think the Nuestra Familia gang is involved in this mess at all."

Lola yawned, and mumbled an unintelligible reply. Ben kissed the top of her head, pulled her just a bit closer, and closed his eyes. He really didn't think he'd sleep, not after the past couple of hours, but the bed really was comfortable, and Lola fit perfectly against him.

The next time he opened his eyes, sunlight was streaming in through the blinds.

And Lola was still in his arms. Sniffing him? He blinked, and lay there for a moment, trying to figure out just what in the hell his woman was up to.

She'd never slept with a man before who actually held her during the night, but she'd quickly decided she loved waking up in Ben's arms. Lola didn't think she'd ever grow tired of it. He smelled so good, sort of a combination of whatever soap he used and his own unique, delicious scent.

She'd long been aware of the way men smelled—not the acrid stench of sweat, but their unique scent. No one had ever affected her the way Ben did. Ben was different, and she caught herself burrowing her nose against his chest, breathing deep, as if she were inhaling a drug.

"What are you doing?"

His voice was a deep rumble in her ear, but even half asleep it was tinged with laughter.

"Sniffing you." She raised her head and shoved her tangled hair out of her eyes. "I think your sleep pheromones have aphrodisiacal qualities." She nipped his shoulder and went back to his chest, sniffing her way down to his belly, nipping at the taut skin over his hipbone, nuzzling the thick, dark curls at his groin.

"I had no idea I had sleep pheromones, though it appears that your interest in mine has aphrodisiacal qualities all its own." He chuckled. "I like that word. Aphrodisiacal. Did you make that up?"

"I have no idea." His morning erection appeared to have grown. She buried her nose against his hard length now standing at attention and took a deep breath. Her body's response was instantaneous.

So was Ben's. He groaned.

She crawled over his thighs, reached for the bedside table, opened the drawer and pulled out a condom. Then, making a rather large production of crawling back, she ripped open the packet with her teeth and carefully rolled the condom over his full length.

When she tore her gaze away from the job she'd done, she realized Ben was lying there with his arms behind his head, just watching her.

"Umm, should I have asked first?"

Smiling broadly, he slowly shook his head.

"Then what are you looking at me like that for?" She rolled away from him and sat up on her heels.

"Thinking I'd like to wake up like this every morning, and trying to figure out how to talk my CO into letting me come in late every day."

"Well, you work on that one while I work on this." She straddled his thighs, rose above him, and came slowly down over his full length. She noticed he wasn't smiling anymore. No, it was more a look of intense concentration. Slowly rising, then lowering herself just as slowly, she took complete control. Planting her hands on his chest, Lola picked up speed, loving the way his expression changed with each move she made, loving the way he felt inside her, filling her up so perfectly.

Her climax was building, the pressure growing. She knew she was close, knew that when she came, he'd be right there with her.

Except he grabbed her hips and suddenly Lola was on the bottom trying to catch her breath while Ben laughed, kneeling between her legs and lifting her thighs so she could hook her heels at the small of his back. He didn't miss a stroke as he so easily took control.

Mere seconds later, Lola arched into orgasm, her body splintering into a million pieces.

And somehow she kept splintering, muscles clenching, chest heaving, bright spots behind her eyes. Each orgasm with Ben was distinctive; each time their bodies peaked together a unique and unrivaled experience. Why was this time so different? What had changed? Still sucking deep breaths, her fingers and toes tingling, her inner muscles clenching around Ben's slowly receding erection, she knew shattered when she felt it, knew without doubt that Ben had knocked her personal reality into a million different pieces.

But her heart? Her heart was whole, filled with joy, but no longer hers. That's when the pieces fell into place and it all made sense: Ben owned her heart. Owned her, body and soul. She wasn't sure exactly how or when that happened, but she knew it was right.

She only hoped Ben didn't figure it out. She wasn't sure Ben Lowell was entirely ready for Lola Monroe.

CHAPTER 15

Ben poured himself a cup of coffee and leaned against the counter while he watched the activity in the kitchen. Marc had popped in right at nine, followed shortly thereafter by Jake and Kaz. A few minutes after their arrival, Ted Robinson showed up.

It was way too easy for Mandy to talk him into staying for breakfast.

Lola was at the stove with an apron around her waist, flipping pancakes on the griddle, laughing at whatever Kaz was saying. Bacon and sausage and a growing stack of pancakes filled the warming oven above the stove.

Mandy and Marc had put the leaf back in the table and Ted had been sent to collect an extra chair from Lola's bedroom. Kaz left Lola's side to put out silverware and napkins.

Ben couldn't have wiped the grin off his face if he'd tried.

He'd seen things like this on television—sitcoms with families that seemed to exist in a congenial form of coordinated chaos, but he'd never been part of it. Certainly not in the cold and unfeeling home where he and Jake had been raised, and while the army had provided friends over the years, it hadn't been anything like this. This was better than any fictional scene he'd ever watched and wondered about. He turned and caught Jake's eye, caught his brother watching him, and the two of them shared a very private smile above the din.

"Ben?" Immediately he turned to Lola. "Would you put the platter of pancakes on the table, so everyone can get started? And there's sausage and bacon in there, too. That needs to go. Thanks." She whipped around and snagged Kaz's arm. "You. Get the strawberry jam, the butter, and the syrup."

"Yes, Ma'am." Kaz saluted.

"Wiseass." Lola smacked her butt and then added more pancakes to the already huge pile on the platter as Ben held it for her.

He set it on the table and went back for the plate of sausage and bacon. By the time he got that to the table, the pile of pancakes had begun to shrink. Lola took a seat next to him and they both loaded up their plates. Ben raised his coffee mug. "To the chef!"

Then he leaned over and planted a kiss on Lola. "And she can cook, too," he whispered.

She blushed. He was absolutely certain she was thinking of all those other things they'd been up to all morning that had nothing to do with food.

Though it had definitely helped him work up an appetite.

Half an hour later, Ben and Ted had the kitchen cleaned up and he finally knew the reason the agent had stopped by so early—beyond the fact he'd been hoping for some of Lola's cooking.

"We're keeping this under wraps right now," he said, "Because we don't want to alert anyone, but the individual who requested the vehicle that the guys were shot in was Mrs. Ewing's personal assistant. His name is Dustin Thorpe, and he handles everything from household staff to Mrs. Ewing's personal security. He also handles occasional work for the senator. As far as we can tell, the men who died were not part of her staff, or the senator's. They might have been working for the senator, but we have no way of knowing. Not yet, anyhow. He could have all kinds of people who aren't part of his official staff."

"That's a link to him, though. More than you had before." Ben finished wiping down the counter and hung the towel to dry. The he turned and stared out the back window. "How does Mrs. Ewing fit into all this?"

"The senator's wife? Her family money got him into politics; that's what paid for his first election, and numerous elections since. Of course, her father's companies, the source of her money, profited quite handsomely over the years from legislation backed by the senator, but for all intents and purposes, she's hardly a mover and shaker. She's written before about her father, and it was obvious she idolized the man, but it appears that daddy's little girl turned into the senator's little girl. She's always kept a low profile, even more so since her parents died."

"At the same time?"

Ted shook his head. "No, her father had a stroke and was left almost comatose for more than a year before he finally passed. Her mother died during that period from lung cancer. Caroline Ewing's father smoked throughout their entire marriage, but her mother was the one who developed lung cancer. Go figure."

"That secondhand smoke's a killer." Ben studied a hangnail and let his mind go blank. They were missing something. Something important, but for the life of him he couldn't figure out what it was. "What do you hear of the media break on this story? That article was supposed to come out a while back."

"I know." Ted shook his head. "They're continuing to 'fact-check' the story. I'm guessing when the senator got wind of it hitting the news, he pulled in a few markers and his very sizable legal team to threaten action should they run a story with, and I'm quoting the media source, 'any unsubstantiated rumors.' Right now, that's holding it up. I haven't seen all the material, but information that came up during the paper's investigation essentially nails the senator's ass on a lot of illegal activity over the years.''

"What's the source for the information? Is it bullet-proof?"

Robinson shrugged. "Oh, yeah. A lot of it's that material we talked about, the notes and tapes from the Secret Service investigation back in the eighties that's been in the hands of a retired agent. When he died last year, his daughter turned copies of everything over to the press."

Kaz had just stepped into the kitchen. "You're talking about Colonel Mac. I didn't meet him, but Jake may have told you that his daughter, Cassie, is the winemaker at the winery where we're getting married. She's married to the vineyard manager, Nate Dunagan, and she and her husband recovered the briefcase. Her father didn't want it to go to the government because it was the government agency he'd worked for that buried the stuff for all those years. But Cassie and Nate were concerned with the legalities. They ended up making copies of everything for the press, and turned the originals over to the Secret Service."

Ted nodded. "That investigation was before my time in the service, but it's a black mark against all of us, that politics so often wins out over the truth. The colonel conducted an amazing investigation, followed orders, then was forced into an early retirement when he discovered things that made his bosses uncomfortable."

"So true," Kaz said. "It was ugly."

Ted nodded in agreement. "That it was, but I understand that the reporters working the story have taken things a lot further. I'm sure that's why they're being so cautious about releasing the story. They want to make sure everything they have is correct. On that note, I need to thank Lola and Mandy for feeding me once again, and then be on my way. I'm starting to feel like a bad penny. You know, the kind that turns up everywhere?"

"Which reminds me," Ben said. "Thanks for turning up last night. I appreciate it."

Ted chuckled. "I figured it was payback for walking out of here with the last of that pot roast your girl made. It was wonderful. And yes, I ate it when I got home around four this morning. This might be the only case I've ever been on where I gain weight rather than lose it."

He shook hands with Ben. "Thank you. I'm on my way to check in with the arresting officer from last night."

"Ah," Ben said. "The one who didn't make an arrest?"

"That would be the one. I'm curious how those boys did when they had to take the nice policeman home to meet their parents at four in the morning. I'll see you folks later."

He was still chuckling when he left the room. As soon as he was gone, Kaz turned to Ben. "He's different than I expected," she said, "Not nearly as stuffy."

"Good food tends to have that effect on a lot of people."

Kaz laughed, and shared a smile with Ben, who wanted to tell Kaz she was different than he'd expected as well, but he managed to keep his mouth shut.

"Ben, Jake and I are making a run up to Healdsburg for the afternoon," she said. "We wanted to check out the site for the wedding, see how many we can invite, that sort of thing. If you and Lola want to ride along, you're more than welcome. I checked with Mandy, but she's hanging out with a couple of her girlfriends later today, so she's not interested, but I'm sure Jake would rather not be surrounded by just women."

"You're sure about that?" Ben replied. When she laughed, he said, "I'd like that. Did you ask Lola?"

This time she winked. "Of course. I wouldn't have asked you without her permission."

"I see. There's a lot I need to learn about this relationship stuff. I'm still a newbie at it."

Kaz poked him in the ribs. "You're doing fine. Anyway, we're planning to leave as soon as you're ready. You okay with that?"

"I am. You guys want to take the green machine? The tank's full."

"That would be the strange vehicle out in front with the dealership happy sticker instead of a license plate?"

"That would be the one."

"I thought so. Let me check with Jake. I have no idea if he's a control freak who needs his own vehicle or not, but then he might like the chance to make out in the back seat."

"There will be no making out in the back seat."

She let out a dramatic sigh. "You are such a poop. Okay. I'll ask him."

They took Ben's Subaru and were on the road shortly after ten o'clock. Traffic was surprisingly light for a Saturday morning in early May, and they pulled into Healdsburg just before noon. Jake had been on the phone for the last few minutes, but now he directed Ben toward a small Mexican restaurant on the main street into town. The lot was almost full.

"I just talked to Cassie," he said. "We're picking up lunch and taking it out to them. She loves this place."

Kaz jabbed him in the side with her elbow and grinned at Lola in the front seat beside Ben. "Actually, Jake is the one who loves this place. It's where we had our very first dinner together, and the chile rellenos are amazing."

"Yeah, well Cassie loves them, too, and since we agree, that's what we're getting."

Ben glanced over his shoulder at Kaz. "Is he always this bossy?"

Kaz rolled her eyes. "You've obviously been away from your brother for much too long."

Yeah, he thought. I have. Too long. But that was changing. Had changed, and he was still smiling when they headed out Dry Creek Road and turned to cross Yoakim Bridge to West Dry Creek. It was a typical Saturday in May, which meant the valley was filled with bicyclists and wine tasters, tourists enjoying the gorgeous countryside, and locals and visitors alike shopping for wines and enjoying the scenery. Ben hadn't been here in at least twenty-five years, but he vaguely recalled a trip out Dry Creek Road, for a picnic at a winery somewhere.

Jake said, "Remember that picnic we came to out here with the parents? It was something one of Dad's clients put on, and his boss told him he had to bring his family."

"Yeah. We had to wear suits, sit, and behave." Jake's comment reminded him of more of the details. "I remember hearing someone say we acted like the Stepford family. At the time, I didn't get it."

"I bet you do, now."

Jake might be laughing, but the memory made Ben feel sad. If he ever had children, they'd get to be normal kids. Of course, first he'd have to figure out what normal felt like.

Lola liked Cassie Dunagan from the first moment they met. She was exactly as Kaz had described her—pretty and smart and so in love with her sexy husband it made all of them smile. Nate was big and good-looking—every bit a farmer from his callused hands to the grape-colored stains on his worn jeans, and the sun-creased laugh lines around his eyes.

They ate their Mexican lunch in the big kitchen of the

beautiful old farmhouse, a farmhouse Marc Reed had deeded back to Cassie and Nate as a wedding gift. It was the house her father had built for her mother before Cassie was born, part of the vineyard and winery Marc had bought before it fell into bankruptcy.

After lunch and a few minutes to clean up the mess, Kaz, Jake, and Cassie walked down to the tasting room to check out the facility with a wedding in mind. Nate took Ben and Lola across the road to see the wine cave and a field—Nate called it a block—of the very old dry-farmed vines that grew some of the grapes Cassie used to blend her award-winning wines.

They wandered down near Dry Creek where restoration had been done to the creek to increase the salmon run, and then Nate took them up to the tasting room. There were half a dozen cars in the small lot, and a metal bike rack with almost a dozen bicycles.

"It looks like they're busy. I'm going to drop you folks off here and get back to work." Nate held the door open for Ben and Lola. "It's too easy to get roped into pouring wine for the tourists, so I need to hightail it out of here before Cassie spots me."

He grinned when they laughed. "I'm glad I got a chance to meet you."

He and Ben shook hands, and he still managed to stay back behind the door and out of Cassie's view. "You've done this before," Ben said. "Sneaky."

Nate was laughing and walking quickly away when Ben and Lola slipped inside after a quick thanks for the tour, and carefully closed the door behind them. The tasting room wasn't at all what Lola expected. Its former life had obviously been as a country barn, but now there was a beautiful kitchen area with granite counters, a huge stainless-steel sink and a modern six-burner gas range. Racks of wine bottles filled one wall, and there were beautiful photographs on canvas of the valley, and the Intimate vineyards, and winery covering the walls.

Ben slipped his arm around her waist and leaned over. "I think those are Jake's photos," he said. He went to take a look, grinned at Lola and gave her a thumbs up. She walked over and stood beside Ben.

"These are amazing." The photos were absolutely breathtaking, proof once again that Ben's brother was a talented artist.

"I know. Hard to believe the same guy who was such a cocky young Olympian grew up to do sensitive work like this."

Lola squeezed his arm. "I'm glad you're getting the chance to know him now."

"He's not the same guy. That's for sure."

She touched his cheek with her fingertips and turned his face toward her. "Neither are you."

Ben had no response for Lola. He hoped he'd changed, hoped like hell he wasn't still the same loser who'd done so much awful shit when he was a kid. Silently he turned away from the photo he'd been studying and checked out the rest of the tasting room. There was a young woman pouring wine at the counter, while Kaz and Cassie stood in a far corner, talking a mile a minute, gesturing with their hands, obviously making wedding plans. Jake stood off to one side, watching the women. He had an amazingly self-satisfied grin on his face.

Ben studied his brother for a moment, and realized he was finding joy in Jake's obvious happiness with his intended bride, but then his gaze shifted once again, this time back to Lola. She was like a lodestone, drawing him no matter which way she went. At the moment, she was watching the people around the granite counter who were talking and laughing and tasting wine. After a bit, she pulled her cell phone out and snapped some pictures.

It was definitely a jovial crowd. Ben was surprised by the mix of ages—everyone from the barely twenty-one-year-olds, to folks their parents' ages, and even much older people mixed in with the younger crowd.

One couple in particular caught his eye. The older lady stood off to one side watching while a young man selected a number of bottles of wine that the young woman working the counter was adding to a box. There was something about the guy that looked familiar, though for the life of him, Ben couldn't tell who he was or even if he'd actually seen him before.

Maybe he just reminded him of someone.

On the other hand, maybe it was because they just didn't seem to fit. Whatever. Before he thought about what he was doing, Ben had his phone out. It was easy enough to delete an unwanted photo later, so he took a picture—first a couple of Lola because she was absolutely beautiful and he realized he didn't have any shots of her, but then he focused his camera on the woman, and then on the young man who appeared to be with her.

He took another shot of Lola just as she turned, realized he was taking her picture, and smiled at him. That was worth a few more, until she was laughing at the huge number he managed to snap in a very short time.

He followed her when she wandered over to the far side of the room where Jake stood with Cassie and Kaz in front of some beautiful old stalls filled with fresh straw and decorated with colorful blankets.

"Kaz?" Lola slipped her arm around Kaz's waist. "Is this the honeymoon suite?" She gestured toward the straw.

Kaz laughed, but at the same time she turned beet red. Lola grabbed her by both hands. "Ohmygawd! You and Jake? In the straw?" When Jake burst out laughing, Ben knew she had them, and he absolutely lost it when Lola shot Jake a glance, raised one eyebrow and said, "I bet that made the dangly bits itch."

It took him a bit to stop laughing, but when he finally caught his breath, Ben turned and grinned at his brother. "You didn't?" Jake just rolled his eyes, and Ben turned to Lola. "Damn, girl. You're right. They did."

Kaz folded her arms across her chest and glared at Ben. "How can you tell?"

"Umm, because your face is the same color as that pretty red purse you're carrying, and Jake's is even brighter."

Kaz spun around and stared at Jake. "He's right. You know, I don't know if I've ever seen you blush before." She tapped the end of his nose. "You're kinda cute when you get all red and flustered."

Jake glared at Ben. "You, brother dear, are in deep shit."

Ben figured his smile was too sweet for words. "Aren't I always?"

Lola got pictures of Kaz and Jake in front of "their" stall, much to Kaz's embarrassment and Cassie's hysterical laughter. Then Cassie got shots of the four of them, and Ben took one of all three women. Lola got a picture of Ben and Jake standing beside each other, and then another when Jake draped his arm around his older, shorter brother's shoulders.

"I've got a picture of the two of us from years ago," Jake said. "You were just about as much taller than me then as I am next to you now. I think they'll look good in the same frame."

"Smart ass," Ben said, but damn, he was having a wonderful time with Jake. And he was touched that Jake had kept a photo of the two of them. He glanced at Lola and had a feeling she knew what he was thinking, of all the years he and Jake had lost, but it was hard to dwell on the bad times because now things were just so good.

What made them even better was having a woman beside him who understood. Who knew what a jerk he'd been
and cared about him in spite of himself. When Lola finally
put her phone away, Ben grabbed her hand. "Let's go pick
out a couple of bottles to take home. It's not fair that we're
always drinking Marc's stash."

They ended up buying a mixed case of different vari-
etals and blends. Ben paid for the wine, thanked Cassie for
her hospitality, and then followed Kaz and Jake back out
to the car.

They left early enough that traffic wasn't too bad. At
least it moved at a steady, if slow, pace. After a while, Lola
brought up the pictures she'd taken in the tasting room.
Ben glanced at them and saw a photo of the same older
woman he'd noticed. "I took one of her, too. And the guy
with her. Not sure why, except he looked sort of familiar."

Lola stared at the photo for a long time. Finally she just
shook her head. She wasn't sure what had made her take
the picture of the woman—at the time she'd looked familiar, but now she just wasn't sure. She passed her phone
back to Kaz. "Do you know her? Or the guy with her?"

Kaz took a look and shook her head. "I don't think I've
ever seen her." She showed it to Jake. Lola had turned in
her seat and watched while he studied them for what
seemed like a very long time.

Finally he raised his head and tapped the screen on the
phone. "I don't remember him, but I think I've seen her
before. She was at Marc's premiere for Intimate." He
glanced at Kaz. "I think I remember seeing her arrive just
before you showed up."

"Ah, that would be around the time I threw the envelope in your face so I could run outside and get kidnapped?"

"Exactly. I think she got there a few minutes ahead of
your histrionics."

"They were very good histrionics." Kaz sniffed.

"The best." It was obvious Jake was teasing, but the minute the words were out of his mouth, he wrapped his fingers behind Kaz's head, tugged her close and kissed her. Lola was almost sure she'd glimpsed tears in his eyes, and she turned around, giving both of them privacy.

She imagined it would be a long time before either of them got past the horror of that night. She turned and caught Ben looking at her. Then he reached across the console with his right hand and took hold of her left, twining his long fingers around hers.

He held on to her hand almost the entire way back to the city.

It was almost dark when Ben pulled up in front of the house. The lights inside were on, so Mandy was probably home, but it was Kaz who first noticed the change.

"Look," she said. "The garage door's been painted."

They all got out of the car and walked over to take a closer look. "It looks like they did a really good job." Lola stood back and checked it out from different angles. "The black doesn't show through anywhere. It looks great."

"Hey! You're home." Mandy came down the front stairs. "I wondered who was talking down here. I really don't want any more graffiti."

"Did the boys do this?" Lola was still checking out the job.

"They did, with Mom and Dad standing watch and making sure they did it right and cleaned up afterwards."

Ben checked his phone. "They must not have called. The officer gave them my number."

"The parents came by with the boys right after you guys left, I think to see the damage more than anything. I heard them out here talking, and came out to see what was going on. Turns out I know the mom—not her name or anything—but she comes into the coffee shop after her yoga class sometimes. She and her husband were very nice, extremely unhappy with their sons, and asked if they could paint it over today. I told them to have at it, that I was leaving before noon, but as long as they didn't leave a mess, they were welcome to cover up their unappreciated artwork. When I left, the boys were already out here painting, and their dad was making sure they did a good job. I let them have the can of paint the landlord left in the garage, along with the brushes and a tarp, so they were able to get right to work. The job was done, the tarp folded, and the brushes clean when I got home."

"You knew their mom? I swear, you know everyone, Mandy." Lola gave her sister a quick hug. "The whole world must come through the coffee shop."

Ben pulled his cell phone out of his pocket. "Maybe she knows our mystery woman." He opened the photo of the older lady at the winery.

Mandy looked at it and laughed. "Where did you run into Cissy?"

"Cissy? That's a real name?" Ben took the phone back and looked at the picture again.

"That's what her son calls her. At least I think he's her son. Maybe her grandson. He brings her in on occasion and they always order whatever the daily special is. He calls her Cissy. They started coming in a few weeks ago. I'm not sure if they live around here or just visit the area, but they're very nice."

"Well, that solves that mystery." Lola deleted the pictures. "I've probably seen them at the coffee shop when I've stopped in."

Ben grabbed the case of wine out of the back of the Subaru, but Lola stopped him. "Aren't you taking that home?"

He kissed her nose. "I'm paying rent here. I tend to

think of this place as home. I may lock it in my room to protect it from the female inhabitants, but . . ."

Mandy slipped her arm through his. "Not a problem. Give it to me. I'll watch it for you."

"Yeah. Right." Laughing at his dry response, the girls headed into the house, talking a mile a minute. Jake hung back with Ben. "Do you have pictures of that lady on your phone?"

"I do," Ben said. "Why?"

"Let's show them to Marc and Ted, just to be on the safe side."

"Okay." Ben glanced at Jake. His brother merely shrugged. Then the two of them followed Mandy and Lola into the house.

CHAPTER 16

Jake and Kaz stayed long enough for a bowl of soup and a sandwich and then headed back to Jake's apartment. Lola had laundry to do and Mandy was curled up on the couch next to Rico, halfway through a thriller one of her buddies had told her she had to read.

Ben asked her how she liked it.

"Honestly?" She rolled her eyes dramatically. "It's scaring the bejeebers out of me. I don't think I'm a fan of thrillers, especially with all that's been going on around here lately."

He sat down next to her. "I'm glad you mentioned that. I'm a little worried about going back to Camp Parks tomorrow night. Are you guys going to be okay?"

Mandy shrugged. "What could happen? We have Rico here to guard us."

Grinning broadly, he shook his head. "Now I'm even more worried. Seriously, Mandy. Do you mind if I put better locks on the doors tomorrow? Make this place a little tighter than it is?"

She stared at him for the longest time. Finally she put the book on the coffee table and said, "You'd do that for us?"

Her softly spoken question floored him. "Of course I

would. I mean, all this trouble is because of me. I couldn't handle it if anything happened to you or Lola because all this crap has followed me here. Damn it, Mandy!" He took a long, slow breath. "Remember when you guys said I mattered to you? Well, it works both ways. You and Lola matter to me. A lot. I want you safe. You need a better lock on the door from the kitchen into the garage. It wasn't even locked when I went through it last night to go after those kids, and the garage door wasn't locked, either. That means your house is wide open—simple access into the house through the kitchen, which has the kind of lock any idiot can open with a sharp point, and that's if you remember to lock it. Your front door has a deadbolt that doesn't work, so you use that stupid latch on the handle that anyone could break through."

She gave him a sheepish grin. "Okay. It sounds like we're going to the hardware store tomorrow."

"Exactly. And I'm buying."

Lola walked out of the kitchen with a basket filled with freshly washed and dried linens. "Okay, but who's folding?"

Ben raised his hand. "I'll do it." He glanced into the basket filled with sheets and towels. "What? No sexy little thongs?"

"Sorry, big guy. Next load. Think of the joy of anticipation." Lola set the basket on the floor in front of him. "What's all the talk about locks?"

Mandy shot Ben an eye-rolling look; clearly, she was making fun of him. It didn't matter, as long as they were safe.

"Ben's going to put new locks on all the doors tomorrow so we can't get in or out. We'll probably end up trapped in here forever. Unless he puts them up while we're gone, in which case we'll be stuck outside."

Ben shook out a towel and carefully folded it, and then

looked over at Mandy. "You really are a drama queen, aren't you?"

"The best." She picked up her book. "Point being, darling sister, we're getting new locks on all the doors tomorrow courtesy of your man friend. Make sure you get the new keys to the landlord."

Lola leaned close and kissed him. "Thank you, Ben. Ignore Mandy if she's being mean to you. I've been wondering if we needed to do something like that with all that's been going on lately."

"I know. I was telling Mandy that I really hate to leave you guys here alone."

"We could probably get Kaz and Jake to move back in on the nights you're gone." Lola glanced at Mandy to see what she thought of that.

Her sister just shrugged. "Or Marc. Then he'd be here to give you a ride into work in the morning, and home at night. We could pay him to stay by offering to feed him. He's a sucker for a free meal."

"I don't think it's the free part he likes. It's the fact that it's home cooked and he's not eating alone." Ben liked the idea of Marc staying here. It beat leaving the girls by themselves. "Why don't you call him?"

Mandy blushed. "I can't do that. I just wouldn't know what to . . . Lola? You can call him."

"No, I can't. He's my boss. I think it would be a little awkward."

Ben stood. "I'll call him. Does he get my room or yours, Lola?"

"Sheets on my bed are clean. I can get some of my stuff out of my drawers—there's plenty of room in yours, but I'm assuming you want to share with me and that Marc will agree."

"He'll agree. And yes, I definitely want to share." Ben

headed into his room where he'd left his phone charging. He dialed the number and Marc picked it up on the first ring. "Marc? Ben here. How would you feel about a week of Lola and Mandy's meals in return for staying here while I'm gone? I have to be at Camp Parks tomorrow night, and I'm worried about leaving the girls alone until this mess settles down."

"Are you serious? Because the unit above mine had a fire this morning. I got home from your place to all kinds of water damage. I've been scrambling to find a place to stay for the next few weeks until the repairs are done. In fact, I'm planning to stay at the office tonight because I hate hotels, but the creature comforts are lacking." He sounded grumpy.

Ben figured at this point, Marc's sense of humor was lacking as well. "Hell, man. Why didn't you call us? Just pack up some stuff and come on over tonight. We'll all be very grateful. I'm sure you can stay as long as you need."

"That would be wonderful, but check with Mandy and Lola first, okay? You invited me for a week; I'm talking about moving in for what could be a couple of months. There's a lot of damage to repair. Call me back. I don't want to pressure them into anything. They're too nice for that."

"Okay. I'll get back to you."

He went back into the front room and explained Marc's predicament.

Lola held out her hand. "I'll call him."

Ben handed over the phone and Lola called. "Marc? This is Lola. Why didn't you let us know you needed a place to stay? Pack up what clothes and stuff you need and come on over. I'll clear out my room for you." She laughed. "Nope. Ben would prefer that I not use it at all. You can stay as long as you like, but remember, you'll be sharing a bathroom with two women. Girl stuff. Yep. A lot of it. No, it's not contagious. You won't lose your man card." Laughing, she hung up.

Marc showed up about two hours later. The Tesla was loaded. Mandy and Lola had just about emptied Lola's room out and moved everything but the furniture into Ben's room.

Ben decided the better part of valor was just to stay out of the way, but once Marc arrived, he stayed busy helping Marc carry his stuff inside.

Ben grabbed the last of the boxes out of the back seat. "Did you get everything, or do you still have more in the apartment?"

Marc laughed, but he looked exhausted. "I ran out of room in the Tesla. They're supposed to start working on the place Monday. I figured I'd get the rest of my things out of there tomorrow." He looped a heavy clothes bag over his shoulder. "Honestly? My lease is up in a couple months. I don't like the place that much and I'm tempted to start looking for something else to rent, but it's not easy to find places in the city, even when money's not an issue. I've got room in my office building, but it's not legally zoned for living space, and I haven't had time to check into changing the zoning on it."

Mandy held the door open for them. "Thanks, Mandy." Ben went through first. "Does Jake have an extra room you can rent?"

Marc shook his head and followed Ben down the hallway to Lola's room. "No. It's a one bedroom, and I wouldn't want to intrude. He and Kaz are still getting to know each other. I don't think they need an extra guy on the scene."

Lola was organizing Marc's belongings in the bedroom. "You can stay here until your apartment is repaired, Marc. We're not going to throw you out, and we've got the space."

"Thanks, Lola, but I was just telling Ben that I'm thinking of looking for another place to rent, and it might take me a while."

Lola glanced at Mandy, who merely said, "Works for me."

Marc dumped his clothes bag on the bed. "What works for you?"

Lola unzipped the bag and started pulling shirts and pants on hangers out of it. "We were having a sister's conversation. No words necessary. Mandy and I are perfectly willing to sublet this bedroom as long as you need it. Then Ben won't have to worry about leaving us here alone at night, we won't have to worry about being here alone, and you'll have a place to stay. Split four ways, the rent's pretty cheap. And I cook."

She went back to hanging his clothes in the closet.

Marc watched her for a minute. "You're serious?"

"Of course. But, there will be rules. You can't be my boss when we get home. We can talk about work if it's something important, but I'd prefer not to, and when you're here, you're our friend Marc, not Mr. Reed."

Shaking his head, Marc just laughed. "I always feel so uncomfortable when you call me Mr. Reed. It's just wrong, you know?"

"No, it's not. In the office you are Mr. Reed. Here you're Marc. Or you might be, 'hey, you, get your big feet off the sofa.'"

"And I can almost guarantee that you're going to be the one who gets to take the garbage out," Ben added. "That appears to be a designated man job. Oh, and one other rule—you can't bring dates home to spend the night. Not allowed."

Lola bumped hips with Ben. "You notice how Ben got around that one, however."

The three of them looked at Mandy, who blushed a

deep, dark red. "Don't look at me, guys. I'm staying out of that one."

On that note, she turned and left the room. Ben glanced at Marc, noticed he looked pretty uncomfortable, and decided it was a good time to keep his mouth shut.

"Marc, tomorrow I'm picking up some better locks for the doors on this place, but I can help you haul the rest of your stuff out of your apartment. The only problem might be furniture. I don't think there's enough room in the garage to store it."

"Not a problem. It's a furnished apartment, so it all stays there, water damage and all. I didn't want the hassle of buying stuff. I've been too busy setting up Intimate Jewels and all the details with the winery, along with my other companies. You have no idea how many problems staying here is going to solve." He turned to Lola. "I really do appreciate it, and I'll make a point of being here as much as possible when Ben's not around."

By ten, Lola had gone in to get a shower and Ben was helping Marc get his belongings put away in what had once been Lola's room. It was slowly but surely taking on a more male-oriented appearance. Mandy had even brought in a plain navy bedspread to switch out with Lola's floral print, and then she went back to the front room and her book.

About half an hour later she was back. "Ben, there's a dark sedan parked across the street but in the opposite direction from the last one. I know there's no one home there because the owners are in Hawaii for a month."

"Well, crap. How'd you spot them?"

"I took Rico out in front to piddle and saw them back into the driveway. I don't know if they saw me or not. They came from the other direction and didn't go past the house, at least not while I was out there."

"Stay here. I'm going to call Ted, but I want to get a look at them first. Marc, you're on girl duty, okay?" Marc nodded and Ben left. The porch light was off, so he went down the front steps and slipped around the front of the house, using the shrubs for cover. The sedan was right where Mandy had said it would be, though with the glare from the streetlight, he couldn't tell if anyone was in it or not. He went back to his room where he'd left his phone on the charger, and called Ted. Then he pocketed the charged phone and walked back to Marc's room.

"Ted's coming out and said he'd check on them. Which reminds me . . ." Ben pulled his phone out of his pocket, tapped the screen, and turned it toward Marc. "Who is this lady? Jake said she was at your premiere for the jewelry line the other night."

Marc took the phone and stared at the picture. Finally, he shook his head. "I don't know. I mean, I recognize her face and I know she was there, but the PR firm brought in a bunch of local personalities and their friends. I didn't know half the people who showed up. I turned the guest list over to my security guy." He rolled his eyes. "They definitely enjoyed the food. That crowd can really go through the caviar. Send a copy of it to me and I'll check with Bill. He worked directly with the PR firm that set up the premiere and organized the guest list—in fact, the guy who runs the firm is a friend of his. I'm sure he'll know who she is."

Ben leaned close and kissed Lola. "Thanks, I'm going out to wait for Ted. Got anything to feed him? I swear that guy is always hungry."

"Actually, I do. I made a chocolate cream pie while I was doing laundry. It should be set up by now."

Ben glanced at Marc. "You realize you're going to have to take up running or you'll get fat living here."

Marc just chuckled. He was about an inch shorter than Ben but close to thirty pounds lighter. "I already run. Actually, I look forward to gaining a pound or two."

Ben waved on his way out the door. He felt a lot better about leaving Sunday night with Marc staying here. His phone vibrated and he checked the screen. Ted had sent a text. *I'm here. If you see trouble, call 911.*

Ben texted back as he went down the front steps again and stood in the shadows beside the bushes. He had a clear view of Ted's sedan blocking the one in the driveway. Ted was walking toward the vehicle, approaching the driver's side. *I see you. Yell if you need back up.*

Before he sent the text, a shot rang out. Ben dialed 911 as he raced down the street, but he had to dive for cover when the car sped out of the driveway, cutting across the yard to get around Ted's vehicle blocking the way, and sped by him.

Ted was down. Ben reached him as the car disappeared at the end of the street and turned west, toward the ocean. The dispatcher came on and Ben gave her a quick description and a location. He told her he didn't know yet if they needed an ambulance. Ted was moving. Ben helped him sit up. Ted rubbed his hand across his head and it came away covered in blood.

"Shit, Ted. Where'd you get hit?" He pulled off his clean T-shirt, folded it up and pressed it against the bleeding wound.

"Grazed my head. Hurts like a sonofabitch. At least I got their license number, but not a very good look at either man. Caucasian, late thirties, early forties, both had dark hair. Ben heard a voice and remembered the dispatcher on the line. "Just a minute. Ted, you need an ambulance?"

"Can you take me to the ER?"

"I can." He gave Ted's information including the license number to the dispatcher as a squad car pulled in behind the agent's.

"Never a dull moment with you folks around, is there?"

Ben glanced up. "Officer McGowan. Fancy meeting you here."

The policeman knelt beside Ted. "Sheesh, Robinson, you're bleedin' like a stuck pig." He took a closer look with his flashlight. "Looks like a shallow graze. You want to go to the ER, get that cleaned up, and we can talk tomorrow?"

"Works for me. You've got my number. Any sign of the vehicle?"

"There are two squad cars working the streets between here and the Great Highway, though as I recall, the last guys watching your place had changed the numbers on the plates, so I'm not sure if they'll pull over the right car."

"Thanks for the reminder." Ted groaned and focused on Ben. "You sure you don't mind hauling me in to get this cleaned up?"

"Not a problem, but we need to go tell the girls. I'm sure they heard the gunshot." Ben helped Ted to his feet. "And I'm gonna need a clean shirt."

McGowan's radio crackled. He listened and turned to leave. "I've got a call," he said. "I'll get in touch with you tomorrow afternoon, okay?"

McGowan jumped into his squad car and raced down the street.

Ten minutes later, Lola sent them off with a wad of gauze covering Ted's head wound and a slice of chocolate cream pie in a plastic container. Ben wore his ACUs, since all his other clothes were currently on spin in the washer downstairs. They made the trip to the ER in under ten minutes, but it was close to midnight before Ben dropped the agent off at his hotel, an extended-stay inn not far from the house on 23rd Avenue.

"You sure you're going to be okay?" He'd followed Ted inside, and left the medical supplies and the directions for wound care. His injury had turned out to be a shallow but bloody furrow across the left side of Robinson's scalp.

"Yeah. I'm just pissed off that idiot nailed me. I'm usually smarter than that."

"You should be feeling grateful the bastard's a lousy shot."

"There is that. I'm going to take a shower and go to bed. Thank you. And thank Lola for the pie. If she wasn't your girl, I'd be putting the moves on her for her cooking alone."

"She's taken." Ben held out his hand. "Give me your keys, and we'll get your car to you in the morning."

Ted handed them over and headed for the shower. Ben was back home in under five minutes, moved Ted's car so that it was now in front of the house, and quietly let himself inside.

Marc was sitting in the front room, working on his laptop. He glanced up as Ben shut the door behind him. "Girls are asleep," he said. "I waited up to see how Ted was doing. He looked like a mess, but sounded more pissed off than hurt."

"Yeah, you nailed it. We had to wait for over an hour at the ER. This town has all kinds of action after dark." Ben glanced at the craft beer in Marc's hand. "Got any more of those?"

"In the refrigerator. Help yourself. I brought my stash with me."

Ben grabbed a bottle and popped the lid off, then walked back out to the front room. "When did the girls go to bed?"

"Mandy disappeared right after you and Ted left, and Lola wasn't far behind. Lola said she had a really good time at the winery today. What'd you think of it?"

"Gorgeous. Jake told me he's an investor. Smart move."

Marc laughed. "He wanted to participate in the first crush after I bought it, and I told him only owners and employees could do that because of liability issues. I'd wanted him as a partner from the very beginning, but for whatever reason, he wasn't willing to get involved. Then when he saw how much fun I was having, he bought in."

"Why? I mean, it's not like you need the money. I don't get it."

Marc studied him for so long, Ben began to feel a little uncomfortable. He had no idea what the guy was thinking. Marc closed the laptop and set it aside.

"That's because you've always had Jake. Even when you two were apart, you knew your brother was out there. In a way, even though you don't want any part of them, you had your parents, too. I was an only child. My parents fought over me when they divorced, not because they really wanted me, but because they each wanted to hurt the other. My father prevailed and my mother gave up all rights to me— by choice. That wasn't part of the custody agreement, but I never saw her again. My dad hired people to raise me, and they came and went like the weather. The only constant in my life was Jake." He shrugged, as if he'd not expected anything else in his life.

"I think, in some way, I figured if I could get Jake legally tied to me in a business, he wouldn't leave, even though I know he'll always be there for me. It was just that added insurance that made me more comfortable."

"Does Jake know this?"

Marc laughed. "Yeah, I told him, but he'd already figured it out. When we signed the papers, he looked at me and laughed, and asked if that made me feel better. I tried to act like I didn't know what he meant, but he saw right through me. He said then that I was his brother, that I'd always be his brother, even when you finally got your shit together and came back."

Ben stared at him for a moment. "He didn't really say that."

Laughing, Marc grabbed his beer and took another

swallow. "Yes, he did. Ask him if you don't believe me. Your brother is amazingly perceptive, which is why he's such a good friend, but it's also what makes him a brilliant photographer. He understands his subjects, whether they're inanimate objects, neurotic buddies, or the woman he's going to marry. Look at these."

He opened his laptop again and brought up a file of pictures Jake had taken of Kaz for their photo shoot at the vineyard a few weeks ago. Ben had seen a few of these, but now, knowing Kaz, and knowing his brother better, he was even more amazed. Each shot was more beautiful than the last, and his brother's talent blew him away. After he'd run through the entire file, Marc closed the laptop once again. "See what I mean?"

"Wow. I could say it's because Kaz is such a beautiful model, but that's not all of it. Not at all. You're right. It's like he sees beyond the way she looks, almost as if he's uncovering the fantasy."

"Exactly." Marc sat back on the couch and stretched his legs out on the coffee table. "I'm not sure if this is breaking the rules or not."

Chuckling, Ben leaned back at the other end and stuck his feet next to Marc's. "I think you're safe, but don't quote me."

"I'm glad you're back, Ben. Your brother has missed you something fierce. He's had some tough times, but now he's got Kaz and he's got you."

"And the shitload of trouble I've brought with me."

"Well, it's not trouble you caused. Witnessing a crime isn't the same as committing one, and he's honestly forgiven you for that one. And yes, I was surprised about that, but it's a testament to who Jake is." Changing the subject, he continued, "Anyway, this will end at some point and we'll move on with our lives. For now, I'm glad I'm here with the girls and I just hope that I'm totally unnecessary."

"I doubt you'll ever be that, Marc. And whether or not you wanted one, I think your family is growing." He finished off his beer and stood. "I need to get some sleep. You want to help me deliver Ted's car tomorrow before we go empty out your apartment? I promised I'd bring it over. He's not staying far from here."

"Sounds good." He stood and then paused for a moment. "Are you sure it's not an imposition, my staying here? Mandy and Lola are just so damned nice, I guess I keep waiting to find out it's all a big mistake."

"Marc, you're doing us a favor—definitely doing me a favor. After all the shit that's been happening here, I don't think I'd sleep nights thinking of the two of them here alone. Just knowing you're here eases my mind. Hell, they wouldn't be in this position if not for me, so you're definitely welcome." He began to head for his room and then stopped. "And I imagine that if there wasn't anything to be afraid of, you'd be just as welcome. They're good people, Marc, but so are you. Don't forget that."

CHAPTER 17

Ben and Marc had returned Ted's car, picked up new locks for the house, filled Ben's SUV with a load of stuff from Marc's apartment—including an old, beat-up Schwinn bicycle he said he'd had since high school—and had gotten back to the house on 23rd before Lola and Mandy were even awake. The guys carried everything into the garage where Marc wanted to sort through the boxes to see what was essential and what needed to be stored, and Ben went into the house to check on Lola.

Quietly, he opened the bedroom door. Lola still slept, the blankets pulled up over her head until only her thick tangle of dark hair was visible. It was almost nine o'clock. She couldn't be too upset about his waking her at this hour, and he needed her. Needed her more than he'd ever imagined wanting or needing another. Like a panther stalking his prey, Ben crawled across the bed, leaned over her, and kissed her in that sensitive spot beneath her ear.

She scrunched her shoulder up and wriggled deeper into the blankets. Ben rolled over the top of her, pinning her against the mattress, and then peeled the comforter down from her face. "Boo," he said, grinning like an idiot.

She glared at him. "Boo yourself. What time is it?"

"Almost nine. Your man is hungry and horny, not necessarily in that order."

"I see. Which need am I supposed to take care of first?"

He rolled his hips against her.

"I think you should be more specific."

He peeled the blankets down far enough to expose her breasts. Such pretty breasts, too, not large, but they filled his hands perfectly. He cupped both of them to make sure, gently tugging her nipples between his fingers.

She groaned and arched against him, but there were all those blankets in the way.

"Good morning, sleepyhead." He kissed her, and thought about kissing this woman every morning for the rest of his life. Then he waited for the panic to hit, the sense that no, he wasn't ready, he was a soldier, a man who didn't want to be tied to one woman, one life.

But it wasn't panic he felt. No, it was a sense of coming home, of finding whatever it was that had been missing for as long as he could remember. Was this what Jake felt with Kaz? How he'd known she was the one?

How could Lola not be the one?

She reached for him, pulled him down and kissed him, and any doubts, any questions he'd had seemed to drift away on the sweetness of her mouth, the taste of her lips, the soft sigh as he slowly pulled the blankets further down her long, lean body, bared her to his greedy touch.

She was entirely naked; he wore jeans and a cable-knit sweater. He'd slipped his shoes off in the front room, but he rubbed his sock-clad toes along her calves and over the tops of her feet. Then he fumbled with his belt and zipper, freed himself and took the condom she handed him. There was something so decadent about taking her like this, fully dressed, his hands and face chilled from the morning fog while she lay warm and naked beneath him.

He sheathed himself, found her wet and ready. He teased her for a moment, rubbing his fingers along the heated center of her, listening to the soft, breathy whimpers when he circled her clit and teased her with what must be frustrating gentleness.

"More," she said, and her voice broke on the words. "I want you Ben. Now. More."

He didn't speak. He merely thrust his hips forward, sliding perfectly deep inside her heat, watching her face as he filled her, reveling in the tight grasp of her slick sheath. She closed her eyes and shoved at the waist of his jeans, pushing his pants down far enough to bare his butt even as she arched against him, her head tilted back, her throat bared to him. He pressed his lips against the pulse at her throat, licking and sucking her sensitive skin, filled with a need to mark her, to make her his in the most primitive way he could.

His lips sealed against her throat, over the line of blue beneath her fair, fair skin. He sucked hard, listened to her whimper as he loved her, felt the flutter of her fingers against his buttocks, stroking his hips, trailing over his skin and then digging in with fingernails, pulling him close.

She cried out. Her legs came up, wrapped around his thighs, and she held him tightly against her until it was no longer a question of Ben taking her. She took him back, held on to him with her hands, with her thighs, with the tight contraction of those powerful inner muscles as her climax took her over the edge.

Her fingers tightened against his butt, her nails dug into his ass, scraping over his tightly clenched muscles until he lost it, until he came harder than he'd ever come before, caught in the maelstrom of his orgasm, every part of his body reacting at once, expanding, contracting, connecting. Shivering, though he wasn't cold. No, he was fire itself, trapped in the inferno of Lola's heat, caught in her passion.

Breath catching in his lungs, his head thrown back as he gasped for air, hips thrusting forward, Lola holding him deep inside, the sound of her soft cries, hearts thundering, lungs straining for air, minds absolutely blown.

Something more than sex had definitely happened here.

He lowered his body over hers, propping himself on his forearms to keep some of his weight off of her, and he took a quick glance at her face, thankful that her eyes were closed. She lay there beneath him, her head turned slightly to her left, lips parted as she drew in one deep breath after another.

He had no idea what she was thinking, what she felt beyond the aftermath of orgasm. He knew her heart pounded because he felt it against his chest, knew that she drew deep breaths from the rise and fall of her own chest. All physical reactions.

The artery in her throat pulsed, a rapid tattoo beneath the dark strawberry mark he'd left on her tender skin. The mark fascinated him—he wasn't one to leave love bites on a woman. That had always seemed so childish, but this was something more, something as profound as what had just happened between the two of them.

Did she feel it? Did she wonder the same way he wondered?

A little bit of sex before breakfast had somehow become so much more—had somehow changed him. Somehow he knew this was the beginning of something larger than either of them. The gut-deep sense that she wasn't alone anymore, and neither was he. They were something more, something strong and enduring. United. Powerful.

She was his. He was hers. Such a simple concept, really. He didn't doubt it, didn't question why or how it happened, but he easily accepted the certainty of it.

It should have terrified him, but it didn't. He felt whole for the first time, complete. At peace. And it was all because of Lola, the missing piece to his own personal puzzle.

One week with this amazing woman, and his life had changed. He just hoped like hell Lola felt the same.

She opened her eyes to the steady gray-eyed gaze of the man who continued to rock her world. The moment he realized she was looking back, he smiled and lifted his weight off of her, carefully holding on to the condom. She reached for him, an automatic reaction she couldn't have stopped if she'd tired.

He paused, leaned close and kissed her. "It's after nine, lazybones. Time to get up."

And just that quickly, the spell was broken. He rolled off of her, disposed of the condom, and pulled his jeans up over that perfect butt.

Except it was covered with red scratches. She'd definitely marked her man, but he didn't seem to notice, thank goodness. Hopefully he wouldn't. Men didn't check out their butts, did they? Not like women did. She grinned at him. "Sure you need to hide that?"

"If I want to get anything done today. Can't very well leave the bedroom with my pants around my knees. You're insatiable."

"Me?" She pushed the covers away and sat up, totally enjoying the look in his eyes when she sat on the edge of the bed wearing nothing but the tiny gold loop earrings she'd forgotten to take off last night. "I'm the innocent one here, big guy. I was sound asleep when you so rudely accosted me."

"Rude, eh?" He swaggered back across the room, planted his hands on either side of her hips and kissed her.

She hadn't expected a kiss like this. Maybe a quick little peck, but his mouth covered hers and she tasted him, opened to him and had to wrap her arms around his neck to keep from ending up on her back again.

"Rude like that, you mean?" He nuzzled the side of her neck, kissed the pulse point on her throat. "Actually, I guess this was kind of rude." She felt his tongue sweep over a particularly sensitive spot.

"What?"

"I left a mark. I'm sorry. I've never done that before, but I sort of got carried away."

"Well, I'd prefer you didn't make a habit of it." She gave him a sultry glance. "At least not where they'll show."

"Excellent point. I'll try and remember only to nibble on less public areas. Should it happen again."

"You do that. Now go. I need to get dressed. I'm hungry."

He saluted, and she laughed. "That's Kaz's response. You need to think of something more original."

He kissed her. Thoroughly.

When she came up for air, it was with both hands planted on his chest. "That works. Now go. Oh, and if you go into the bathroom, you might want to check out that perfect ass of yours."

He lifted one eyebrow and gave her an inquisitive look, and then he left, thank goodness, because her knees were weak and her heart was pounding. What was it about him? And what exactly had just happened between them?

She felt as if he'd been part of her life forever. As if he belonged with her and she with him, but that couldn't be possible this quickly. Could it?

She thought of other boyfriends, not all that many considering the fact she'd turned thirty-one in March. She thought of how they'd affected her—or not, as the case had always been. Why was everything with Ben so different? So good but also so scary, because it was all new, all uncharted territory.

Maybe she needed to spend some time with Kaz, find out how she'd known with Jake, ask her what clues had convinced her he was the only one for her.

Because that's how Lola was thinking of Ben: that he was the one. She'd always thought that was all a myth, that in reality you met a guy you were compatible with and it sort of grew from there, but it hadn't grown with Ben. No, everything with Ben had exploded. She'd felt a connection from the moment he'd first walked into their house last week, and that connection had only grown stronger in the past few days.

They connected on so many levels and obviously had some damned good sexual chemistry. She took that into consideration when she dug through the clothes she'd moved in here last night, and finally found a perfect dark red, sleeveless sweater top, one with a sleek turtleneck style that covered her little strawberry mark. The color was definitely apropos. She paired it with a pair of faded blue skinny jeans and pulled her hair back in a high pony tail.

Then she made a quick run to the bathroom, glad it wasn't occupied. She hadn't thought of the logistics of sharing this apartment with not one, but two men. She was only in there a couple of minutes, got her face washed and her teeth brushed, and then redid her lopsided ponytail and fluffed her bangs. Her color was growing out—again. Ben said he liked it black, but she was getting tired of the hassle of keeping it dark. She wondered how he'd like it if she went back to her natural dark blonde.

Wondered what he'd have to say once he checked out his butt.

She was giggling when she left the bathroom and almost ran into Marc in the hallway. "Hey, roomie," she said, still grinning like a fool. "Did you sleep okay last night?"

"I did," he said. "You've got a really comfortable bed. A lot better than the one in that apartment I've been living in for the past few years."

"Marc." She stood there with her hands on her hips, laughing at him. "There are stores that sell comfortable beds. You should have gotten something better."

He shrugged. "Guess it didn't seem important."

"Men." She was still grinning when she headed toward the front room. Ben was kneeling at the front door, changing the deadbolt.

"When did you get that?"

He shot her a grin. "Unlike some of us, Marc and I have had a very productive morning. We've already returned Ted's car to him and checked to see if he's okay—he is, by the way. We made a stop at the hardware store for locks, and picked up the rest of Marc's stuff at his trashed apartment. Boxes are in the garage, by the way, but he said he's going to go through them and get everything out of there as soon as he can. Oh, and I also managed to put a smile on my woman's face."

She loved that he thought of her as his woman. Smiling, she leaned close and whispered, "And a hickey on her neck."

He whispered back just as dramatically. "Matches the claw marks on my ass, sweetie."

She felt the blush and knew she probably went beet red. "You looked, huh?"

He wagged his finger and she moved closer. "You drew blood," he whispered. You've probably scarred me for life."

"I didn't! Did I?"

He laughed so hard she wanted to smack him. "No, but you could have."

She kissed him. "Be nice to me. I'm going to make breakfast. I might just make enough for you to have some. Is Mandy up yet?"

"In the kitchen. She's made a fresh pot of coffee."

"Now you know why I love my sister."

Mandy handed Lola a cup of coffee as she stepped into the kitchen.

"Thank you. Perfect." She took a sip. "I can't believe I slept so late. You hungry? I smell sausage. Did the guys eat already?"

"No." Mandy refilled her cup and sat on the barstool near the stove, her favorite place when Lola was cooking. "There was a package in the fridge so I went ahead and cooked it. There's a lot there, but how much do you want to bet Kaz and Jake will show up?"

"Good point. I'll scramble some eggs. Do you want to make toast?"

Mandy didn't answer. She was staring at the front room. Staring at Marc, actually, who was talking to Ben. Lola hadn't asked Mandy how she really felt about Marc living here. She knew her sister had had a crush on the image of the man before they'd ever met, but Lola had no idea how she felt about him now that he was actually living here, sleeping in the next bedroom.

She hoped it didn't get awkward, that Mandy wasn't still crushing on the guy, that Marc didn't feel uncomfortable about it if she was. There'd been so much going on all week, they'd hardly talked. Mandy had been working some truly awful hours. At least that was something they could talk about with the guys here.

"What's with the crazy hours at the coffee shop? This is the first time you've had a weekend off in months." Lola started cracking eggs into a bowl. She had just decided to cook the entire eighteen pack when she heard the front door open, and Jake's voice in the hallway, talking to Ben.

She focused on Mandy again. "You've been working way more than usual." And she'd been so quiet, hiding away in her room at night to read, almost as if she were depressed. Lola might blame it on the guys being here and the changes in their comfortable—albeit boring—routine, but it had started a while back, even before Ben showed up.

Mandy just shook her head. "I don't know. Something's going on. I have a feeling that Lynette might be thinking of selling the place. You know she's opened another shop downtown? I think it's turned into more work and expense than she was planning when she decided on a second shop, but we talked the other day and I told her I can't keep working this many hours without a raise. She didn't go for that at all."

"You're kidding?" Mandy was so easygoing most of the time, Lola had a feeling her boss was taking advantage of her good nature. "Have you looked for anything else? There are a lot of coffee shops, and you're good at what you do. You've got great people skills. Better than mine, that's for sure!"

Mandy just shrugged, which was a good indication she didn't want to talk about it with everyone in the other room. Lola added butter to the frying pan and threw in some chopped green onions. Lately, she'd felt like a short order cook more than an office manager, but it was fun to have everyone here at mealtimes. It made meals more fun. With Marc living here, she doubted they'd be taking the table down—that extra leaf was the only way they could all fit.

Kaz waltzed into the kitchen, quite literally, in Marc's arms. He spun her in front of the table, dipped her backwards in a deep bow, and then made a quick exit.

Laughing, Lola reached for a coffee cup. "What was that all about?"

Kaz grinned when Lola handed the filled cup to her. "I told him he was going to have to dance with me at the wedding, and suggested he might need dance lessons. He informed me he was instructed in the finer points of ballroom dancing at a very young age." She took a sip. "He actually seems to know what he's doing. He's cute, but he's shorter than me."

Mandy rolled her eyes and stuck more bread in the toaster. "You're six two, Kaz. Everyone's shorter than you. Except Jake."

Laughing at Mandy's snarky comment, Kaz went to the drawer and pulled out silverware for everyone. "I don't see Ted. Is he coming for breakfast?"

"You don't know, do you! Crap, I forgot all about the fact you weren't here last night. Ted's recovering this morning. He got shot last night."

"What?!"

Lola told her what had happened, about the guys watching the house and Ben's call to the agent. "He's lucky he was only grazed, but Ben took him to the ER and they got him bandaged up. I'm planning to take some food over to him later. I bet he's got one hell of a headache today."

Jake walked in. "You talking about Agent Robinson?"

Lola nodded. "Yeah. Did Ben tell you what happened?"

"Just now. But they didn't catch them?"

"As far as we know." Lola went back to cooking, but she looked over her shoulder toward the front room. Ben was finishing up the deadbolt installation. "I just wish they'd get it all solved so we could get rid of all the unwanted attention and Ben could quit worrying."

"I know. I'm glad Marc's here, though. I know Ben's been worried about leaving you two alone all week. Kaz and I talked about staying here on the nights when Ben can't, but this is a lot better for all parties involved. Marc's a fan of regular meals and beautiful women, and Kaz and I are . . ." He laughed. "Let's say we're not necessarily all that quiet at night. Strikes me as an outstanding solution to a really crappy problem."

"It certainly solves the problem of how I'll get to work every day, having the boss in my bed." When everyone laughed, she added, "While I'm in Ben's." Lola checked the eggs. "Would you call everyone in? Tell them to come eat."

Jake looked over her shoulder. "Got enough?"

Lola raised an inquisitive eyebrow. "Doesn't your woman cook for you?"

Kaz walked in just then. "Not if she can help it." She kissed Jake on the cheek, and then told Lola that Marc and Ben were on their way.

Ben arrived in time to set the skillet of eggs on a trivet in the middle of the table. Marc poured coffee for the guys and Mandy set out the platter of sausage and the toast and jam. Kaz carried a big bowl of fresh fruit in from the front room with a sheepish grin on her face. "I forgot I brought it," she said.

"That's because I swept you away with my brilliant dancing skills."

"Is that what it was?" She patted Marc on the head after setting the bowl in the middle of the table. "I hope that's everything, because we're officially out of room."

Ben sat beside Lola. Laughter and silly jokes seemed to ebb and flow around them, and he thought how much he was going to miss this all week while he was at the base. All those years of deployments, one after the other at bases all over the world, and he'd never really missed anything. He'd never had anything he'd cared enough about to miss.

Now, his life was so full, he began to truly comprehend what he'd be leaving behind each time he went back to Camp Parks. It gave him a new sense of empathy for all those soldiers, men and women both, who went off to war and left their loved ones behind. When there was no one waiting, going home wasn't all that big a deal. When there was someone at home you loved, it was everything.

There was a knock at the front door. Lola started to rise, but Ben touched her hand. "Don't. You cooked; you eat. I'll get it."

CHAPTER 18

When Ben opened the front door, Ted Robinson was standing on the front porch. His head was bandaged. "I should have known it was you. Lola just put breakfast on the table. Come on in."

Ted stepped in, but he wasn't smiling. "I got some news about the two guys who were watching your place last night."

"From the look on your face, it's not good. What happened?" He saw Ted glance toward the kitchen. "Follow me. That way you'll only have to tell us once. And you'll get a good meal."

"Thanks." Almost sheepishly, he added, "You know I'll never turn down Lola's cooking."

He followed Ben into the kitchen. Everyone had already squeezed closer and Jake had put another chair in place. Mandy handed Ted a plate and silverware. "Whatever it is, can it wait until you've eaten?"

"Thanks, Mandy. And yes. It can wait. This looks wonderful. Thank you."

He sat and filled his plate, and conversation went on as before. Ben couldn't help but identify with Ted. The agent's work took him all over the country, and his home was one long-stay hotel after another. Even here, where they'd done their best to make him feel welcome, he was on the job. And from the look on his face, whatever news he brought wasn't good.

Finally, when the plates were cleared and Marc and Jake were at the sink doing dishes, Ted folded his napkin and set it on the table. "The two men who were watching the house? A couple of officers in a squad car spotted them on Judah, heading west. They followed them at a distance until the men pulled over near Sunset Boulevard. When the officers got out of the car to see if they had the right pair, the passenger opened fire. One of the officers was hit. He's in critical condition at UCSF Medical Center with multiple gunshot wounds, though it sounds as if there's a good chance he'll make it. The driver of the car is dead. The officer's partner got him."

Lola covered her mouth with one hand, and grabbed on to Ben's with the other. He held hers just as tightly, glanced at Lola, and then focused on Ted. "Any idea who they are? Who hired them?"

"Not yet. I mean, they've got identification, and both men have long criminal histories, but we have no idea who hired them. From what I heard this morning, they might not know who it was. It could have been arranged through a third party. We don't know yet, but we will. The bad news is that we now know they have no qualms about using their weapons."

"We knew that last night," Ben said. "How are you doing this morning?"

"I'm sore, and really grateful the bastard was a bad shot. He's the one who died."

"Good." Mandy's comment surprised Ben. She was usually so quiet and sweet-natured, but he agreed with her, and said as much.

She gave him a wobbly smile. Damn, none of this would

be happening if not for him. "I'm really sorry I've brought all this to your doorstep," he said.

Mandy just shook her head. "No. Not your fault they're horrible people."

Lola squeezed his fingers. "She's right. It's not your fault, and it will end."

"Not soon enough." He glanced at Jake and knew his brother understood. As did Marc, and it came as a huge shock when he realized they were all on his side. Everyone in this room.

"I . . ." But he couldn't say anymore. He glanced from one person to another, all of them watching him, worried about him, and he couldn't handle it. He left, but he didn't go far, just out the back door to the small yard where Lola had found him that first night when he'd had his meltdown.

But it was entirely different today. Today he was so damned grateful for the family he'd suddenly acquired that he didn't want to embarrass himself by blubbering like a damned fool. He heard Lola follow him as he went down the stairs.

That was okay. She'd already seen him at his worst.

She slipped behind him and slid her arms around his waist.

"For what it's worth," he said, "I'm not running away. I just didn't want to make a fool of myself."

"Do you want me to go?"

She rested her head against his back. He imagined he felt her lips between his shoulder blades. He shook his head. "No. You've already seen me when I was totally fucked up. This is only a minor meltdown." He sniffed.

"What is it? You looked as if you'd lost your best friend."

That startled a laugh out of him. "Hardly. It just hit me

so damned hard, that even though I've put all of you in danger, you're still behind me. All of you are like my own personal platoon; you've each got my back."

"Of course we do. We love you Ben. Each and every one of us."

He swallowed, thought about what she'd said. "Do you love me, Lola? Really?" He turned and pulled her into his arms. "Because I realized this morning that I love you. That I can't imagine not having you in my life, but it's too soon, isn't it? I mean, how do you know when it's the real thing? It sure feels real." He grumbled and added, "I was planning to ask Jake how he knew that Kaz was the one, even though it happened really fast."

This time Lola was the one overcome with emotion. She buried her face against his chest, and her shoulders shook so hard, at first he thought she was crying. When he tipped her chin up to kiss her, there were tears on her cheeks. "S'okay," she said. "Laughing tears. Not crying ones."

And then she took a deep breath and brought herself under control. "When you left the bed this morning, I knew I was in love with you. And my first thought was to ask Kaz." She snorted, and that made her laugh harder. "Sometimes our minds work so much alike it's scary."

"I hate to imagine what our kids will be like. Combining our DNA could be dangerous."

"If they're like you, Ben, they'll be wonderful. C'mon. They're all probably wondering what's wrong."

"Yeah. Okay." He'd never had to escape an audience before. Nor had he ever had to walk back in and apologize to one. He took Lola's hand and hauled her back up the stairs. She'd come after him. She'd said she loved him. He could do this.

Right now, he figured he could do just about anything. Ben led her back to the kitchen. The table had been cleared, and everyone sat around with their cups of coffee, talking as if nothing had gone wrong. She was so proud of Ben that she knew she must be glowing.

"Okay," he said. "Meltdown's over." He pulled Lola's chair out for her, and she took her seat, but she tipped her head back and smiled at him, encouraging him. He stood behind her and planted his hands on her shoulders. He wasn't hiding. No, he was looking at each of them as he spoke. Definitely a man worth loving.

"This has been a really emotional morning for me." He paused and cleared his throat. "I apologize if I upset anyone. I needed a moment to get my shit together. You see, this morning I just realized that I'm in love with this woman, and that's not an easy thing for a man to wrap his head around. At least not one like me, because I don't like to do the introspective shit or talk about feelings or anything like that, but I was still sort of reveling in the feeling when Mr. Good News showed up."

He glanced at Ted. "Nothing personal Ted, and I mean that, but what you said reminded me that not only the woman I love, but all the others I love are in danger because of their association with me, and yet that association has quickly become the best, most important part of my entire life. I'm too selfish to walk away from you people, my family, so we need to figure out a way to end it. Passively waiting for someone to hurt one of us isn't working, because we're getting hurt."

Ted had been sort of smiling all the way through Ben's little tirade, but now he frowned and interrupted. "Who's been hurt? You're all perfectly safe, or you have been, so far."

Ben pointed his finger at Ted. "You, numb-nuts. You eat at our table, you're part of our family. At least I think that's how it works." He glanced at Lola.

Smiling up at him, she nodded. Then she covered his

left hand with her right. "That's how it works." Ted looked sort of stunned by the inclusion, but that was fine with her. He actually fit into this group fairly well, in spite of the age difference. He had to be close to fifty, but he was every bit as much a misfit as the rest of them.

Forty-plus years old, still single, no one important to him? His life sounded way too much like the direction Ben's had been heading.

Ben leaned over and kissed the top of her head. "Good. We've got that cleared up. So Marc has moved in here, which means Lola and Mandy won't be alone all week while I'm gone. Ted, I don't know if you've got the authority to do this, but is there any way you can get some extra police presence for this neighborhood? If a squad car was occasionally rolling up and down the street, not on any set schedule, but the cops were aware of the issues here, it might discourage some of the blatant intimidation we've been getting. That's what it has to be, this business of parking across the street and watching the house. If they're trying to scare me away from whatever I'm supposed to testify about, they're choosing a really bad tactic, because they're just pissing me off. They're certainly not trying to hide what they've been doing."

Ted was nodding in agreement. "I can do that. I spoke with officers McGowan and Macias this morning, and they've promised to keep a close eye on your place, but I'll make sure the request goes in at the precinct level. I just wish that damned article would hit the newspapers. I have a feeling that once it busts wide open, all this sneaking around will come to a very quick end."

"I know," Ben said. His hands tightened on Lola's shoulders. She felt the tension in him. In the deep growl of his voice and the taut strength of his hands. "That's what concerns me."

* * *

Ben packed up his duffle for the trip back to Camp Parks. He'd decided to leave shortly after dinner, when he was hoping traffic wouldn't be quite as heavy. Mentally he went over the chores he'd wanted to complete today—Marc's apartment was empty, except for the furniture that belonged to the complex, and there were new locks throughout the house, including deadbolts on the bedroom doors, should anyone break in.

That had been Marc's idea, and it made perfect sense. While Ben worked on the locks, including an inside bolt on the main garage door, Marc had replaced the batteries in the smoke alarms and carbon monoxide detectors, and he'd called an alarm company José Macias had recommended. They'd set up an appointment for early Tuesday morning, before he and Lola needed to leave for the office, to see about wiring the house.

The place was as tight as they could make it, but Ben still hated to leave them. Truth? He hated leaving Lola. The idea of sleeping alone all week wasn't at all appealing, and he knew he'd worry about her.

Marc's presence helped, but Marcus Reed was no fighter. He was a truly gentle soul, but he was protective of the girls, and his thoughtfulness today had given Ben an added sense of comfort, knowing he honestly cared about both Lola and Mandy. Ben was going to have to trust him to keep them safe. Officer Macias had stopped by this afternoon. Ben wondered if he had a crush on Mandy—the guy certainly followed her every move while trying really hard not to be obvious.

He hadn't seemed at all pleased to learn that Marc had moved in, until Mandy had explained that no, Marc wasn't her boyfriend. He was just a good friend, staying there to add a level of protection.

Ben had watched Mandy when she'd given Officer

Macias her explanation, and he noticed Lola watching her sister just as closely. He was certain she was thinking the same thing he was, that Mandy was protesting just a bit too much. Marc had seemed oblivious, but he was such an introverted guy that it was hard to know what he was thinking.

Of course, little by little they had all gotten to know Marc better. And the more Ben saw, the more he understood why Marc and Jake had such a close friendship. Marc was loyal, and that was a trait Jake had always valued. It was also the one way in which Ben had totally failed his brother. He was determined to redeem himself, to be worthy of Jake's trust.

He heard the door open and he turned. Lola stood there with an insulated tote bag in her hands. "I packed leftovers for you. Things that will be easy to heat up for dinner. The twice-baked potatoes and some of that pork roast. There's a bowl of Kaz's fruit salad, and . . ."

He'd walked toward her the moment she entered. Now he took the heavy bag from her and set it on the floor beside his boots and wrapped his arms around her. "Thank you. I'm going to miss you like crazy. I'm glad I'm just going across the bay, not across the world." He kissed her and then shook his head. "Gives me a whole new appreciation for the grunts who leave their wives and kids behind. I used to wonder what the big deal was. Did you know that even moms get called up and have to leave their babies, little kids that hardly even know them? It's tough."

Lola wrapped her arms around him and held him close. "I think of how much I missed you last week, and I know I hate it. Were you serious about getting out?"

"Very serious. I'll have my twenty years in by the end of this year. I'm not scheduled for any more overseas deployments, so this is the last leg of my enlistment."

She leaned back in his embrace and studied him for a moment. He loved the way she looked at him, sometimes as if she had to think of which question to ask next, other times as if she was trying her best not to laugh.

This was a serious look. "Will you miss it? Miss the people you met, the guys you served with?"

He shook his head. "All those years, sometimes in horrible situations where we didn't know if we'd get out alive, where some of the guys didn't make it and it was only blind luck that any of us did . . . all those years, all those men, and some pretty tough women, too, and I never once felt the connection the others talked about. That brotherhood that's honed in battle? I didn't feel it. I did my job, followed rules, broke them when I had to, but I didn't feel anything. They were good people, but I didn't want to get close to anyone. There were a lot of good folks I knew I could count on, but I was afraid to have anyone count on me. I didn't know if I had it in me to stick. To actually be there if I was needed."

"Because of Jake?"

"No. Because of me. Jake did everything right, but I failed him in the worst way possible. I believe him when he says he forgives me, but it's going to be a long time before I forgive myself. Before I trust myself. But I will promise you this, Ms. Lola Marie Monroe, I will not fail you. I will do whatever it takes to keep you safe, and I will love you like you've never been loved before."

He kissed her then. Held her close against him and tried to absorb as much of her as he could, her warmth, her scent, the sound of her heartbeat, the feel of her hands clutching his shoulders. He'd never been more afraid in his life. The power she held over him was both terrifying and wonderful, and he never wanted to know what it felt like to be without her.

He hated leaving with so much danger lurking, but he had to trust Lola and Mandy's good sense, and Marc's good nature. Marc wouldn't let anything hurt them. He'd promised them. Promised Lola.

Marcus Reed had proved he was a guy you could count on. All Ben had to do was remember what Marc had done for Jake. What he continued to do for him.

Ben grabbed his boots and his duffel bag, made a detour to the bathroom for his overnight kit, and stuffed it in with his clothes. Lola carried the tote filled with food, and he made a stop in the front room where Mandy and Marc were watching television.

Marc held up his cell phone. "Hey, Kaz just sent an app to me you might want to consider. Look."

Ben leaned over the back of the couch and checked out Marc's screen. "It's a thing that locates your friends. You have to sign up and allow your location, and it pinpoints whoever you're searching for, as long as they're in your app network." He showed Ben where Mandy was, and it pinpointed her here in the house.

"That seems pretty invasive." Lola looked at it. "I might be playing hooky from work, you know, hanging out at the mall and telling you I'm working from home."

Marc laughed. "And I'd catch you. Except I'm now living with you so I'd probably already have figured that out."

"Wiseass." Lola took a swipe at his head and he ducked.

Then Marc quit laughing, his expression went from teasing to serious. "Kaz is worried, as she should be, that there is a risk one of us could get nabbed by whoever is essentially stalking Ben. If Jake hadn't had her tablet with the phone location app, she might have ended up dead. I want you to at least think about adding it to your phones, and adding the rest of us."

Ben grabbed his phone out of his pocket. "I'm in. What is it?"

Marc gave him the name and Ben added it to his phone, as did Lola. While it was loading, he put his boots on because it was getting late and he needed to leave. The longer he stayed, the harder it was to go.

Once the app was loaded, they all added each other. Ben checked and discovered Lola in a heartbeat, and it really did make him feel easier about leaving. "I'll get in touch with Kaz and Jake tomorrow. This really is a great idea. Just don't lose your phone."

"If any of us do, we can have one of you guys find it." Mandy glanced at Ben's duffel bag and then looked at him. "Now I'll be able to tell when you're on nighttime maneuvers, running around in the dark playing soldier with the rookies."

He'd told them about his training missions during the week and some of the stupid stuff that had happened with newbie recruits and reservists. For whatever reason, Mandy had thought the whole concept of pretend battles with reservists was totally off-the-wall. He'd suggested to her it was obvious she had no military background, which had led to Mandy saluting him whenever the timing was as inappropriate as possible.

Damn, he was going to miss Mandy, too. He leaned over and kissed the top of her head. "I'm going to miss your perceptive observations of military life," he said.

She just snorted. He told Marc he'd keep in touch, and then it was just Ben and Lola walking out the front door, down the stairs to the walkway, and down the walk to his car. He stowed the duffel bag and the tote filled with food in the back.

Then he took a good look up and down the street. He didn't see anyone suspicious parked anyplace close enough to worry him. He pulled Lola into his arms and hugged her.

"Call me tonight, let me know you got there okay, and that you're safe."

He could suggest she check the app, but then he thought of those sexy phone calls. "I promise," he said. "Make sure you wear something sexy."

She was laughing when he got into his SUV. He waved, made a U-turn in front of the house and drove north toward the street that would take him across the city to the Bay Bridge. He watched Lola in the rearview mirror, and she stood there on the sidewalk until he finally turned the corner at the end of the street.

It was Sunday night, and he was already counting the hours until Friday.

CHAPTER 19

One month later
Camp Parks, Dublin, CA, June 10

Ben checked his watch for the tenth time in as many minutes. It was a little after ten A.M. and he still had almost seven hours before he was free to bail out for the weekend, but he was feeling so antsy it was hard to sit still. Damn, but he was ready for a break. He and Lola had absolutely nothing planned, which, after the week he'd had, sounded fantastic.

He glanced up as the CO stepped into his office. Booker didn't look happy about something. One thing Ben had learned in his few weeks at the base—the guy had a face you could read like a book.

"What's up, sir?"

Booker took a seat in the chair across from Ben's desk. He sighed, stared at the wall above Ben's head for a minute, and finally looked straight at Ben. "That article's going to hit the *San Francisco Chronicle* in the Sunday morning edition, which means that any shit that hasn't hit the fan already will hit this weekend. Most likely before the paper's on the streets. There'll be Internet teasers, lots of bits and pieces ahead of time. If we know it, you can be god-damned sure the senator knows it."

The air left Ben's lungs, seemingly all at once. "I need to text Lola, let them know." He checked his watch. She would be at Marc's office. Mandy had gone in to work early. He had to go to Lola. He wasn't about to let her deal with this on her own. Before he could ask for permission to leave early, the captain spoke up.

"I'm putting you on leave, beginning immediately. I've got authorization to give you up to thirty days should you need it, with pay, but I expect you to report back as soon as you feel the danger has passed. You may be contacted during this time by US attorneys from the Department of Justice who are working on Senator Ewing's prosecution. Theirs is the office that called so I could warn you about the article, and said your leave was approved should you need it. If you have any questions, be sure and call me."

"Thank you." Ben honestly didn't know what else to say. His car was packed, as he'd been planning to head straight for San Francisco as soon as his workday ended. "I've been both dreading this and just wishing it would happen. I still don't know what my testimony can do or why it's important enough for all this cloak-and-dagger crap. I just want it to be over."

"I understand." Booker held out his hand as he stood. Ben stood as well, and grasped it.

"Good luck, Ben. And I do mean for you to call me, officially or otherwise. Jia and I care what happens to you. Be safe, but please keep in touch. My wife's an even better worrier than I am."

Ben glanced at their clasped hands and felt that stupid lump in his throat. He'd tried to explain it to Lola, how the connections he was building with people scared the crap out of him because they made him feel so vulnerable, and yet here was another one.

She'd told him he was looking at them all wrong—that those connections made a man stronger, not weaker. That the vulnerability made him better; it meant that he was feeling normal, healthy reactions to important human connections. He'd have to take her word on that one, because that wasn't how he felt right now, but he managed a smile. "Please assure Jia I will do my damnedest not to get myself killed. Thank you, sir."

He turned away and grabbed his briefcase, stuffed his laptop inside and checked his desk to make sure he hadn't left anything important undone. He stopped for a moment and went through a quick mental checklist. "I think everything that was at all time-sensitive is done, my reports are filed, and there's no dog to feed. I'm outta here." He started for the door and then paused a moment. "If you hear anything, anything at all that might help me figure out what the hell's going on that's got everyone on my ass, will you call me?"

"Definitely. Now go."

"Yessir!" Ben saluted. "And thank you." Then he turned away and raced out to the parking lot. As soon as he got in the car, he sent Lola a text. He told her the story was coming out Sunday and to tell everyone to be careful. He let her know he was on his way home, and would stop by Marc's office. There was no telling what could be building right now, but Booker was right.

The shit was about to hit the fan.

Lola glanced at her watch. It was almost ten, Ben should be home by six-thirty or seven, depending on the traffic. It was really awful on Friday nights, and this weekend it was bound to be bad, as a lot of schools were letting out and kids were gearing up for the summer.

Marc had gone to a meeting with Jake and Kaz to work on a new advertising campaign for Intimate, and he'd mentioned they might do some test pictures around town. It sounded exciting, tying the jewelry into the wines that were coming out in the fall. Kaz was already becoming a household name, so famous, in fact, that Cassie and Nate had told her—quite seriously—that they'd need to keep all the plans for their August wedding a secret to keep the paparazzi away.

"Paparazzi." Lola laughed as she went through the bills she needed to organize for the accountant. "Who'da thunk it?" She glanced up as the front door opened. "Hi, Bill. What's up?"

Bill Locke, Marc's head of security, was a taciturn, grumpy sort, but Lola thought she got along with him okay. Ben had never cared for the man. He said there was nothing in particular that bugged him, he just didn't like him.

He wasn't all that likable a man, but he appeared to do a good job and Marc trusted him. Lola figured a good working relationship was a better strategy than disliking a man on principle because her boyfriend didn't care for him.

Bill glanced at his watch and then looked at the door to Marc's office. "Is the boss here?"

Lola shook her head. "Mr. Reed had a meeting with his photographer and the model. He promised he'd be back by lunchtime. Anything I can do?"

"Damn." He shook his head. "I'm not sure. There's a really nice lady who's been showing a lot of interest in investing in one of Mr. Reed's charities, that one that sends homeless kids to music camp, but she's leaving this afternoon and won't be back for a couple of months. She wanted to talk to him about the extent of support he wants, what the tax deduction would be, that sort of thing. I got the feeling she was talking a six-figure donation. It's a great charity. I'd hate for him to miss the opportunity."

Marc had sent Lola out a couple of times to talk to po-

tential donors, and both times she'd gotten hefty dona-
tions to his philanthropic causes. "Let me check and see
if Mr. Hadley is going to be here for a couple more hours.
If he is, I can go and talk to her."

"You sure it wouldn't be a problem? I can take you."

"No. I'm fairly well caught up here today." She smiled
as she put her work away in the side drawer of her desk.
"My boyfriend's coming home for the weekend. I don't really have my mind on my job, to be perfectly honest. Getting out of the office yet still accomplishing something
work-related sounds perfect."

Lola headed back to Theo Hadley's office. She'd seen
him come in earlier, but he often left so quietly she didn't
even know he'd gone. The door was partially open, and
Theo sat there at his desk with his laptop open and fingers
flying.

"G'morning, Mr. Hadley. Bill Locke asked me to go
with him to speak to a potential donor for one of Mr. Reed's
charities. Mr. Reed's unavailable this morning, and I wondered if you could cover the phones until I get back? It's
been really quiet all morning and I shouldn't be more than
a couple hours, tops."

"Not a problem. Good luck." He waved and went back
to his computer.

Then she sent a text to Marc, letting him know what was
going on, that she'd be with his head of security. She
grabbed the folder of information about the camp on her
way out the door. Bill was waiting by the elevator.

He glanced at the folder she was stuffing into her over-
sized handbag. "What's that?"

"Information for the donor about the camp. You know,
the cost of running it, hiring teachers, and renting the site.
Mr. Reed paid for the entire camp out-of-pocket last year
and was planning to do it this year, too, until one of his
friends offered to help fund a couple of campers. It sort of

spread, with several other people wanting to help. He hasn't had to ask for money. It's a great program, so he had the brochure printed up in case anyone else showed interest."

They reached the ground floor and went out to Bill's car parked directly in front of the building. It was a dark gray sedan. She wondered if this was the standard security-guy-slash-stalker model of vehicle.

Bill glanced down as he opened the door for her. "What are you smiling about?"

"Gray sedan. This must be the official security-guy car."

Laughing, Bill walked around to the driver's side. "It is. Nondescript, big enough to be comfortable, and gets good mileage."

"I never thought about the mileage. Guess that's important when you're following someone."

"Or parked with the engine running. Ya gotta remember stuff like that." He was still chuckling as he pulled out into traffic.

"Where are we going?" She hadn't even thought to ask him.

"Beautiful digs over in Pacific Heights."

"Really? Hope I'm dressed okay for this." She took a quick glance at her outfit. She'd chosen a black pantsuit this morning with her dark red sleeveless turtleneck sweater. Every time she wore it, she thought of Ben. Knowing he was coming home tonight, she'd thought it might be fun to greet him wearing what he still called her "official love-bite cover-up sweater."

She wondered what he was going to think of her hair. She'd finally had it with the black and had gone back to her natural dark blonde. When she'd had it done, the hair-dresser had added some lighter blonde streaks and she knew she looked good. She also looked a lot different than the girl Ben had fallen for. She could always dye it again, but . . .

Bill glanced over at her. "You look nice. Very professional." He smiled. "Don't worry. You girls always worry about how you're dressed, how you look to everyone. Guys don't think of that stuff."

She sat back and relaxed. Bill was never this talkative. She liked him much better this way. "I know," she said. "And for that alone we women will always carry a certain amount of resentment toward the male gender."

"I knew there was a reason I'd missed." He grinned at her and then focused on his driving.

The traffic was heavy this early in the day, but Fridays were usually a bit crazy in the city. Lola stared out the window as they headed west on Broadway. Before long, they were driving along roads flanked by houses the size of some of the office buildings downtown. Lola hadn't been out here in years. She'd forgotten how beautiful it was, bound by the Presidio to the west and a view of San Francisco Bay to the north.

Bill parked the car in front of a massive home on Baker Street. Lola grabbed her handbag that doubled as a briefcase, and got out of the car. Bill walked with her up the front steps, and she had the craziest sense that he should probably be taking her around to the servants' entrance. She had to force herself not to stare at the beautiful gardens spreading over every inch of ground that wasn't covered by house and high stone wall.

They reached the front door and Bill grabbed an ornate door knocker. He'd barely let it fall when the door opened and a young woman in a maid's uniform opened the door and quietly stood to one side.

Bill nodded to her and led Lola through the massive doors. She had the strangest sense she'd just left reality behind. The interior was immense and open, an entryway that went the full three stories, and while the front of the house was all stone, the walls to the side and the ceiling were glass.

Her first thought, that this wasn't such great planning in earthquake country, flew out he proverbial window as an older woman accompanied by a young man approached the foyer. Lola blinked. And then she blinked again. She knew this woman, had seen this man. "Cissy?"

The woman stopped and glanced at the young man. Then she leaned close and stared at Lola. "Have we met, dear? I don't recall meeting you."

Lola shook her head, but shivers coursed along her spine, and she realized they'd never asked Ted if he recognized the woman in the photo, the one she'd taken at the winery. On the other hand, if she was a fan of Marc's wines, donating to his cause made sense.

Cissy had to be in her seventies, though she was very attractive, probably a combination of good genes, a lot of time with a personal trainer, and some very expensive plastic surgery.

"We haven't met," she said. "You were in some of the photos I took a few weeks ago at the Intimate Vineyards Winery in Dry Creek Valley. My sister was looking at the photos and said she knew you from the coffee shop on Irving Street. Mandy's the barista."

"Oh, she's a lovely girl, don't you agree, Dustin?" She smiled at the man beside her, and then nodded pleasantly to Bill. "It's nice to see you, William. Thank you for delivering Ms. Monroe. Ms. Monroe? Will you follow us, please?" She turned and walked toward a large set of double doors.

Shivers raced down Lola's spine, the horrible realization that something here was not quite right, and Ben was right not to like Marc's head of security. Lola glanced at the man. "Do you want to explain what the hell is going on, Mr. Locke? Why do I have the feeling this has nothing to do with the music camp for homeless children."

His smile wasn't very encouraging. "You're right, Ms. Monroe. Now move it."

He planted his hand in the middle of her back and shoved her forward. Hitching the strap of her bag over her shoulder, Lola followed Cissy and Dustin into the next room.

Ben made great time until he reached the Bay Bridge. He'd just gone past the exit to Treasure Island when traffic came to a screeching halt. There was a California Highway Patrol car up ahead with lights flashing. Ben waited a moment, decided they weren't going anywhere for a while, and got out of his SUV. At least in his ACUs he looked a little more official than if he'd been wearing jeans and a T-shirt. He walked past the stopped cars to find out what the problem was, and how long they'd be.

The CHP officer was pulling a bag of flares out of the back of his vehicle. He turned and grinned at Ben. "Sergeant Lowell! Good morning. Just a fender bender, Sergeant, but there's glass and metal all over the road. They should have everything cleared out within the hour."

Of all the people to run into. "Well, hell. Corporal Benson, right? You were in my training class last week. I don't always get records on what you guys do in the real world."

"This is what I do. Keep good men from going home." He grinned as he shut the trunk. "I'm assuming that's where you're headed."

"You assumed right. Haven't seen my girl all week long."

"I'm sorry to make you wait, but they said it shouldn't take too long. Fridays are bad enough without a couple of drunks getting into it on the bridge."

"Well, damn. Thank you." He went back to the car and settled in to wait. After about twenty seconds of twiddling his thumbs, he got his cell phone out of his pocket and checked to see if Lola had answered his text.

Nothing. He checked e-mail, and then looked at a couple of websites he liked. That held his attention for about five seconds, so he decided to check the app he'd loaded and see if it found Lola in her office. He loved picturing her in there, sitting at her desk, looking so prim and proper. He logged in, did a search, and found her.

Except, what the hell was she doing in Pacific Heights? That was a long way from Marc's office on Battery.

He pulled up a map and looked closer and finally got an address on Baker Street. Took the address and went to street view and got a look at the place. It was massive, one of those older mansions with a view of the bay, not too far from the Presidio. He knew she'd been doing some work for Marc's charities. The guy had his fingers in way too many pies for Ben to keep track of, but Lola loved all the different things she got to do on the job.

He went back to the app and once again found the little dot that identified her. Then he got curious and did a search for Marc, but his dot showed up in Golden Gate Park. Curious, Ben searched for Jake, who it appeared was with Marc, and then Kaz, who was also with them. Photo shoot, obviously. The only other person he had in the app was Mandy, so he ran a search on her.

At least Mandy was right where she belonged, in the coffee shop on Irving. He sent her a text and said he was headed home early, but it was getting close to lunchtime and he didn't want to bother her if she was busy. He checked Lola's location again. Still in the same place, but why was she there if Marc was in the park with Jake and Kaz? He thought they usually went together whenever Lola had an offsite assignment. Marc had once asked him if he was comfortable with Lola going with Bill Locke, but Ben had said no. For whatever reason, Ben just didn't trust the guy. It was weird how his radar went into action whenever Locke was around, but Marc hadn't questioned him, so whatever Lola was doing, she was doing it on her own.

He didn't like that. Not with that damned story ready to hit this weekend, not with chances of it getting leaked ahead of time. Damn.

He sent Lola a brief text saying that he'd be getting home early and he missed her. If she was working, she probably had it on vibrate, so it shouldn't interfere with whatever she was doing, but he hoped she'd answer and put his mind at ease.

He waited a few more minutes and checked Lola's location again.

The light was gone.

"Shit." He turned the app off. Turned it back on. Looked for Marc, and his dot popped up right where he'd been, in Golden Gate Park.

He looked for Lola again. Nothing.

He couldn't find her anywhere, and traffic on the bridge was still at a dead stop.

Lola's cell phone was in her briefcase, and with any luck, Marc would get worried when she didn't show up and he'd use that app to find her. She couldn't call anyone. Bill had brought her into this beautiful room and shoved her down into a chair, and then he'd stood by the big window looking out toward the bay with his arms behind his back, like he was standing watch over a vicious criminal.

"Are you going to tell me why I'm here? And who that lady is? Mandy only knows her as Cissy and her son, Dustin."

"Son?" Bill laughed so hard he had to wipe tears from his eyes. "That guy's not her son, little girl. Dustin's her lover."

"Her lover? Good lord." The woman had to be old enough to be the guy's grandmother. He didn't look more than twenty-five or thirty. "But who is she?"

She heard footsteps and turned toward the door. The woman and her—good Lord, lover?—stood in the doorway. He had his arm around her waist, fingers splayed possessively across her hip. She smiled pleasantly, as if she were meeting Lola at a social event. "My name is Caroline Belinger Ewing," she said. "I am the only child of Thaddeus Ambrose Belinger."

And wife of Senator Burl Ewing. Well, crap. It all made perfect sense, but the old broad didn't need to know that Lola recognized the name. "I would say it's a pleasure to meet you, Mrs. Ewing, but to be perfectly honest, it's not. I've obviously been brought here under false pretenses, and I have no idea what you want with me. I was told you were interested in becoming a donor for Marcus Reed's music camp for homeless kids. If that's not why I'm here, I really need to get back to the office. I have work to do."

She stood and hitched the strap for her bag over her shoulder. Nothing like trying to bluff her way out the door.

Mrs. Ewing and Dustin blocked the door. "You have to give her credit for trying," Bill said. Then he laughed. Lola lunged forward. If she could just get as far as the front door and start screaming bloody murder. . . .

Dustin blocked her way and grabbed her around the waist. Her bag fell off her shoulder and bounced when it hit the floor, and part of her brain registered that the floor was Italian marble and probably cost more than Marc's Tesla. Her cell phone popped out of the side pocket, skittered across the slick surface, and bounced off Bill's shoe. It buzzed loudly, vibrating against the marble.

Bill leaned over and picked it up. "Hmmm . . . looks like a text from the soldier boyfriend. It's not anything important." He held the power switch down until the phone turned off, and then stuck it in his back pocket.

Lola slumped in Dustin's grasp. The app wouldn't work without power.

No one would be able to find her.

CHAPTER 20

Ben punched in Ted Robinson's number. The agent answered immediately.

"I was just going to call you," he said. "That article's going live on Sunday."

"I heard. My captain let me know, said he'd gotten word from one of the attorneys for the prosecution, but I'm afraid we've already got a problem. Do you have any idea who owns this house, or possibly rents it?" He gave Ted the address on Baker Street.

The man didn't even have to look it up. "It's Caroline Ewing's family home, the one her father left to her. Why?"

"I think they've got Lola. I'm stuck in a traffic mess on the Bay Bridge. I have one of those friend location apps on my cell phone. She should be in her office, but she's not. The app placed her at that address on Baker. I tried to send her a text a couple minutes ago. She didn't answer, and the identifier on the app has disappeared. I'm concerned that someone heard her phone and shut it off."

"I'm on my way. Might take me twenty, thirty minutes to get there."

"Thanks, Ted."

Ben spotted the CHP officer walking up from behind, and got out of his car. "Corporal? I've got a really odd request, but it's important. Is there any way you can get me off this bridge? It's a long story, but essentially I'm a witness in a big case that's supposed to hit the news this weekend. I've just gotten off the phone with one of the FBI agents on the case, and . . . shit, man, we think my girlfriend's been kidnapped, probably to keep me from testifying. I think I know where she is, and an FBI agent is on his way, but I need to be there. Can you get me off this fucking bridge?"

"Hold on." He grabbed his radio and turned away, waited a moment with his hand in the air, signaling, Ben guessed, for him to keep his frickin' mouth shut. Damn it all.

Then the officer was running for his car, shouting, "Get in your vehicle, and stay on my ass. There'll be another black-and-white behind you. And let me know what happens."

"Thank you. Will do."

Ben slammed the door on his SUV and pulled in right behind the officer in the emergency lane on the left. A second CHP car raced into the spot immediately behind Ben, and both vehicles used their lights and sirens. They couldn't move at top speed, but they were moving, and Ben had a feeling his new best friend was probably breaking more than one rule.

Both cops peeled off as soon as they got him past the accident and the automobile parts that were scattered across all the lanes. Ben pulled in alongside Benson's squad car and grabbed the card the CHP officer thrust through the passenger side window. "Call me."

"I will. And thank you." Ben saluted the man and headed for San Francisco.

The bridge ahead was entirely clear of traffic.

Lola glanced at her watch. It was almost noon and she'd been sitting in this room with Bill standing guard for at least an hour. The waiting was making her crazy. What were they going to do to her? There was no way anyone would have any idea where she was, not with her phone turned off. And she hadn't told Theo where Bill was taking her, just that she was leaving with him on business.

At noon, the maid walked into the room where Lola sat thrumming her fingers on the arm of the chair. She held the door and gestured politely toward the next room. "Lunch is served. Please follow me."

Lola stood, shaking her head. This was just too f'ing bizarre. She shoved the strap to her handbag over her shoulder and followed the maid with Bill close behind her. The maid held out her chair. Instead of sitting, Lola stood behind it and glared at Dustin, who was already seated next to the old lady. "I would like to know why you're holding me against my will. What have I ever done to you? I don't even know you."

Dustin had remained quiet throughout the morning, but this time he raised his head. "You might not know Mrs. Ewing, but your boyfriend does. Please be seated."

"And if I choose not to sit?"

Bill grabbed her by the shoulders, and shoved her into the chair so quickly she hardly had time to struggle. "You don't have a choice. Stay put."

Dustin merely smiled. "Thank you, Mr. Locke."

Mrs. Ewing turned to him and, with her hand on his arm, said. "Actually, Dustin, that's not quite correct. I believe her boyfriend only knew a few of Burl's associates."

Dustin sighed. "I know, darling, but it's enough to put Burl behind bars for many years. And then think of what will happen to your name? To your father's good name?"

This time it was Mrs. Ewing sighing dramatically. "You're so right. Daddy would be horrified at what Burl's gotten himself into this time. He thought it was all taken care of once that horrible Secret Service agent was gone, but no, the man had to save all his records! And now drugs?" She looked at Dustin with dismay, reminding Lola of a spoiled, petulant little girl.

It was absolutely the creepiest thing she'd ever seen.

Dustin was patting Mrs. Ewing's hand. "We can't do anything about the records, but those things all happened years ago. This latest could not only take Burl down and put him behind bars, it could come back on you, my love."

"But I don't understand how." She shook her head. Then she straightened in her chair and took a deep breath. "We've gotten through other terrible times, Dustin. Terrible times. We'll get through this."

"Actually," Lola said, "I don't think you will. The men who've been watching us? We thought they were hired by your husband, Mrs. Ewing, but that's not right, is it? That was you. But what about the thugs who killed them? *You* hired those men, didn't you, Dustin? That whole Nuestra Familia link was your idea. I'm just wondering what your part is in all of this. The drugs? The connection with the security company in Spin Boldak? Or was that connection between you and Senator Ewing and the security contractor? And with you, too, I imagine, huh, Bill?"

"Shut up, bitch."

Shutting up was the last thing Lola planned to do. The maid was serving them, now. Perfect little plates with perfect little canapés and tiny sandwiches. It was absolutely surreal to know she was sitting here quite possibly in grave danger, pointing out to a killer just how guilty she knew he was.

Probably not her smartest move. Mrs. Ewing picked up a small sandwich and glanced at Lola. Her signal it was time to eat? But what if the food wasn't safe? "I'm really not hungry," she said. "But thank you. It looks lovely, but somehow being held prisoner has a horrible effect on my appetite."

Mrs. Ewing merely looked confused. She took a dainty bite of her sandwich. Dustin stared at Lola. "I'd suggest you enjoy your lunch, Ms. Monroe. It might be a while before you have another meal."

Food was the last thing she wanted, but she sat there quietly while Mrs. Ewing carefully cleaned her plate, with Dustin eating his meal beside her. Lola watched the two of them calmly. At least she hoped she looked calm on the outside, because her mind was spinning in a thousand different directions. Unfortunately, not one of those directions looked very good for her future.

Ben and Ted connected by phone and arrived at the Belinger estate at almost the same time. Ben parked a couple of doors down, but Ted was right in front of a dark gray sedan that had parked in front. He walked down the street and met Ben beside his car.

"Now what?" Ben glared at the huge mansion. He was certain Lola was inside. He recognized the car behind Ted's. "I think that gray Buick belongs to Bill Locke, Marcus Reed's head of security. I've never trusted the bastard. If he's got Lola I . . ."

"You won't do anything. Ben, use your head. Let this play out within the legal system, because I really don't want anything to screw up putting these bastards in jail. Do not jeopardize this operation."

Ben glared at Ted. He hated that the agent was right. "Got it," he said. "Do you have a warrant?"

Ted shook his head. "At this point, there's no probable cause. We have no proof Lola's inside there, or if she is, that she's being held against her will. According to Theo Hadley, Marc's business manager, Lola was going out with Bill Locke to talk to a potential donor for one of Marc's charities. That could be all she's doing."

"She wouldn't turn her phone off. She's very aware of the potential for danger right now."

Ted nodded. "I agree. I plan to go knock on the front door and ask to speak to Lola. I've brought my supervisor into the loop, and Renteria is headed this way, but it would help if you'd pull back just far enough to block the driveway, in case anyone decides to leave."

"Got it." It wasn't much, but at least he was doing something. Ben moved his SUV back about six feet and parked directly in front of the driveway. The garage was built for three cars, so he could only cover a fraction, but it might be enough to slow someone who was trying to escape.

Ted waited for him on the front walk. Ben joined him, and followed Ted to the door, but he stood to one side where he'd be less visible to whoever opened the door.

Ted grabbed the huge brass knocker and brought it down on the door. And then they waited.

Lola sat quietly at the table while Mrs. Ewing, Dustin, and Bill ate dessert. Finally, Mrs. Ewing raised her head and smiled at Lola as if she were a favored guest.

Lola glared at the woman.

A loud knock on the front door startled everyone. Mrs. Ewing dropped her fork. Bill cursed. The maid started for the door, and Dustin shoved his chair back and stood. "Evie? I'll get it."

Lola thought the maid looked frightened, but she nodded and backed away.

Dustin threw his napkin down on the table, and glared at Lola. "Not a word if you want to live through this."

"Dustin?" Blinking slowly, Mrs. Ewing gazed at him. "That's not a very nice way to speak to our guest."

"Quiet, Cissy. This is a job for a man." Dustin patted her shoulder.

Lola couldn't believe it when the older woman blushed and lowered her head. "You're quite right, Dustin. I'm sorry." Then she went back to her dessert.

Lola sat quietly after Dustin left the room. She didn't want to do or say anything that would focus Bill's attention on her. She listened, heard the front door open. First she heard Dustin's soft voice, and then Ted's! She was positive it was him, but she couldn't make out what he was saying.

She shoved her chair away from the table and screamed. Bill's open hand caught her across the jaw, knocking her to the floor. The chair clattered against the slick marble. Bill immediately hauled Lola to her feet, his forearm pressed tightly against her throat so she couldn't make another sound.

"Lola! Move, you bastard!"

That voice was decidedly Ben's. She'd know it anywhere, but she couldn't breathe, couldn't speak. Bill was dragging her out of the room and she couldn't stop him. Everything looked fuzzy, out of focus. Vaguely, she heard Mrs. Ewing cry out, but she sounded much too faint . . . so far away.

Ben shoved past Ted and the idiot trying to keep him outside and raced into a fancy dining room to the right of the entryway. He caught just a glimpse of an older lady sitting at the table, and what looked like the soles of Lola's boots as she was being dragged through a door at the end of the big room.

Jumping over a fallen chair, Ben reached the door just as it slammed shut, but he had his shoulder on it, his weight against the door fast enough, hard enough that the guy couldn't close it. They struggled for a moment and then suddenly the pressure was off. Ben shoved, but something was blocking the door.

He glanced down. Definitely Lola's black boots, but she wasn't moving. Heart pounding from both fear and adrenaline, he carefully opened the door, pushing against her slight weight. He had no idea how badly she might be hurt, so he slowly shoved against the door, pushing against her, sliding her body across the floor far enough that he could step through the opening.

But, was it Lola? Long, dark blonde hair had come loose from a twist of some sort, but he knelt beside her and saw that it was definitely Lola, with a badly bruised face and blood trickling from a split in her lip. He leaned over and checked the artery in her throat, touched the spot where he'd marked her just over a week ago. Her pulse beat strong, if a bit too fast, but at least he'd found it.

He breathed a sigh of relief, leaned close and kissed her. "Sweetheart? Are you okay?"

Her eyes flew open. She sucked in a deep breath, and then another.

"What happened to your face? Did Locke punch you?"

She touched her throat. Whispered roughly, "Yeah. It was Bill. When he dragged me out, he had his arm pressed against my throat. Choking me. Couldn't breathe." She tried to sit up, and Ben got his arm around her, helped lift her until she was upright.

"Want to stand," she gasped, and her voice sounded raw, filtered through broken glass. He helped her to her feet.

She wrapped her arms around him and burst into tears. "So scared, Ben."

"I'm sorry, Lola. So damned sorry." He swung her into his arms and carried her back into the dining room. The man who'd answered the door sat at the dining room table, his blonde hair disheveled, hands cuffed behind him. He was the bastard who'd tried to keep Ben out. The older woman sat next to him, and Ben immediately recognized them as the couple from the winery, but whereas the man looked irate, the woman merely looked confused.

Ted was standing near the door, talking on his phone and looking quite pleased with himself. "Just a minute." He held the phone to his side. "Lola? Are you okay?"

She'd wrapped her arms tightly around Ben, but she nodded her head. Ben hugged her closer to his chest. "Bill Locke got away," he said. "I think he went out through the back. He punched her in the jaw and then dragged her out holding her in a stranglehold. She was unconscious when I got to her, so I stayed with her."

Ted chuckled. "I think you would have stayed with her anyway. Lola, I'm really sorry you've been hurt, but don't worry about Locke. Renteria's got him cuffed out in front. We're waiting for backup."

Ted went back to his call and Ben carried Lola into the next room. The maid was standing against a wall, shaking like a leaf. Lola touched the side of Ben's face. "Put me down, Ben. I want to make sure she's all right."

He lowered her feet to the ground and helped her stand. "Are you okay?"

Lola nodded. She was still shaking when she carefully approached the maid. Ben stayed a couple of steps behind her, in case she stumbled. She still wasn't all that steady on her feet.

Stopping in front of the girl—and being this close to her, Ben realized she was only a girl, barely into her teens—Lola softly asked, "Are you all right?"

The maid sniffed and wiped the back of her hand across her face. "They'll send me back."

"Where? Are you illegal?"

"No." She shook her head for emphasis. "Foster home. The people were awful. I don't want to go back." She grabbed Lola's hands. "I'm so sorry they hurt you. I had no idea what they were doing. I've only been working here a week. The old lady's real sweet, but that guy can be scary."

"Did he hurt you?"

She rolled her eyes, obviously feeling a little less afraid hanging on to Lola. "Not yet, but he keeps watching me. I know that look."

Lola glanced at Ben. It wasn't easy controlling his anger as he dug into his back pocket, pulled out his wallet and extracted one of his cards. No young girl should ever have to "know that look."

"My name is Ben Lowell," he said. "You have any problems, call me. We'll do what we can to help."

"Thank you." She took the card and stuck it into her apron pocket.

"How old are you?" Lola was still holding her hands. Ben wondered if anyone could ever lie to Lola, especially if she was hanging on to you. He knew he couldn't.

"Sixteen."

Lola glanced at Ben, eyes pleading. He wanted to say this was not a puppy to take home to keep, but he only said, "It's entirely up to you, sweetheart." He squeezed her shoulder, and knew exactly what she was thinking. Lola was good at taking in strays.

She'd kept him, hadn't she?

She glanced at him. The bruise on her face was getting darker. What he really wanted to do right now was go outside and punch Marc's security chief. "I just want to make sure she doesn't go back into the system," she said. Then she turned again to the girl. "What's your name? I'm Lola Monroe."

"Evie Saunders."

"Okay, Evie. Stick with me." Lola took the girl's hand and led her back to the foyer where Ted had set up his own little headquarters. City police had arrived while Lola was talking to Evie, and they all appeared to be trading information, so Ben herded the two of them outside to a beautiful little garden off the entryway.

"We're out of the way here, but we should wait. I'm sure they're going to want a statement. Lola? Where's your handbag?" They needed to get in touch with the rest of their group, let them know what was going on.

"Probably still on the floor in the dining room."

"Wait here. I'll go get it." He leaned close and kissed her soundly. Then he left Lola and Evie waiting in the sunshine.

The dining room was empty, but he grabbed a familiar black leather handbag lying under an upended chair. He righted the chair, grabbed the bag, and carried it out to Lola. She grinned at him when he handed it to her. Then she frowned, and cursed.

"What?"

"My cell phone. Bill has it in his pocket. Or he did."

"I'll get it. He's still in the squad car out in front, I think."

He went back outside and found Agent Renteria. His right hand was wrapped in gauze, and there was some blood showing around his knuckles.

Ben pointed toward Locke, visible behind the tinted glass. "The bastard in the back of the squad car took Lola's cell phone. Any chance we can get it back?"

"Hi, Sergeant. Let me check with the officer. He patted Locke down and probably has it."

He was gone less than a minute and returned with Lola's phone. "The officer had it. He thought it was Locke's, didn't realize Locke had taken it from her. This look like hers?"

"That's it. I bought the cover for her."

"Camo?" Renteria laughed.

Ben glanced down at his ACUs. The pattern on the

phone case matched his uniform exactly. "It's so she'll think of me when I'm on base. Thanks."

"You're welcome, and I'm sorry."

"For what?"

"For not warning you in time. We've been watching Dustin Thorpe and Mrs. Ewing, and had our suspicions about Locke, but nothing we could confirm. Ted and I just found out this morning about the article coming out on Sunday, but it appears that Mrs. Ewing has known for a couple of days now. Plenty of time to plan this."

"Are you sure she planned it?"

Renteria snapped his gaze from the front of the house to Ben's face. "Who else?"

"Think about it. Thorpe works for Mrs. Ewing, and, strange as it sounds, he's also supposedly her lover. He's also linked to Senator Ewing and has done some stuff for him. That's what Bill told Lola. Mrs. Ewing doesn't sound as if she's cooking on all burners, to put it bluntly, and I wonder how much of this is Thorpe's doing, with the old lady footing the bill."

"I don't know, but it's something I'll definitely be checking on. Thank you. Is Ted still inside?"

Ben turned and started back toward the front door. "Last time I saw him, he was." He walked back to the house with the agent on his heels, passed Ted, and went straight back to the kitchen, poked around until he found a plastic bag and filled it with ice. Then he wrapped it in a clean kitchen towel he found in a drawer. He took it back to Lola and handed her the bag of ice and the cell phone. "Keep this on your face; it'll keep some of the swelling down. You're gonna have a nasty bruise, though. Can you send a text to everyone, let them know what's going on? I'm going to call Marc. He needs more than a text—I want to tell him about Bill's role in all this, and that you'll be okay."

Lola took the ice and held it against her face. "You're awfully bossy, but thank you." Then she cocked an eyebrow at him. "Don't rub it in, the part about Bill. Marc's going to be really upset that he's vouched for Bill all this time." Then she went to work with the texts.

With Lola's comment in mind, Ben called Marc. "Hey, it's Ben. I'm with Lola over in Pacific Heights. Some bad stuff went down. And Marc? Bill Locke was involved, but Lola's okay.

There was a long silence, than a litany of curses that sounded nothing like Marcus Reed.

"Yeah," Ben said. "That was my reaction, too." He gave Marc the address. "Bill's still sitting out in front, cuffed in the back of a squad car. I thought you might want to come over and have a little chat with your guy."

He ended the call and turned to Lola. "There. I didn't say 'I told you so' even once."

She smiled. "And I appreciate it. A lot."

"One more call," he said. He dialed his CO. "Cap'n Booker? Thank you. Lola's okay now, but she was kidnapped around the time you were giving me leave. Yeah, I got her back. I'm here now, at Mrs. Ewing's house in Pacific Heights, but I wanted to let you know." He glanced out the window as the news vans started rolling in. "I think if you watch the nightly news, you'll get all the details."

Lola glanced up. "Uh-oh. Looks like the cops are headed our way." She squeezed his hand as he ended the call to his captain. "I love you, Ben. Thank you for saving me."

He leaned close and kissed her. "Thank you for loving me." Then he thought of something. "Don't let me forget to make one more important call."

"Who?"

"I need to thank the CHP officer who broke all the rules

and got me across the Bay Bridge when traffic was stopped for a wreck."

Lola sat there and just grinned at him. "I think we really need to talk tonight. Among other things."

He leaned close and nuzzled her neck. "After the other things," he said, and then he kissed her.

"After." She smiled and kissed him back. She was safe, she loved him, and he loved her. It was all good.

CHAPTER 21

"Evie, you're sure you're okay going with Mrs. Bradley?"

The social worker had arrived after a call from the police. She and Evie appeared to know each other, so Lola figured she should stop worrying about the girl. *Should* being the operative word.

She was still worried. Everything this afternoon had her keyed up. She'd been at the house on Baker Street for hours, now, while the investigation went on.

And on.

She really wanted to go home. With Ben.

"I'll be fine. And thank you. Both of you, for everything." Evie hugged Lola, smiled at Ben, and went with Mrs. Bradley to get her things out of the bedroom where she'd stayed last night. Lola watched the two of them until they'd gotten into Mrs. Bradley's car and pulled away from the curb. Then she let out a long, frustrated sigh. "I'm not usually so wound up," she said.

"Getting kidnapped will do that to you." Ben gave her a hug. "Try to relax, hon. Dustin's on a no-bail hold and Mrs. Ewing is on her way to the hospital for a checkup. I don't think she even realizes what's happened here today."

Lola shook her head. "I dunno, Ben. I don't believe for a second that the old bat's as far gone as everyone seems to think. She knew exactly what was going on today, and she didn't even flinch when Bill hit me. I think she actually enjoyed it."

"I'd really like to kill the sonofabitch."

"Good." She kissed him. "If you get the chance, I won't stop you."

Ben hugged her close. "Bloodthirsty wench, aren't you?"

"Maybe a little. I think it's worse, because I trusted him. Marc trusted him."

Ben shrugged. "I didn't."

She raised an eyebrow and glared at him. She really didn't need to hear any I-told-you-so's right now.

Ben kissed her. "Sorry. Guess that was uncalled for."

"Ya think?" But she kissed him, just so he'd know there were no hard feelings. "Though I do intend to pay more attention to your hunches in the future."

"Lola?" Marc stepped into the dining room where they'd been sitting. He had Mandy with him. "Are you okay?"

Lola stood and gave him a hug. "I'm fine. Ben was my white knight, riding to the rescue, though I think it was Ted's partner who euphemistically slew the dragon."

"Renteria?" Marc glanced toward the front of the house where the two agents were talking to the police. "He told me he thinks he busted a couple of his knuckles on the bastard's jaw. I am so sorry, Lola. Guess I should have trusted Ben's instincts. Ben, you're going to have to vet any of my future security people. For now, I think I'm staying away from all of them. I can't believe he suckered me like he did. I like to think I'm smarter than that."

"For what it's worth, you're not the only one." Lola still felt like an idiot for trusting him. "I should have known something was wrong when he was so friendly. Before today, he was barely civil to me."

Mandy had moved close to Lola and slipped her arm around her waist. "The sad thing is," she said, "It's human nature to want to trust people. Scum like Bill and Dustin, and even Mrs. Ewing, make it hard not to be cynical."

Lola rested her head on Mandy's shoulder. "That really does make me sad. I'm glad you're here," she said. "What a day."

Mandy hugged her tighter. "Marc told me what happened. Are you okay?"

"I am. I think I was more pissed off than scared, if that makes any sense. I only got scared when Bill took my cell phone and turned it off. I'd been thinking that someone would notice when I didn't show up at home; they'd use that app to get to me. But when Bill turned off my phone . . ." Lola's voice cracked.

Ben leaned over and kissed her. "That's how I found you. Sitting in traffic on the Bay Bridge while they cleared an accident, I looked you up and saw your dot at this address. I texted you, but you didn't answer, and then when I went to check back on your location, you were gone. That's when I just about had a heart attack, stuck in traffic for what could have been hours. It was pure luck that I knew the CHP officer controlling traffic. He got me off the bridge."

"When you sent me a text, Bill had just picked up my phone. He saw your name come up on the screen and that's when he shut it down."

"Poor timing on my part. I'm sorry."

"I'm not. I'm safe and so are you. The fact that he turned it off made you worry enough to come rescue me. I can't imagine them going after any of us again after this plan went so badly."

"I certainly hope not."

Ted walked in. He looked exhausted. "I think we can all clear out for today. I still need to talk to you guys, but

I'm beat and I imagine you'd like to get home. I'll get in touch with you tomorrow."

"You're welcome to come for dinner," Lola said. "Marc's buying."

"I am?" Marc actually chuckled. There hadn't been much cause for laughter today. "Not a problem. It's the least I can do. This is my fault, Lola. I'm so sorry."

"No, it's Bill Locke, Dustin Thorpe, and Caroline Ewing's fault. Quit apologizing. You're buying dinner because I doubt you want to cook, and Mandy fixed it last night. As the kidnappee, I'm claiming a night off."

Marc hugged her. "I think you're entitled. Ted, please join us. Any questions you have, you're welcome to ask over dinner and some good wine."

"That's the best invite I've had today. I'm too hungry and grumpy not to take you up on it. Can I bring anything? I hate sponging off you guys. You've all been so generous."

"Yeah," Ben said. "Real generous. We're keeping you gainfully employed and all."

"There is that. Let's get out of here. The police are ready to lock up. Lola? Did you get all your stuff? Did anything spill out of your bag in there?"

"I have no idea." She turned to go look, but Ben put a hand out and stopped her. "I checked when I got it for you. The floor was clean—no sexy girly stuff or anything the least bit interesting lying around."

She made a face at him. "Then I'm good to go."

Mandy leaned over and gave her a hug. "I'm going with Marc. I want to make sure he picks out edible stuff."

"You're no fun." He grabbed Mandy's arm and hauled her out the front door.

Lola and Ben followed Ted, but Lola stopped on the front porch and gave Ted a hug.

"What's that for?"

"For showing up with Ben today. For saving my butt.

This could have been a whole lot worse if not for you, and I want you to know I do appreciate you, horrible FBI agent that you are. Come and eat, but if you want to stop by your place first, you've got time. We'll save a place at the table for you."

"Thanks. I'll be over in about half an hour. That okay?"

"Perfect. See you later." Lola waved and then got into Ben's car when he held the door open for her. "Did you remember to call the CHP guy?"

He chuckled. "I did. Told him that thanks to him, I'd saved the lady in distress and all was well, and to be sure and watch the nightly news for details."

"I was so out of it when that news guy stuck the microphone in my face. I probably sounded like an idiot."

"You sounded sharp and brave, and very fed up with these people who keep bothering us. I was so proud of you."

He kissed her, closed her door, and walked around to his side. She sat there, thinking of what he'd just said. He was proud of her. She couldn't remember anyone ever saying they were proud of her. Certainly not her mother, who considered both Lola and Mandy to be dull, uninteresting young women who led boring lives. After today, Lola figured she was just fine with boring. And Ben was proud of her.

She held his praise close to her heart all the way home.

Mandy had directed Marc to a place that specialized in takeout comfort food. They'd brought home a couple of roasted chickens, mashed potatoes and gravy, and mixed fresh veggies roasted in some sort of vinaigrette that had everyone eating way too much and dipping their sourdough French bread in the sauce.

Mandy had been setting everything out on the table when Kaz and Jake showed up. They'd already left the photo shoot before Ben got in touch with Marc, and only knew what was going on from the text message Lola had sent.

Kaz got Lola and Ben off to one side after dinner. "Are you okay? That's a horrible bruise. I can't believe Marc's security guy did that to you."

Lola ran her fingers over her swollen jaw. "It still hurts, but I'm okay. I keep telling myself it could have been a lot worse. Ben got there just in time."

"I know." Kaz grabbed Ben's hand. "You and your brother are pretty good guys to have around."

Ben wrapped his arms around Kaz and hugged her. "Kaz, neither of you would have been targeted if not for us. Actually, if not for me, because Jake was totally innocent. I will never forgive myself for putting you and my brother, and now Lola, in danger."

"Never's a long time, bro." Jake looped his arm over Ben's shoulders. "I keep telling you, let it go."

Ben snorted. "I'd love to, but it won't let me go. Not when it keeps messing with our women."

"There is that, but this had nothing to do with our incident twenty years ago. This was something even you're totally innocent of, as hard as that is to believe."

"Gee, thanks."

"Kaz and I are headed out. She has to be bright and perky for a morning shoot in Marin."

"What is it with these damned photographers and their morning shoots?" she grumbled. "Why can't you take photos at sunset?"

"It's all about the light, sweetheart." Jake glanced across the room at Marc and Ted. "Thanks for dinner, Marc. We're gonna go. I'll have the proofs from today's shoot for you by tomorrow afternoon."

"Thanks, Jake."

Ted left shortly after Jake and Kaz. The house seemed

quiet after so much noise, and even though it was early, Lola was yawning and looked ready to collapse. Ben went in and took a quick shower, but when he got back, Marc was the only one—besides Rico—left in the front room. He sat on the couch looking very much alone, holding a beer and staring at nothing. A couple of empty bottles were lined up on the coffee table in front of him.

He'd been really quiet since everyone left after dinner, and while he was normally a fairly quiet guy, Ben wondered what else was going on in his friend's head. He went into the kitchen and grabbed a beer for himself, and then sat on the couch on the end opposite Marc. Rico sprawled across the entire center cushion with his head in Marc's lap.

Ben sat there, sipping his beer, thinking of all the emotional highs and lows he'd been through today. And then he tried to see it from Marc's point of view. The guy had to be a wreck. He cared about Lola and Mandy. And his employee, someone he was quite close to, had betrayed him. In fact, Locke had probably been plotting this for quite some time.

"You going to be okay, Marc?"

Marc turned his head and stared at Ben. He shrugged one shoulder, but he didn't say anything.

"What does your chief of security do? What were Bill's duties?"

Marc blinked, and Ben could almost see the wheels spinning. All he needed was something to think about other than what had happened to Lola.

"He handled everything. All of it, from the physical property I own around the city, to the computer equipment, artwork, and that sort of thing at the office on Battery. Some of the software projects I'm getting into are classified, which means the computers have to be stored in a special locker when I'm away from the office, and Bill was cleared to keep an eye on the equipment."

He rolled his eyes. "Obviously that clearance is no good, and I'll have to have a security check run on stuff to make certain nothing's been compromised. One more issue to deal with." Sighing, he took another sip of his beer. "He was supposed to make a physical check of the various properties I've got around the city, make sure there aren't any problems with tenants, but I told him when I hired Lola that his most important job was to be there to keep Lola safe when I wasn't in the office." He took a couple of deep breaths, and then buried his face in his hands. "Shit, man. He could have killed her. You kept telling me you didn't trust him, and I just figured you were being paranoid."

He raised his head and stared at Ben as if he still couldn't believe what had happened. "His credentials were excellent, references were good." He cursed, low, harsh words aimed at himself. "Of course they were. They were written by Dustin Thorpe and Senator Ewing. I'd never made the connection until I pulled up the files on my laptop tonight and checked to see who'd written his letters of recommendation. Burl Ewing and Dustin Thorpe, except he's been with me for a couple of years, and they had no idea I'd ever be a link to you guys."

"No, but if Thorpe's a crook, you're a link to a lot of big money projects. Is Bill your only security guy, or did he have people working under him?"

"He hired temps when we had need of extra bodies. A couple of guys that he calls on regularly for events and such. Like for the premiere a couple of weeks ago." Suddenly he sat up and stared at Ben. "The accident! The guy driving the Toyota that slammed into my Tesla? I knew I recognized him. It was one of the men Bill hired to work security for the premiere. Damn it all. I need to call Ted tomorrow and let him know. That's too big a coincidence for Bill not to be involved. But does the regular work he did for me have anything to do with what happened today? I can't imagine how they could have known of a link between you and me."

Ben took another swallow of beer. "I think he used his position to find out more about you. You're worth a lot of money, but I imagine that when Lola went to work for you, that was like a gift from the gods."

"I know. I thought I was offering her a good job that would keep her safe. Look what happened . . ."

"It was not your fault, but you need someone you can trust handling your security. That's what I do, Marc. I run security operations for the army. I've always reported to an officer in charge, but essentially, I'm the one who calls the shots. Embassies, dignitaries visiting war zones, contractors doing work for the government in hot areas, that sort of thing. I've got security clearance up the ass. If you're willing to take a chance on me—and to wait until I get my discharge in a few months—I'd like to apply for the job."

Marc's head came up and he stared at Ben. "Are you serious? You'd work for me?"

"Why wouldn't I? You're smart, you've got great ideas, and you're successful. Plus, you're really well-diversified." He chuckled softly. "I doubt I'd have time to be bored. And you've got a really hot office manager. Of course, this would only work as long as you don't have trouble with office relationships."

"Ben, I don't know what to say. Of course I want you. Hell, I'd hire you today if you were available, but I can get a temp service in until you're free to come to work for me." He held out his hand. "You willing to shake on it? I don't want you backing out."

"Not a chance." Ben shook hands with Marc. "Thank you. That's been my one worry, that I didn't know what

I'd do once I got out of the military. If you need any background info, education, that sort of thing . . ."

"You're smart, obviously know your way around weapons." Marc shrugged. "I don't know that a formal education is necessary to do a good job."

"Yeah, but I'm proud of the fact that I got my MBA along with a degree in history. Originally, I wanted to be a teacher, but then I got interested in business. I've taken classes the entire time I've served. It's funny, because Jake and I were talking about our education, the fact that neither of us took the traditional route, and yet we both ended up getting higher degrees than we might have if we'd done things like normal kids."

"That says a lot about the kind of men both of you are. It's all good." Marc stood and gathered his bottles. "I think I've had enough to drink tonight. Ya know, in a way, I'm jealous of both you and Jake. I never finished college. I've made a bloody fortune in software development and I still think of it as playing with code, but I dropped out midway through my freshman year. I've often felt that I missed the college experience."

"Jake and I did most of ours online. I needed that degree to help me feel better about myself. Jake said he did it to find out for sure what he liked best, what he wanted to do with his life once he was out of the CYA. Point being, you do what works. Marc, don't feel badly about any of what happened today. We're going to get through it, and we'll all be fine. It's not your fault, just as it isn't mine or Lola's. She's feeling guilty for trusting Bill, but she'll get over it. So will you. Hopefully, Bill will have some time behind bars to think about it, too. Have a good night."

Marc nodded and went into the kitchen to dump his bottles in the recycling bin. Ben took a quick look outside. There weren't any cars parked in driveways along the street, and a patrol car rolled slowly by as he stood in the shadows at the top of the stairs.

Rico got up and waddled down the hallway to Mandy's room. Ben followed the dog and pushed the door open so the old dog could go sleep beside his favorite person. Then he went into the bathroom, brushed his teeth, and got ready for bed.

Lola would be waiting for him, but he wouldn't bother her. Not tonight. Tonight he just wanted to hold her close.

When he got to the bedroom, however, Lola, appeared to have other ideas.

She pulled the covers back when he walked into their room, and he crawled in beside her. "I thought you were asleep. Hope I didn't wake you."

She slid up close beside him, laid her head on his chest and wrapped her arms around him. "I was awake. I heard you and Marc talking." She kissed his chest. Parts lower began to stir. "I feel so badly for him, and at the same time, I feel really stupid for not listening to you. You never did trust Bill."

He ran his fingers through her hair. Her long, dark blonde hair. "But Marc did, and he's the man you work for. And I couldn't give a good explanation about my feelings toward Bill, so there was no reason to pay attention."

"I will from now on."

He laughed and pulled her up over him so he could kiss her. "I certainly hope so. By the way, have I told you how absolutely gorgeous you are with your hair this color? I mean, the black looked great, but this is even better. Why'd you color it?"

"Have you noticed how much I look like Mandy?"

"Now that you mention it, yeah. Much more noticeable with the lighter hair color."

"Exactly." She propped herself up on his chest and glared at him, though the slight twitch to her lips was a dead giveaway. "I do not want my man fantasizing about sex with my sister when he's doing the hot and nasty with me. Got it?"

"Not a problem." He laughed out loud and shook his head, but something in her eyes didn't ring true. "So that's the only reason?"

Her smile slipped and she glanced away. Rarely did Lola not make eye contact. He used two fingers beneath her chin and turned her face to his. "What?"

She shrugged. "Mandy and I both look like our mother. I don't ever want to be anything like her, and I colored my hair so that I wasn't looking at her face every time I looked in the mirror."

He leaned close and lightly kissed her lips. "So what made you change it back?"

Her smile was wide and beautiful. "You. The stuff we've had to deal with. The way you make me feel about myself. I wanted you to know who I really am, what I really look like." She kissed him, but then she pulled away before he could deepen the connection. "I realized that I'm not my mother. I'm strong. I've done a lot with my life without any support beyond Mandy's, and I have nothing to be ashamed of. I'm a better woman than my mother will ever be, and I'm not going to let her make me feel like I'm less than I am."

"Good, because you're all the woman I could ever want." He kissed her longer, deeper this time. "And I promise never, ever, to pretend you're Mandy. Mandy doesn't do it for me. You do."

She laughed. "Good to know." Then she reached for a condom and started working her way down his body, nibbling and kissing until she reached the crease above his left thigh. The thick fall of her hair swept over his erection and tickled his balls. Working behind the curtain of her hair, she slipped a condom over him, and the gentle touch of her fingers behind all that blonde hair was the most erotic experience he could recall. Lying still was a struggle.

When she dragged her hair across his belly, he quit trying, wrapped his arms around her and rolled the two of them over. She was giggling, but Ben was deadly serious.

He settled between her raised thighs and filled her in a single thrust. Her laughter ended on a soft sigh, and a quiet whimper. She wrapped her legs around his waist and held him close, and Ben groaned, caught in the silken beauty of her skin, the warm clasp of her hands clutching his shoulders, her legs locked tightly around him, her feminine sheath rippling around his thick length.

"I love you," he whispered. "God, how I love you. I can't believe you're mine."

"Always," she said, planting kisses along his jaw, against his throat. "Always. You are mine, Ben Lowell. Don't you ever forget it."

CHAPTER 22

Lola went straight for the coffee on Saturday morning. Ben's side of the bed had been empty when she woke up, but it was still early. She took her cup to the table and had just spread out the morning paper when Ben walked in from the garage.

"Good morning, sleepyhead."

She scrunched up her face to focus on the clock. "It's not even seven. It's Saturday. Why are you up so early?" And why did he look so damned good? Wearing boots, old jeans, and a faded sweatshirt, and he still looked yummy. Men had it easy. Life was so unfair.

He grinned and she had a feeling he knew exactly what she was thinking. "Unlike some in this room, I've been working. Marc and I have been going through his boxes, figuring out what can stay and what needs to go. I had no idea you had such a big storage area behind the garage— or an extra bathroom. Why didn't you say anything? Marc and I can use that one so we don't intrude on your girly domain."

"I forgot it was down there." She, Mandy, and Kaz had actually done just fine with the one upstairs, and it was cold and dark down in the garage. "It's all yours. You use it, you clean it, though."

"I think we can handle that." He laughed.

Damn, he had the sexiest laugh.

"Get some clothes on, comb out the tangles in that beautiful blonde hair of yours, and get your sister out of bed. Be ready to go in ten minutes. I'm taking you and Mandy to breakfast."

She sipped her coffee and glanced at the door. "Where's Marc? Isn't he coming, too?"

"Yes, he's coming, too." He leaned over and kissed her. "Are you always this grumpy in the morning? Maybe we need to rethink this being in love stuff."

She flipped him the bird, grabbed her coffee, and headed back to the bedroom to change, with a quick detour to pound on Mandy's door. She had no intention of rethinking anything. She loved him. He was hers. She almost told him to get over it, that he knew she was not a morning person, but he'd obviously figured that out.

She'd told him about a tiny little cafe on Irving, east of Nineteenth Avenue, and it was early enough that the place was just about empty. Ben herded them all inside and they found a table. Within a couple minutes they'd ordered, had their coffee served, and Lola felt as if she was actually beginning to relax.

Yesterday had been a harrowing experience, one she didn't care to repeat.

Before long, Marc had them all laughing with a story about one of his first software projects that had gone totally haywire. She'd not realized what a good sense of humor he had, but he'd really loosened up a lot since moving in with them, and even though he was her boss, he was a terrific roommate.

Life was looking good.

Ben's phone chimed. He glanced at the screen and stood. "I have to take this—it's a two-oh-two area code." He went outside.

"Two-oh-two?" Lola glanced at Marc. "Any idea where that is?"

He nodded. "Washington, DC. I imagine it's someone from the Department of Justice. Ben said yesterday's attack on you and the article coming out tomorrow could finally get this case moving."

"Great. I had just had the thought that things were finally looking good. I guess that's tempting fate, to think happy thoughts." She shook her head. "What a talent. I guess it's nice to be good for something."

Marc reached across the table and took her hand. "You're good for a hell of a lot more than tempting fate, Lola. Don't you ever forget it."

He was so serious that she turned her hand into his and squeezed. "Thank you. I was being snarky, but I think it's going to take me a while to get over all the excitement yesterday."

She glanced up as Ben stepped back inside the restaurant. He was stuffing his phone back into his hip pocket, and his expression wasn't at all promising.

He sat down and sipped his coffee. "That was the US Attorneys' Office. I didn't think I'd hear from them this weekend, but they've got all the copies of my notes from the time when I was in Spin Boldak. It appears they've found a lot in there they can use, and want to go over it with me."

"Do you have to fly to DC?" Lola hated to think of him leaving again. He'd just gotten home.

"No. They've got a local team and they're coming out this afternoon to talk to me, so it looks like I'll have to hang around." He wrapped his fingers around Lola's. "I'm sorry, hon. I was hoping we could take a ride, get out of town. Maybe tomorrow."

The waiter arrived, set their food on the table, and quickly left.

"Not a problem." Lola took a big bite of her hash browns. "You got me out of the kitchen and this is so good! When will they be here? We've got laundry to do, anyway."

"Around one. Think of some chores to keep me busy, okay?"

She knew he wasn't very patient. Why did she keep thinking this whole situation still had all the markings of turning really ugly?

"Working off a little nervous energy here?"

Ben looked down from the branches of the huge old tree he'd been trimming. Lola stood at the bottom of the steps by the back door with her arms folded across her chest. The pile of branches and deadwood he'd cut out of the old ficus tree was taller than she was, and Lola wasn't short. He had no idea what he was going to do with all of it, but it really had needed a good pruning.

And he'd really needed to work up a sweat. "What time is it? I left my watch in the bedroom."

"It's twelve-thirty, and you need a shower."

"Ya think?" He started down the tree, climbing hand over hand on branches spaced like the rungs of a ladder. "I'm going to need some twine so I can tie this stuff up, haul it out of here."

"You can carry it through the back of the garage after the attorneys leave. That door on the back wall goes through the storage area you and Marc found yesterday, and then into the main garage. We can call and have it hauled off."

"Sounds good." He set the clippers on a workbench at the back of the house and stopped long enough to give Lola a kiss before heading inside for a shower. Twenty minutes later, he was clean and dressed in relatively presentable jeans and an ivory knit V-neck sweater. He'd even taken the time to shave, but that was more for Lola than who-ever was due to show up.

He had no idea what they were going to talk about, what they wanted to know, or what they already knew. He couldn't even be sure the people coming had read the material he'd turned over to them.

There'd been a lot of stuff, and he'd kept copies of all of it, though he'd given them his original notes. Schedules, names, places, questions he'd had about what they were doing. So many questions, but his CO in Spin B had told him to keep his mouth shut and follow orders, that there was a pretty powerful senator behind whatever was going on.

The CO, a major, had been a career officer with less than a year until retirement. There was no way in hell he wanted to make waves, and he'd figured if he didn't know what was going on, then no one could ask him about it, but Ben had been curious. He might not have asked, but he'd written those questions down and wondered about an awful lot.

He still wondered about the bombing, the death of the security contractor and the innocent folks around him. That was no terrorist attack—according to Captain Booker, it was a hit, pure and simple. Everyone over there seemed to know about it, though no one had ever indicated that he was a target, not until Captain Booker had come along. The captain had filled in some of the empty spots in Ben's theories, but he hoped the two people coming today would be able to tell him more.

He heard Mandy talking out in front. She'd taken Rico for a walk, and as far as he knew, she was out there talking to the dog, but he went to the front door anyway. Mandy was leading a young man and a middle-aged woman up the stairs.

"Hey, Ben. These folks are here to see you." She squeezed by him and took Rico inside.

Ben stepped aside and held the door open. "I'm Ben Lowell," he said. "Come in."

Dara Janns and her assistant, Jerome Zeeder, showed their Department of Justice ID badges to Ben. He took the time to look at them and check the names against their photos. Not that they couldn't have been forged, but he was definitely growing more paranoid about this case as each day passed. He shook hands with each of them and closed the door behind them. "I thought we'd go into the kitchen in case you needed to use the table."

"Perfect. Thank you." Janns was obviously in charge of the team. She followed directly behind Ben with Zeeder trailing as he led them through the front room to the kitchen. They all took seats around the table.

"Before we start," Ben said, "I wanted to ask if my roommates could be in here for the discussion. I'm not sure if you're up on the latest, but my girlfriend was kidnapped yesterday by Senator Ewing's wife and her twenty-something-year-old boyfriend. The man who actually snatched her was head of security for another of our roommates, so they're involved in this to the point that their lives are being impacted by the case."

Ms. Janns stared at him, sort of a deer-in-the-headlights look. Then she grinned, as if she wasn't sure if he was putting her on or not. "You're saying Caroline Ewing has a boyfriend in his twenties? You do realize she's seventy-six years old, right? Her husband is almost eighty, but he's still a powerful figure in the senate."

"Yes, ma'am."

She just shook her head. "Actually, we'd heard a bit about yesterday's events, and had hoped to speak to the young woman involved." She glanced at her notes. "That would be Lola Monroe? And you're saying the other room-mate's employee was involved in the kidnapping?"

"Marcus Reed. He owns Reed Industries, Intimate Wines, the Intimate jewelry line, and a number of other businesses, and his head of security, William Locke, is currently being held at the county jail. So is Dustin Thorpe, the boyfriend."

"What about Mrs. Ewing?"

"She was not booked, most likely due to her age. My girlfriend disagrees with that—she said, and I'm para-phrasing here, 'The old bat knew exactly what was going on and actually seemed to like the fact that I got punched in the face.'"

"Is she here? Your girlfriend? Is Mr. Reed available as well?"

"I'll get them."

He brought Mandy, Lola, and Marc back to the kitchen, introduced them, and everyone took seats around the table.

Jerome Zeeder opened his briefcase and brought out a tripod and small video camera. He asked everyone's per-mission to use it, and then set it up. Then Ms. Janns began her interview. She asked pointed questions of Marc, Lola, and Ben regarding the events of the day before. She had a copy of the police report and made notes all over it. Her atrocious handwriting explained the need for the video camera, and Ben said as much.

She laughed. "My father always said I should have been a doctor because I had the penmanship for it, but I'm much too cynical. Law's a better match."

She questioned Marc about Bill Locke's background and the work he'd done for Marc, got Lola's entire story in more detail than Ben had gotten from her, and then asked Mandy if she had anything to add.

"A couple of weeks ago, Lola, Ben, and Marc, and Ben's brother Jacob and his fiancée, Kaz Kazanov went to Marc's winery up in Sonoma County. Lola was showing me some of the photos she'd taken in the tasting room, and I recognized a couple of customers of mine from the coffee shop where I work. I didn't know their full names, but I definitely recognized them. We didn't find out until yesterday who they were—Cissy Ewing and Dustin, only I thought Dustin was her son. I only knew her as Cissy."

"Okay, so they were at the coffee shop where you work, the winery you," she pointed at Marc, "own," and then to Lola, "And Mr. Lowell says that you don't think Mrs. Ewing is nearly as befuddled as she tries to appear."

Nodding, Lola said, "Exactly. Something's not quite right, but I definitely suspect she's not as confused as she'd like everyone to think. To be honest, the whole thing with her and Dustin is just creepy. Anyway, I was brought to her house, invited in for lunch, and when I quickly realized that things were not what they appeared, I said I was leaving. It was then I was told that I couldn't leave. They all sat at the table and forced me to sit as well—that's when Bill slammed me into my seat—and they proceeded to have a very formal lunch. With maid service, I might add. And that's another thing. The maid said she's only sixteen years old. Apparently, they hired her from a foster family that treats her badly, which is why she went, but she was afraid of Dustin. Said she didn't like the way he watched her. Her name is Eva Saunders. She goes by Evie. She left yesterday with a social worker named . . ." She turned to Ben. "What was her name?"

"Mrs. Bradley," Ben said. "I didn't get a first name."

"Have you given this information to anyone?"

Ben glanced at Lola before he answered. "Ted Robinson, the FBI agent who's been working on the case. He's the one who helped me rescue Lola yesterday."

"Fascinating stuff. None of this is why we're here, except it sounds as if it's all part of the same case. It has to be. We'd heard about the kidnapping, but none of the particulars." She glanced at the clock on the wall over the door. It was almost five. "Is that the right time? I'm sorry. We didn't intend to ruin your entire Saturday."

"It's not a problem," Ben said. "These people, whoever they are, are the problem. They've turned our lives into a nightmare. Marc moved in so the girls wouldn't be alone while I'm at Camp Parks because we've had stalkers and vandalism, which has kept us on edge. I'm currently on a thirty-day authorized leave, thank goodness, because I'm more comfortable with the two of us here keeping an eye on things."

"Do you mind if we take a bit more of your time? We haven't even gone over the material you brought back from Spin Boldak. I'm hoping you can fill in some of the blanks."

Mandy and Lola excused themselves, but Marc stayed on. It was after six before Zeeder and Janns turned down Lola's invite to stay for dinner, and finally left.

"You've been extremely helpful, Mr. Lowell." Ms. Janns shook his hand again. "Your dated notes corroborate a number of shipments of morphine base that DEA officers were able to pinpoint and tag coming out of that area. The photo you'd taken of that one shipment of cash in the torn box has been invaluable. There's a serial number showing on the partially exposed hundred dollar bill that's linked to a money exchange that matches a list of bills the DEA sent over as evidence in this investigation. Corroborative evidence like that is pure gold."

"I've got one question I just thought of" said Jeremy Zeeder, who had remained in the background throughout most of the day. "Did you ever meet the owner of the security company, or were all your dealings with Arnold Hendrickson, the on-site security manager?"

"I met a guy in the very beginning named Robert Lassiter. He seemed awfully young to be the owner of a security firm—I don't think he was even thirty when we met. Seemed pretty sharp. The only reason I thought he might be the owner, or at least a manager, is because Hendrickson deferred to him on everything. I only saw him the one time. The date's in my notes. I can't recall if I wrote out his full name or just noted it as 'RL.'"

"Thank you." Janns jotted the name down, finished gathering her papers, and stowed them in her briefcase. "You've got my card. If you think of anything, or if anything happens that might be connected to the case, please give me a call. I appreciate your willingness to spend your day off going over all of this."

"Like I said earlier, I just want it to go away, and if my testimony will speed things along, you're welcome to it."

He stood in the doorway and watched them leave, aware he was also checking to make sure there wasn't anyone parked nearby, watching.

What was that line from *Catch-22*? Oh, yeah . . . *Just because you're paranoid doesn't mean they aren't after you.*

Dinner was simple. Lola heated up soup and Mandy made sandwiches. Kaz called to make sure everyone was okay, that no one had gotten kidnapped or shot at, and they all laughed at her flip comments, but when the call ended, Lola felt like a balloon that had lost all its air.

"I don't get it." She sat at the kitchen table with a glass of wine. Mandy had taken Rico for a short walk, and Ben and Marc were cleaning up. "I haven't done anything physical today, but I'm absolutely exhausted."

Marc glanced over his shoulder. "It's stress. I feel the same way."

"Like someone pulled your plug?" Ben laughed.

"Though in your case, Marc, I imagine someone would have to take out the batteries. You strike me as a wireless sort of guy."

Marc just laughed. "Sort of the same way you're coal powered?"

Ben pulled an imaginary steam whistle and made train noises.

Mandy walked into the kitchen in the midst of the sound effects and looked at the guys like they were nuts. She glanced at Lola.

"I have no idea," Lola said. Then she put her head down on the table and laughed until she cried.

Ben sat down next to her and draped his arm over her shoulders. "Are you crying or laughing? Because I really need to know if I should commiserate or join in the jocularity."

She raised her head, not really certain exactly what she was feeling, yet so aware of Ben, of the fact she was feeling something powerful and yet couldn't name it, couldn't describe it. She could certainly enjoy it, though, because in spite of the terrible things that had happened, that might still happen, this wonderful man was here in her life, he was funny and smart and so caring, and he loved her.

"I love you," she said, loving him even more when his eyes lit up, and his smile spread slowly until his focus on her was so absolute, so all-encompassing, that she wanted to wallow in being the obvious center of his attention.

"I love you, Lola Marie. So much." He ran his fingers through her hair. "So pretty. I can't even picture you with it dark, now that I've seen it this color, Though it doesn't matter what color you want it. You're so much more than the way you look. You amaze me. You're smart and funny and compassionate—you know what it is to care about others in a way that truly has meaning. And did I mention, the way you look is pretty spectacular?"

"Yeah, but you can say it any time you want." She turned and kissed the palm of his hand cupping her cheek. "I love that you like looking at me. You make me feel beautiful."

Ben suddenly realized they had an audience. He'd been so focused on Lola, the others hadn't even existed. "On that note . . . Mandy? Marcus? Good night. I'm taking my woman to bed."

He lifted her in his arms, held her against his chest, and she realized she was crying again. Too much. They'd dealt with too much during the past couple of weeks, and she didn't know if she could handle anything else.

But Ben kissed her forehead and then carried her out of the kitchen, through the front room, and into their bedroom, and she realized that yes, she could handle just about anything, as long as she had Benjamin Lowell beside her.

Later, Ben lay there awake, his body sated, his mind whirling. He'd never really understood why people referred to sex as making love until Lola, but it finally made perfect sense. Touching her, running his hands over her sleek body, tasting her, joining with her in the most intimate way possible was so far beyond mere sex, he had no way of defining it, other than making love.

Making memories, making stronger ties between them, making those first tentative steps toward a future together. He knew that he wanted her for all time, wanted to grow old with her, have children with her. Make a life with Lola.

The whole idea of marriage should scare the crap out of him, but it only made him more determined to put all of this mess with the trial and his testimony behind them and put the bad guys away, anywhere, so they would stop bothering him and leave him to court his lady.

She slept so soundly, trusted him so completely that he felt powerful, able to do anything necessary to keep her safe. He certainly understood now where his brother's heart and mind were, and how they got there so quickly. He'd wondered if Jake and Kaz really understood what they were getting into, falling in love so quickly.

He'd never said anything at all to Jake about his worries, but he still felt as if he owed his brother an apology for harboring the doubts he'd had when he'd first met Kaz, had first seen how gorgeous she was and wondered if she was as real as Jake seemed to think. Beautiful women weren't to be trusted—hadn't he heard that over and over from the guys whose wives were screwing around on them while they were facing death in places like Wanat and Kamdesh, or the nightmare that was Ganjgal?

He'd seen too much death, done too many unforgivable things to be lying here in a bed with Lola, but he knew he'd fought bravely, knew he'd done the best he could, and he'd done it without a woman waiting at home for him.

Not every wife or girlfriend cheated, but he wondered how many were like Lola. She was amazing, and she was his. And he'd be out of the army in a few more months, free to start his own future—one that had to include this wonderful woman sleeping so soundly beside him.

He'd worn her out tonight, but it was like he couldn't get enough of her, couldn't taste or touch or love her enough not to want more. Of course, her appetites were just as voracious, her need for him felt as strong as his for her, and wasn't that just the most amazing thing ever?

She snuggled close against his side, slipped her arm over his chest and curled her fingers against his throat. And just like that, his mind eased. His body relaxed. His eyes closed.

He drifted off, imagining a lifetime of nights like this.

CHAPTER 23

A vibration against the bedside table woke him. He lay there a moment, trying to identify the sound, and it took a few more buzzes before he realized it was his cell phone. Moving carefully, he reached for the thing, intending to turn it off, but something had him sitting up in bed, answering the call.

He recognized the voice immediately—Evie, the maid from Caroline Ewing's house.

He felt Lola stir beside him when he asked Evie what was wrong, because there was no way in hell the girl was making a social call at three-fifteen in the morning.

"You said I could call you if I was in trouble. I need help."

She was whispering, but Lola was stirring and Ben put the phone on speaker. Evie's frightened voice seemed to fill the bedroom.

"What happened? Where are you?"

"They took me out of my bedroom. Mrs. Ewing and Dustin. I thought he was in jail, but she must have bailed him out and I don't know why they want me."

"Where are you?"

"I think I'm at Mrs. Ewing's house. They blindfolded me and wouldn't say their names, but I recognized their voices, and it smells like her house. Like her stinky perfume. I think I'm in the same bedroom that I stayed in when I was here, the one in the back. Can you come get me?"

"I'll be there. Just hang on." He ended the call.

Lola kissed his cheek and whispered in his ear. "Ben, she's lying. It's a trap."

He turned and kissed her mouth. Damn but he loved the taste of her. "I know. No way in hell would anyone kidnap a teen and not check for a cell phone."

He was dialing Ted's number as he spoke. "Get dressed, sweetheart. I want you to go with me. I might need help with . . . Ted. Sorry to wake you, bud, but I just got a call from Evie, the maid at Mrs. Ewing's. Yeah, the kid who left with the social worker, though I didn't check the lady's ID. Did you? Yeah, you're right. We probably should have, but it was a police operation at that point. Anyway, Evie said she's been kidnapped and she's at Mrs. Ewing's, that Dustin's there, so somehow he's gotten out. She wants me to come rescue her. Exactly. It's a little bit too convenient for me, too, and Lola agrees. Meet you there in twenty minutes. Okay. Twenty-five."

He grinned at Lola. "Ted says he's not that fast 'cuz he's old." Then he kissed her.

She was already dressed—black jeans, boots, and black turtleneck. She tucked her hair into a dark stocking cap and grabbed a maroon jacket and then raced down the hall to tell Mandy where they were going. Ben slipped on jeans and a black sweatshirt along with his well-worn desert boots. He tucked his knife into a horizontal scabbard on the back side of his belt and dropped the sweatshirt down to cover the blade.

When he stepped out into the hallway, Marc was waiting. "Do you need help?"

"I called Ted, so we're covered, but thank you. I'd rather you stayed to protect Mandy, just in case. I'm taking Lola because there's a teenaged girl involved. If it's a setup, I don't want to make it any easier for them."

"Probably a good idea. Good luck. Call and let me know how you are, okay?"

"I will. Thanks."

Lola came out of Mandy's room. "I let her know where we're going. Have you got your phone?"

Ben nodded and Lola checked to make sure she had hers. "C'mon," he said, taking her hand. "We need to meet Ted."

It was a fast fifteen minutes to the house on Baker Street. Ted was parked across the street and down the block, out of sight of the house, so Ben pulled in behind him. Ted walked over to the Subaru and got into the back seat. "I contacted Officer McGowan. If it's a setup, and I have to agree with you that it sounds damned suspicious, we need to have an officer here."

"I agree," Ben said. "Though if it's not and she really is in danger, I'm going to feel like crap about this. Something's going on, though, because there are a lot of lights on at the house."

"Don't you dare feel bad," Lola said, and Ben thought she sounded pretty pissed. "I am really tired of everyone screwing with our lives. Besides, I thought Dustin was on a no-bail hold. Did he get out?"

Ted shook his head. "I don't know." He glanced up as a squad car pulled in ahead of Ben. No lights or siren, and he was also out of sight of the house. "Good. Looks like McGowan."

They all got out and walked over to meet the officer. Quietly, Ben relayed the gist of the phone call to him. "So, I did tell her to call me if she had trouble, and I promised I'd come, but this just sounds way too implausible. And we're not even sure that the woman who came for Evie the other day was actually a social worker, but since they seemed to know each other, I didn't think anything of it."

"Did you get her name?"

"Mrs. Bradley. That's who Evie said she was."

McGowan made a quick call to check. "If the girl's a minor, there are protocols that have to be followed. Someone should have the info on her. It may take a while to hear back." He glanced at the house. "It's lit up like a damned Christmas tree in the middle of the night. Something's sure as hell going on."

"Okay, Ted." Ben glanced at the house, the sense of something really wrong growing by the second. "We might not have time to wait. I called you as a courtesy, so I'm not sure how official your presence is here right now. How about I just go knock on the door, tell whoever answers the truth, that Evie called and said she's in trouble and wanted me to come here and help her? That I'd prefer not to involve the authorities."

"Works for me." Ted stared at the house for a moment longer. "Just be careful, okay?"

"I can do that." Ben leaned over and gave Lola a quick kiss before adding, "As long as you boys have my back."

"Right behind you," McGowan said, "But for now I'm going to stay out of sight. Ted, you do the same. Close enough for back up, but let's just see what they have to say to Ben. Lola, why don't you wait here in case we need help with Evie. You okay with that?"

"I'm going to move a little bit closer, but I'll stay out of sight."

"Not too close." Ted gave her a worried look.

"I won't. Now go."

Ben kissed her once again and then strode boldly up to the front porch and knocked on the heavy wooden door.

A moment later, the door flew open and Dustin Thorpe stood there. He was shirtless, wearing a pair of designer jeans, but his feet were bare, his hair disheveled. Ben thought he looked like he was either drunk or stoned. He was definitely pissed off.

"What the fuck are you doing here?"

"I could ask you the same thing. Look, I got a call from Evie. She said you and Mrs. Ewing had taken her against her will, and brought her here. I just want to check and see if she's okay."

"Who the fuck is Evie?"

"Your maid, you bastard. The underage girl who was working for you."

"She called you?" He shook his head. "Haven't seen her since she left with that social worker." He stepped back from the front door. "Come right in. See for yourself."

"I think I will." Ben stepped through the door. And he hoped like hell McGowan and Robinson had some sort of contingency plan.

Dustin led him into the dining room where they'd held Lola. "She's not here."

"What room was hers the night she stayed here?"

"I think the little bitch suckered you." He shook his head in disgust. "It's back here. Follow me."

He stumbled as he walked down a long hallway, taking a couple of turns through the huge house, and Ben was hoping the idiot wasn't so stoned he'd gotten lost. Finally, he stopped at a door at the very end, as Evie had said, near the back of the house. Dustin opened it.

"Holy shit!" Dustin stumbled back, tripping over Ben's feet. "Cissy? What the fuck?" He spun around. "I didn't know about this. I swear."

Evie sat on the bed wearing a cami top and flannel pajama bottoms. Her hands were tied together, the rope looped over the top of the headboard. She wasn't blindfolded, and she'd obviously been crying. Mrs. Ewing stood near the bed holding a double-barreled shotgun, trained on Evie. The girl stared at Ben and her eyes filled with tears. "I didn't think you'd come. I told her you wouldn't."

Ben stared at her, trying to figure out what the hell was going on. "I promised, didn't I? I always keep my promises." Then he leveled a long stare at Mrs. Ewing. "Do you want to tell me what this is all about?"

"It's simple. You keep your mouth shut about all that nasty business in Afghanistan, and this little girl won't end up dead. Tonight, at least."

Dustin stayed behind Ben, but he cursed again. "Evie, I'm sorry, sweetie. I had no idea you were here."

"You did too. You helped her. I recognized your voice." She tugged at the ties holding her hands to the bed. Tears ran down her face. "You're lying."

Ben shook his head and laughed. "I can't believe you guys. This is a freaking circus. Dustin, she says you're lying, and Mrs. Ewing? I'm never going to live this down. Lola said you were a lot sharper than you let on, and I told her I thought you were just a sweet old lady. You need to realize, though, that threatening this girl to get me to refuse to testify in a case that I've already been deposed on isn't going to work, either. It's too late. You need to put the gun down and turn Miss Saunders loose."

He recognized the tell, that split second when Caroline Ewing decided it would just be so much easier to kill Ben than to deal with the girl. She swung the heavy gun around like she knew how to handle the thing, and he dove to one side, going low and rolling well beyond the door.

Dustin didn't move as fast. The gun roared, Evie screamed, and then all Ben could hear was a ringing in his ears from the deafening thunder of two twelve-gauge shotgun shells blowing out the side of the doorway where he'd been standing.

McGowan came flying down the hallway with Ted right behind him. Both men had their guns drawn. Stunned by the blast, Ben lay on the floor covered in blood, but he was almost positive it wasn't his. His head was still spinning, but he slowly rolled to a sitting position.

Dustin's upper body had caught just a fraction of the blast, but at such close range, it was more than enough to do a lot of damage. He was still alive, but blood pumped from a massive wound in his chest and right shoulder. McGowan jumped over him and went straight for Mrs. Ewing, who was trying to shove another shell into the chamber. He grabbed the shotgun and spun her around before handcuffing her.

Ted ran to Evie and untied her. She was sobbing hysterically when Lola ran down the hallway. "Ben! Oh my God. Are you . . . ?"

"I'm okay. I'm not hurt. I saw her swing the gun this way and dropped and rolled. Dustin didn't move fast enough."

"There's someone else here," she said. "A man ran through the dining room. He went out that door where you found me."

"I'll check." He shoved himself to his feet, but Robinson stopped him.

"I'll check. Stay here."

"Yessir." His ears were still ringing, and he was sticky with Dustin's blood. At least he hoped it was Dustin's. Now that the adrenaline was wearing off, he was starting to notice some pain of his own.

A uniformed officer raced down the hallway with his gun drawn. Ben's and Lola's hands both went up. "Not us," Ben said. "Officer McGowan's in the bedroom with the one who shot this guy. His name's Dustin Thorpe and he obviously needs an ambulance."

The officer holstered his weapon and reached for his

radio. "We just caught a guy out in front. He claims he lives here, that there's a crazy old lady with a gun."

"She's in there," Lola said. "And hang on to that guy out in front. I think he's part of a big drug ring that's under investigation by the Department of Justice." She took Ben's hand. "There's a bathroom over here. I need to wipe the blood off of you and see if any of it's yours."

"Let me check Dustin first." He knelt beside the guy and then turned to Lola. "Grab some towels, hon. I need to apply pressure." He shook his head. His ears were still ringing.

Lola ran across the hall to the bathroom and returned with an armload of towels. She handed one to Ben. He found the area where the blast of pellets had torn a large section of Thorpe's shoulder away. Thank goodness the guy was unconscious. This was going to be an agonizing injury, if he lived through it.

He turned to Lola. "I think Evie really was kidnapped. Do you mind checking on her? She was tied to the bed when I got in here, and Mrs. Ewing was aiming the shotgun at her."

Lola slapped her hand over her mouth. "Good Lord! Take care of this jackass if you have to, but then you need to get cleaned up. I think some of that blood is yours, tough guy. I'll be with Evie."

He kept pressure on the wound until the paramedics arrived. Once they took over, he grabbed a couple of the towels he hadn't had to use on Thorpe and stuck his head through the open door. Lola was in a far corner with Evie, hugging the girl who was sobbing loudly.

This was way out of Ben's comfort zone. He caught the policeman's attention. "Officer McGowan? If Lola asks for me, please tell her I need to go wash some of this blood off. I'll be in the bathroom across the hall."

McGowan nodded.

Ben went into the bathroom and stripped his shirt off before dunking a thick towel in warm water and washing the blood away from his chest and arms. Then he turned and looked at his back in the mirror. It looked as if he'd caught close to a dozen pellets across his shoulder blade and the back of his left arm, but Dustin had definitely gotten the bulk of the blast.

He wondered who the other guy was—maybe Dustin really hadn't been the one to kidnap Evie. He wondered if Dustin was going to make it, if they'd ever know for sure who did what?

He glanced at his watch. It was after four in the morning. He finished cleaning up as best he could, and paid attention to the places that kept bleeding. All on his back. Maybe he'd get Ted to take him to the hospital. It was his turn, after all. Except he liked the idea of Lola taking him. That was the sort of thing a woman did for her man, wasn't it?

He decided not to put his blood-soaked shirt back on. Instead, he threw it in the sink, walked down the hallway, and found what appeared to be a man's bedroom. There were a number of designer shirts hanging in the closet. He found a dark green Henley that looked about his size, and put it on before going in search of Lola.

The paramedics were moving the gurney with Dustin on it toward the front door. One of the men glanced at Ben. "You the one who kept pressure on the wound?"

"Yes sir. How's he doing?"

The men with the gurney went on ahead, but this one stayed behind. "I think he's got a good chance. Shotgun wounds are always ugly." He squinted at Ben. "Are you bleeding?"

"Probably. I'm the one she was aiming at. I moved faster than he did."

"Better get those pellets out. She was shooting lead shot."

"Just my luck. Thanks." Ben started back toward Lola, but he saw Ted out in front with a guy on the ground in front of him in handcuffs, and made a quick detour. "I'll be damned," he said. "It's Robert Lassiter. Haven't seen you since Spin B, Lassiter."

He took a closer look at the guy, who hadn't said a word, but if looks could kill, Ben figured he'd be dead. Real dead. And it suddenly made sense to him, why Dustin Thorpe had looked so familiar. Why Evie thought Dustin had kidnapped her.

Ted hadn't said a word. Ben hunkered down to put himself at eye level to Lassiter. "What's the relationship?" he asked. "You and Thorpe? Brothers? Cousins? He's older. Not by much, but you guys certainly look alike."

"Shut up, you son of a bitch."

"Sound alike, too." He glanced at Ted, who grinned at Ben.

"You know this guy? Crap, Lowell, I thought you had better taste in friends."

Ben shook his head. "No friend of mine, but I think he's the one who helped kidnap Evie. She said she was blindfolded but she heard Thorpe speaking. This guy sounds just like him. I have a feeling it was Mrs. Ewing and Robert Lassiter that took her."

"Lassiter is her nephew. Senator Ewing's sister's son."

Ben turned and stared at Robinson. "And Dustin Thorpe?"

"That's where it gets interesting. He's the senator's bastard son—his mother is a college girl who interned for him. His sister raised the boy. These two are first cousins."

"So his wife is screwing her stepson-slash-nephew?" Ben gave a long, low whistle and shook his head. "Lola wasn't kidding when she said the old lady was creepy."

"Appears so."

"Do you have any idea what's going on?" Ben needed to go check on Lola, but he still couldn't link all the dots together.

"Getting close. I'll let you know as soon as I figure it out. Don't forget to buy the Sunday paper." He glanced at his watch. "In fact, it should be showing up any minute now. But Ben?"

"What, Ted?"

"Get to the hospital. You're bleeding all over yourself."

His back was beginning to hurt, and the shirt was definitely sticking to him. He went in search of Lola. Mrs. Bradley was there with Evie and his girl. Ben went straight to Lola and kissed her. Then he turned to Evie and took her hands. "You okay, sweetie?"

She nodded. "Is Dustin going to die? How come he lied? I know he was the one who took me. I'm positive."

Ben shook his head. "Maybe he didn't. The police have arrested another man. He looks a lot like Dustin, and when he spoke, he sounds like him, too. I think he's Dustin's cousin. The thing is, their voices are really similar, and he's a real scum."

"Dustin's not scum," she said. "He could be grumpy, but mostly he was nice to me. Mrs. Ewing treated him like her pet, but he was always nice to me. That's why I was so upset, because I thought he loved me, but then tonight I thought he kidnapped me."

Lola had her arm around Evie's shoulders. "You told us you didn't like the way he looked at you. Were you lying?"

She turned to Lola and nodded. "I'm sorry. He asked me to say that so you'd feel sorry for me. I'm not sure what they were planning, but I did what he asked."

Ben glanced at the older woman. "Mrs. Bradley? Are you truly with Child Protective Services? We should have checked when you picked up Evie the last time."

"I am." She reached in her purse and pulled out an official ID. "I should have shown this yesterday, but I had no idea that Evie wasn't with her family, and I'd not gotten her message, that the father was frightening her." She looked at Evie. "I told you we take your fears very seriously, Evie. When it's an emergency, you talk to anyone at the agency, and you let them know."

Ben looped his right arm around Lola's shoulders. "Hon, can you take me to the ER? You were right—a bunch of those pellets hit my back and they're starting to hurt."

She kissed his cheek. "Do I get to say I told you so?"

"I guess so, but you're driving."

"Just a minute." She left his side for a moment and then returned with a couple of thick towels to put over the leather seat in his car. "I don't think Mrs. Ewing will need these where she's going," she said.

Then she drove him to the hospital.

CHAPTER 24

Ben rolled over in bed, carefully, because it appeared that digging shotgun pellets out of a guy's back hurt more than when they went in, especially when the ER doctor turned out to love her job, and insisted on removing the pieces of shrapnel still embedded from the bomb at Spin Boldak. But none of that mattered because Lola was lying beside him, smiling at him as if she had the world's biggest secret.

"What are you grinning about, Ms. Monroe?"

"You." She kissed him. "It's almost eleven and you're just now waking up. I've never seen you sleep this late."

"I'm injured. There were eleven pieces of lead in my back. Big pieces of lead." He whimpered. "We didn't get home from the ER until after six." When he added a moan, she laughed and he grumbled, "Where's the sympathy, woman?"

"I have none. And it's true. There were eleven shotgun pellets, i.e., pieces of lead in your back. Little. Tiny. Pieces. Although I think it was the other stuff the doctor removed that's hurting you now. You also know, those half dozen pieces of shrapnel? Were you just planning to leave that metal in there?"

"Makes it more entertaining going through airport

security. Besides, it wasn't lead. No reason to put me through the pain and suffering of removing it. What's your point?"

"My point?" She sighed. "Please tell me you're through getting shot. Will working security for Marc require dodging bullets? Because I called Kaz early this morning while the doctor was getting your lead out, and we've agreed that we don't want our men stopping any more bullets of any kind."

Ben pretended to think about that one for a while. "Jake didn't stop his. He let it get away. Went right past his arm, albeit rather close. I don't think getting grazed by a bullet counts. I, on the other hand, stopped every single one of mine. And then some."

She cupped his face in her hands, her smile gone. "Don't you ever, ever scare me like that again. I was outside when I heard that gun. It sounded like a cannon, and Officer McGowan and Ted took off like the hounds of hell were chasing them. Evie was screaming, but I didn't hear you. And then when I saw you, you were covered in blood."

Tears rolled down her cheeks. Ben wrapped his arms around her and pulled her close. He'd worry about the stitches later. "I'm sorry I didn't scream. I would have felt like such a girl. And I moved as fast as I could."

She giggled and hiccupped and cried even harder.

There was a soft tap on the door. Ben took a quick look to make sure they were both decent, and said, "Come in."

Jake shoved the door open. Kaz was right behind him. "You okay, bro? Kaz told me what happened."

"A little sore. When the ER doc started digging around for the blasted shotgun pellets, she decided to cut out some shrapnel that had been there since Spin B."

"Did they get the lead out?"

"It was funny the first time I heard it. Not so much the fifth, sixth, or seventh time."

"Damn. I thought I was being original. So what do we know?"

"I have no idea. Ted's coming over for dinner tonight and we're going to compare notes."

"CliffsNotes, or the whole story?"

"I guess we'll have to wait and see."

As it turned out, there wasn't much news. Ted showed up for dinner, exhausted and grumpy, and more than ready for this case to end. Dustin was alive. The paramedics had told Ted that Ben's intervention was what saved him. Evie was staying with Mrs. Bradley and her husband. The social worker had been handling Evie's case since the girl had been orphaned at age thirteen, and decided that the least she could do was give her some good family years during high school. They were already talking formal adoption.

Robert Lassiter was in jail and so was Mrs. Ewing. Because of their financial resources, neither one would be granted bail because the risk of them leaving the country was too high. The judge who'd allowed Dustin out was going to be explaining why he'd deferred to Mrs. Ewing's attorney's request to free Dustin on bail after his initial arrest.

Ted took a swallow of wine and sighed. "Other than that, we just have to wait and see what comes out. Did you guys read the Sunday *Chronicle*?"

"Oh, yeah." Ben adjusted his position in his chair. He'd forgotten how much it hurt to get stuff dug out of his body.

"You okay?"

"I'm fine. This sort of thing didn't used to hurt as much. I'm obviously getting older."

"Aren't we all," Ted muttered.

Ben merely shook his head. "That article was something. All the stuff that the first stories merely hinted at now spelled out in detail with confirming statements from so many well-known and highly respected people . . . it's all pretty damning."

"Agreed," Jake said. "I found myself reading between the lines, though, now that we know what Ewing's wife is like. Makes me wonder if she was the power behind the throne, so to speak. I wonder how many of Ewing's strings were pulled by either Caroline or Daddy dear."

Ted merely smiled. The smile told Ben that Ted knew a whole lot more than he was letting on, but couldn't quite talk about it yet.

One week later . . .

Ben pulled his undershirt off and turned so he could see his back in the bathroom mirror. Everything was healing well and the stiffness was mostly gone. He'd gotten the stitches out this morning, and nothing was bleeding, but he'd definitely added to his collection of scars.

Why any woman could want a guy with a body this messed up was a mystery, but damn it all, he was sure glad Lola didn't seem to mind.

"Ben? You about ready? Jake just got here."

"Out in a minute." He slipped the shirt back on and pulled a dark gray sweater on over that. They were meeting Ted at a Mexican restaurant for dinner. The FBI agent was heading back to Virginia, but he'd promised to update everyone on the status of the ongoing case before he left. And, in a small way, pay them back for all of the meals he'd eaten at their table.

Ben was going to miss the guy. Ted had been a lot more open with them than he'd had to be, had done everything he could to include Ben and Lola in what was going on, even when what was going on hadn't hit the papers yet.

Ben opened the door and stepped out. Lola was just coming out of Mandy's room, so beautiful she literally took his breath. Short, deep blue fitted dress, killer heels, and a cute little handbag that hung from her shoulder and rested against that perfect butt.

And all that long, blonde hair.

He wanted to say something worthy of her. All he could get out was, "Wow."

She spun around, laughing. "That works," she said.

"Good, because you're so damned beautiful and sexy that I'm speechless."

"That works even better." She took his hand. "You feeling okay?"

"I'm not bleeding anywhere. That's good." He tugged and she followed him down the hallway.

"Well, now all your scars make sense. You're like a magnet for metal, aren't you?"

"God, I hope not. How would I explain Kaz's nose ring stuck to my butt?"

Lola snorted. "I'd slap you for that, but you'd probably start bleeding again."

Ted had arranged for them to have a private room, and it seemed like a huge waste of space until Ben realized he'd meant it when he said he was inviting a few extra people involved in the case. It was actually a big party, everyone from the police officers who'd been on the case to his partner, David Renteria and his wife, and the CHP officer who'd gotten Ben across the bridge.

And more. "Ben, how are you doing?"

"Captain Booker? I didn't expect to see you here, sir." He shook hands with his CO, gave his wife Jia a hug, and then introduced Lola.

After introductions, Booker said, "Hope you don't mind. Your FBI guy invited us." He wrapped his arm around his wife. "Any time I can offer Jia dinner in the city without picking up the tab, I'm game." He laughed at his own joke. Jia poked him in the side.

Ben chuckled. "You get him, Jia." Then to his CO, "Seriously, thanks for coming. Hopefully, I'll be back at my desk in another week. My back still looks like hamburger, but it's healing."

"We'll need to talk about that in a few days," Booker said. "I know you're anxious to get back to civilian life, and we've come up with a solution that won't actually shorten the time to your retirement, but should let you start moving forward with your life. You're going to be attached to the FBI for the duration of the investigation. If you want to start on your retirement packet, I'll make sure it doesn't get lost, and we can have you approved for retirement in about six months, which is when your twenty is up. You'll be posted to their office here in San Francisco while you're working with the FBI. Come in as soon as you're cleared for duty and we can start the process."

He hadn't expected that. Not at all, but he felt Lola's fingers tighten around his, and gave her a returning squeeze for luck.

They made a point of speaking to everyone before finding a couple of stools at the bar. Ben ordered a tonic and lime for himself and a margarita for Lola, and they sat, sipping their drinks, watching the way this group interacted. Mandy and David Renteria and his wife were laughing about something, and Craig Benson, the CHP officer who'd gotten Ben across the bridge, was talking cars with Marc Reed. After a few minutes, Ben turned to Lola and planted a big kiss on her lips.

"What was that for? Not that I'm complaining." She kissed him back.

"Look around us. Most of these people didn't even know each other before tonight, but look at the way they're all getting along. This is fascinating—they have nothing in common except that they've each played a part in this case."

Ted walked up in time to catch Ben's comment. "That's not entirely true, Ben. Think about it. Everyone who's here is someone who's interacted with *you* in the course of the last few weeks, all helping out with the case in one way or another, but they've been involved through you. And every single person who's here tonight has, at one point or another, expressed their admiration for what you've done to help solve this case."

Stunned, Ben had absolutely nothing to say. What could he say? Instead, he squeezed Lola's hand. She held on tight, probably so he couldn't run for cover.

Lola almost laughed. Finally, Ben was in a position where someone was saying something nice about him, and he'd just have to deal with it. She wanted to shout, "Thank you, Ted!" but she kept her mouth shut.

Ted leaned against the bar beside Ben. Poor guy. Ben wasn't very good at accepting praise, even though he deserved every single bit. Then he surprised her. Really surprised her.

He actually sounded gracious!

"Thank you, Ted. I find that hard to believe, but thank you." Ben glanced away for a moment, and then turned to Ted and grinned. "So, have we solved it?"

Ted laughed. "Actually, I think we have. We have an older interrogator who looks like Caroline's daddy; he even boned up on the man's speech patterns. He was able to work wonders. I'm going to get everyone together at dinner in a few minutes and we'll go over the main points, but for what it's worth, Lola was right."

"I was? That never happens. When?" She laughed when Ben gave her a dirty look.

"Caroline Ewing was behind a lot of this."

"I knew it." Lola took a sip of her margarita. "And you thought she was just a crazy old lady."

Ted said, "Oh, she's batshit crazy." Then he laughed at Ben when he just about choked on his drink. "The woman's loony as can be. She's also one sick old broad. She's a pedophile. Turns out she started grooming Dustin for sex when he was about twelve years old."

"That's horrible." Lola felt sick. Dustin was a sleaze, but . . . Wrong. Just so wrong.

Again, Ben squeezed her hand, even as he focused on Ted. "How's he doing?"

"He would have died if you hadn't been there to keep pressure on the wound. He may lose his right arm unless they can rebuild his shoulder. It's a mess. Most of the joint is gone. But he really was the lady's lover. Has been since he was around thirteen years old—he's spent almost fifteen years playing the boy toy. She was around sixty when it all started."

"That's horrible. I don't want to feel sorry for him, but . . ."

"For what it's worth, Lola, I'm kind of with you. He didn't have a chance. His whole life has been twisted. Robert Lassiter is the senator's nephew—his sister's only child. Dustin is Ewing's bastard son, which makes them first cousins, hence the resemblance you noticed so quickly, Ben, and the reason Evie thought Dustin had kidnapped her. Their voices sound almost exactly alike.

"Dustin's not innocent—he's been blackmailing Robert Lassiter for years, ever since figuring out that the security company Senator Ewing financed for Lassiter was a front for drugs. Of course, the seed money was Caroline's, but the senator seems perfectly comfortable spending it, while not paying attention past cashing the checks. The trade-off is, he's always looked the other way where Caroline and Dustin were concerned, but Dustin threatened to tell the senator what Lassiter was up to. The old bastard actually appears to be innocent as far as the drug running in Afghanistan. Lassiter's been buying Dustin's silence and Dustin's been happily stashing the money in the Cayman Islands."

Ben interrupted to ask, "But why the tail? Who was following us, and why?"

"Lassiter kept a tail on you through Bill Locke, who hired them. He wanted to know where you were and who you were meeting with, but he was doing that mostly because he wasn't sure what, if anything, you knew. He requested the government vehicles using Dustin's name and hired the guys who were murdered across the street, and the two who got me. He didn't particularly want to kill you; he just wanted to know if that might become a necessity. He called the hit in Spin Boldak. Arnold Hendrickson was his primary target. Lassiter had discovered Hendrickson was skimming funds, had his favorite mullah convince a jihadist it was a political hit, and you were invited in at the last minute in case you knew something. Which you do, thank you very much, Sergeant Lowell."

Ted just shook his head as he continued. "They're all nuts, Ben. It was just pure luck you didn't end up dead. Somehow, Caroline got wind of the security company running drugs. We're still not sure if Dustin told her or if she found out some other way, but she sent Dustin to take care of the two men following you. She was afraid the media would connect the drug operation to her name and it would sully her father's reputation. The family name is everything to her. She says she didn't tell Dustin to kill anyone. She claims she just asked him to see why Lassiter had men following you. Dustin says otherwise, that she told him to take care of the two men. It appears he shot them with the same twelve-gauge shotgun that Caroline shot him with. He got panicky when Caroline blew up at him for the murders, and that's when he started putting the word out, implicating Nuestra Familia. Dustin's the one who hired the kids to paint the garage. You were right on that one. It was all a red herring to throw attention away from him. Other than that, Caroline had him completely under her control."

"But you said Caroline knew about Lassiter and the drugs, yet he was staying at her house. What's going on there?"

"She hadn't said anything to Lassiter yet. I think she's afraid of him, of what he might do. She doesn't control him the way she can Dustin." Ted took a deep breath, let it out. "I keep wondering what Dustin would have been like if he'd had a normal life. He's smart and personable when he's not lying to you. He pulled a lot of stupid shit, but I believe Caroline made him what he is. Robert Lassiter is just bad all the way through, and she had a right to be afraid of him. Typical rich kid who's never had to think of the consequences of any of his actions. The sister raised the boys together. Robert was always favored, which set up a lot of Dustin's hatred for the guy, so when Caroline Ewing offered to take Dustin under her wing, everyone thought it was a great idea."

Lola just shook her head. There was nothing to say to something like that.

"As far as the senator, it looks like he's guilty of everything that Colonel Mac Phillips uncovered back in the 1980s. That bastard has used all his years in office to make a fortune, very little of it legal. His father-in-law bought his senate seat and continued to buy each election until he died, then Caroline took over. That was her way of controlling the senator. He kept his mouth shut about her relationship with his son, and she forked over the cash, but the guy is still a crook. There's so much in the colonel's notes that's been verified by the newspaper's investigation, it will be impossible not to send the man to prison.

"When they kidnapped Lola, the plan was for you, Ben, to come hunting for your woman and Dustin was supposed to kill you. The thing is, no one clued Dustin in on the plan. When Locke showed up with Lola and explained she was bait, he refused."

"Where did Locke come into all of this?" Lola shuddered, hating how she'd trusted Bill when she shouldn't have. "Marc hired him a couple of years ago, before any of this was news."

"That appears to be pure serendipity. Locke worked for the security firm Lassiter owns and originally had Hendrickson's job, but he got tired of life in the Middle East and came back to California. Lassiter guessed there'd be good money in stolen software and figured that placing Locke with Marcus Reed would give him some inside knowledge. The fact that all of you were involved with Ben and his wonderful notes, was pure luck."

Ben glanced at Lola. "Remind me to quit taking notes. They get you in trouble."

Ted laughed, but he looked exhausted. "For now, everyone who should be in jail, is in jail. I guess it depends on how good their attorneys are as to how long they'll stay there. Only the senator is out on bail. His wife Caroline, Robert Lassiter, William Locke, and the guy Locke hired to run into Marc Reed's Tesla are all behind bars. Dustin's been charged, but he'll be in the hospital until he's healthy enough for a cell."

He rested his hand on Ben's shoulder—the one without the healing injuries. "I'm going to miss you kids. It appears my part in the investigation, at least until the senator's trial, is done. Caroline, Dustin, Robert, and the rest will be tried out here in California, since their charges are all separate from Senator Ewing's, though I'm sure they're going to try and tie him to the drug business in Spin Boldak. There's a

very slim chance he could be involved, but I imagine I'll
be called back to testify in their cases."

He sighed. "We could be missing all kinds of things.
The investigation is still pretty fresh. I'll be heading back
to Virginia in a couple of days, but I wanted to tell you,
this job hasn't been like any other I've ever been on. A lot
of it was the usual crap, but there's been a lot of good. A
lot of laughter, which is generally lacking in my life, and
all the good parts are due to you and your friends. For that,
I thank you."

He pushed himself away from the bar and clapped his
hands, drawing everyone's attention. "Okay, folks. I think
everyone's had enough time for beer and margaritas. Let's
get this show on the road."

It was late when they got back to the house. Kaz and Jake
headed straight home after dropping them off. Mandy went
into her room to change into her pajamas and Marc disappeared into his room to work on a software problem. Ben
had a feeling they were all a little shaken by the details
they'd gotten from Ted tonight.

He grabbed Lola's hand. "Walk outside with me?"

She smiled. "Sure. Still feeling a little overwhelmed?"

"You figured that out, eh?"

"I did, but I was really proud of you. Even when Ted
was praising you, you didn't run for cover."

"Yeah, but I wanted to. There just wasn't anyplace
to go."

She laughed. "Probably why Ted picked an enclosed
room inside a crowded restaurant."

Chuckling, Ben led her through the kitchen door and
down the steps. It was an unusually clear night. No fog,
but no moon, either. Holding on to his hand, she followed
him through the yard that he was pruning further into

submission whenever he had the chance, until they reached the old bench under the dogwood tree.

Lola sat and looked at him as if wondering why he hesitated. She had no idea he didn't intend to sit beside her.

No, this was the woman he wanted to kneel before. So he did.

The moment he went down on one knee, she pressed her hands to her mouth. He reached for both hands and pulled them away from her face, held them in his. "I tried to think of the best place to do this, because I wanted to get it right. There's Ocean Beach, Point Lobos, Golden Gate Park, all those beautiful places around the city where guys take the ones they love.

"Then I realized there's no better place in the world than right here in the backyard where you saved my life, no better place than here, where I had my first of what may be many meltdowns, to ask you, please, to keep saving my life. Will you marry me, Lola? Will you promise me forever, promise to try and love me even a fraction as much as I love you? I love you so much, sweetheart. I want to spend the rest of my days convincing you I can be a good man. Will you give me that chance? Will you be my wife?"

She was crying. Crying and laughing, and she wrapped her arms around his neck and hung on for dear life. He got up with Lola in his arms, sat on the bench, and held her in his lap—and then he remembered the ring. He'd stuck it in his rear pocket, and he had to dig around to find it, but he did. He slipped it on her ring finger, left hand. It was a perfect fit.

Still sobbing, she held her hand up and the tears almost stopped. Almost. "It's beautiful, Ben. So different. What is it?"

"It's tourmaline and diamonds. I know you liked Kaz's ring, and it's not traditional, but if you'd rather have a diamond, we can trade . . ."

"No." She kissed him. "This is so beautiful! What made you choose it, though?" She laughed. "It looks like it's the same color as your car."

"Silly." He kissed her. "It's the same color as your eyes. I saw it and thought of you. Of course, everything I see, I think of you. I won't rush you. I know we haven't known each other very long, but I'm not getting any younger. I want you to take whatever time you need to think about setting a date, about where you want to live, and what kind of a future you want, as long as it's with me."

"Any time. Any place. It doesn't matter. Only you matter, Ben. I love you. I loved you the first time I saw you, only I didn't realize the depth of what I felt. I don't know if I really know even now, because it grows stronger every day."

"We've got plenty of time to figure it out." He kissed her. Sweet, loving kisses that got hotter and sweeter with each breath they took.

Finally, he stood with Lola in his arms, and for a brief moment he thought of the first day he'd come here, before he'd settled anything with Jake, before he knew Lola and Mandy, Marc and Kaz; before he really knew the man his brother had become. He'd been so damned scared, but for the first time in his life, he hadn't run from his fears.

He'd finally found the courage to face them, courage he hadn't realized he even had. Courage Lola had given him.

He leaned close and kissed her gently. "I wasn't kidding, you know. You really did save my life."

She touched his lips with her fingertip. "I know," she said. "So you'd better take good care of it."

Laughing, he carried her up the stairs and into the house.

Into a future he'd never dared dream.